THE ROYAL RUNAWAY

A Royal Romcom

Royally Kissed
Book 3

KATE O'KEEFFE

Wild Lime
Books

For my sister-in-law, Donna, who reads everything I write and still claims to like me anyway. xx

Introduction

Good people of Ledonia! I'm excited to be back in Tleurbonne, capital city of Malveaux, for The Games, the scintillating annual competition between our two countries. Who can forget what happened last year when the then single Prince Alexander, aka Europe's most eligible bachelor, chose the newly minted Princess Madeline to be his partner in the Wife Race? Of course, the two then fell in love and got married, and the country fell into depression until the once drab Princess Sofia emerged from her chrysalis as a dazzling heir to the throne on the arm of the delectable Marco Rivera.

With the two older royal siblings married off within a year, that leaves only two from the House of Canossa left: tomboy Princess Amelia, and Prince Alexander's successor in the McHottie stakes, Prince Maximilien, now training with the Royal Ledonian Air Force.

Shall we all take a moment to reflect on how very well our Max has grown up?

So *very* well.

Now, where was I?

Oh, yes. Princess Amelia.

My sources at the palace tell me that she's leaving for India for a silent meditation retreat. Yes, you read that correctly. Our vivacious, never-stops-talking, full of the joys of life Princess Amelia—who once challenged three diplomats to a tree-climbing contest during a state dinner, much to her parents' horror—is going to spend a full month in complete silence.

Silent meditation? Our Amelia? I'd sooner expect our King to take up breakdancing.

I'm sure I'm not the only one who finds this a little hard to believe, so I have devised a list of more likely possibilities:

She's secretly training to become the world's first royal astronaut for Ledonia's ambitious, but previously unheard-of, space program.

She's running away to join the circus as a blindfolded knife-thrower to learn how to slice an apple off the head of some poor volunteer.

She's apprenticing with a team of professional tree surgeons (and knowing our princess's propensity to climb trees, this seems the most likely).

Whatever she's doing for the next month, you can be sure I will get to the bottom of it.

But really, isn't it time she fell in love and gave us all something to enjoy?

Yours breathlessly awaiting the next royal love story,

Fabiana Fontaine xx

#NamasteYourHighness
#MeditatingPrincess
#TimeForAnotherRoyalLoveStory

Chapter 1

Amelia

I live my life by a set of unflinching rules of things a Ledonian princess is forbidden to do. And today, I can add another one to the ever-growing catalog. Rule number 1,247: *A princess may not escape her royal duties by faking attendance at a silent meditation retreat.*

Well, I'm about to break that one somewhat spectacularly.

I've always kept my list of rules in a leather-bound journal, carefully hidden behind one of the many artworks in my rooms—an attempt by Father to make me appreciate the history of my country. Which of course I do, and I don't need some painting of a bunch of wilting flowers and a moldy old orange by some dead guy hanging on my wall to make me appreciate where I live.

I get it. I'm a princess of Ledonia, and that means I've got certain privileges—and certain expectations.

The privileges I'm down with. Who wouldn't be? But the expectations? They're a bit of a sticking point for me. Hence my journal is rather full of things I'm not allowed to do.

Things like:

- Rule number 124: *No climbing trees.* In my defense, those diplomats were totally up for it.
- Rule number 657: *No wearing jeans to official events.* Which is utterly ridiculous because, as I pointed out to Mummy, half the population wears trousers. To which she replied, "Quite, dear. The men."
- Rule number 908: *Never wear orange fingernail polish covered in little spiders, even if it is Halloween.* Can't a girl have some harmless holiday-themed fun? Not if she's a Ledonian princess, it would seem.

So, yes, there are way too many rules for a princess like me. In fact, there are rules for every aspect of my life. From what to wear to how to wave to what shade of lipstick one should wear to a ball.

And you know what? I'm looking forward to breaking each and every one.

All of these silly rules come so naturally to my sister, Sofia. Seriously, I think she swallowed the rulebook as a baby and has followed every single rule contained in that book ever since.

Well, not *every* rule. She did leave the palace grounds without an official escort when she and her now husband, Marco, took a trip to a village in the mountains and kissed under the light of a hundred lanterns, breaking Rule number 511: *Never, ever leave the palace grounds without security detail.*

If Sofia and Marco's little adventure has taught me anything it's that if you're going to break the rules, you must make it thoroughly worth your while.

Go big, or go home.

That's the way I see it.

As I wrote a new entry last night in the room I always stay in when we visit the Tleurbonne Palace in Malveaux —Rule number 1,246: *Don't snort laugh and then slap your thigh when talking with a member of the public, no matter how funny they might be*—I could almost see Father pursing his lips at my penmanship, even now that I'm twenty-four and three quarters.

Not that I'd *ever* let him read what I write in my book.

And anyway, these days, he's more focused on my social media presence than my penmanship, which he says should be impeccably elegant and regal. He clearly doesn't know that all I want to do is post funny memes of cats as well as photos of me with Max or Alex or Maddie, having a great time, like any normal person would.

"Such images are not becoming of a princess, Amelia," Father decreed. "And don't even get me *started* on those videos you made last week. Thank goodness our PR team managed to take them down from Tickery Tockery before too many people saw them."

"It's TikTok, Father," I corrected, but of course it fell on deaf ears. Father is about as interested in my opinion as anyone else in this palace, aka *Amelia is talking but no one is listening*. It goes with the territory when you're the third-born child whose role in life is to look regal and not a lot else.

Today, my journal is safely tucked away in my handbag at my feet as we sit in the royal Ledonian enclosure to watch The Games, the annual competition between our two countries, Ledonia and Malveaux. They involve everything from archery and polo to large, burly men picking up things like logs and hurling them across lawns in a show of strength.

Soon, the real fun will start when we royals compete in the more lighthearted activities. One such activity is Cheese Rolling, in which we nudge wheels of cheese with a stick down a gentle slope. It's always fun, but my absolute favorite is the Wife Race, which isn't quite as old fashioned and sexist as it sounds. Well, it was until Alex insisted last year that we could all compete in the event, married or not, at which point I chose the largest, most strapping chap I could find—a rather easy-on-the-eye rugby player called Liam Cartwright—and successfully crossed the line first.

I plan on doing exactly the same at this year's event.

"What are you smiling at?" my younger brother, Max, asks as we applaud the winners and prepare to compete ourselves.

"Nothing," I reply evasively.

"I assumed you were making eyes at Liam Cartwright. He's going to be your partner again in the Wife Race, isn't he?"

"Of course he is. I have every intention of winning this year."

"I'm not sure *you* did a whole lot to win last year, dear sister, what with the fact the women get carried."

I rise from my seat and adjust the ridiculous hat I've

been sweltering under for the past few hours, an elaborate thing involving pheasant feathers. "It's all in the technique, you know, Max."

"And I suppose you're going to tell me it's got nothing to do with the fact that Liam Cartwright is six foot five and built like a—"

"Do *not* finish that sentence!" Mummy's voice sounds out in warning.

"All I was going to say was he's built like a jolly sturdy building that may or may not house a toilet," Max replies with a mock innocent look on his face that absolutely no one believes.

"My dear boy, you can speak like that with your compatriots in the Royal Air Force, but not in mixed company," Father scolds.

"Of course, Father," Max replies.

"Come on, you two. We've all got to get ready for the Cheese Rolling and the Wife Race," Mummy says to Sofia and Marco, who have spent half the morning gazing at one another like a couple of lovesick puppies.

You know there's a certain irony in the fact that Sofia once planned on marrying somebody she felt no attraction to whatsoever, and now she's married to a man she clearly has major sizzle for.

I take it as a personal success. It was me who told her that using a series of boxes to be checked off on a spreadsheet was a terrible way to find a husband.

I was right.

Now, I want it to be my turn to find the sizzle with a dashingly handsome, totally dreamy man.

Which is exactly what I plan on doing after The Games finish tonight.

Before you go thinking I'm going to do something reckless, I have it all planned out. I have the perfect alibi.

According to the official line, once The Games are over here in Malveaux, I'm travelling to India with my cousin, Stefania, where we're going to enter a month-long silent meditation retreat.

I know what you're thinking. Me, silent? But for reasons yet unknown but nevertheless rather convenient, everyone seems to believe my story.

And as for Stefania, even if she wanted to tell my family that I'm not on the retreat she won't be able to without breaking her silence, which I know she takes awfully seriously because she's one of those rule-following oldest siblings who suck the joy out of everything.

Really, it's the perfect cover! I can have a grand adventure all of my own, with nobody breathing down my neck and telling me to follow the rules and all the other things I hate about being a princess.

I'll be free.

Free to do what I want when I want. I'm going to break every rule that's kept me trapped in this gilded fishbowl, especially the climbing trees rule.

The very thought makes me giddy.

A short while later, with my strapping, oversized rugby player at my side, we wait at the starting line, ready to head across the grass in the Wife Race.

"I warn you, Ami, I've been working out harder than usual in preparation for this," Alex tells me.

I raise my eyebrows at Maddie, his wife.

"It's true. He's been training for weeks," she says, with that goofy loved-up look on her face as she smiles up at my brother.

"So has Marco," Sofia says, and she and Marco share just as much of a goofy loved-up look as the other two.

Me? As strapping and altogether manly as Liam Cartwright might be—and he is awfully strapping and altogether manly—I don't have the urge to look at him with anything other than "let's win this thing" eyes. And besides, Liam told me he's met someone and fallen in love, so even if I did look at him in that way, it would not be reciprocated.

It needs to be my turn. *I'm* the one who wants a grand love affair. *I'm* the one who wants to be swept off her feet by an impossibly wonderful man whose eyes light up when he looks at me, just the way my brother's and sister's do when they gaze at their loves.

You see, I've not once been in love. Not even a little bit. Sure, I may have had short lived relationships with a few men and have fancied the pants off some others, but I've never felt that deep sense that I know beyond a whisper of doubt that this is my person. That he and I are better together than when we're apart. That the world is somehow so much more wonderful because he's in it.

Not to mention the sizzle.

Oh, how I want that sizzle! Feeling that hot, all-consuming electricity searing through me, consuming my every thought?

Bring.

It.

On.

That's why I'm not going to India to stay mute for a month. That's why I'm escaping this royal prison. To experience life. To lap it all up. To meet the man of my dreams and—hopefully, *hopefully*—to fall in love, sizzle and all.

And it's not just anyone I want to meet. On, no. I know exactly who.

Greg Smith, the man I've been talking with for the last couple of months. The man whose dark eyes make my breath hitch. The man whose jaw is razor sharp and stubbled, whose lips curve into the most delicious of smiles, whose broad shoulders fill out his shirt to perfection.

I let out a sigh.

I might not have met Greg Smith in person yet, but with everything we've shared over the last two months, I just know he's the man for me. Yes, he's utterly gorgeous, but more than that, he's sweet and thoughtful and knows exactly what to say and when to say it.

He's my fantasy man.

To meet him in real life, I need to get to the Côte-des-Papillons, aka the Butterfly Coast, where we'll meet at a bar overlooking the sea. He'll be holding a single red rose —clichéd but nevertheless romantic—and then our adventure will begin.

"Ready, Princess Amelia?" Liam asks, his arms outstretched to pick me up.

"Let's win this thing," I tell him.

He flashes me his smile. "Is that a royal commandment, Your Royal Highness?"

"Would it help you go faster if it was?" I ask and he nods. "In that case, I command you to run like the wind, Liam!"

"As you wish, ma'am," he replies, as though he's Wesley from *The Princess Bride*.

But I'm not *his* princess. I'm *Greg's* princess.

Or at least I hope I am.

I leap into his arms, the horn blares, and Liam takes off, each of his footsteps reverberating through me as he pounds across the field. In only a few short strides we've left everyone for dust: Alex and Maddie, Sofia and Marco, Max and the teeny tiny girl he chose for the event, slung over his shoulder, and Mummy in Father's arms, whose face has gone bright red from exertion.

Our family is nothing if not competitive, and we are all giving it our absolute best as we aim for the finish line.

"We're gonna beat you this year!" Maddie calls out from her position in my brother's arms, her words coming out in short bursts with each step Alex takes.

"No, we are!" yells Sofia from her position atop Marco, who, I admit, is alarmingly close to us.

Max doesn't say a word. He's too busy giving it his all, his face a study in determined concentration.

"Have ... you ... not ... seen ... Liam?" My words come out as though I'm trying to yell while jumping on a trampoline. "Legs ... like ... tree ... trunks!"

And within a few more bounds, with my internal organs now feeling like they're playing a game of musical chairs, Liam strides across the finish line ahead of the others, and we are the victors for the second year running.

Hazar!

Panting hard, he lowers me to the ground, his face shining red. "We did it," he says between heaving breaths.

"The dream team!" I raise my hand and we high five.

I can feel Father's judgement without even looking at him. Another rule to add to the journal. Rule number 1,248: *No high fiving rugby players in public, even if you have just won the Wife Race for the second year running.*

But I don't care one bit. Not only did we win, but I'm about to throw that rule book and all of its silly, nonsense princess rules right out the window.

My family congratulates me—Alex, Max, and Sofia somewhat begrudgingly—and after the evening celebrations finally begin to wind down, I'm itching to go.

I find Max and pull him away from the girl he's flirting with, much to his annoyance.

"This had better be important. Claudette was just telling me how bendy she is."

9

"How fun for Claudette, and yes, it's important." I glance around to make sure that we're totally out of earshot. "I'm going to tell you something, but you have to promise not to tell a soul," I begin in a low tone.

"Is it something worth knowing?"

"Trust me, it is."

"Go on, then."

"Promise?" I offer him my hand.

"We're not kids anymore, you know."

"Promise."

"Okay. Promise." He takes my hand, and we do our special handshake, the one we devised when we were eight and six respectively.

"I'm not going on the meditation retreat," I say, a grin claiming my face.

"Can't say I'm surprised. You're not built for silence, Ami."

"I'm going on an adventure instead."

"What do you mean?"

"I'm leaving tonight for a grand adventure!"

"You can't do that. Father will kill you. And so will Mummy."

"But don't you see? They'll never know, and I'll return to the palace after the retreat is done and no one will be the wiser."

He shoots me a dubious look. "It will never work."

"It will. You'll see."

"Father will have you followed, that Fabiana Fontaine woman will track you like a bloodhound, and you'll get recognized the moment you set foot outside the palace."

I shake my head at him, counting them off on my fingers. "Father won't have me followed because he thinks I'm going to India. Fabiana Fontaine will have no clue I'm even gone. And I'll wear non-princess clothes so no one will recognize me."

"You wear non-princess clothes half the time anyway, unless you count jeans and high tops as princess-wear."

"But only when I'm off duty and no one sees me. Can't you see? It's the perfect plan."

He pulls his brows together. "Are you sure you should be doing this?"

"One hundred thousand billion per cent. I need to break free of this life I lead. I need to see what else is out there."

He studies my face for a beat. "Just be careful, okay?"

"Promise," I tell him with a quick arm squeeze.

"There she is," Mummy says as she and the rest of the family crowd Max and me. "Have the most wonderful but silent time, darling," she says as she pulls me into a hug. "Make sure you look after her, Stefania."

"I will," my cousin replies.

"I still can't imagine you not talking for an entire month," Alex says with a light punch to my arm.

"I'd reply but I'm already practicing for the not talking part of the retreat," I say, and Alex raises his brows at me as though I've just proved his point.

Which I have.

Dang it.

"And it's only twenty-eight days," Stefania corrects.

"Oh, I'm sure those last two days will make all the difference to Ami," Max replies, and receives a rapid shove from me.

Sofia pulls me into a hug, "Take care of yourself."

"Try not to get Delhi belly," Marco adds. "It's not pretty. I've been there, literally in Delhi."

I scrunch up my nose. "TMI, Marco," I reply, but he just grins.

It's Alex's turn to hug me goodbye. "Why are you doing this again?"

"Can't you see? It's because she wants to find herself, like Julia Roberts in that movie. Ami's pulling an *Eat, Pray, Love*," Maddie replies for me.

Pulling an *Eat, Pray, Love*? Sure, let's run with that. After all, I may not be heading to India on a silent meditation retreat—*yawn*—but I am hoping that meeting Greg might at least cover the love part.

"The car is here, your Royal Highness," Cooper, one of the footmen, says.

"Thanks a lot, Coops." Beaming at my family, I say, "Well, this is it. See you all in a month."

They encircle Stefania and me, hugging us and telling us they love us, and to take good care of ourselves while not speaking.

"Remember, you won't hear from me for the full twenty-eight days. I'm starting my silent meditation from the moment we land in India," I say.

"Good luck with that," Alex says.

As I turn and wave at them all one last time before I climb into the car, my heart feels like a snow globe someone's shaken right up. It's time to embrace the terror of what I'm about to do and lap up every last second of my adventure. After all, the royal family of Ledonia might be expected to find their spouses through arranged marriages and royal balls, but this princess? She's going rogue.

Rule number 1,249: *A princess must never, ever feel giddy about breaking the rules.*

Well, there goes another one.

Chapter 2

Ethan

"Do something sexy."

Seriously? That's the seventh time I've been told that tonight, and I still have no idea what it means. Give a smoldering look? Flex? Pretend I'm interested in whatever inane question is about to follow?

"Ethan Roberts! Ethan!"

"Hey, Ethan! Over here!"

"We love you, Rowan Thornheart! 'Learn to wield the winter's curse!'"

I blink at the crowd like a clichéd deer in headlights, hearing my name, and my character's name and his famous line hurled at me from the sea of photographers and journalists. I take a breath, my chest tight as I glance down at my black lace-up shoes, so shiny I can almost see my reflection in them, dark against the red of the carpet.

I take a breath. *I've got this.*

You can't be the lead in the smash hit Netflix show, *It Came One Winter*, without getting this kind of attention on awards night, particularly when the show has a bunch of nominations.

Only this year it all seems so much more intense.

Sure, Season 3 has been a huge success, even rivalling Bridgerton in the ratings—but for a type of audience who's less into love and more into blood, death, and mindless violence.

You know how these fantasy shows go.

But the thing is, I've never liked these events. The posing, the frivolous questions, the having to be on show.

The being judged.

My date for the evening is no help. Well, I say "date" but even that's just for show. Chelsea Hutchinson, my co-star. On screen, we have a love-hate thing going on, alternating between raging war on one another and hooking up in random places like fur-lined, candle-lit caves and castle turrets during dramatic snow storms while our armies battle it out below.

You know, just your regular relationship stuff.

The network's publicity team tells me the audience laps up our "relationship," assuming our on-screen chemistry is replicated in real life.

It's not.

Chelsea is beautiful, but she's so much more interested in Chelsea than anyone else, me included.

The next twenty minutes become a blur of microphones and less than genuine smiles. A journalist, who introduces herself as Karina Wallace, asks about my nomination.

"I'm honored to be in such talented company," I say.

"Who are you wearing?"

"A suit by Jonathan Lunsford."

"Oh, look, Ethan. Here's Pageant Morris. She's your ex, right?" Karina says, already knowing the answer.

I lift my chin at Pageant. "Hi," I murmur.

Seeing an ex is always awkward, but on a red carpet? Criminally so. And it's all documented by eager photographers and journalists.

"Ethan Roberts, you look delectable," she purrs as she air kisses me, her dress almost painted on it's so tight. "Why did I ever give you up?" she says softly in my ear.

"I think it had more to do with the fact you started sleeping with your co-star than you 'gave me up' exactly," I say under my breath, the banal smile on my face at odds with my words.

"What can I say? You just weren't ambitious enough for me, even though you and I would have had such totally hot babies together," she replies before she blows me a kiss over her shoulder and shimmies away.

Hot babies?

Paige and Hollywood are made for one another.

I endure the SlowCam, being asked once more to "do something sexy," before a journalist so skinny her head looks like a lollipop asks, "How amazing is your life now that you're dating your co-star, Chelsea Hutchinson?"

Yeah, a fake relationship Chelsea's and my agent has orchestrated is just amazing.

"It's amazing, as you say," I reply, moving along the carpet.

But no sooner have I escaped one journalist, when I'm accosted by another—this time a guy in a perfectly cut white suit, pink hair, and no shirt—or chest hair, for that matter. He introduces himself as Timoth*ay* and then asks, "What tips did your brother, Dan Roberts, famous NHL player, give you about fame?"

A conversation we had back home in Maple Falls, Washington state, flashes into my mind. It was the month the first series was released, and my fame had gone from "total obscurity" to "the hottest name in Hollywood" overnight. I was reeling.

Dan sat me down on our parents' sofa and told me that all I had to do was be myself and trust that people will like who I am, no matter what character I play on screen.

I know he was trying to help me, but I had no clue what fame was really like. Dan's the kind of guy who signs autographs with a genuine smile. Me? I'm counting the seconds until I can escape.

"With Dan now retired from the NHL, you're the only currently famous one left in your family. How does that make you feel?" He thrusts his microphone in my face with an expectant look.

How do I answer *that*?

I'm struggling on with the help of my fake girlfriend?

I must carry on in the name of fame?

In the end, I go with something sarcastic and entirely made up.

"Actually, my mom just went viral on TikTok with her sourdough bread making, so I'm pretty sure I'm like second famous in the family now? Third, if you count my parents' cat, who keeps photobombing her videos."

Timoth*ay* blinks at me, thrown.

"Cleo really is a very special cat," I explain.

Landing this role has been the highlight of my career, a

career punctuated only occasionally with small roles and ads, bit parts on established TV shows, stage productions so off-Broadway they're practically in New Jersey. Or literally, as the case was for one of the plays I did a couple years back.

But the thing is—and I know I'm going to sound ungrateful when I say this, but that doesn't make it any less true—all I ever wanted to do was act. I wanted to be involved in a cast with talented people who loved doing what they do. I wanted to create something incredible for an audience, embodying my role, giving it all I've got.

It's my passion. My reason for being.

Not this.

Not the personal questions and endless photographers and questions as you pose like an idiot on a red carpet, flashing bulbs blinding you as you sweat through the suit a designer lent you so you could help them sell more suits.

Don't get me wrong. Being a part of this show is amazing. I feel like I've grown so much as an actor, and I can honestly say I love what I do. But for every positive there's always a negative, and that negative for me is right here, right now, at an awards show in Hollywood, surrounded by people wanting you to be something you're not.

Finally, I make it into the auditorium.

I've been hit with more camera flashes than this carpet has faced stilettos, and I've acknowledged my fans, posing for a few selfies. And now I sit through the awards show along with the rest of the team. We get up on stage when the show wins, and I make sure to express the appropriate level of humility when another hot young actor wins my category.

As I'm heading toward the exit after the ceremony, hoping to slip away before the after-party madness begins, a firm hand clamps down on my shoulder.

"There he is," Dion Chambers, my agent, materializes beside me in one of his trademark suits. His smile is all perfect white teeth, but his eyes are calculating behind designer frames.

"Hey, Dion. Just heading home."

"To the after-party," he corrects, steering me toward a quiet corner. "But first, excellent work with the meeting today. Crystal Clear Productions is going to take you places, kid."

I resist the urge to point out that at twenty-eight I'm hardly a kid. "About that—"

He lowers his voice, his smile never leaving his face. "I've already got the ball rolling on this. Big things, Ethan. This is going to change the game for you. You're hot right now. You need to milk it for all it's worth."

"What if I don't want to milk it for all it's worth? What if all I want to do is my job?"

He laughs as though I've said something funny. "Trust me, Ethan, you're gonna need this. Your show is hot right now, but if you don't ride that wave, you're gonna be forgotten once this show is done. I would say you're not exactly in a position to be picky right now."

Fear grips my belly. "What do you mean? The show's doing great—"

"Shows end, Ethan. Then what?" His phone buzzes and he checks it, his smile widening. "Interesting. We're tracking your social media mentions right now, and they're through the freaking roof."

"You're tracking how many people are talking about me?"

He gives me a look like I've asked whether he breathes oxygen. "Now, listen. This is about building your brand beyond Rowan Thornheart." He glances over my shoulder, his attention already elsewhere. "We'll talk more next week." He slaps my back.

As he strides away, I can't shake the feeling that I've just been managed rather than heard. I've learned it's a familiar sensation with Dion.

I make my way from the auditorium and when I climb into the sleek black car, I let out a relieved breath of air.

I always thought of myself as sitting somewhere close to the extrovert end of the spectrum before I began working in Hollywood. But, *man*, these people are "on" all the time. I seriously don't know how they do it. Maybe it's because I grew up in a small town where I was on a first name basis with all the kids in my high school, and the fall festival was the biggest thing to happen each year. I don't know. What I do know is this adulation, this infamy, this whole circus, has never been what I wanted.

Just as I'm closing my eyes, the door flies open, the car instantly filling with people's chatter, as Chelsea slides in beside me.

"That was *amazing*!" she exclaims, her eyes bright as she leans back in her seat in a cloud of perfume and pulls a mirror from her clutch. She peers at her reflection. "Oh, my hair! Why didn't you say something."

I flip my gaze to her. She looks just as perfectly put together as she always does. "Your hair looks great to me."

She bats my upper arm. "You're a guy. What would you know about hair? It's a mess. Oh, no!"

"What?"

"My aura has faded."

"That's… bad?"

"Ethan, it's a disaster! I need to see Daphne, like, *now*." She taps at her phone. "Daph. Crisis. Come meet me in the car? We're on our way to the party now."

"How do you fix an aura?" I ask.

"You'll see. Did you talk to Dion?"

"I *listened* to him."

"He's working on this new project for us and he's super excited about it."

"What is it? Did he tell you? All I got was banal platitudes."

She waves my comment away with a flick of her wrist. "I don't know. Something *amazing*. He's really got his finger on the pulse."

I harrumph. "Sure."

As the car begins to crawl away from the curb, joining the stream of silver vehicles, Chelsea chats about all the people she's seen, being her usual hyper self. Only after talking for at least ten minutes does she actually notice I'm not exactly engaged in the conversation.

"You seem a little glum, Eth. Is it because you didn't win? Because you know you usually have to be nominated a bunch of times before you win these things. And you look hot. That's what really matters."

Sure.

"Nah, I'm just a little tired," I reply.

"I know what you need."

I arch a brow. It's not likely someone like Chelsea would know what I need.

"You need champagne."

And there it is.

I shake my head. "I'm good."

Ignoring me, she pulls a bottle from the icebox and hands it to me to open. I dutifully do, the pop of the cork punctuating her pearls of wisdom on how to stay relevant even if you don't win an award.

"I've been in the industry much longer than you," she says, as though the extra six months more than me make all the difference.

I pour out a couple of glasses, although I'm not in the mood for champagne. Despite the 90° outside, I'm in the mood for a cup of hot cocoa in front of a fire at my family's home in Maple Falls.

Man, does that life feel far away right now.

She takes a sip of her champagne and then sizes me up. "You're no fun tonight, Eth."

"Sorry about that, Chels," I reply.

"Do you know what you need?"

I hold up my untouched glass. "Champagne. You already told me."

"What *else* you need. You need a vacation. Somewhere fabulous where you can relax and forget about all of this for a while. Then, you can return and be hotter than ever."

I turn to her, surprised by her uncharacteristically astute observation. "You know you might be right?"

"Of course I am. So go take one. We're not due back on set for a month."

"I guess I could head home. See my folks. My brother and his wife have just had their first child, who I've not seen a lot of." The tightness in my chest loosens for the first time this evening.

But then it tightens right back up when I picture having to be locked away inside as paparazzi wait for me or any member of my family to emerge.

I won't do that to them.

Chelsea makes a face. "Yawn. You could do something way more exciting than that. I've got an idea." She starts tapping at her phone again and then turns the screen around, showing me a world map.

I raise my eyebrows at her in question.

"Pick a place. Which continent?"

"You want me to just randomly pick a place to go on vacation for a month?"

"Why not? You need your glow back. I don't want some half-baked version of Rowan Thornheart when we start filming again." I begin to think she's generally concerned about me when she adds, "It'll make me look bad. Like I can't get a hotter version of you."

I resist the urge to roll my eyes. "I don't know. Europe? I've never been."

"Good start. Now, close your eyes and choose a place."

"Why?"

"So you can choose a country free from your conscious self, instead tapping into your deeper, spiritual being and allowing it to guide you to where you're meant to be."

Oh, good grief.

"Trust me, Eth. You need this, like, *so bad*. Dion told me so."

"He did?"

"Mm-hm. Just before, at the ceremony."

Is it weird that he told Chelsea I should take a break and not me?

I close my eyes. I like the idea of escaping to Europe for a while, and Chelsea's way of choosing where I go could be as effective as any other.

"I'm placing the phone in front of you and all you have to do is point your finger."

I do as she says, jabbing my finger at the screen. I open my eyes to see the spot I've chosen is in the middle of the Mediterranean Sea. "Does this mean my spiritual self wants to go for a swim?" I ask with a smile.

"*Duh*. It means your aim is off. Here. Take the phone in your other hand, then close your eyes and point."

I do as she says and when I point, my finger lands on southern France. "France. I could eat French bread and cheese for a while."

She takes the phone back. "Actually, you chose a small

country next to France. Malveaux," she says, pronouncing it as "Mal-vox." I might not have been to Europe, but I remember how to pronounce that small country's name from a news article a while back. A Texan became the queen of the country, I think. Or princess. Something like that.

I don't exactly follow royalty.

"So, I'm heading to Malveaux?"

She clicks her phone off. "Of course you are. Go. Have an adventure. Do something fun. Your soul will thank you, you know."

I have no clue how my soul will thank me. Maybe send me an ecard? A fruit basket?

But I do like the idea of going to a small country on the Mediterranean. I can breathe in the sea air, feel the sand between my toes, the sun on my face—and forget about what's become of my life for a while.

As the car comes to a stop outside the party venue, the hairdresser-slash-aura-fixer Daphne climbs inside, acknowledging me with a nod before she gets to work on Chelsea. She waves her hands like an enthusiastic air traffic controller directing invisible planes, and I get lost in thought.

The idea of escaping solidifies in my brain. Malveaux. A place where the media won't find me, where nobody will ask me to "do something sexy" or care "who" I'm wearing.

A place where I can breathe again.

My mind is made up. By this time tomorrow, I'll be gone from all of this. Anonymous. Free. Just a guy on vacation figuring out what matters to him.

For the first time all night, I feel something like hope.

Chapter 3

Amelia

"Is that everything?" the vendor asks, wrapping the sandwich in paper.

"Yes. Just the ham and cheese, please," I reply, trying to sound like I buy my own food from bakeries every day of my life.

He nods, holding out his hand. "That'll be eight euros."

I hand over the crumpled bill. No gloves. No bowing. No *Will that be all, Your Royal Highness?* Just a simple transaction between two ordinary people.

It's nothing short of thrilling.

When you've lived your entire life in the spotlight from the very moment you entered the world, with enough stupid rules to make even the strictest teacher rub their hands together in glee, strutting down this beautiful Tleurbonne street in my favorite scuffed high tops—*gasp!*—while eating a sandwich purchased from a bakery? Well it feels like I'm starring in my own personal revolution.

A princess revolution.

I take my first bite, the still-warm bread crunching perfectly against the melted cheese and savory ham. Oh, my goodness. This might be the best sandwich I've ever eaten, and I've had many meals prepared by a Michelin chef. The palace chef would faint if he knew I was eating food prepared by someone without a team of health inspectors monitoring every move.

Rule number 257: *A princess never eats food while walking down the street.*

Well, there goes another rule broken, and I've barely even started my adventure.

As I wander down the busy street, people actually bump into me. And some don't even say sorry! Nobody curtsies. Nobody has called me "ma'am" or insisted I replace my jeans and sneakers with a conservative nun-like dress and sensible heels.

My security detail would be having a collective heart attack watching me wade through this river of humanity.

But I'm too busy grinning like a tween who's just discovered their parents' Wi-Fi password.

And yes, I've broken Rule number 443: *Never travel without security detail.* But this feeling is nothing short of exhilarating! And besides, how can I truly be myself while being watched constantly by men in dark suits and sunglasses with grim looks on their faces?

Today, I'm just another young woman, casually strolling through the city streets of Tleurbonne, enjoying the warmth of the day and the beauty of the city, spending a few pleasant hours before my train is due to leave to whisk me away to meet the man I hope will prove to be my grand love.

The thought of finally, finally meeting Greg tonight has my belly positively swooping.

His last message keeps playing in my head. *I can't wait to see those beautiful eyes of yours in person.*

He doesn't even know I'm royal. In fact, he thinks I'm a lady's maid at the palace. But he's still interested in me, the *real* me. Not my title, not my family connections. Just Amelia.

Or "Mia," as he calls me online.

Two months of late-night messages sharing our dreams —his vineyard expansion and my carefully generic aspirations so as not to give away my true identity. Two months of him sending me photos of sunsets from his terrace with captions like *How I wish you were here.*

No one's ever wanted just me before. They're always looking for an angle, a way to use me to get what they want.

I remember making a new friend in my first few days at boarding school when I was 13 years old, only to overhear her mother telling her to use "the princess connection" in whatever way she could.

That's what makes Greg so special. He's interested in *me*. Not my royal blood. Not my family's money or position.

Just me.

And I'm going to meet him at a bar overlooking the sea

at sunset tonight! Will he be nervous? Will his voice sound the same as it does in the voice messages he sends, that delicious deep rumble with his Malveauxian accent?

I've imagined our first meeting a hundred different ways: him standing as I approach, his eyes lighting up with recognition, perhaps taking my hand or even pulling me against him into a hug. Not because I'm Princess Amelia of Ledonia, but because I'm the woman he's been connecting with all these months. The woman who laughs at his terrible jokes and sends him song recommendations and who finally worked up the courage to escape the confines of her life just to meet him.

IT WAS easy enough to give Stefania the slip at the airport last night. I pretended I'd forgotten my passport, sending her ahead to the meditation center while I "arranged" for the royal jet to come back and get me later. By the time she realized I wasn't coming, she'd be committed to twenty-eight days of silence.

Just to be safe, I messaged her that I'd been unexpectedly called back to Ledonia, and that I'd see her next month on her return when I begged her to tell me all about the retreat.

She'll be none the wiser, and I'll be free.

I've switched my phone off and bought a new one, complete with a new number no one knows. Well, no one other than Max, that is. I sent him a quick message, telling him that if he absolutely had to, he could reach me on this number but only if it was a life-or-death emergency.

He responded in his typical Max way, telling me not to get myself murdered or taken hostage because he was unlikely to pay the ransom.

Brothers.

After leaving my suitcase at a storage space at the main train station, just as the travel sites recommended I do, I meander down a narrow cobblestone street, pausing to smell the flowers outside a florist. I've sat in the sun and munched on a delicious pastry and drunk a rather horrible cup of Malveauxian tea—to which I promptly added several teaspoons of sugar to make it palatable. I've marveled at the city's grand Gothic cathedral, trailed my fingers through the water in the famous Fontaine de Lumière, and meandered through a pretty city park, its majestic trees towering above me, making me feel small and insignificant.

I'm enjoying the sun on my face, dreaming about Greg, when I spot several members of what look like paparazzi charging toward me at a rapid rate of knots.

No! They can't have spotted me! I've only been gone for twelve hours. How could they know I'm here when I'm meant to be on my way to some remote mountainous spot in India to not talk for a month?

Desperate, I take flight, bumping into an elegant middle-aged woman, weighed down with shopping. "I'm so sorry!" I call over my shoulder in my best Malveauxian as I dart around the corner. I spot a door of a nearby shop and fly inside, closing the door firmly behind me, my heart beating double time.

I peer through the glass to see them charging down the street, passing me by.

I let out a relieved breath. My adventure could have been over before it had even begun!

Amelia: one. Paparazzi: zero.

I turn to look at what sort of shop I've come into, and spot rows and rows of unusual clothes. Mannequins are dressed as pirates, another as Marilyn Monroe in her famous subway dress, and another as what could only be described as a question mark.

It's a costume shop.

Serendipitous? I think so.

What runaway royal doesn't need a good disguise when the paparazzi are hot on her tail?

Gambling on the public not recognizing me in jeans and a T-shirt was clearly amateur. I need to step up my game, and I've accidentally landed in the perfect spot.

"Can I help you, miss?" an older man with a balding head and thick salt and pepper sideburns asks me in a doubtful tone.

Miss not *Your Royal Highness*. It's a good start.

"Yes, I'd like a costume, please," I say in Malveauxian as I step further into the shop, the anxiety from only moments ago disappearing into the ether.

"Well, I'd say you're in the right place then," he replies with a kind smile, and I like him instantly. "What did you have in mind?"

Before I have the chance to reply, there's a crashing sound as someone bursts through the door, toppling over the mannequin in Marilyn Monroe's famous dress.

Oh no! The paparazzi are here!

I'm seized by panic. I grab the closest thing to hand, a blur of orange and black, and reply hurriedly, "This one. I'll take it to the changing rooms right now." I make a beeline for the back of the shop, collecting the first wig I can find before I pull back the curtain and leap inside, my heart pounding like an electronic drum machine at a dance party.

Once safely inside, I catch my breath.

It'll be okay, I tell myself. *They didn't get a good look at me. They think I'm halfway across the globe. And they've never seen me in jeans. I'm fine. Totally fine.*

Carefully, I peel back the curtain, just enough so I can see who's out there, but they can't see me. I'm shocked to spot a tall man rushing toward me with a determined look on his face, his jaw locked.

The shop proprietor calls after him. "Sir? Can I help you, sir?"

The guy ignores him. He's getting closer and closer to me. I glance around in wild desperation, heart thudding, mind racing, panic rising and rising... until he darts into the neighboring stall and pulls the curtain over with a dramatic *woosh!*

What the...?

I blow out a breath, my frantic heartbeat beginning to return to normal.

This escaping the palace thing is so much more nerve-wracking than I ever anticipated.

He wasn't looking for me. He's not paparazzi. He's just some guy in a hurry who needs a costume. A grim, anxious looking guy who needs a costume at that.

I wonder what his story is.

But I've got my own fish to fry, as my lady's maid, Theresa, puts it. Not that I've ever fried a fish. Princess, remember? We're too busy holding our pinkie fingers out as we sip tea from fine china cups.

Gingerly, I pull the curtain open a crack and check the rest of the shop. Other than the now somewhat confused proprietor, thanks to not one but two of his customers making a hasty beeline for his changing rooms, the place is empty. I let out a relieved breath. They weren't following me. No one knows I'm here.

I'm safe.

I close the curtain over again and inspect the items I hastily grabbed as I flew in here. I've got a bright orange costume with big black dots that looks something like Fred

Flintstone from the movie would wear, and a long blonde wig.

How incognito would I be if I stepped out of this shop dressed as a character from a Flintstone movie? It would be like wearing a huge target on my back with the words "runaway royal right here" in bold letters.

I collect the items and pull back the curtain.

"How were those, miss?" the proprietor asks, and I notice he has a name tag which reads *René*.

"Not right, thank you, René," I say, handing him the costume.

"Did you want other Flintstone costumes to try?" he asks and then adds tentatively, "Perhaps one for a woman? Betty or Wilma? Or Pebbles, perhaps?"

"Actually, I've decided against going to this party as a Flintstone," I reply, looking around.

It would need to be a much more realistic costume than something from the time when humans and dinosaurs supposedly cohabitated in a town called Bedrock. Something an everyday person would wear.

My eyes land on a pink cowgirl costume, complete with a matching pink hat. No. Margot Robbie already did that one in the *Barbie* movie.

"What do you have for women my size, René?" I ask.

"That depends on what you're looking for. Something like this, perhaps?" He pulls a costume from a nearby rack that looks something akin to a swimsuit, only skimpier. "Might I suggest Wonder Woman?"

Yes, great idea.

I shake my head.

"A Playboy Bunny?" He holds up an equally skimpy costume, this one with a bunny's tail and ears.

Seriously?

A firm shake of my head.

"Sexy nurse?" This time René shows me a costume with a little more material, but low enough cut that the world could see right down to my navel.

Another shake of my head.

"What about a sexy angel?" He pulls out another white costume, this time with a split that could quite well reach my navel from the other direction.

Before he has the chance to offer me another sexy costume—a sexy embalmer, perhaps?—I say, "I'm looking for a costume with a little more... material. Something I could wear to a children's party, for example."

Aka, something that leaves a little more to the imagination than these tiny pieces of fabric posing as costumes.

"Oh. I understand. I've taken you to entirely the wrong section. Come this way, miss."

I follow René, reminding myself that in a few short hours I'll be safely on a train to meet Greg. The right disguise could be the difference between freedom and being dragged back to the palace in disgrace, a laughing-stock, as I'm sure that woman Fabiana Fontaine will refer to me. Or worse.

As we move toward the back of the shop, I catch a glimpse of the determined man in the adjacent changing room. His expression is still tense.

For a moment, our eyes meet in the mirror, and I offer him a smile, saying, "Hello."

He doesn't smile back.

Rude.

I push him from my mind, focusing on the task at hand. Princess Amelia might be recognizable out there, but whoever emerges from this shop won't be. And that new person is that much closer to the coast, to that bar by the sea, and to Greg.

That much closer to the possibility of love.

Chapter 4

Amelia

I'm still rifling through costumes when the curtain to the changing room the rude man darted into flies fully open, and the man himself steps out into the shop.

He's tall—taller than my brothers—with closely cropped dark hair and a presence that inexplicably fills the small shop.

"This is the wrong size," he says to René, his voice sonorous and smooth. "I might just go get something else."

Huh. He's an American.

"Certainly, sir," René replies in heavily accented English. "I'll be right with you once I've served this young lady. But of course, feel free to peruse the racks in the meantime."

The rude American's gaze flicks briefly to mine, and I'm momentarily struck by how starkly deep blue his eyes are. The same eyes that had looked so intense and focused when he'd rushed into the shop now seem much warmer against his strong jaw and perfectly proportioned features.

But he's still rude.

"Right. My bad," he says, appearing to notice me properly for the first time.

"If you're in a hurry—" I begin in English, but he shakes his head. Although I'm Ledonian, I do speak several languages fluently, English being one of them. You can't be a member of a European royal family and not speak several languages. Mummy made us all learn Latin, too. Not that I exactly have much call for it, like, *ever*.

"It's fine. I thought I was pressed for time, but it turns out I'm not." He glances out the window before he turns back to me and pulls his lips into a smile. "What are you looking for?"

"A costume," I reply elusively. This guy scared the crap out of me, charging toward me with what appeared to be ill intent only a few moments ago, and then he was rude ignoring my greeting. I'm hardly going to get all chummy with him.

"Well, I would say you're in the right place for that," he replies, and when I flick my gaze to him, I see his face is lit up in a smile.

It works to soften me a fraction and I smile back. "I suppose I am."

"This section is where you'll find the more modest

women's costumes, miss," René says as the doorbell tinkles and a group of people walk into the shop.

I turn to them in alarm, but I relax when I see it's only a group of teenage girls, giggling amongst themselves.

"If you'll excuse me. I'll be right back," René says as he makes his way toward them.

I begin to rifle through the costumes, keeping my head down. I find quite a few nun's habits and medieval dresses, when I notice that the American guy hasn't moved. Instead, he's standing like a statue, his eyes flicking from me to the teenagers and back again. When one of the girls pulls out her phone, he turns his back completely to them and pulls out a nun's habit.

"Are you going to party as a nun?" I ask pleasantly.

What is with this man?

"Err, no. I was lost in thought for a moment there."

When the teenagers burst into high-pitched giggles, he visibly tenses. They look our way, and he plucks a Snow White dress from the rack, holding it up like a shield.

I'm not judging. If the guy's a cross dresser, he's a cross dresser. That's his business, not mine. Though hiding behind costumes seems a bit extreme.

"Do you know them?" I whisper, gesturing subtly toward the girls.

"No," he says quickly. Possibly too quickly. "I just don't like having my picture taken, and I thought that's what one of them was doing just now."

Interesting. Is he camera-shy or hiding from someone? Perhaps he has an ex-girlfriend in town. Or maybe he's on the run from the law—though criminals probably don't typically hide in costume shops. They'd have a secret lair somewhere in the rough end of town. Or in a cave.

I take a surreptitious look at him once more. He seems to be assessing the costumes he's got in his hands, a perplexed look on his face, and I notice him glancing nervously at the group of girls once more.

Who is this guy that he would be afraid of a bunch of teenage girls? Actually, scratch that. I have first-hand experience of how vicious teenage girls can be. Thank you, boarding school and supposed friends who only want to use me for my royal status.

But he's a grown man. Surely he can't let a bunch of teens bother him?

"I'm in the wrong section, aren't I?" he says with a short, self-effacing chortle.

"I don't know. I can see you as a nun. The big headpiece would certainly add allure to your look, although getting through narrow doorways may prove a challenge."

He smiles at me, his face lit up, and it strikes me that not only does he cut a rather fine, tall figure, but he's clearly struck the genetic lottery with his handsome features, too.

"I'd probably choose to be Mother Superior."

"You're the type who likes to be in charge, then?"

He shakes his head. "I'm the middle child. I've never got to be in charge of anything in my life."

"Same! Bossy older siblings?"

"I'm grateful to only have one. A brother. You've got more than one?"

"I have an older brother and an older sister. She's the eldest and really, really bossy."

"I think it goes with the job description."

As he steps a little closer, I notice more details—broad shoulders tapering to a slim waist, the kind of athletic build that comes from exercise, the kind our security team all seem to have. The women *and* the men.

"Between you and me, I'm glad I'm not the first born.

Being the middle child might have its drawbacks, but I think it's the best," he continues.

"You don't have to be bossy, and you're not the baby."

"Right?" he replies, his eyes alight. "I'm Maverick Mitchell, by the way," he says with a confident, pearly white smile, his hand outstretched.

I take his hand in mine. "Your parents called you Maverick?"

"Sure did."

"Well, I suppose there's an actress called Rebel, so why not Maverick?" I say, more to myself than to him.

"Are you saying my name sounds feminine? Because it's very manly where I'm from."

I glance at the nun's habit and Snow White costume in his hands. "Oh, I believe you," I deadpan, and win another smile from him.

This is surprisingly fun. He's got no clue who I am and he's not bowing and calling me *Your Royal Highness* or any of the things I detest. He sees me as an equal, a fellow shopper who happens to be looking for a costume to wear to a party.

"And you are?" he asks.

"Amel—," I begin, realizing too late that the last thing I should be doing is using my actual name. Surely a fake name is Subterfuge 101. Basic, entry-level stuff. In all my careful planning for this adventure I've failed at the very first hurdle.

"Amel?" he asks.

"Amel-ikintoflin," I say.

Amel-ikintoflin? Where did that come from? I had all the names in the world to choose from, but somehow I've managed to land on quite possibly the most ridiculous name ever.

Maverick raises his brows. "Amel-ikintoflin? That's... unusual."

Scrambling to fix my frankly ridiculous faux pas, I reply hurriedly, "It's Dutch."

Because it could be Dutch. It *sounds* Dutch. And I did meet a woman from The Netherlands at a charity function last month whose name was equally long and contorted. I think. Or was that a man?

I channel my inner Sofia by lifting my chin to show him that not only is Amel-ikintoflin my name, but that I'm mildly offended he's questioning its validity.

"Dutch?" he asks, his features visibly relaxing as René shows the girls some 80's costumes and they giggle and chat among themselves.

"Dutch. In fact, I'm from a long line of Dutch Amel-ikintoflins."

I'm doubling down. There's nothing else I can do. Don't they say the first rule of successful lying is to fully commit to the lie?

Well, I'm committing.

"A long line of Dutch Amel-ikintoflins?" he questions.

I offer him my most pleasant princess smile. "Indeed."

He pulls his brows together. "So, Amel-ikintoflin is your last name?"

Dang it!

Time for some quick thinking.

"No, actually, it's my first name. All the women in my family are called Amel-ikintoflin. Have been for genera-tions upon generations."

By now his brows are pulled so closely together he could hold a one Euro coin between them. "Isn't that confusing?"

"Not in the least. Why would it be?" I ask, lifting my

chin a fraction more, because I need all the Sofia I can get right now.

He presses his lips together. "Tell me something. If all the women in your family are called the same name, how do you tell each other apart?"

Luckily, I land on an idea to dig me out of this self-inflicted hole. "We have nicknames."

Yes! That's good. Believable. Now all I have to do is think of a plausible nickname.

"What's your nickname?"

"Mine's Amy, like Amy Adams from *Enchanted*." When he looks at me blankly, I add, "You know, the Disney movie?"

He shakes his head. "I don't."

"It's very good. You should watch it. It's about a beautiful cartoon princess who gets sent to real life New York City, a land where there's no happily ever after."

He looks at me as though I've just made that all up and have quite possibly forgotten to take my meds today. "Noted."

The chattering girls make their purchases and leave the shop, and Maverick's shoulders relax.

"So, should I call you Amy?" he asks.

"That depends."

"On what?"

"If I can call you Mav?"

"I'd like that."

Fake it 'til you make it.

"Pleased to meet you, Mav." I offer him my hand and we shake.

"You, too, Amy."

"So, you're American?" I ask, keen to move on from my allegedly Dutch name and movies about princesses leaving their royal lives behind.

Far too close to reality.

He raises his hands in the air. "Guilty. What gave me away?"

I shrug. "Everything."

He chortles. "Right."

"What are you doing in Malveaux?"

"I'm on vacation."

I twist the sleeve of one of the costumes. "Oh. I thought you might have been here for The Games."

I'm sounding him out to see if he actually does recognize me and is just toying with me before he produces a camera and destroys my life.

Well, my next twenty-eight days, anyway.

"What are The Games?" he asks, and I feel a rush of relief. He genuinely doesn't know who I am.

Which is refreshing, I admit. His relaxed demeanor and easy smile now that the teenagers have left are so different from the stiff, formal interactions I'm used to.

"The Games is an annual competition between Malveaux and the neighboring country, Ledonia. They only finished last night. Lots of people are here in the city for them. They're very popular."

"I'm sorry I missed them."

"The Royals compete in the lighthearted games, too, you know," I lead.

"Is that so?" he asks, his tone suggesting he's not at all interested in hearing about the royal families.

I blow out a breath.

I think I'm in the clear.

René rushes over to us, and I notice that the shop is now empty but for us. "I'm sorry about that. How did you get on with finding a costume, miss."

Costume. Right. I'm not here to converse with American tourists called Maverick.

"Not very well, I'm afraid, René. I don't think I'm looking for one of these sorts of costumes." I wave my hand at the selection. "I think I'd like to look like the sort of person you might see walking down the street, rather than a character. Does that make sense?"

"You mean like a rocker or punk or a goth?" Maverick suggests, and it's like a bulb alights in my brain.

"Yes! Exactly that. I want to be a goth," I declare, remembering a girl from school who used to dress all in black, with black-rimmed eyes and black lipstick, and never, ever smiled. She was rather severe looking, and quite the opposite of me. The perfect disguise for a runaway princess!

With my dark hair I know I could pull the look off. I might not have the porcelain skin, what with my skin tone being decidedly olive, but that's nothing a touch of makeup can't take care of.

"I like the idea of being a goth, too," Maverick says. "If that's okay with you, Amy?"

"I'm sure we're going to entirely different parties. It won't matter at all if we're both goths," I assure him.

The fact I'm not going to a party at all is a mere detail he doesn't need to know.

René leads us to a section of the shop filled with entirely black clothes. Both Maverick and I gather all the elements needed to look like a goth and disappear into our respective changing rooms. For my part, I pull on a black T-shirt featuring a large skull front and center, a slim-fitting black skirt covered in a fine skull pattern that hits mid-thigh, and some stick-on tattoos in the shape of—you guessed it—skulls.

I've got a theme and I'm sticking to it.

I gaze at my reflection. Not bad. Quite goth, but I'm missing something.

I pull my black eyeliner from my handbag and draw a ring around my eyes and blacken my lips, the result being I look a lot less me and a lot more unapproachable and moodier.

Now all I must do is make sure I don't smile and I'll have this whole goth thing down pat.

I pull back the curtain and step into the shop, where René runs a critical eye over me. "That's what's called a clean goth aesthetic, miss. Are you sure you don't want to be more extreme for your party?"

"Quite sure," I reply with a smile and then stop myself, instead arranging my features into appropriately brooding, dark, and macabre.

Whatever macabre looks like exactly. Doesn't it mean "dead?"

Maverick's curtain rustles, and I turn to see him in all his dark glory. Like me, he's wearing a black T-shirt, but he has a moon on the front, with the silhouette of a gnarled tree. He's wearing it loose over a pair of black trousers, which he's paired with entirely the wrong shoes: white sneakers.

Unlike me, he's wearing a long black wig that looks a lot more like a wig than it does actual hair. The darkness of his outfit makes him look paler and more intense, entirely appropriate for a goth.

"What do you think?" he asks, holding his arms out to the side.

"Fabulous! But the wig? It's not great," I say.

He reaches up and touches it. "It doesn't work?"

I shake my head, and he pulls it off. Instantly, the color returns to his skin, and he looks a thousand percent ... less dead.

"Might I suggest you lose the shoes, as well?" René says.

"René's right. Those shoes scream American tourist to me," I say.

He looks down at his feet. "Yeah. Not very goth, huh?" He looks at me and his face lights up in a smile.

"You need to stop doing that, too, to get into character," I tell him.

"Doing what?"

"When did you ever see a goth smile, Mav?"

"Good point," he says, his smile moving in entirely the wrong direction.

"One final touch." I collect my black eyeliner. Holding it up I ask, "May I?"

His brows crease up again. "What are you going to do with that?"

"I'm going to put black freckles right across your nose and draw an upturned moustache on your top lip," I say, holding my expression.

"You are?"

"Of course not. I'm going to put some eyeliner on you."

"In that case, be my guest."

"You're very tall. You might need to sit."

"You bet."

"How tall are you, exactly?"

"6'4". My brother's taller."

"Goodness."

He takes a seat on the wooden stool in his changing room. I lean in and run my pencil below his lash line. As I do, he looks up at me and I notice the blue of his eyes is like swimming in a moonlit ocean, with tiny bits of gold scattered around his pupils.

Coupled with his square jaw, it strikes me how handsome he is. I've seen this level of physical perfection before. At state dinners with visiting dignitaries' handsome sons who are paraded in front of me, all groomed since birth to be the perfect escort.

But there's something so much more authentic about Maverick, a lack of practiced charm that's refreshing.

I pull back and inspect my handiwork. With the eyeliner, his eyes are accentuated, lending him an almost haunted look, transforming him from the American tourist who walked into the shop to a convincing goth.

With his eyes still trained on mine, he says, "Thank you, Amy," in a soft tone that feels almost intimate.

Which is crazy. We've only just met.

"All part of the Malveauxian service," I reply lightly, pulling my gaze from his.

"I think you both look splendid. Just enough goth to fit the bill," René pronounces.

Satisfied with our looks, we both pay for the costumes, and despite me telling him he looks better without the wig, I notice Maverick paying for that, too.

"You're not changing out of your costume either?" I ask as he slides his regular clothes into a paper bag, just as I did myself.

"Nor you, by the looks of things," he replies.

"I like the look so much I want to wear it before my party."

"Yeah. Me, too."

We thank René and leave the shop, blinking in the bright afternoon light.

"Well, I suppose this is it," I say, turning to him. "It was lovely to meet you, Mav. I hope you enjoy the rest of your stay here in Malveaux and enjoy your party tonight."

"Thanks. You, too. You ... err ... make a gorgeous goth. If that's a thing."

Did he just tell me I'm gorgeous? I think he did, and

he's not trying to slither his way into my affections because I'm a princess, either.

"Thanks. You do, too," I say, heat rising in my cheeks.

We stand in awkward silence for a moment. Somewhat inexplicably, I find I don't want to say goodbye to this American stranger with whom I've spent an enjoyable hour not being Princess Amelia. I'm not clear if it's because I've enjoyed his company or simply enjoyed not being the real me.

"So," I say to break this odd silence.

"Yeah. So."

"Bye."

"Bye."

I turn and walk down the street, knowing I wouldn't mind seeing him again. He's interesting. He's the kind of person who would make a good diplomatic ally at one of those interminable palace functions where you need someone real to talk to.

But I have Greg waiting for me, and he's where my focus needs to be.

Chapter 5

Ethan

"Bye," she says, and then she's gone, walking away down the narrow cobblestone street before I can think of a better response than my own lame "Bye."

Nice going, Roberts. Real smooth.

I watch Amy—or Amel-whatever-Dutch-name she'd said—disappear around the corner, her goth outfit making her blend into the shadows.

Is it weird that she wanted to wear her costume, too? Of course she looked absolutely stunning in it, but then she looked equally attractive in her jeans and T-shirt.

And there was something oddly familiar about her, though I can't place it. Not her looks so much as something in the way she carried herself. The confidence beneath her wide-eyed enthusiasm, I guess.

I throw on my black wig and walk in the opposite direction, already regretting my purchase despite Amy's advice to ditch the thing. It's itchy and uncomfortable, making my head sweat in the warm afternoon sun.

But Amy doesn't get it. She's in costume for a party. Me? I need all the disguise I can get. That scrape with paparazzi before I dived into the costume store has made it clear that even in Malveaux, Rowan Thornheart has fans.

The "Maverick Mitchell" alias was a stroke of genius on my part, borrowing from my childhood hero in *Top Gun*. My parents would always smile when I suggested it for family movie night, despite the fact we'd watched it only the week before. Dan and my kid sister, Emmy, were not so kind. I'm pretty sure they grew to hate that movie because of me, completely missing its genius.

Back then, fame looked so different in my imagination. I pictured creative freedom and respect. Sure, there was some adulation thrown in there, too, but that was never the main objective for me, and I sure as heck didn't think I'd be hiding behind an itchy wig in a foreign country just to feel human again.

The thing that bothers me the most about fame isn't the cameras or even the invasion of my privacy, even though those are hard enough to stomach. It's how fame seems to have hollowed out the meaning from my interactions with people. Every conversation seems to have an agenda, everyone wanting something from me.

Somehow, in this new life of mine, I've lost that

genuine connection to people, the connection that was a given before I reached Hollywood.

Talking with Amy was refreshing for a bunch of reasons, but also because she had no idea who I was. For those brief moments in the costume store, I wasn't Ethan Roberts, TV star, aka heartthrob warlord, Rowen Thornheart. I was just a guy in the wrong section, accidentally plucking a nun's costume from the rack.

If I'm being totally honest, it also helped that she was cute.

Okay, she was more than cute. She had an uncomplicated beauty to her that's sorely missing in Hollywood. When she put on her goth costume, she looked so sexy I virtually had to pick my tongue up from the floor, Jim Carey style in *The Mask*. Coupled with her easy and positive vibe, I was sorry to have to see her go.

Shame we had to part ways.

But I'm not here to meet a woman. I'm here for a change of scene. Getting involved with someone would only complicate matters, and complication is the last thing on my list.

I look around as I make my way down the boulevard. The picturesque streets of Tleurbonne, with their old stone architecture, manicured hedging and trees lining the sidewalks, couldn't be more different from the wide, traffic-filled, often soulless streets of LA. Here, life seems to move at a more sedate pace, no horns blaring and people in a rush, making demands into their phones as they hurry along.

It's exactly what I'd hoped for when I pointed blindly at Chelsea's phone.

If only the paparazzi hadn't found me here.

Right now, there's no sign of any photographers, but then they're famous for lurking in the shadows, pouncing when you least expect it. I've got to be on high alert, even in my costume, which I know can only go so far in hiding my true identity—there's not much you can do to disguise your height when you're 6'4", let's face it. But I hope it's enough to put them off the scent and allow me the freedom to move about this city undetected.

I round the corner onto a main thoroughfare and try to blend in as much as a goth can. The aroma of freshly baked bread fills my nostrils, and it strikes me how hungry I am. I've not eaten since breakfast, and that was just a croissant and a cup of coffee.

I locate the source of the delicious aroma, and order myself a *croque monsieur*, which turns out to be a fancy way of referring to a ham and cheese toasted sub.

I munch on it as I make my way back to my small hotel, purposely chosen for the fact it's not part of a big, international chain, and hopefully discreet enough for me to hide away in. I'll retreat to my room to read a book, which is something I don't get to do a lot these days.

As I pass a small park with people sitting in the shade under majestic trees, my phone vibrates in my back pocket. I pull it out to see a message from Chelsea.

CHELSEA:

I thought you wanted to hide.

Accompanying the message is a grainy photo of me, sitting outside the coffeehouse I enjoyed my breakfast at only this morning. My once delicious sub turns to cardboard in my mouth as a cold chill runs down my spine.

What the …? They know where I am?

So they *were* after me. I wasn't just being paranoid, darting into that costume store. What's more, I know with sickening certainty that they won't let up until I give them a story, something salacious—or worse.

49

ME:

I'm clearly not very good at this hiding thing.

CHELSEA:

Rookie mistake number 1: going to a big city. You need to get out of there. Go where there are less people for a start. Less people equal less photographers. It's basic math.

I stare at her message, a familiar heaviness settling in my chest. Is this what my life has become? Mathematical equations to minimize human contact? Three years ago, I was begging for callbacks and celebrating when I got a commercial for hemorrhoid cream (true story).

Now, I'm reduced to calculating population densities to find somewhere I can breathe.

The worst part is I still love acting. I love becoming Rowan Thornheart and bringing that character to life.

What I don't love is how the show's success has turned me into a commodity, something to be photographed and sold alongside the show's merchandise.

And yes, they do sell dolls of me.

ME:

I guess I could go camping somewhere?

CHELSEA:

Camping? Are you insane?!! People get murdered by serial killers when they go camping, not to mention the shocking toilet arrangements. Ugh.

Despite my current predicament, I smile at my screen. That is so Chelsea. Ever the drama queen. Before I have the chance to reply another message arrives from her.

CHELSEA:

I have a friend who has a house in the most beautiful spot just outside a small town not too far from Tleurbonne. It's close to the sea, I think.

ME:

Do you mean the Mediterranean?

I add the face with rolling eyes emoji because surely even self-absorbed Chelsea has heard of the Med.

CHELSEA:

Sure.

It's called Montelac and it has a population of only 653 people, a large proportion of which are older residents who have lived there their whole lives. It's one of the last places in Malveaux that isn't on the tourist map.

I blink at my screen. She knows the town's population and the average age of the residents. I tap out my reply.

ME:

Did you just swallow a travel brochure?

CHELSEA:

It's called Google. You should get acquainted.

ME:

Noted.

CHELSEA:

Let me check with my friend, although he has so many houses, I'm sure he won't miss it if you stay in this one for a couple weeks.

I sift through the idea. A town of only six hundred or so people could be small enough that, if they do recognize me, they won't care. Either that or I could hide away and forget about the rest of the world for a while.

My phone vibrates in my hand.

CHELSEA:

Dion says you can have the house!

ME:

Dion? As in our agent Dion?

Why didn't she just say that it was his house?

CHELSEA:

Duh.

Helpful.

CHELSEA:

He's super excited about you visiting. Says it's on a lake that's called Lake of Dreams. It sounds amazing! You should def go.

ME:

Are you with him right now or something?

I glance at the time on my phone. It must be the middle of the night in LA.

CHELSEA:

We're hanging out.

ME:

Hanging out?

CHELSEA:

You know how it goes.

ME:

Uh, no?

CHELSEA:

So, the house?

ME:

Let me think about it.

CHELSEA:

Dion says don't take too long deciding.
Love you! xoxoxoxoxo

I may be leaping to conclusions here, but if Chelsea is with our agent at this time... No. She wouldn't. Would she?

I push the idea from my mind. Whatever Chelsea is up to, I've got bigger things on my mind. On edge, I glance around. People seem to be minding their own business, talking on their phones, relaxing in the sun, walking their dogs.

I relax a notch.

So there was one photo of me. Big deal. I won't eat breakfast at that café again. Easy. I don't have to go running away to a house Dion owns in a town filled with the elderly. That's taking things a step too far.

I'll be fine here, particularly now that I have my ingenious disguise.

I take another bite of my sandwich, only now there's not even a hint of cardboard. Finishing it off, I drop the wrapper in a trash can on the street outside my hotel. When I pull open the glass door, I spot a group of men lounging on the lobby sofas. Dressed in dark, practical clothing, heavy camera gear strapped across their bodies, and a disheveled appearance, they're such a paparazzi cliché they look like they'd taken a visit to the costume store.

My heart instantly begins to beat like a drum, the pressure in my chest I felt that night on the red carpet returning and pinching hard.

How do they know I'm staying here? Did someone tip them off?

And, most importantly, will they recognize me in my new disguise?

Without pausing to find the answer to any of my questions, I put my head down and make a beeline for the stairway. I dash up flight after flight until I reach my floor, thankful for Jorge's cardio drills at my regular PT sessions. Outside my room, my breath labored from exertion, the room card opens my door with a *beep*, and I step inside, closing and locking it behind me.

I need to get out of this place.

I need to go somewhere else, somewhere that's not a main city. A place less populated, preferably a place that doesn't have TV or streaming services.

Yeah, I might need a time machine for that.

Who knew the show was so big in Malveaux? I knew it had a global audience, but no clue that I was this famous in this little country.

What is clear to me is I can't stay in this city undetected, which means I can't get the break I so desperately need to get my head together.

I blow out a breath. Two days. That's all it took for them to find me. Forty-eight hours.

I stuff my clothes into my backpack, grabbing all my toiletries, and changing my shoes from my comfortable sneakers to the only black shoes I've got: another pair of sneakers. I glance in the mirror and see my pale face staring back.

I collect my phone and do a quick bit of research. That small town Chelsea mentioned, Montelac, sounds perfect right now. A quick google tells me I can get a train to Côte-des-Papillons and then transfer there by bus.

Decision made.

As I sling my backpack over my shoulders, I catch a glimpse of myself in the mirror. The dark eye liner Amy applied makes my eyes look huge. Combined with the black of my wig and T-shirt sucking any color from my skin, I don't look much like me at all. Maybe I can get by the paparazzi in the lobby, and then on to a train station, without being spotted?

Man, this is what my life has become?

My mom asked me only last month if my life was everything I'd hoped for. I lied and said yes because I had no clue how to explain that achieving my dream feels a lot like losing myself.

I rush down the staircase, pausing at the door on the ground floor to peer through the small window into the lobby. The paps are still there, eagerly expecting their prey, like lions lying in the long grass, awaiting their lunch.

It's now or never, Roberts.

I take a breath, edge the door open, and put my head down as I aim for the exit. As a man pushes through the door to come inside, one of the men says something that sounds a lot like my name. I don't react. I don't even look at them. I just keep moving with purpose, as though I'm a random goth who's got places to go and people to see—all the while hoping against all things holy these guys don't work out who I really am.

My hope is in vain.

Looking over my shoulder, I see the men rising to their feet, their cameras at the ready. Have they worked out it's me? Or do they think the poor schmuck I passed as I exited the hotel is someone worthy of documenting?

I'm not about to hang around to find out.

I stride down the street, following the path plotted on Google Maps to get to the train station. As I turn onto a main street, I dodge groups of kids and businesspeople, keeping my head down. After a few minutes, there's no one calling my name. I look over my shoulder.

No sign of the paps.

I slow my pace, letting out a breath I hadn't even realized I was holding.

Eventually, I reach Tleurbonne Central Station, where I line up along with others to buy a ticket to Côte-des-Papillons. When it's my turn, I fumble my way through, not knowing a word of Malveauxian. Luckily, the woman behind the desk speaks some English, and I learn that the next train departs from Platform 12 in less than twenty minutes.

I climb on board and find my row. The carriage is empty but for a couple of older women in floral dresses who are too busy talking to notice me. I pull off my wig, now damp from my exertion, and stuff it into my bag before I take my seat, hoping to blend into the dark interior.

I pull up the browser on my phone and search for my name. Staring back is the image of me enjoying a cup of coffee this morning. The headline reads *Warlord Rowan Thornheart Thaws in Malveaux.*

Not exactly original.

What the article doesn't capture is how desperately I just want a cup of coffee without it becoming news. Or how much I miss conversations that don't involve my career trajectory or relationship status. The last real conversation I had with someone who wasn't trying to get something from me was… well, it was with Amy in that costume store.

Maybe that's why I'd felt that strange pull to keep talking to her. When she looked at me, she *really* looked at me. She didn't look through me or past me or wanting to know what I could do for her. She saw Maverick, not Ethan Roberts, not Rowan Thornheart. And somehow that felt more real than anything I've experienced in months.

Ironic, I know.

The carriage begins to fill with travelers, some heavy-laden with luggage, some with shopping bags. I slink down further in my seat and concentrate on reading a book on my phone, hoping I look different enough for no one to recognize me.

I take a deep, calming breath, hold it, and then let it out.

The next thing I know, a whistle sounds, and someone calls out something in Malveauxian, which I can only assume is "All aboard!" by the fact a guard dressed in a dark blue uniform and hat steps onto the carriage and the doors begin to close over.

No sooner have they almost shut when they ping back open.

I slide further down in my seat. A woman's voice rings out. The Paparazzi don't appear to be an equal opportunities employer, most of them men, so my bet is she's not a pap. She's speaking in rapid Malveauxian, but there's something familiar about it.

I push myself up in my seat to catch a glimpse of her.

What I see takes me completely by surprise.

Standing there, speaking rapidly to the guard as she thrusts a ticket into his hand, is none other than my fellow goth, Amy.

My heart does a strange little skip. It's her. The one person who sees me as just a person, not a photo opportunity or a celebrity sighting.

For a split second, I consider slinking further down in my seat, avoiding any complications. But something pulls me toward her. Maybe it's the chance for one more genuine conversation before I disappear into Dion's lake house to lick my wounds in solitude?

Or maybe it's just that in a world where everyone wants a piece of Ethan Roberts, here's someone who simply wants to debate the merits of goth wigs with Maverick Mitchell.

Chapter 6

Amelia

Does anyone still believe the official royal line that Princess Amelia is currently on an Indian mountain, seated in the lotus position, aggressively thinking about not thinking, following a vindaloo and some naan bread?

The answer to that question must be a resounding *no*.

She may not have run away to join the circus or taken flight into space, as I suggested in the past, because there are rumors abound that she hasn't in fact gone anywhere at all.

Spotted walking down a busy street in Tleurbonne was one young lady who, despite her casual attire, bore a striking resemblance to our Amelia.

Could it be that instead of embarking on a journey of mindfulness she has instead escaped for an entirely different journey, one we all hope will involve romance?

Has Princess Amelia swapped silent contemplation for silent rebellion?

Sadly, she has only been sighted once, but this royal correspondent shall not be deterred.

Watch this space, good people.

Yours in Tiara-tipping and tea-spilling,

Fabiana Fontaine xx

#RoyalEscape
#AmeliaOnTheLoose
#DontDrinkTheTea

"Thank you so, so much," I say to the guard with my best smile. "You're an absolute lifesaver. I don't know what I would have done if I'd missed this train."

"Take your seat, miss. We're departing now," is his bland, expressionless reply.

But my excitement won't be dented. I'm simply happy I'm here and have made it safely onto the train before it left the station.

"Of course," I reply, taking my ticket from him.

Right now, I'm breaking Rule number 511: *Never take public transportation unless you are in a private carriage*. And the fact that the guard treated me with casual disdain proves my disguise is working. I'm just another ordinary passenger on this ordinary train to Côte-des-Papillons—and Greg.

The thought has my belly doing cartwheels.

"Down there on the right." He gestures down the carriage, and I flash him a grateful smile before I drag my suitcase down the surprisingly narrow aisle. I try not to think as a princess—first class private carriage where you have your own roomy space, complete with whatever you want to eat and drink, with staff at hand to ensure your comfort—but it's impossible not to compare it with this cramped carriage, full to the brim with people, packed in like sardines.

I turn back and ask him, "Where do I put my suitcase?"

He gives me a look that tells me I'm some kind of idiot before he looks up, and I notice overhead compartments, stuffed full of people's luggage.

"Up there? All right. Thank you," I tell him, wishing I'd worked harder on my upper body strength with my trainer, Raoul, and wondering if I can in fact lift my suitcase up that high.

But needs must, as they say, and as I move along the aisle, apologizing as I bump up against people's feet, I remind myself I chose to travel like a regular person, and regular people place their suitcases in overhead racks on trains.

I find my seat, which is next to a man of about eighteen or nineteen, who glances at me briefly before returning his attention to his phone, a surly expression on his pimply face.

"Good afternoon," I say, but he ignores me completely, continuing his scroll through social media—all about something important to humanity, I'm sure.

Well, at least he won't be chatty.

I run my gaze over the luggage rail until I find a spot two seats down from mine. I pick my suitcase up, careful not to swing it into anyone's face, before I take a breath and heave it up over my head with all my strength, aiming for the rack.

Just as I touch the edge of the suitcase to the railing, the train lurches forward which, combined with my frankly pitiful upper body strength—clearly an area to work on with Raoul—my arms give way.

Panic rises as I become aware that I'm powerless to stop the inevitable heading my way. I stagger, trying to right myself and not let go of the suitcase at the same time.

It's at this point my shoulder meets what I can only assume is the back wall of the carriage. But then the wall's arm encircles me, preventing me from falling as the weight of the suitcase reduces to practically nothing.

Wait. Walls don't have arms.

I look up in alarm to see my rescuer.

"You?" I gasp, my eyes wider than the palace's most generous of dinner plates.

"Is that any way to thank your knight in shining armor?" he asks in his smooth American accent, his black eyeliner-ringed eyes sparkling in amusement.

In one deft movement he slots my suitcase neatly on the rack as though it's no big deal at all. Which for a man of his size, it probably isn't. He's all contradictions. He's as solid as the palace walls yet somehow soft. His chest rises and falls with steady breaths that don't betray any exertion from catching both me and my ridiculously overpacked suitcase, and through his T-shirt, I can feel the unmistakable contours of someone who clearly spends his days at the gym.

It's an objective observation, nothing more. The same

way one might note that the abdominal muscles on a statue in the royal gardens have been particularly well-crafted.

And then his scent reaches me. It's vanilla and something woodsy, like the forest at the palace in Villadorata after it's rained. Not that I'm intentionally breathing him in. That would be decidedly un-princess-like, not to mention the fact the only man's scent I want in my nostrils is Greg's.

Wait. That doesn't sound right.

Oh, I know what I mean. I don't want to go enjoying any man's scent other than Greg's. End of story.

My side remains pressed against Maverick for longer than royal protocol would permit. But then let's face it: I threw royal protocol right out the window the moment I escaped the palace.

"Or should that be 'goth in shining armor?' I guess I'm a confused metaphor right now," he says as the train lurches again, reminding me that I'm essentially wrapped in the arms of a stranger in the middle of a public train carriage.

As the train movement evens out, I step back with the practiced grace of someone who's spent a lifetime maintaining appropriate distances from people. Rule number 543: *A princess must keep an appropriate distance from others in public.*

Yup, another rule smashed.

"I'm awfully sorry, Maverick," I murmur as heat crawls up my neck.

Traitorous biology.

And yes, there's a rule for that, too. Rule number 149: *A princess never blushes except when diplomatically advantageous.* Whatever in heck that means.

"Hey, no problem, Amy. I'm just glad I was here to

catch you before you fell and hurt yourself. Or someone else, for that matter."

I glance at his face. His eyes dance with amusement. The black eyeliner suits him, making the blue of his eyes stand out like sapphires against black velvet.

Not that I'm cataloging the precise shade of Maverick's eyes.

That would be ridiculous, not to mention a betrayal of Greg.

I pull my lips into what I hope is a composed smile, channeling Mummy's expression when I've committed some ghastly social faux pas—like the time I asked the Archduke of Scottopia if his toupee was made from a dead squirrel (and in my defense, it really did look like a dead squirrel, tail and all).

A shadow crosses his face, transforming his features from amused to suspicious in the space of a heartbeat. "What are you doing on my train?"

I raise my brows as they practically reach for my hair-line. "*Your* train?"

"You know what I mean. It's quite a coincidence, don't you think? Twice in one day?"

His words don't quite slap me with accusation, but they certainly tap me firmly on the shoulder with suspicion. Has he somehow worked out who I am? Is he actually paparazzi in disguise? But surely even the most dedicated royal photographer wouldn't go to the lengths of following me into a costume shop and pretending to be an American goth just for a chance photo.

"I'm on my way to meet a friend, if you must know," I say, straightening my spine to my full, albeit much more modest, height.

How did this guy get so tall, anyway? He's like a giraffe

and a basketball hoop had a kid they raised on protein shakes.

"A friend?" His question hangs between us, loaded with doubt.

"I do have them. Friends, that is," I reply, my tone defensive because come on! *He's* the one who could be following *me*, not the other way around. Why would I follow a random American tourist, no matter how attractive he is.

Which I've noted purely objectively once more.

"Look," he begins, his voice softened. "I didn't mean the way that sounded. I thought you were going to a party, because of the costume."

I glance down at my black clothes. The costume shop alibi. Right.

"The party was earlier today. Right after I saw you at the costume shop, actually."

"A party in the middle of the day?"

"That's right. It was a children's party." The lie rolls off my tongue with ease. When you've spent your life attending events where you can't give too much of yourself away, you develop a certain talent for fabrication, aka lying.

The role of a princess isn't as straightforward as people think.

He widens his eyes. "You dressed as a goth for a children's party? That's new."

"Why ever not?" I reply, as though it's perfectly normal to terrify small children at birthday parties by dressing like I've been raised from the dead.

Or is that zombies?

The guard, clearly lacking the patience of the royal staff, throws us a glare. "Passengers must be seated at all times while the train is in motion."

"Is that really a rule?" I ask, genuinely curious. In my admittedly limited experience with public transportation, the rules seem arbitrary at best.

The guard's already thin lips compress further, transforming into a paper cut across his face, and his hands land on his hips with all the authority of someone who takes their polyester uniform very seriously indeed.

"I would take that as a firm yes," Maverick suggests, his eyebrows lifting in a way that conveys both amusement and warning.

"All right. I'll take my seat," I concede to the guard, before turning back to Maverick. "Thanks again for catching me."

"Anytime," he replies.

"And just for the record, I'm not following you. You have my word."

He remains rooted to the spot like one of the ancient oaks in the palace grounds, his eyes searching my face. "Do you—? Nah. Forget it."

My curiosity gets the better of me. "Do I what?"

"I was gonna ask if you want to come sit with me, but you've got a perfectly good seat over there." He gestures toward my assigned spot beside the teenager whose relationship with his phone appears to be more intimate than most marriages.

I make a snap decision. I may be on my way to meet the man of my affections, but I can still enjoy the journey. Besides, Maverick is infinitely more interesting than Monsieur Phone. No competition, really.

"I'd love to sit with you, Maverick," I say.

"Great. I'm down the carriage." He gestures with his thumb over his shoulder.

I follow him along the narrow aisle, navigating the obstacle course of protruding knees and bags with all the precision of a royal procession—minus the ceremonial trumpets.

Clearly.

The train lurches around a bend, sending me stumbling against a seat back. Twenty-four years of deportment lessons from Madame Bisset, and I'm pinballing down a train carriage like a toddler learning to walk.

I've spent my life in perfumed palace hallways where even the dust is imported from somewhere exclusive.

Just a joke.

This is different. Real. Totally intoxicating in its ordinary-ness.

Maverick stops at a pair of seats and gestures for me to take the window. "Your royal carriage awaits," he jokes.

He has no idea how close he's stumbled on the truth.

I play along. "Why, thank you, kind sir," I reply as I slide past him into the seat, safely ensconced by the window. My goth skirt, which is so much shorter than anything my princess wardrobe contains, rides up as I sit, and I tug it down with as much dignity as possible. Princesses aren't accustomed to fidgeting with their clothing, as royal tailors ensure everything sits precisely where it should at all times.

I make a mental note to tip them more generously in the future.

I wonder what my family would say if they knew I was on a train with an American who just caught me in his arms, both of us dressed as goths, and me on my way to meet the man I've been dreaming about for months?

Reckless, that's what they'd say. Particularly my parents. Alex and Sofia would lecture me in stereo about responsibility and dignity. My only ally would be Max, though he'd hide his approval beneath layers of brotherly teasing.

But then, none of them are here. And for the first time

in my life, neither is anyone whose job description includes *Keep Princess Amelia from doing anything interesting.*

And besides, my family doesn't feel the way I do, hemmed in and restricted. Controlled. They seem happy with the life they've been born into and even managed some changes to make themselves even happier, aka finding their soul mates and living happily ever after with them.

Well, I want my shot at that too, and I can't stand all the dull, weak-chinned aristocrats and handsome but dull as pond water diplomats' sons who get paraded in front of me in my parents' vain attempt to provide me with suitable partners. They're all so predictable. They either want to tell me all about how incredibly amazing they are at fishing and hunting and riding horses, or how clever they are at spending their family's money, or worse yet, tell me how incredibly amazing I am, with my pretty face and polite manners.

Who gives a fig about a pretty face and polite manners? It's total nonsense! I'm so much more than just that. I have dreams and passions and a drive within my soul to live my life to the absolute fullest.

The last thing I want is those tepid men with their tepid feelings.

That's not enough for me. Not now, not *ever*.

I want someone who's all-consumed by their love and passion for me. Someone who cannot bear to be away from me. Someone who looks at me with eyes filled with sizzle and intensity and love.

Will I find that with Greg?

I have no idea, but I'm more than willing to find out, and I'm on my way to doing just that.

I look out the window as we whizz past buildings and trees, the city slowly giving way to the rolling hills of the

Malveauxian countryside. The window is smudged with the fingerprints of previous passengers, a roadmap of other journeys.

Beside me, Maverick drops from his great height into his seat and I become aware that oddly, I'm suddenly conscious of my breathing. I breathe all day every day without giving it a moment's notice. But now, sitting so close to Maverick that my shoulder could easily brush his arm, I find I need to remind myself to both suck in and expel air.

It must be the physical awareness that comes from sitting inches away from a virtual stranger with whom I've already shared two bizarre encounters today. The universe must have an odd sense of humor, throwing us together. It's almost like we're characters in one of my favored romantic comedies that my brothers pretend to hate but still watch.

Not that this is romantic. That's not what I'm saying in the least.

It's simply coincidental. That's all. Coincidental and *not* romantic.

"Great view. It's a stunning country. Kinda like Northern California meets Montana," Maverick says, breaking the silence that stretches between us.

"Malveaux is really quite lovely. Although I must admit, I haven't spent all that much time traveling by train. Only a few trips, really."

And they were all in the royal carriage with a butler and servants and the whole shebang.

"Let me guess. You're more of a private jet kinda gal?" he asks, the edges of his mouth lifting in a smile.

Although he's joking, the uncanny accuracy makes my heart perform a gymnastics routine.

"Nothing nearly so glamorous, I assure you," I lie with

practiced ease, most certainly not thinking of the royal jet I only just flew to Malveaux on for The Games.

And just like that, we fall into conversation and the initial awkwardness of physical proximity fades, and it's like we're back in that costume shop, chatting about random, inconsequential things.

"Good call on losing the wig," I say. This close, I notice the faint scar that bisects his left eyebrow, barely visible unless you're paying close attention. Which I'm not. *Obviously*. "But tell me, why are you still in your goth costume? Don't you want to keep it fresh for your party?"

"How come you're still in yours?"

Touché.

"I find I quite like this look. In fact, I'm thinking of going goth. For a while, anyway."

The train whistles as we pass through a small town. A child across the aisle presses her nose against her window, drawing imaginary shapes with her finger.

"Is your 'friend' also into the whole goth thing?"

"The way you say that makes me think you don't believe I have a friend in Côte-des-Papillons. But I assure you, I do. We're due to meet tonight in fact."

"Where are you meeting her?" he asks, and I wonder whether he purposefully chose to make my "friend" female.

"I'm meeting *him* at a bar."

"Your friend is a guy? Huh. So, this is a date."

I bite back a smile. "Yes. I suppose it is."

"I find that generally you either know it's a date or you don't."

"It's a date then."

"A first date?"

"Yes, but I know him very well," I reply, purposely elusive.

Is he just making conversation? Because this feels a lot like the sort of interrogation I would get from a member of my nosey family.

His eyes search my face, and I lift my chin as though to show that I do know Greg Smith well. Because I do. We've spent hours and hours chatting online. Sure, I've never technically met him, and I've only seen a few photos of him, but those are just minor details in our relationship. Meeting him will be the icing on the already very sizable cake.

And so what if I haven't given Greg my real name and I've pretended to be part of the palace staff rather than a princess? He'll understand perfectly when I explain it all to him, I'm sure.

When you think about it, it's the kind of thing we can look back on and laugh about in the future. *Remember when I thought you were a lady's maid and you were in fact a princess?* he'll ask as he gazes tenderly at me, and then he'll kiss me softly, which will be his way of telling me it made the whole experience that much more exciting.

At least that's how I hope it will all turn out.

"You met this guy on the internet, didn't you," Maverick says.

"That's maybe how we met, but we've got to know one another extremely well over the past couple of months, and now that we finally get to meet, I'm sure things will work out perfectly. For both of us."

There's a small voice in my head that sounds suspiciously like Sofia. *Really, Ami? You're pinning your grand romantic adventure on a man you've never actually met?*

I squash the unwelcome thought immediately. I don't need my bossy older sister's voice in my head while I'm on my grand adventure.

I'm writing my own fairy tale here, one that starts with a goth costume and a dashing winemaker called Greg.

AND SITTING HERE WITH MAVERICK, who seems genuinely concerned—even if I don't need his concern, thank you very much—I can't help but wonder if Greg would have offered to help me with my suitcase or caught me when I fell.

Wait. What am I thinking? Of course he would have. Greg is perfect. Greg is wonderful. Greg writes me paragraphs about his hopes and dreams and asks about my day with such genuine interest. He's everything I've been looking for.

"It's a good thing for you there are no weirdos on the internet in that case," Maverick says.

I catch his sarcasm, but he doesn't understand. Greg isn't like the people he's thinking of. Greg is different. Greg is... well, he's Greg.

Though the fact that I can't come up with a more specific defense is slightly concerning.

"Don't a lot of people meet online these days?" I sound defensive even to my ears.

"I guess they do," he concedes.

"I'm on the internet and I strongly suspect you are, too. Are *we* weirdos?" I ask, pleased with my comeback.

"No, but that's not to say this friend of yours isn't," he replies in measured tones, as though he's talking to a child. "What's his name?"

I narrow my eyes at him. "Why?"

He holds his phone up. "So we can Google him or course."

Knowing exactly what he'll find because I've already

Googled him a number of times myself, I reply, "Be my guest. His name is Greg Smith."

"Greg Smith. Got it." Maverick's thumbs move across his phone screen, and I watch his face carefully, waiting for the inevitable look of embarrassment when he realizes he's been wrong all along.

Instead, his eyebrows draw together slightly, his mouth tightening. "Greg Smith is probably a pretty common name, you know. Let's narrow it down. What does he do?"

I smile as I think about how Greg spends his time working with his hands to produce fine wines. It's so very romantic, like a hero in a romance story.

"He's a winemaker," I say with pride.

There. That should narrow it down. Not that many Greg Smiths can be winemakers in a small coastal town in Malveaux. Only my Greg.

"And this Greg Smith lives in Coat dess Pa-pill-ions?"

I let out a giggle at his pronunciation. "It's pronounced coat day papyon," I say, pronouncing it so he will hopefully understand.

Maverick shows me his phone screen and I see familiar photos of Greg, looking debonair in a suit and tie, and in his working clothes at his vineyard.

"This is the Greg Smith you've been chatting with online?" he asks, and there's something in his tone I can't quite place.

"It's so much more than 'chatting.' We've dug deep, right into one another's souls."

"Sounds painful."

I ignore his silly joke and instead point at the screen. "See? Greg is real. He's exactly who he says he is. And in a few hours, I'll be sitting across from him at a bar over-looking the sea, finally in the presence of the man I've been dreaming about."

"You know, I find that really interesting because this guy?" He holds his phone in place. "This guy is Noah Francis."

"No, that's Greg Smith. Noah Francis is someone else," I say carefully.

Poor Maverick. All those good looks of his must be at the price of intelligence. *Pretty and smart? You can't have it all, Maverick.*

"I have no idea who Greg Smith is, but I can tell you that this guy is Noah Francis, and I know that because he's an actor on a TV show in America. It got canned after the first series, but it wasn't half bad. I know he has a decent following on social media, though."

No. That can't be right. Greg isn't an American actor. Greg is a Malveauxian winemaker. He's the reason I'm on this train, dressed as a goth, heading to a coastal town. Greg can't be someone else.

Can he?

For a brief, dizzying moment, I feel like I did when I nearly dropped my suitcase—off-balance and out of control.

But he can't be right. He must be confused.

I reach for his phone, needing to prove him wrong. "May I?"

"Be my guest."

I scroll through the search results, my heart pounding. I find the photo I know best. It's of Greg on a trek with a mountain backdrop, the broad smile I've thought about more times than I care to admit pasted on his face.

But as I click on it, it jumps to a social media profile of someone called "Noah Francis."

I blink at the screen, my belly tying in knots.

There must be an explanation. Perhaps this Noah

person stole Greg's photos? Perhaps they're twins? Perhaps—

Cold builds in my chest. Perhaps I've been a fool.

But I absolutely and resoundingly refuse to believe it because the alternative is that I've built up an entire romantic fantasy in my head about someone who doesn't exist.

The idea is far too humiliating to even contemplate.

I go to Greg's Instagram and see the photos I've gazed at too many times to count. I know every part of Greg's face, from the creases at the edges of his eyes to the way his hair always flops over the left of his forehead, to the curve of his smile.

Turning the phone around, I say, "See? Greg and your Noah Francis may look alike, but this is the real him."

The words sound hollow even to my own ears, but I cling to them desperately. Because if Greg isn't real, then what am I doing here? What is this whole adventure for?

Maverick looks from the photo back to me before he presses the side of his phone, and the screen turns black.

The finality of that gesture makes my stomach drop.

"Does that mean you believe me?" I ask.

"That means I'm coming with you to the bar tonight to make sure this guy is who he says he is."

Part of me wants to refuse, to insist that I don't need a babysitter, that I'm perfectly capable of handling my own romantic affairs, thank you very much.

But another part, a part I'm not ready to examine too closely, is almost relieved. I'll have an oversized goth body-guard with me when we meet. A backup plan, if you will.

Because what if Greg isn't Greg at all?

Chapter 7

Ethan

Was it a rash decision to offer to go with Amy to meet her date?

What am I saying? *Of course* it was. I now run the very real risk of being spotted in this town I can't pronounce right, too.

Smart move on my part? Nope.

More like stupid.

But there's something about Amy, something intangible that makes me want to ... I don't know. Protect her? Yeah, that's what it is. I want to protect her. But not in a *she's some poor, defenseless girl who needs my protection simply because I'm a guy* kind of way. This is the 21st century. I know women are perfectly capable of looking after themselves.

In fact, they're probably a whole lot better at it than us guys.

With Amy it's like she's new to this world and everything seems so amazing to her because of it. Which is totally ridiculous. She's a grown woman, probably in her early to mid-20s. She knows this country and she speaks fluent English as well as Malveauxian.

Huh. Maybe *she* should be looking out for *me?*

But despite her obvious credentials, there's something in her manners and the way she speaks that tells me she could do with a friend.

A friend. Yeah, that's what I'll be. I'll just push away those inconvenient feelings I get whenever I look at her. Easy.

Good job, Roberts. Tell yourself that enough times and you might actually start believing it.

Dion would be crying with happiness if he could see me right now. Ethan Roberts, Netflix heartthrob and brooding anti-hero, now moonlighting as a goth bodyguard for mysterious women from costume stores.

Sounds like the logline for a show I would never audition for.

And yet here I am, living it in real time.

I slide my gaze to look at her, sitting beside me, watching the view as the train whizzes through the countryside. Sure, she's beautiful. And sexy. Don't think I haven't noticed. Her black T-shirt is slim fitting enough that it more than hints at a curvaceous figure beneath, and the length of her skirt, hitting her mid-thigh, perfectly straddles the line between classy and sexy.

But she's also smart and funny and looks insanely cute as a goth. Not that I think goths want to look cute, exactly. But Amy sure does with her heavy eye makeup that brings out the chunks of gold in her brown eyes, her dark hair down her back, thick and long.

Black works with Amy's skin tone, even if she comes across more Disney Princess than a serious goth. She's all wide-eyed and excited about life. I half imagine her living in a tower, gazing out at the world longingly, waiting for her Prince Charming to come and rescue her.

I wonder if she can summon woodland creatures with a song to do her chores for her, too?

I bite back a smile.

Man. Three seasons of playing a cynical warlord must have warped my worldview. Next thing you know, I'll be suspicious of kittens and children's birthday parties. *Sorry, kid, but I don't trust that piñata. What's really inside it? What are you hiding?*

She's just an enthusiastic person who takes joy in life's little things.

And I admit, I was skeptical when I saw her climbing onto my train. But then she does have a legitimate reason to be here, even if I'm pretty sure she's being taken for a ride by this guy. She's meeting a jerk who's pretending he's someone else and has probably strung her along for months.

I glance at her profile, her button nose pointed straight ahead. She's chewing on her lip as though she's deep in thought.

Nah. I'm being paranoid. It's just a coincidence that she was in the same two places as me today. Nothing more than that.

Man, I miss that carefree small-town guy I once was. That guy would never second guess something like a woman turning up in two places in one day. The guy with the happy home, living an uncomplicated life, acting in high school plays with big dreams of making it one day.

Now that I've "made it" it turns out it's not all it's cracked up to be.

She turns to look at me, her face creasing into an easy smile as her eyes land on mine. Yup, I was staring at her and yup, I've been totally busted.

If things were different right now——? Nope. I can't think that way. She's on her journey and I'm on mine. End of story.

My phone vibrates and I check it to see a message from Chelsea.

CHELSEA:

Dion is sending a helicopter to take you to his house. What time works for you?

"What time are you meeting your mystery guy?" I ask.

"Six o'clock. And he's not a mystery guy. He's Greg."

"Greg. Sure."

The name 'Greg' has all the mysterious allure of a beige wallpaper sample. Even serial killers have more interesting names.

Not that I'm hoping he's a serial killer.

I'm just pointing out that if you're going to create a fake persona online, at least give yourself a name with some pizzazz. Lord Darkblade or The Duke of Danger. Anything but *Greg*.

"Think what you like," Amy says.

I tap my reply.

ME:

Can he make it 8pm? I've got a couple things to do on the coast before I go.

Two hours will give me plenty of time to accompany Amy to meet this guy and help her make a plan for when he turns out to be some creep. Then I can say my good-byes and hop on that helicopter to take me to the lake house.

The smalltown kid in me would do a happy dance that this is my life now.

Current me? I'm not so excited about it.

When your childhood dreams come true, but the reality involves paparazzi and pretending to be someone you're not, the whole thing starts to feel a lot like a cosmic practical joke.

Our train slows as it begins to pull into an old station with huge metal pillars holding up a massive glass roof. With its ornate stone arches running along the walls, covered in a mosaic of butterflies, it doesn't look anything like a train station I've visited before. There's a sign that says "Côte-des-Papillons" in elegant gold lettering.

"Wow," I murmur under my breath.

Amy nudges my arm. "You're such a tourist, Mav."

I turn to see her full lips pulled into a smile, her pretty eyes sparkling. "What? Objectively speaking it's an amazing train station."

"Are you telling me you don't have amazing train stations in the United States?"

"To be honest I wouldn't know. I don't use trains a whole lot."

She blinks at me, looking every inch the Disney princess. "Why ever not?"

I mime driving. "'Cos I've got a car. Plus, there's the small fact that this is the 21st century."

What I don't mention is that I don't use public trans-port these days because I'd be swarmed by fans before we even reached the first stop. Nothing kills the romance of train travel like being asked to sign someone's forehead with a Sharpie while their friend livestreams the whole thing.

"But what if you want to sit back and see the countryside as you travel between cities?"

"Yeah, I don't do that."

I know what she's going to ask before the words have even left her lips. "Why ever not?"

Is that her Disney princess catchphrase? I swear, if she bursts into song right now, I'm jumping out the window, emergency procedures be damned.

"Because I'm from a small town in Washington state, and I live and work in Los Angeles, so I fly."

That's the sanitized version of the truth. I fly private when the studio's paying, and commercial in disguise when they're not. Either way, there's no staring dreamily out of windows at rolling countryside. There's just me, trying not to make eye contact with anyone who might recognize me while simultaneously looking normal enough that I don't attract attention for being weird.

It's a delicate balance.

"You're missing out, Mav. Trains are so romantic, so old world and charming. I would travel on them every day if I could. Maybe with a slightly cleaner window, though." She indicates the smudges on the glass. "Couldn't you catch one between Los Angeles and your hometown?"

"Sure I could, if I had a spare thirty-five hours." Plus, a desire to be trapped in a metal tube with no escape route when someone inevitably recognizes me.

I'd rather eat glass while getting a root canal.

She does that doe-eyed thing again. "Thirty-five hours? Gosh, America is jolly big."

It's my turn to smile. "You're right. America is jolly big."

"I've been to New York before. I'd love to jump in a car and drive across the country someday. Like Thelma and Louise."

"Without the driving off a cliff part though, I bet."

Her eyes dance when she replies, "Best not that part."

The train doors slide open and people begin to disembark, the noise of the busy train station filling the carriage.

I bounce out of my seat to collect Amy's suitcase, noticing as I did when I put it in the overhead rack that it's made of soft, expensive leather and definitely not the sort of suitcase you would expect a young woman to have.

Maybe she's rich? She hasn't said anything about her family in the time we've been together. Maybe she's Malveauxian old money and lives in some impressive ancient house with a tree-lined driveway?

As I set it on the floor, I notice a sticker that says something in a foreign language, with an image of a peacock. Why would anyone put a sticker on such an expensive leather suitcase? It's hiding something metal underneath, but I can't see what.

Amy is becoming more enigmatic by the minute. A multilingual woman with expensive luggage who's dressed like a goth, speaks like she swallowed an etiquette manual, and has the wide-eyed wonder of someone seeing the world for the first time.

It's like she's playing a character herself.

Takes one to know one, Roberts.

"Thank you ever so much, Mav," she says as she slides out of the seat.

I grab my backpack—not made of expensive leather, and definitely not from old money—and sling it over my shoulder, standing back for Amy to head down the aisle before me.

"A gentleman goth. How rare," she comments with a pretty smile.

"We are a dying breed. It's us and the gentlemen vampires. We formed a club."

She lets out a giggle. "I suppose you sit around drinking whiskey and smoking cigars, discussing how to best one another in the gentleman stakes."

"Less that and more trying to dodge having our blood sucked by the vampires," I quip. I gesture down the aisle. "Shall we? Côte-des-Papillons awaits."

"Nice pronunciation, Mr. America."

"What can I say? I learned from the best."

My comment wins a smile from Amy before we make our way down the aisle and step out onto the platform. Someone is playing the violin, which makes the place seem even more whimsical—and as a guy, that is not a word I ever thought I would use, especially about a train station.

Next thing you know, I'll be describing things as *delightful* and *simply marvelous* and my high school hockey coach will revoke my man card on the spot.

Good thing I don't have to care about his opinion anymore.

We catch the attention of several people, but only briefly. I suspect it's more because we're dressed in our goth costumes, which makes us stand out from the otherwise regular looking crowd.

We make our way through the train station and spill out onto the street along with the hordes, where taxis and buses wait and people fill the sidewalk.

"Where are you meeting 'Greg?'" I make air quotes with my fingers and Amy rolls her eyes.

"You're going to be proven wrong, you know. And we're meeting at a bar called La Belle Vista overlooking the sea. He's going to be holding a single red rose. Awfully romantic, don't you think?"

More like cheesy.

"Sure."

"Shall we get a taxicab into town? I don't know about you but I'm rather hungry. Shall we eat before I meet him?" she asks, and my belly rumbles, right on cue.

"Sounds good to me."

I find us a cab, and we crawl out of the busy station, heading down the hill toward the ocean, deep blue and glistening in the early evening light. The buildings are at least a couple of hundred years old, and unlike in Tleurbonne, they're all painted bright colors, everything from green to blue and yellow. Even the spire of an old church is painted orange.

"This place is magical," I mutter, more to myself than to anyone else.

"Wait until you see the promenade," Amy replies, and as though she timed it herself, we turn onto a street that runs parallel to the glistening sea, where palm trees move in the light breeze.

It's the kind of backdrop they'd use for a romantic montage in a movie. Cue the upbeat indie song, two attractive leads laughing in slow motion, perhaps a gelato cone and some meaningful glances.

"Nice place."

"It's pretty, isn't it? I haven't been here for so long, but I do so love it. Oh, look, there are some restaurants. Driver! Drop us off here, please."

After a discussion in which Amy offers to pay and I insist that I pay instead, I hand the driver some notes and pull our luggage from the trunk. As I place Amy's case on the sidewalk, I say, "That's a pretty nice looking suitcase you've got there."

I'm fishing. Sue me.

She looks from her suitcase to my tattered backpack, practical but old, my dad's from back in the day when he travelled around the country and met and fell in love with my mom while in a small town in Wisconsin.

"This suitcase?" she asks, as though she brought a bunch with her. "It's part of a set my family owns."

I was right. Family money.

Amy continues to be an enigma wrapped in a mystery wrapped in a very cute goth outfit.

"Where do you want to go?" she asks as our taxi is immediately occupied by a couple of middle-aged American tourists, if their stars and stripes T-shirts are anything to go by.

I spot a table for two on the street outside a restaurant beside us and suggest there. After all, we've got our luggage in tow.

The hostess, a woman in a black pencil skirt that hits her mid-calf and a stiff white shirt, purses her lips as her gaze trails over us. It's clear she's found us unworthy of her establishment before we've even opened our mouths.

She looks us up and down, her top lip curling in the universal language of hospitality snobbery.

Some things, it would see, transcend cultural barriers.

I paste on my best Hollywood smile. "How are you doing tonight?" I ask, but she simply raises her brows at me. I'm not deterred. "I don't speak Malveauxian, so I hope you understand me."

A curt nod.

"We would like a table for two, thanks. That one." I point at the vacant outside table.

"It is not available," is her heavily accented reply as she continues to look down her nose at us—which is no small feat, considering I'm a good foot taller than her.

"But there's no one sitting at it and I don't see a reserved sign," I reply.

"You can have a table inside. At the back by the conveniences." She collects some menus and turns on her heel, her mind made-up.

"I guess it's reserved?" I say to Amy with a shrug.

If I wasn't hiding my identity, I could pull the famous actor card out for the first time in my life to get the table, even if it does go against the way I was brought up.

"Leave it to me."

"Okay, but I don't think she's gonna cave."

I watch as Amy trails after Ms. Superior and begins to speak in Malveauxian, pointing at the table. A moment later, she returns, a triumphant smile on her face. "Care to join me at the outside table?"

"How did you manage that?" I ask as I follow her, stacking our luggage against the wall.

"I told her that we are here for a convention at the Palais Papillon, and that we will bring all our goth friends here tomorrow to occupy each and every one of their outdoor tables from noon until night unless she allows us to sit where we want tonight."

I smile at her, impressed. She's got hidden depths, this one. "So, she's not a fan of goths."

"Especially when I told her that we're the only two who don't take our ravens with us to dinner."

I chortle. "Ravens?"

"You can't get much more goth than a raven, Mav."

I'm struck once more by how competent Amy is, despite her whole Disney princess in the real world vibe.

She's like one of those Russian nesting dolls. Just when you think you've figured her out, you discover a whole other layer underneath.

And the most concerning part? I find myself wanting to discover every single one of those layers.

Which is a complication I definitely do not need.

But as we settle in at our hard-won table with the spectacular view, I can't help but feel there's nowhere else I'd rather be. Because despite the picture-perfect view, I find my gaze drifting back to Amy. The mesmerizing way the evening sun catches the gold flecks in her eyes, the quirk of her lips when she finds something amusing.

Yeah, I could get used to this.

I lean back in my chair and let out a breath, my shoulders fully relaxing for the first time since I darted into that costume store this morning. It feels good to breathe in the fresh sea air, and to get to sit here unrecognized with a woman who I find so very attractive. I can feel like a normal guy—well, a normal guy wearing eyeliner, that is. But this is Europe. Probably half the guys wear makeup.

The irony isn't lost on me. I spend my professional life in makeup far more elaborate than this—three hours every morning with a team of artists transforming me into Rowan Thornheart, coating my face with prosthetic scars and that ridiculous white wig that makes me look like a heavy metal Santa Claus. And yet somehow this simple black eyeliner feels more like a disguise than all of that production-grade artifice ever did.

On set, I'm being someone else while everyone knows exactly who I am. Here, I'm technically being myself while pretending to be someone else.

The mental gymnastics would make my acting coach's head explode.

"To adventures," Amy says, clinking her glass against mine.

"To adventures," I echo, the chilled Chablis slipping easily down my throat.

Part of me wonders what she'd say if she knew who I really was. Would she be impressed? Starstruck? Disappointed? Most people's behavior changes the moment they discover I'm "somebody." Their eyes get that glassy, calculating look, their laughter gets a little too enthusiastic, and their questions become thinly veiled attempts to extract something useful, perhaps a story they can tell at parties about the time they met Rowan Thornheart.

I guess I've grown so accustomed to that treatment that normal human interaction now feels strange to me. Case in point: Amy's genuine smiles and unfiltered comments.

Our meals arrive and we eat hungrily. The food is incredible, and with the amount of butter and cream I bet my cholesterol has risen at least a handful of points since we sat down. But what's life if you don't get to enjoy little pleasures?

My nutritionist would be having heart palpitations watching me right now. But then, Jorge would probably just add another set of punishing weighted squats to tomorrow's workout and consider us even.

I've been training so hard in the gym to build muscle for my role, thanks to the fact my character is often shirtless. "It's integral to your character's personality," one of the producers told me when we began filming Season One.

Really? It's an important character trait that a guy who lives perpetually in winter not throw on a shirt every once in a while?

"Tell me about your family and their fancy luggage," I ask, swallowing a particularly tender piece of steak. "Is all the food in Malveaux this amazing?"

"Everything but the tea. Don't touch it."

"That bad?"

"Terrible. To answer your question, I'm the third of four, with a very bossy older sister who recently got married, an older brother who is also married, and a younger brother. Unmarried."

"Marriage is a big deal in your family, huh?"

"Sadly, yes."

"Why? Don't you want to get married someday?"

"Of course I do."

Ok*aaa*y.

I'm none the wiser.

"Where do you live?"

"Where do *you* live?" she retorts.

"I live in Los Angeles these days, but I'm from a small town in Washington state."

"Los Angeles is very busy and full of very beautiful people."

Beautiful is one word for them.

"And I live in a country that way." She points to her left.

Surprised, I ask, "You're not from Malveaux? But you speak the language so well."

"I'm from Ledonia, a nearby neighbor." She takes another sip of her wine. "You know, Mav, we have a saying here on the Continent. There are three types of people: multilingual, bilingual, and American tourists."

"Do you?" I ask with a laugh. "What can I say when the world speaks English so well? What other languages do you speak?"

"Malveauxian and Ledonian, of course, but also French, Spanish, German, some Italian. And English. Obviously."

I blink at her. "You speak seven languages?"

"Eight. I forgot Latin."

I've spent the last three years learning an entirely fictional language for my role as Rowan Thornheart—complete with its own grammar and phonetic structure designed by a linguistics professor employed by the studio —and here's this woman who casually tosses out that she speaks eight actual languages.

There's that Russian doll at work again. Layer upon layer.

I'm suddenly aware that my attraction to her isn't just about her obvious beauty, but something more substantial. It's about *her*.

"I guess Latin must come in handy for all the times you're in ancient Rome," I tease, feeling unsettled by how strong this pull to her is.

She lets out a giggle, her shoulders shaking. "I do so love a good time travel at this time of year."

"Don't we all?"

We share a smile.

I've spent my career portraying people who don't exist, saying words someone else wrote, feeling emotions that aren't mine. But sitting here, pretending to be Maverick while actually being more myself than I've been in years, I'm not sure what that says about who I really am anymore. The layers of performance have become so intricate that I sometimes lose track of which version of myself I'm supposed to be playing.

Maybe that's why Amy fascinates me so much. She seems to contain these remarkable contradictions—naiveté paired with worldliness, enthusiasm alongside sophistication—yet somehow, they're all part of this one person.

A clock tower somewhere chimes, and Amy checks the time on her phone.

"Goodness! I have to go!" she exclaims as she springs to her feet, thoroughly flustered. "I'm meant to be meeting Greg right now and I need to wash all this makeup off my face and change before I do. I can't believe I'm going to be late!"

"I'm sure he'll wait for you," I reply, trying not to feel cynical about this whole thing.

Yup. Fail.

The part of me that's trained to analyze character motivations already knows exactly how this evening is going to turn out. It's so formulaic I could practically story-board it.

But still, as Amy returns from changing back into her regular clothes, her eyes no longer ringed in black, I find myself hoping I'm wrong. I'm going to find it hard to see the light dim in her eyes when she realizes she's been deceived by this guy who she seems to have pinned so much on.

Woah! Back up the bus a minute.

When did I become so invested in Amy's happiness, a woman who I didn't even know twenty-four hours ago?

I'll take her to the bar, wait for her to meet Greg, hope that he is who he says he is, and then leave.

And if he isn't?

I don't know what I'll do.

We say goodbye to a relieved Ms. Superior, and I take our bags and follow the map on Amy's phone to the bar. It turns out it's only about fifty yards away, down some steps in a sort of rustic shack. It's totally at odds with its elegant clientele, lounging on seats as soft music plays, the view of the sparkling ocean through its large windows breathtakingly beautiful.

"He's got good taste in bars, I'll give him that," I say as I take it in.

Amy is too flustered to reply as she scans the guests, searching for her guy. "I can't see him," she says, her brows pulled together, her lips forming a line. "Do you think he's coming?" She looks up at me with such apprehension in her eyes, I have the urge to reach out and smooth away her worry with the tips of my fingers.

The gesture would be pure Rowan Thornheart—dramatic, intense, borderline inappropriate—yet the impulse comes from somewhere entirely genuine inside.

"I'm sure he'll be here," I soothe, hoping rather than believing it to be true. "Let's take a seat at the bar and watch the door."

"Great idea. Oh, I'm so glad you came here with me, Mav. I'm a box of butterflies."

I order us some drinks at the bar, my mind a battlefield of contradictions.

The trained actor in me is already anticipating the scene about to unfold.

The protective new friend wants to shield Amy from potential disappointment.

The cynical Hollywood veteran expects the worst of people's intentions.

And somewhere beneath all those layers, there's just Ethan Roberts, a smalltown boy who once dreamed of being a famous actor, only to discover that being famous means never getting to be just himself anymore.

Man, I need this break from my life.

When I turn around, drinks in hand, I see a man holding a single red rose, and it's then I know for sure part of me has been hoping that Greg wouldn't show up tonight all along.

Chapter 8

Amelia

My heart leaps, then immediately plummets to somewhere in the vicinity of my sneakers. The man bearing the rose looks nothing—and I mean absolutely *nothing*—like the photos Greg sent me. Instead of the chiseled jawline and tanned, muscular build I'd been expecting, I'm faced with someone who appears to be sweating profusely despite the pleasant evening temperature, with pasty skin, thinning hair and a gap-toothed smile.

"Is that him?" Maverick asks.

"I don't know," I reply, even though I do.

Looking at the sweaty man clutching the rose, I get the distinct feeling I know exactly what's happening right before my eyes. I just don't want to believe it.

The man's eyes land on me and light up with recognition. He makes his way over, rose extended like a peace offering before the battle has even begun.

"Mia?" he asks.

I swallow hard and nod, vaguely aware of Maverick stiffening beside me. In this moment, I wish more than anything that I could summon the Royal Guard with a snap of my fingers. To do what, I'm not sure. Make Greg not have lied to me about his appearance for the last two months?

That would be a good start.

But I'm not Princess Amelia here. I'm just a naive girl who's been thoroughly catfished.

I blink at the man holding a red rose in front of me, an eager look on his face. "Greg?" I manage. My voice is so high-pitched nearby dogs must be cocking their ears.

He's got sandy brown hair and a pleasant looking smile as he gazes at me with eager eyes—eyes that are significantly deeper set and devoid of the dreamy quality of the man I thought I was talking with online—but that's where the similarity with the photograph I've cherished for months ends. The difference between him and his image is stark, and it cannot be explained by something as trite as bad lighting or a bad hair day.

"In the flesh," he replies, his smile showing his lack of not one but two teeth.

I resist the urge to inform him that the "flesh" before me doesn't match the digital version I've spent months messaging.

Maverick hasn't moved from my side, and I'm unexpectedly grateful for his looming presence. If there's one thing royalty teaches you, it's how to maintain composure in the face of disaster. I've smiled through state dinners with food poisoning and danced with dukes who stepped on my toes. I can certainly handle one disappointing date.

Can't I?

"This is for you," Greg says as he thrust the rose at me.

I take it automatically, years of protocol dictating that I accept gifts with practiced grace. A thorn immediately pricks my finger, and I drop the flower with a small yelp of surprise.

The rose tumbles to the floor in what feels like slow motion, and it's hard not to feel like this is the perfect metaphor for my romantic hopes as they come crashing down around me.

Both Greg—or whatever his actual name is—and Maverick dive for it simultaneously, their hands colliding by the floor.

"I've got it." Maverick's tone makes it clear this is about more than just a fallen flower.

As they both straighten up, I lock eyes with Maverick, and a silent acknowledgment that everything he warned me about on the train was right

Which means everything I'd hoped for was wrong.

Greg, oblivious to our wordless exchange, smiles at me again, sweat visibly collecting on his upper lip.

"Shall we sit?" he asks, gesturing to a table. "I reserved a table by the window for us."

"Yes, let's," I reply, my voice coming out as satisfyingly human once more.

What else can I do? I've come all this way for this meeting. The least I can do is see it through.

As Greg leads the way to a table overlooking the water,

I feel Maverick's hand briefly touch my elbow. I glance back to find his eyes filled with concern.

"I'll be right here," he mouths.

For reasons I can't fully explain that simple promise feels like the most comforting thing I've heard all day.

"You look like your picture," he says as we sit.

"True, but you don't," I say pointedly.

He has the good sense to look ashamed. "About that. I … err … I need to explain."

Good. An explanation.

"I used an actor's photo."

"Really?" I deadpan.

"I'm sorry, but I thought someone as beautiful and amazing and incredible as you would never go for a guy like me if you saw what I really looked like."

I think my heart just cracked.

"I'm sorry you felt the need to do that," I reply, berating myself for being so shallow. It wasn't Greg's looks I was so attracted to. It was *him*, Greg and his clever mind and humor and humanity. The man who I sat up late messaging night after night while the rest of the palace slept, telling me all about his travels throughout the world, making wine in Napa Valley, New Zealand, and Chile.

So what if he looks different from the guy in the photo? So what if he's perspiring so hard he needs to keep using a handkerchief to wipe his forehead? So what if he smells a little funky? It's because he's sweating so much, which must be because he's so nervous to meet me and show his true face to me.

It's rather sweet when you think about it.

I look up at him and he smiles at me, which prompts me to add that a perfect set of teeth aren't necessary to win my love. Indeed, if there are teeth missing, even several, there's nothing wrong with that. And who really needs front teeth, anyway? You don't chew with your front teeth. They're just for show.

So, instead of agreeing with Maverick that Greg isn't who I was expecting to meet here tonight, I plaster on a smile and reply, "Thank you for your honesty."

"Can you find it in your heart to forgive me?" Greg asks, and he has such a puppy dog look in his eyes—like a bulldog, complete with the droopy jowls—I can't help but do just that.

"Of course I can, Greg. It doesn't matter how you look." Or how much you sweat. "I'm interested in the man you are inside. Not the chiseled jaw and six-pack in the photo."

Although the chiseled jaw and six-pack were rather nice.

Stop it, Amelia!

"You know, I've long since admired this bar, and I thought it would be a special place to bring you." He wipes the sweat from his forehead once more with his now limp handkerchief and stuffs it back into his pocket before he reaches the same hand across the white linen table cloth. "May I?" he asks.

I swallow. "Of course."

As I place my own hand in his I try hard not to think about sweat. Instead, I put my efforts into hoping to feel the same surge of attraction I felt for him each time we messaged.

But all I can think is that his hand is hot and sticky, and as his skin touches mine, I have to work hard at resisting the urge to snap it away.

I'm sorry, but I do. I feel utterly terrible about it. I tell myself it's only sweat. Everyone sweats. Only some seem to sweat somewhat more profusely than others.

Perhaps I am that shallow after all?

I chance a look Maverick's way, and, just as expected, he's watching us closely, like a guard dog, awaiting the moment to pounce.

"Now that you're here, I'd love to tell you more about the vineyard."

"You would?"

"I don't suppose you've ever considered investing in one, have you?"

"In a vineyard?"

He nods his head quickly. "It's a unique opportunity," he says, leaning toward me, and I can't avoid catching his scent, although in this case "scent" is a euphemistic way of describing body odor.

Sorry, but it's true

Greg stinks.

Anyone would if they'd sweated as much as him in the space of ten minutes. The man is quite possibly in danger of dehydrating completely at this rate.

"Mia?" he asks, and I realize I've not been following a word he's said.

"Sorry, Greg. Tell me about this vineyard."

"It's a small vineyard in the hills not far from here. The soil and climate are perfect to grow grenache grapes. All it needs is just €75,000 to secure our future together."

I blink at him. "You want me to invest in a vineyard?" I manage to squeak out, my voice mouselike.

His eyes light up with an intensity that makes me want to shrink into my black goth T-shirt. His eyes certainly don't hold the warm, gentle gaze I'd fantasized about during our countless messages.

In fact, I would go so far as to say they're calculating, almost predatory.

The look of someone who's finally spotted their mark.

"Not just any vineyard. *Our* vineyard," he replies as he

squeezes my hand. "You and me. Our future together. All I need is the money and we can be happy together."

My heart plummets to the bar floor. I've spent months imagining this moment, dreaming of our perfect meeting, of finally connecting with him.

And all he wants is my money.

What an absolute idiot I've been.

I chance another look at Maverick. His eyes are still on us, his brows pulled into that worried look he seems to get.

I press my lips together. "I didn't plan on investing in anything, Greg. I just wanted to meet you."

Greg's demeanor shifts faster than you can say "online scam." He pulls his hand from mine, saying, "After everything we've shared, you're hesitating? Mia, all those nights talking about our dreams? Sharing parts of ourselves with another? Does that mean nothing to you?"

"I just think it makes sense to spend some time together first, before we do anything like invest money or anything like that."

I'm saying the words but I'm not feeling them.

I think I already know everything I need to know about this man.

"Spend some time together first?" His voice rises, drawing attention from nearby tables. "Mia, we've been talking for months! What more do you need to know? Unless—" His eyes narrow, which is quite a feat, considering how small they were in the first place. "Unless you've been playing with my feelings this whole time."

Yes, the pot has well and truly called the kettle black now.

But still, the accusation hits harder than it should, because in one way, he's right. I have been playing a role. It's just not the one he thinks. I've been the lady's maid seeking romance, while he's been... what? A conman with a collection of photos of a handsome actor.

The thought hits me in the solar plexus.

What a fool I've been.

Just as I'm working out quite how to respond, a woman approaches our table.

"Greg? Greg Smith?" she asks in Malveauxian, clutching a red rose in her hands.

The universe, it seems, can have a particularly cruel sense of humor.

What follows is a blur of accusations and revelations between Greg and the woman, but I barely hear them over the roaring in my ears. Two months of hope, of planning, of dreaming, has been shattered in this one horrifically enlightening evening.

I look up to see Maverick looming over us, his back-pack over his shoulder and my suitcase in hand, and I can't help but feel every inch of his impressive height.

"I believe this is an excellent time for us to leave," he says.

"I couldn't agree more." I stand on shaky legs, grateful for his steadying arm. I've run away from my life as a princess only to end up here, fighting back tears, being duped by one man and rescued by another, a man I've only just met who's shown more genuine concern for me in a handful of hours than Greg has in months of messages.

Maverick takes my hand in his and together, we head for the door.

"Wait a moment," I say. I turn back to Greg and the woman. Placing my hand on the woman's arm, I say, "It's a scam. I'd run, if I were you."

She looks at me as though I've told her the sky is green.

"No, really. I just met him here myself. All he wants is for you to invest in his winery."

Her eyes widen at me. "Really?"

"Really," I confirm.

"Thank you," she replies.

"You're welcome." I head back to Maverick and when I reach the entrance, I take one final look over my shoulder at Greg. He's so deep in conversation, trying to convince his next target that he's not a con man, that he's barely noticed me leave.

Outside, the cool evening air does nothing to soothe the burning in my chest.

"Are you okay?" Maverick asks.

"I-I don't know," I reply, sniffing back my tears. They're tears of shock and betrayal, and, if I'm completely honest, tears of relief.

Greg is not the man he presented himself to be online, and I've had a very lucky escape.

And then something unexpected happens. Maverick wraps his arms around me, pulling me into a bear hug. I melt into it, the sense of safety enveloping me in his strong arms.

"That was a crappy thing for him to do to you and I'm so sorry," he says softly.

"Thank you for being here for me."

He pulls back and looks me in the eye. "Anytime," he says, and something tells me I can rely on this man. Which is an odd thought to have after I just learned I've been led up a garden path by a con man.

"You okay?"

I shake my head. "He was my whole reason for coming here. I don't know what I'm going to do now."

"You can do whatever you like. You had a lucky escape."

I look up at him, suddenly feeling utterly exhausted by this whole thing. Escaping the palace, pretending to be someone I'm not, the goth costume, the duplicitous Greg.

It's been a lot.

"Just maybe stay away from meeting men on the internet for a while," he adds, and I let out a surprised laugh. Mixed with my tears, I sound like a gurgling drain.

"That's good advice, Mav."

"Shall we get out of here?"

"I think that's a jolly good idea."

As Maverick guides me away from the wreckage of my romantic dreams, at least this disaster has given me something new to add to my journal of princess rules.

Rule Number 1,250: *A princess should never trust a man who seems too good to be true because chances are he sweats more than the royal horses during a summer parade, and his investment opportunities are about as real as my desire to spend a month meditating on the side of a mountain.*

Chapter 9

Ethan

The look on Amy's face makes my chest ache in a way I'm not prepared for. I can tell she's trying hard to hold it together, but her bottom lip gives her away as it trembles with each step she takes, her hand gripping the handle of her fancy leather suitcase so tight her knuckles have gone white.

Maybe I should feel vindicated that I was right about that guy. But you know what? All I feel is an overwhelming urge to comfort Amy—and to punch Greg in his sweaty, duplicitous face.

So, yeah. There's that.

I blow out a breath. I need to look at this logically. Amy seems like a totally decent, genuine person, and definitely a person who doesn't deserve to be duped by some catfishing jerk with a sweat gland problem.

I feel bad for her. That's all.

And that weird protective feeling I'm getting for her? Maybe it's just jet lag? Or something I ate? Or … I don't know.

Whatever it is, the woman is hurting, unshed tears pooling in her eyes, and if there's one thing I hate to see, that's a woman cry.

"I can't believe that happened. I'm such an idiot," she says, more to herself than to me.

"Hey, don't do that." I stop and turn to face her. "You're not an idiot. You thought that guy was someone he clearly wasn't. He's a scammer. A professional manipulator."

My belly twists with irony. Not that I'm a scammer or a professional manipulator, but I'm not exactly being honest with her about who I am.

"So you got duped. It happens to the best of us. Move on. Forget about him. You're worth a hundred of that jerk."

A tear rolls down her cheek, leaving a smear of eyeliner in its wake. "A hundred of me? That's a lot of Amys." She lets out a watery laugh, and the tension in my chest loosens.

The fact that she can joke about this is a good sign. She's stronger than she knows.

"And he's a catfishing jerk," she adds.

"A *prize* catfishing jerk."

"A prize catfishing jerk who used an actor's photo."

"Yeah."

"And he did it to more than just me."

"A guy that practiced at sweating nervously is definitely running his scam on at least twenty people."

She lets out a sound that's half-laugh, half-sob. "Is that supposed to make me feel better?"

"Is it working?"

She wipes at her eyes, smearing her makeup further. "Maybe a little." She looks at the black on her fingertips. "Oh, no. I must look an absolute fright."

"You look like someone who's just had her hopes dashed. So, actually pretty on-brand for a goth, when you think about it. You'd better change back into your goth outfit right away."

This wins me a genuine smile.

"See? You're moving on already."

Amy heaves out of breath. "It might take more than ten minutes. And now it's getting late, and you've been more than kind. I should let you go."

"Have you got a place to stay?"

She nods. "A bed and breakfast. It shouldn't be far from here." She pulls her phone from her purse and taps at it. "It's only half a kilometer, apparently. See?" She turns her phone around and I see the map.

"Let me walk you there."

"Are you sure? I've already used up half your evening."

"I'd like to make sure you're okay."

Her lips lift into a smile that gets me, right in the chest. "You're so kind, Mav. Thank you."

I give a self-effacing shrug. "I'm just trying to be the man my parents brought me up to be."

"Well, your parents did a fine job."

We follow Amy's map, winding through the streets and

getting further and further from the sea, the buildings turning a whole lot less pretty, and a whole lot sketchier. By the time we reach Amy's B&B I've already made my mind up what's going to happen next.

We take in the crumbling walls, the broken windows, and the barbed wire running along the top of the fence. There's a drunk old man I can smell before I see, slumped against a nearby wall, half-drunk bottle in hand.

It looks like a place from a cop show where a grisly murder has taken place.

"It said it was charming online," she murmurs.

"I think we've learned not to trust the internet so much today, right? I don't think you should stay here."

The man groans, muttering something to himself.

"You're right. I'll need to find something else." She looks up and down the street as though the answer might lie close by.

And then the words are out of my mouth before I can think better of them. "Come stay with me. I'm heading to a friend's place on a lake not far from here. Apparently, it's super nice and secluded. There's a small town, but not a lot else."

Wait. Did I really just invite her to the lake house?

Yes. Yes, I did.

Smart move? Time will tell. But it's probably the *right* move—at least for Amy.

For me? The jury's still out.

And referring to my slimeball agent as a "friend" is a stretch, even by Hollywood standards.

Her eyes widen. "Do you mean that?"

"Unless you have another investment meeting scheduled for later tonight?"

Her eyes dance as she grins at me. "No further plans. I'm done with investment opportunities for now. And online dating. And quite possibly human interaction in general."

I nudge her with my elbow. "It's not that bad. Is it?"

"I suppose not. But I did have some rather high hopes for Greg."

"I get that, and you know what? It's probably best you found out now rather than in the next few days when you're in a position where it's not so easy to walk away."

"I suppose you're right. Where is this friend's place? And in no way does that sound suspicious, by the way."

She's teasing me.

"You can trust me, Amy," I say, trying to reassure her and fully aware that Greg would have said the exact same thing.

She bites her lip, and I know she's trying to work out what to do.

I pull up Chelsea's message on my phone and read, "The house is in a small town called Lack dess Reeves."

"Lack dess Reeves?" she questions, and I know I pronounced the place all kinds of wrong.

"How should I say it?"

"No 's' at the end of the words. Lac des Rêves. It literally means lake of dreams."

"Poetic. My friend said the house is quiet, private, and huge. How about you have the west wing, and I'll have the east?"

She blinks at me. "It's a palace?"

"Of course it's not a palace, but there's a helicopter that can take us there, so I'm making an educated guess it's not some small, rundown cottage."

She bites her lip, considering.

"Look, I know it sounds crazy. We just met, and you've had your trust pretty thoroughly destroyed by jerk face back there. I have no interest in getting you to invest in anything, I'm a stand-up guy, and I'm heading there anyway, so it's totally up to you."

She bites her lip. With her eyes, ringed in smudged eyeliner, it makes her look like Bambi. If, you know, Bambi was a human. And real.

"Why would you do that? Help me like this, I mean?" she asks.

And that, ladies and gentlemen, is the million-dollar question.

But I'm not about to tell her that she strikes me as a weird mixture of strength and naivety, an educated woman with fancy luggage who doesn't seem to know how the world works. A woman who's just survived a con man. That no matter how capable she appears, I have this instinctive feeling that I need to protect her.

Then there's the fact that she intrigues me, more so than anyone has in a long time.

Yeah, I'm definitely keeping *that* to myself.

"For starters, I have a kid sister who would never forgive me if I left someone in distress when I could help. Then there's the fact you just got duped by a scammer. Plus, you don't have anywhere to go."

She studies my face for a long moment. "How do I know I can trust you?"

"You don't," I say honestly.

Her face morphs into a smile. "This could be part of your masterful plan."

"Right. My masterful plan to ... what exactly? Teach you the proper way to apply goth eyeliner?"

"It's smudged, isn't it?" She touches her cheek, then looks at her black-smeared fingers. "Oh, no."

It's about now I wish I had a handkerchief like Greg did, although mine would be a whole lot less drenched in sweat.

"Do you want to wipe your tears on my T-shirt?"

Don't judge me. It's all I've got.

I take the bottom edge and lift it up.

She shakes her head as she lifts the bottom of her own T-shirt, and I try to avoid looking at the smooth, soft skin of her belly.

Yeah, okay. I fail. I'm a guy and she's a gorgeous woman. It happens.

But I know I'm meant to be all about comfort and support right now, not thinking about what it would be like to kiss those sensuous, plump lips, to feel that curvaceous body pressed against mine, to have her look into my eyes with the same searing heat just one look from her sparks in me.

I clear my throat.

Where was I?

That's right: comfort and support.

The last thing I want to do is come across as some kind of lecherous creep after what's just happened to her.

I turn my attention to my phone, sending Chelsea a quick message.

ME:

Would it be okay if I invited someone to stay at the house?

CHELSEA:

OMG! Who is it?

ME:

I just need to help someone out.

CHELSEA:

Is she cute? Tell me everything.

ME:

Later. Helicopter?

CHELSEA:

Fine, keep your secrets. For now.

I fully intend to.

ME:

What about the fact your "friend" is in fact our agent?

CHELSEA:

What can I say? You know how it works in Hollywood.

Sadly, I do.

A moment later, a new message flashes up on my screen. This time it's not from Chelsea. It's from Dion.

DION:

Renaldo will meet you and your friend at the hotel helipad in 20. I'll message you the house address. Look for the guy in the navy uniform standing beside a helicopter.

There's Dion's dry wit.

ME:

I totally owe you, Dion.

DION:

Noted.

Why is that so unsettling? And the fact he and Chelsea are together again? I think I'm going to have to unpack that some other time.

He sends me the hotel address and I do a quick search on my map app.

"Is it all right if I come to stay at your friend's lake

house for a night or two? Just to give me some time to get my plans together?" she asks.

"You can stay as long as you like. I plan on being there for a few weeks, four tops." I reply, noticing she's managed to transform herself from raccoon back to regular person.

"Four weeks?" she asks.

"Yeah. Probably."

The drunk guy seems to notice us for the first time, pointing and saying something in Malveauxian.

"Shall we get going?" I ask.

"Definitely."

We begin the trek back toward the sea, the wheels of Amy's suitcase making a clanking sound each time the wheels hit a dip.

"We can catch our ride in twenty minutes from a hotel on the waterfront," I tell her, casually arranging a private helicopter from a hotel helipad like it's an Uber, when only a few short years ago I was eating ramen in a studio apartment and calling my parents when I was short on paying the rent.

There's probably a metaphor in there somewhere, but I'm too busy playing knight in shining armor to properly analyze it.

"You own a helicopter?" she asks.

"No. Definitely not. It belongs to Dion, this guy whose house we're heading to."

"The place with the east and the west wings that's not a palace?"

"That's the one. We need to get to the helipad."

She nods her head rapidly. "Okay. You know, Mav, this evening has taken a very unexpected turn."

"You're telling me. This morning, I was just a guy trying to avoid ... err, tourists. Now I'm apparently running a damsel in distress rescue service."

She nudges me with her elbow. "I might be in distress but I'm no damsel, that I can assure you. I mean, what does a damsel even look like?"

"I dunno. A beautiful woman with her hands and feet tied, lying across some train tracks as piano music plays?"

She giggles and the sound makes me smile.

"So, if you're not a damsel, what would you call yourself?"

She thinks for a moment. "A princess having a temporary setback." She looks up at me, and there's something about the way she says it makes me watch her more closely.

Is there a joke here I'm not quite getting?

I decide to play along. "Well, in that case, Your Royal Highness," I say with a bow. "Shall we quicken our speed to reach the royal helipad?"

She curtsies back, surprisingly graceful for someone in jeans and sneakers. But then Amy is an enigma, as I'm quickly learning. "Lead the way, Sir Maverick."

We reach the helipad on top of one of the town's fancy hotels. Renaldo, the pilot, doesn't even bat an eye at my goth appearance. All in a day's work when you're on Dion's payroll, I guess.

As I help Amy into the helicopter, she navigates the awkward entry with poise, making what should be an inelegant scramble look somehow the opposite. I've done enough wire work and complicated set pieces to recognize exceptional body awareness when I see it.

Who *is* this woman I've invited to stay with me?

As the helicopter lifts off into the dark sky, Amy presses her forehead against the window, watching the lights of Côte-des-Papillons shrink beneath us. The intimate glow of the cabin's minimal lighting sculpts her profile perfectly.

"You know, Mav," she says, turning to me, her voice

muffled and tinny through her headset. "When I planned my great escape, I didn't expect it to involve air travel."

"Great escape?"

She presses her lips together before replying, "You know, my escape from my everyday life."

"And what kind of life is it that you need to escape from?"

"One with a lot more rules than I'd like."

Rules. *Huh.* Maybe she's an athlete on a strict program? That could explain her poise and body awareness. Or maybe she's on the run from some crazy cult? Or maybe, much more likely, she's just got a super strict family, and she needs a break?

I think of her fancy luggage. Yeah, probably the strict family, some wealthy parents with high expectations of their daughter.

"What about you? What are you escaping from?" she asks.

"Who said I'm escaping?"

I'm keeping my secret. At least for now. But that doesn't mean I can't give her a partial truth. So I add, "I needed a break from being me."

She nods, like it makes perfect sense to her. "Tell me something," she begins, and I freeze, wondering how deep under cover I might need to get. "Does being you usually involve rescuing strange *non*-damsels in distress from dating-slash-business opportunity disasters on the southern coast of Malveaux?"

"Only on Wednesdays."

She giggles again, and I decide it's a sound I wouldn't mind hearing more often. "It's Monday."

"Then you must be special."

"That's nice to hear."

For a moment, we look at each other in the dim light

of the helicopter cabin and I'm struck again by her beauty, and there's something real about her vulnerability, something that cuts through all the pretense and secrets we're both maintaining.

Amy's beauty isn't the carefully manufactured kind I've become accustomed to in LA, where everyone's face is artfully crafted with fillers and Botox.

Pageant was the last woman I properly dated. She had a whole team of people, from curating her social media presence to which brand of water she drank, to the "spontaneous" photos taken of us on our morning runs. It had felt like our entire relationship was choreographed with the precision of a military operation, all in the name of publicity and fame.

Amy is the opposite of someone like her. She's who she is, an intriguing mix of capability and naivety, and I'm finding it impossible not to be drawn to her the more time I spend with her.

She grins at me, and for a moment I forget about all the reasons bringing a stranger to a borrowed house in a town I've never been to is probably a completely terrible idea. "Thank you for helping me, Mav. You're a good person."

A good person who's keeping my true identity from you.

Yeah, I'm not sure how "good" that makes me exactly.

But then she's obviously not telling me her full story, either.

I guess that makes us even.

What would she think if she knew the truth about me? Would her expression change, eyes widening with recognition, that familiar transformation I've seen countless times as people mentally replace *Guy I've just met* with *Ethan Roberts, famous actor*? Would conversation suddenly become stilted, peppered with questions about what it's like to work with this director or that co-star?

The thought makes something twist uncomfortably in my chest. I don't want to see that kind of transformation in Amy. I want to keep seeing her laugh without checking how it photographs. I want to keep watching her navigate the world with that strange combination of sophistication and wide-eyed wonder.

And as for me? I want to remain as Maverick Mitchell. A regular guy helping out a woman who's had a rough night.

Chapter 10

Amelia

I am positively vibrating with the most delicious morsel of gossip this royal correspondent has devoured since Prince Max was caught on camera skinny-dipping in the river with a team of no less than eight lady rowers at last year's Royal Summer Regatta—and don't pretend you've forgotten those photographs because I've had them framed.

Would you believe that our very own Princess Amelia, the same princess who is allegedly pursuing transcendental enlightenment in the mountains of India, has allegedly been spotted dashing through the streets of Tleurbonne looking less "namaste" and more "no way"?

Not only that but she was apparently dressed in *jeans* and *sneakers*, my dears. The horror! The scandal! The absolute fashion catastrophe!

Our princess was seen racing onto a train like she was being chased by her dance instructor after missing waltz practice.

One imagines King Frederic downing a whiskey or two as Queen Astrid reaches for her smelling salts at the very thought.

Perhaps it was merely her doppelganger with an uncanny resemblance to our beloved princess? Or, horror of horrors, could the palace have *lost track* of a royal?

Imagine the panic in the royal household! The King checking under sofas, the Queen ringing all her friends, young Prince Max being interrogated about his sister's whereabouts while trying to sneak out himself! It's positively Shakespearean.

I remain your ever-devoted royal correspondent, with eyes peeled and ears perked for any further sightings of our runaway royal,

Fabiana Fontaine xx

#PrincessOnTheLoose
#JeansAndTiaras
#RoyalHideAndSeek

What am I *doing*?

I mean, there isn't exactly a section in the royal rule-book on what to do when you find yourself in a picturesque lake house with a suspiciously handsome American stranger after a narrow escape from a dating disaster.

Maybe someone could insert it between Rule number 813: *Correct cutlery placement when dining with minor dictators*, and just before Rule number 814: *Always maintain a dignified posture while riding camels in the Sahara*.

I'm standing in a house that can only be described as a châteaux, on what looks like a thoroughly picturesque lake thanks to the brightness of the full moon tonight, following a dating disaster with a man I thought I knew, and then escaped here on a helicopter with another man who I've known for only a day, both of us dressed as goths.

Seriously, you couldn't make this stuff up.

I blow out a breath. The big question is, can I trust Maverick Mitchell?

Or should the question actually be, have I got any reason *not* to trust him?

As we separate to inspect the house and all its rooms. I count off the facts on my fingers.

1. We met by chance. Twice.
2. He seems genuine, evidenced by the fact he stuck around at the bar while I went on my disastrous date with Greg—or whatever his name really is.
3. He helped me escape from said disastrous date.
4. He was genuinely sweet to me during my low point tonight, even offering me his shirt to wipe away my smudged makeup. I mean, that's kindness personified, isn't it?
5. He's hot. So there's that.

Not that I should be basing any decisions on the fact that a man I've just met is hot. Even if he is decidedly hot, with his dark blue eyes, thick brown hair he frequently runs his fingers through in that sexy manner of his. And I haven't even touched on his athlete's physique, right down to his impossible height. Seriously, I have to crane my neck just to look into his eyes. But what eyes. Like deep blue pools that draw me in, hinting at the depths that lie behind them. The way the skin around those eyes creases when he smiles his kind smile, a smile that soothed me after the disaster of my "date." Made me feel safe.

And really, can someone truly evil have such kind eyes?

But on the other hand, there's the fact that he told me at the costume shop that he was planning to wear his goth costume to a party. What happened to that party?

"This place is enormous. I think we can actually have a wing each." Maverick's voice pulls me from my quandary, and I wander back to the living room where he's holding a set of towels.

"You never told me about your party," I say and I watch him closely for his reaction.

"Party?" he questions, pulling his brows together in what I'm now learning is his characteristic way.

"Yes. The party you were going to, dressed as a goth."

"Oh, that party," he replies, as though he has a long list of parties to attend and isn't in fact getting away from himself, as he confessed to me earlier in the helicopter. But what do I know? Perhaps "getting away from oneself" means going to a whole string of parties. Although I strongly suspect not.

"My plans changed. I was meant to go to a party in Tleurbonne, but I decided to head to the lake house early."

"I see."

Do I believe him? It seems reasonable enough. People's

plans do change. Maybe he wasn't in the party mood? And besides, I wasn't exactly honest with him about the alleged children's party I said I'd been to before hopping on the train.

Perhaps it's better that I leave sleeping dogs lie.

If I don't question him too closely, hopefully he won't do the same with me.

I file my questions away for another day and pronounce, "This place is just lovely, Mav. I've never been to this particular lake before. I'm looking forward to discovering it's treasures."

"Not a bad spot." He holds out a set of towels. "I got you these. Thought you might want to de-goth."

I take them in my hands, feeling their soft plushness. "Thanks."

"It's all part of the service, Your Royal Highness."

I do a double take before I remember it was my joke from earlier in which I was sounding him out to see whether he really did recognize me. But there wasn't even a flash of recognition in his eyes.

"A knight who provides linens. How very 21st Century," I say.

We stand in silence for a moment, neither of us knowing what to say next.

"Are you hungry?" he asks finally, breaking the mounting awkwardness.

"Starving!" I reply with gusto, because even though we ate dinner only a couple of hours ago, my tummy grumbles at the thought.

Being disappointed by Greg has given me an appetite.

"Let's go see what we can find in the kitchen," Maverick says.

I follow him past an elegant dining room with a large mahogany table and a chandelier rather similar to some of the chandeliers at the palace, then down a wide hallway lined with paintings, and into a kitchen. It's an elegant space. The cabinets are pale blue with gold-hued marble counters. Rustic wood beams sit overhead, and a chandelier hangs over the island, making the room gleam with its warm glow.

Maverick turns in a circle, trying to locate something. "Refrigerator?"

"Over there," I say, pointing at a walk-in fridge with glass doors not unlike the one in the palace back home in Villadorata. I sometimes sneak into it after the kitchen staff have left for the day and devour an extra pudding.

"Huh. Never seen one like that before," Maverick says as he pulls the doors open. Inside the fridge is filled with a colorful display of fruits and vegetables, pots of yoghurt and dips and spreads, milk, and various meats.

"That's a lot of food," I say, stepping into the cool fridge, still clutching onto my towels. "Fancy a little picnic?"

He turns to me in surprise. "It's dark out."

"We could sit on large cushions on the living room floor and throw the French doors open to see the view of the lake. The moon is full tonight and very bright."

"I was thinking more of a quick late-night sandwich at the kitchen counter before hitting the hay, but your idea is better. Let's collect what we need." He glances at the towels. "You might want to put those to the side for now."

"I'd thought the very same thing," I reply, placing my towels on the counter.

We go about collecting whatever looks good from the fridge. We've got everything from some salmon pâté to carrots to an assortment of cheeses, and tubs of strawberries.

Maverick locates the pantry and pulls out a loaf of bread, waving it in the air. "Sandwich?"

"Yes, please."

He locates a thick wooden chopping board and a knife and together with the loaf, he places them in front of me.

Now, I don't want to come across all elite or anything, but really, when does a Ledonian princess ever use a wooden chopping board and a knife to cut up a loaf of bread? Answer: never. That would be breaking Rule number 42: *A princess must never prepare her own food.*

Oh, but how I love to break those rules, so preparing our own food it is, even if it is just slicing up a loaf of bread. I make a mental note to put a big, fat, thoroughly satisfying line through that one in my rule book later.

I examine the items in front of me. How hard can it be? It's logical that the bread sits on top of the board. So far so good. Then, I suppose, I just start cutting it up. Should be easy enough.

I pick up the knife and hold it over the bread, about to start slicing when Maverick says, "Shouldn't you take the bread out of its paper bag first?"

I let out a light laugh. "I knew that!" I insist, when I really didn't.

I pull the bread from its paper bag and line it up in the center of the board once more. I lift the knife into the air and lower it onto the bread with a chopping motion, but the knife bounces right out of my hand with barely a dent to the bread, flying up in the air and landing with a *clank* onto the tiled floor.

Oops.

It turns out that slicing bread isn't quite as straightforward as I might have imagined.

Maverick looks from the knife to me and then back at the knife. He frowns. "What happened?"

"Frankly, I couldn't quite tell you."

He collects the knife from the floor and cleans it under flowing water from the tap, dries it, and places it on the board next to the bread. "Do you want me to give it a shot?

"I'm quite capable of slicing some bread," I tell him with false bravado, because it's quite clear I have no idea how to do this.

He raises his hands in surrender. "You got it."

As he turns away to do something with cheese, I make another unsuccessful attempt, managing only to further mangle the innocent loaf. My cheeks burn with embarrassment. At the palace, everything is discretely managed for me. Other than raiding the fridge at night, I've got no clue what goes on in the palace kitchens. But here in this kitchen, with no royal infrastructure to shield me, I'm simply a woman who can't slice bread.

I can't help but feel utterly useless, unable to complete even the most basic of tasks.

I refuse to be defeated by this loaf. I take another shot, but this time I don't go in for any big movements. Instead, I placed the knife directly on top of the bread and with my other hand, I press it down. Surely this should work? In the battle between bread and knife, knife should win, what with it being made of metal and not … bread.

Sadly, I'm wrong. All I manage to do is squash the loaf to half its original size.

How on earth do you slice a loaf of bread? Particularly when the knife is a little bendy. Yes! That's it! That's my problem. Maverick gave me a bendy knife by accident. I simply need a stronger knife.

I pull open drawers until I locate a knife drawer, filled with knives neatly lined up. I grab the largest one—something that looks very serious indeed—and check its bendiness. It doesn't bend at all. We're making progress.

I've been going about this completely the wrong way. It's now obvious to me I need to use some brute force. I lift the large knife into the air, holding the loaf in place when I feel a hand grip my wrist and gently pull the knife away.

"I was going to use that!" I complain.

I look at him and expect to see pity in his eyes, or worse, a flash of superiority people get when they know something you don't, like Sofia used to give me growing up every day of her life.

But instead, his expression holds genuine understanding.

And humor. Definitely humor.

"Have you never sliced a loaf of bread before, Amy?" he asks.

I need to come clean. The squashed and completely un-sliced loaf is evidence of my lack of bread slicing experience. "I haven't," I admit.

"Because you always get pre-sliced bread? Yeah, me too," he replies, letting me off the hook. "You know, the first time I had to do my own laundry, I turned everything I owned gray, including my sheets and my towels. I told my family that since gray is a sign of maturity my laundry had officially outgrown me."

I let out a laugh. "At least it wasn't pink like Rachel's went on *Friends*."

His brows ping up. "You get that show in Ledonia?"

"Oh, we're right up with the play, you know. We get all the '90s shows."

It's his turn to laugh. "Let me show you how to slice bread." He demonstrates the sawing motion needed for bread-cutting and I watch his hands move as he methodically slices the bread. Slice after slice, his hands are steady and strong. "See? It's easy when you know how."

"Thank you, Mav," I say softly.

"Why don't you wash the strawberries?"

"Certainly. I know exactly how to do that."

"Good to know."

I watch Maverick move around the kitchen with the practiced ease of someone who doesn't need royal kitchen staff to prepare a simple picnic. It's mesmerizing, really, like watching a nature documentary about a species I've only read about in books: *Homo sapiens normalus*, in his natural habitat, performing the ancient ritual of food preparation without cutting off a limb.

"Where did you learn to cook? You seem quite handy."

"Nothing fancy. When you live on your own, you either learn to feed yourself or become intimate friends with the delivery guy."

"And you clearly learned to feed yourself."

A smile tugs at the corners of his mouth. "Let's just say I could recite the entire menu of Golden Dragon Chinese by heart before I learned it's way cheaper to make your food than buy it from a restaurant."

There's something refreshing about his straightforwardness—the way he doesn't seem to be performing. Everyone in my life is performing something: royal duties, diplomatic niceties, appropriate deference for my royalty. Maverick just... *is*.

I lean against the counter. "Were you always so self-sufficient?

"Not really. Growing up, my mom handled most of that stuff. But after college, reality hit pretty hard."

"What kind of reality?"

"The kind where no one magically appears to wash

your socks or make sure you've eaten something other than instant noodles that week."

Instant noodles sound rather thrilling to me.

"What about you?" he asks as he pastes some of the salmon pâté onto a slice of bread. "What's your family like? Beyond the strict rules and fancy luggage, that is."

Now there's one dangerous question.

But there's something about the way Maverick looks at me attentively, like he's actually interested in the answer, that makes me want to give him something real—without giving the game away.

"They're complicated," I say, which is perhaps the most honest thing I've ever said about my family to someone outside the royal bubble. "Like me, my older sister, Sofia, has had her entire life mapped out since birth and she's completely fine with it. My older brother, Alex, spent years rebelling against family expectations before finally finding his place. And Max, my younger brother, pretends nothing bothers him, but I think he feels the weight of it all much more than he lets on."

I stop, horrified that I've revealed too much. If he knows any of my family's names, he could piece it all together. But he just nods, like he understands family dynamics.

"And where do you fit in all that?"

The question catches me off guard. Where *do* I fit? The spare to the spare to the heir? The princess with no clear purpose except to wave and smile and make an appropriate marriage and then quietly disappear?

"I'm still working that out, hence the great escape."

He smiles at me, and something in his eyes tells me he understands. "Are you gonna wash those strawberries any time soon?"

"Strawberries. Of course." I collect the tub of the fattest, juiciest strawberries and take it to the sink. I find some liquid soap and squirt it over the fruit, giving them a jolly good clean. It buffs off some of the skin, so they end up looking a little like lumps of something red more than strawberries.

As I finish, I turn in triumph to Maverick, but he's got an odd look on his face.

"What is it?" I ask.

"You used soap to wash the strawberries?"

I beam at him. "Of course I did. You said to wash them."

"Right." He nods his head a few times, that frown of his returning once more.

Why is he frowning at me? I'm certain I did a good job. Besides, I'm not about to tell him I've never washed strawberries before.

And he really should stop frowning quite so much. He'll get permanent lines. He'll have a resting frown face, and no one will like him.

Except, if I'm completely honest, he looks rather sexy when he frowns.

Which is all the more reason why he should avoid frowning around me. I don't want to develop a crush on this man. Not after what's just happened. I need to lick my wounds for a while. Think about other things. Things like how to be a normal person, doing normal things.

"Do you want me to wash anything else?" I ask.

"No!" he says rather forcefully, and it's my turn to frown. "What I mean is I think we've got everything we need, so let's take our sandwiches and go have our picnic."

"What about the strawberries?"

"Let's … not."

A few minutes later, we've pulled the French doors open that overlook the lawn leading down to the lake and placed some of the sofa cushions on the floor. We both sit, biting into our sandwiches, which taste utterly incredible.

"I grabbed a couple of bottles of beer. Do you want one?" He holds a bottle out to me.

"Oh, yes please. I hardly ever get to drink beer."

He snaps off the cap and the beer hisses. Holding his bottle up to mine, we clink before we both take a sip.

"Ah, that's good," he says, leaning back against the cushions.

I follow suit, gazing out at the lake, glistening in the moonlight as I take another bite of my sandwich. "It's beautiful here," I say between bites, the moonlight casting silver ripples across the water's surface.

"It really is."

"I could imagine staying here forever. Have you decided how long you're staying?"

He shrugs. "I'm not sure yet. Maybe? Depends."

"Well, that's as clear as mud," I say on a laugh. "What does it depend on?"

He thinks for a moment before he replies, "On whether I can get a job."

A *job*.

Perhaps I could get a job, too? I could do something normal people do every day of their lives, something I would never get to experience as a princess—which, let's face it, is pretty much any job anywhere.

"What sort of job?" I ask, my pulse jumping.

"I dunno. Something in the service industry, probably. I've done that before. I'm thinking of looking in the town tomorrow."

"Could I come with you?" I ask, enthusiastic for this new turn my adventure has taken.

"You want to get a job, too?"

"I would absolutely love a job!"

"I thought you were only staying for a couple days?"

That. Right.

"I might stay longer, if you're open to it? I mean, I don't want to outstay my welcome or anything, but it is rather splendid here, and I promise not to be a bother." Then I add, "I could really do with the money."

There. That makes me sound totally normal. I need a job to make money. That's what people do who aren't royal. I did bring some money with me, of course, but I used some of it for my train ticket here, and I'm worried it won't last all that long if I'm not careful.

He studies me for a beat. "How long do you think you want to stay?"

"As long as you're happy for me to?" I chance and hold my breath.

He pulls his lips into a line. "Let's go check out the town and see what jobs we might be able to find."

"Perfect! Thank you so much, Mav. We're going to have lots of fun, you and I. I can tell."

He bites back a smile, and I wonder what I've said to amuse him. But I'm positively brimming with excitement at this idea. A job! An actual job! I've never had one before, and the thought of going to a place of work, of having things to do with my day, tasks to complete, working with other people who don't call me *Your Royal Highness* and bow and curtsy and watch what they say around me, fills me with glee.

"Can I ask you something that might sound somewhat strange?" I set my sandwich down.

"Stranger than whether you tried to use soap to clean strawberries?"

I laugh despite myself. "How was I supposed to know you don't use soap on strawberries?"

"I dunno, by doing life?"

I press my lips together before I ask, "Do you ever feel like your whole life has been one long performance? Like everyone's watching you, expecting you to be a certain way, and if you step out of line even a little, they're all shocked?"

He pauses for a beat, his eyes reflecting in the moonlight.

I may be wrong, but it seems to me there's something in that pause. Perhaps a story he isn't telling me? I only recognize it because I have similar pauses of my own.

But I might be reading too much into it.

"Yeah," he says finally. "Like everyone has expectations of how you're meant to be, and they don't actually care about the real you underneath."

I widen my eyes at him. He gets it. Really gets it. "Exactly that! And then you find yourself doing ridiculous things just to feel—" I struggle to find the right words because I can't finish my sentence the way I intend by saying "like you're not just a princess."

"Real?" he offers, and I blink at him.

He really *does* get it.

"Real," I confirm.

We share a look which feels like a moment of complete understanding. We're two people who recognize the loneliness of being seen but not *known*.

He takes a sip of his beer, staring out at the view. "Can I ask you a question now?"

"Ask away."

"How come you don't know your way around a kitchen?"

"Oh. Well, I have this condition."

It's called being a princess.

He tilts his head to look at me. "A condition?"

"It's a condition that means that you can't make your own food. It's very rare. It mostly affects people with ... err ... very attentive mothers. Yes, that's it. Very attentive mothers."

"What's this condition called?"

I come up with a term as though it's a real condition. "Chronic Culinary Incompetence Syndrome." I suppress a smile at how clever I am.

"Chronic Culinary Incompetence Syndrome."

"You probably haven't heard of it because it's very rare."

"And it means your mom has to do the cooking for you?"

Or the palace chefs. "That's right."

"Amy, that's not a condition. That's called being a kid. But you're what? Twenty-something?"

"Twenty-four and three quarters."

His lips quirk. "I'm sure the three quarters makes all the difference. Does your mom still cook for you?"

"Yes."

"So, you still live at home."

"Yes."

"Huh."

"What does 'huh' mean?"

"It means that it makes sense."

"What makes sense?" I ask, genuinely confused.

"That you think you need to use soap to wash strawberries." He presses his lips together to stifle a smile.

"You don't use soap?"

He shakes his head. "No soap."

"Should I have used dishwashing liquid? That was my second choice."

"Definitely not," he replies with a chuckle.

"I've got a lot to learn."

He shrugs, his features lifted in a smile. "Haven't we all?"

We fall into a comfortable silence as we eat, the kind that doesn't need to be filled with chatter, and I find myself feeling more comfortable with Maverick than I have with anyone in a long, long time.

"I've spent my whole life following rules, and now that I'm breaking them, I keep waiting to feel guilty. But I don't. I just feel free," I say.

"I know exactly what you mean."

I turn to look at him. "Is that terrible?"

He shakes his head. "It's human. We all need space to figure out who we are beyond everyone else's expectations."

"Is that what you're doing here? Figuring out who you are?"

A shadow crosses his face. "I guess I'm trying to remember who I was before ... everything."

I want to ask what "everything" entails, but there's something in his tone that suggests boundaries. And I, of all people, understand the necessity of boundaries.

Instead, I simply nod. "Well, for what it's worth, I like who you are."

He smiles. "Right back atcha, Amy."

And though we're still virtual strangers in many ways, and I've not even given him my real name, there's a thread of understanding between us that feels strangely comforting. It's not a romantic feeling, despite the fact anyone can see he's jolly handsome. I'm certainly not ready for anything along those lines after the Greg fiasco.

I suppose it's the beginning of a real, authentic connection with someone. Perhaps this could be my adventure? A princess getting to make genuine connections with the people she meets. It might not have the excitement of a grand love affair, but as I look at Maverick gazing out at the lake, I wonder whether it might just feel like an adventure after all.

Chapter 11

Ethan

It's early morning and the house is silent. I pull back the curtains in my bedroom—with a massive four-poster bed, its own fireplace, writing desk, and enough space to swing a cat and all her relatives—and blink in the soft morning glow.

This place is incredible. Although we arrived in the dark last night, picnicking by the open doors showed me how amazing the view would be in the light of day, and this morning, I can see down the green grass to the lake, sparkling a deep blue in the sun.

Not that I exactly like the fact this is Dion's place, and I can't help but wonder what price I'll need to pay.

I guess I'll cross that bridge when I come to it.

And really, he's my agent. He should have my best interests at heart.

I take in a deep breath, pushing my concerns to the back of my mind. I can almost feel a weight being lifted from my shoulders, like I've been carrying a backpack filled with all my worries around with me and finally, *finally*, I've been able to take it off.

I look out at the blue sparkling lake. This is so different from the way I start my days back home in LA. By this time, I would be on the way to meet my PT at the gym to work hard at staying in the shape required for Rowan Thornheart.

Then, after a shower and a protein shake, I climb into my car and make my way to the studio for filming. And those are long days. Sometimes I don't get home until the small hours, collapsing into bed and catching some Z's before I do it all over again, like some kind of mouse on a wheel that goes around and around and around.

It feels so dang good to be away from all that.

Assuming Amy must still be asleep, I pad in my bare feet down the grand staircase to the kitchen at the back of the house, where I find everything I need to make coffee, including an expensive looking Italian espresso machine. I learned to use such machines while working as a barista to support myself as a starving actor in LA.

With my cup in hand, I wander outside to drink in the view, coming to a stop part way down the grass toward the lake. My view is framed by a couple of old oak trees, and I watch as a bird lands on one of its high branches, taking my first sip of coffee, thinking over the drama of the last few days—and in particular, my unexpected houseguest.

Amy had been taken for a serious ride by that jerk back at the bar. I knew something was up the moment she mentioned she'd met him online and that he had used another guy's photo. Guys like that are a dime a dozen, and a pretty woman like Amy should know better than to fall for his tricks. But fall she sure did, and I'm only glad I was on hand to pick up the pieces.

And now she's here with me, at the lake house. For how long? I have no idea. What I do know is that having her here is … nice. She's easy to talk to, even if she's got no clue how to slice bread or wash fresh produce. Liquid soap? What the heck was that about? I mean, I've met plenty of actors in LA who are out of touch with reality, but I bet even they would know you don't need hand soap to clean strawberries.

I figure my hunch was right. She's from a wealthy, controlling family with expensive taste in luggage.

No wonder she's a self-professed escapee.

My phone vibrates in my hand, and I see it's Dion calling.

"Good morning," I say, holding the phone to my ear.

"How's my hottest client liking his new digs?"

"This place is amazing. Thank you so much for offering it to me."

"I told you, I'm looking out for you. What are your plans?"

"I'm thinking I might go get a job."

"Why?" His tone is less than complimentary.

"I guess I want to do something different while I'm here, something that will connect me to the man I was," I reply honestly.

He harrumphs. "What do you mean? Poor?"

I don't dignify his question with a response. It was probably rhetorical anyway.

"Who's this house guest you've got?"

"Just a girl I met in a costume store."

"Is she hot?"

I pinch my lips together. My agent is reducing the complicated and interesting Amy into one word. *Hot.*

"She's a nice person."

"Nice?" He chortles, sounding a lot like that cartoon dog, Muttley.

I've never really been able to work Dion out. Chelsea was the one who put us in touch, back when I'd first got the role of Rowan Thornheart and needed some representation. He's always struck me as an oddball, but he's an oddball that gets things done, and no one ever said you should be friends with your agent. Or even like them, for that matter.

"Yeah. Nice," I say.

"Shame she's not hot. For your sake."

"I didn't say that."

"You didn't have to. What kind of job are you looking for?"

"I have no idea."

"There's a café in town. Name of Francine's. You could try there."

He's now suggesting where I can find a job?

"Thanks for the idea."

"I guess I'll leave you to it. Enjoy my house."

Something twists uncomfortably in my belly at the fact my refuge is owned by my agent.

"Thanks again," I reply.

"See you back here in a month," he says, still chortling as he hangs up.

As I take another sip off my coffee, there's a rustling

137

sound in one of the oak tree branches. Must be another bird.

"Good morning, Maverick."

"Hey, Amy," I reply, swiveling around to see her. But she's nowhere. "Amy?"

"Up here," says her disembodied voice, floating down from above like some kind of woodland spirit.

"Up where?" I look around, thoroughly confused. Where could she possibly be? Up a tree? No. She's not seven, and this isn't an Enid Blyton novel.

"Look up."

There's a rustle of leaves once more and, incredulous, I look up to see her draped over a branch, wearing a pair of plaid shorts and a T-shirt, a hesitant smile playing across her now goth-makeup-free face. The morning sunlight filters through the leaves around her, creating a dappled effect that makes her look like she's stepped out of a Renaissance painting—if Renaissance painters had been into capturing women in shorts lounging on branches before breakfast.

It seems unlikely.

"You climbed a tree," I say as my mind races on two parallel tracks.

Track One tells me that Amy's an overgrown kid.

Track Two is a little more concerning. How much of my conversation with Dion did she hear, and did I give myself away? I didn't reference Hollywood, but she's surprisingly perceptive for someone who thinks soap is an ingredient in strawberry preparation.

"Well, I didn't fly up here," she replies, a touch haughty for someone currently draped across a branch. "It's wonderful!"

And there it is again, that infectious enthusiasm for ordinary things. It's as though she's experiencing life for the first time, cataloging each moment with wide-eyed wonder.

"Remind me. You said you're twenty-four, right?"

"And three quarters."

"How many people aged twenty-four and three quarters do you know who climb trees?"

"At least one."

"Not counting yourself."

"Don't be so negative, Mav," she chides. "It really is the most thrilling thing. Why don't you join me?"

"Because I'm an adult enjoying my coffee right now." I hold up my cup as evidence. "And I got tree climbing out of my system years ago."

Which is mostly true, though I did have to learn to scale a particularly gnarly oak for a scene in Season Two. Three days of harnesses and safety briefings so I could dramatically brood on a branch for approximately forty-five seconds of screen time.

And there was definitely no joy in the climb.

Not like Amy, who seems to be loving every moment.

"You could at least have had the common decency to put on a shirt," she says.

I glance down at my bare chest and white boxers, suddenly self-conscious in a way I haven't been since my first shirtless scene. Truth be told, I hadn't expected to see Amy this early, let alone to be up a tree. It hadn't occurred to me to throw on a T-shirt for my solitary life contemplation over my first coffee of the day.

"I'm sorry my bare chest offends you," I quip, though there's something in her expression that suggests offense isn't exactly the emotion she's experiencing.

But that might be more hopeful thinking on my part.

Not that I should be hoping for anything with this woman.

"Well, it does," she sniffs with a primness that's comically at odds with her current position straddling a tree branch. She gives a little toss of her head that nearly unbalances her, her hands clutching the branch tightly as she tries to maintain both her physical and moral high ground.

The way the clash between her free-spirited nature and whatever strict upbringing she's trying to escape is playing out before my eyes. It's endearing.

"Are you stuck?" I ask, the thought occurring to me.

"What goes up, must come down. I got up here, ergo I will get down."

"Ergo?"

"Yes. Ergo."

There it is again, that flash of cultivation beneath her surface. Amy is a completely fascinating mixture of contradictions.

She doesn't know how to slice bread, but she casually drops that she speaks Latin into conversation.

She thinks you need to use soap to wash strawberries, but she handled that snooty woman at the restaurant yesterday with confidence.

She climbs trees like she's an excited kid, but then acts all haughty because I'm shirtless.

I take another sip of my coffee and return my attention to the view. "Suit yourself." When she says nothing more, I begin the walk back to the house

"Mav?"

I know what's coming. I turn and look back up at her. "Yes, Amy?"

"I don't suppose—? Oh, never mind."

"Amy, are you *stuck*?" She's like a kitten who's climbed too high and is now desperately meowing for a firefighter.

"Not stuck, exactly. More, I don't know. Descent impaired?"

"That sounds a little like your Culinary Incompetence Syndrome."

"It's entirely different, if you must know," she quips, her voice all haughty again.

"Look, do you want my help or not?"

"Only if you can. I don't want to put you out."

"Hold tight. I'll be right there," I say as I secure my footing on the lowest branch and reach for the next.

"You're good at this," she says as I climb higher and higher.

"Not my first rodeo."

"What have horses and bulls and other farm animals got to do with climbing a tree?"

"It's an American saying," I grunt as I pull myself up to her branch with considerable effort. She did well to climb this high given her size.

"Well, I suppose that makes sense. You do have rodeos in the United States."

She's keeping her voice slight, but I can tell she's freaked out. She's a grown woman stuck up a tree. I'd be freaked out, too.

"How did you manage to get up this high?" I ask, catching my breath as I edge closer along the branch.

I'm close enough now to catch her scent. It's something subtle and expensive that definitely isn't store-brand shampoo—and it's inappropriate for me to notice such things while we're twenty feet above solid ground.

I'm now close enough to her to reach for her legs, that are still wrapped around the branch.

"I climbed up here, of course," she offers, her full lips lifting into a hint of a smile, and I'm struck by how breathtakingly beautiful she is without all that black goop on her face. Her skin is olive and smooth but for her nose, which is sprinkled with a light dusting of freckles. Her large brown eyes are watching me closely, her hands white knuckled as she holds onto the branch for dear life, like a koala.

For all her cheek and pomposity about my current state of semi-dress, she's just a scared girl who's gotten herself into something she doesn't know how to get out of.

I edge along the branch, channeling every Bear Grylls outdoor adventure episode I've watched. "You need to let go with one hand."

"I don't want to," she replies in a voice so unlike her usual confident and enthusiastic tone, and something in my chest tightens.

I put it down to the rescuer's mentality, feeling empathy for my rescue-ee.

I go for my most soothing tone when I reply, "I get it. It feels counterintuitive. But you've gotta trust me." I move closer until my chest is nearly touching her back, suddenly hyper-aware of how close we are. "I've got you, Amy. Now, very slowly, release your right hand and reach back for mine like a reverse high-five."

"That sounds very American," she replies, her voice strained.

"Kinda goes with the territory. See it as step one in the Maverick Mitchell Tree Rescue Protocol."

She lets out a shaky laugh. "Is there a step two?"

"Absolutely. It's called 'Don't Look Down.'"

Her eyes meet mine, and with the smallest of head nods, I reach out and wrap my arm around her waist, pressing my front against her back.

She's trembling, but I'll admit, there's something about how perfectly she fits against me that makes my breath catch.

Again. *Not* helpful.

"I've got you, Amy. Now, very slowly, release your right hand and reach back for mine."

She lets out a shaky breath and slowly uncurls her fingers from their death grip on the branch. She slips her hand into mine and I begin to help her turn until I have her safely secured against me, her body nestled into mine.

Don't think about how good this feels. That's what I tell myself. But my body is not listening. She fits so perfectly against me, and a part of me wants to stay here on this branch, holding her, keeping her safe.

But that part of me is thinking with something other than my brain, and I override it, quick smart.

I shuffle us along the branch and help her find the trunk of the tree.

"You okay climbing down from here?" I ask, still holding on to her.

"I think so. What goes up, must come down. Remember?"

"Yeah, about that last part? Take it slow."

I don't let go of her until I can see she has a firm grip on the trunk, her feet growing in confidence as she finds each branch, making her way down back to the ground.

I follow her down, and when we reach the ground she rushes back into my arms, squeezing me hard.

Instinctively I wrap my arms around her once more— only this time she's not a frightened little mouse, seeking reassurance. This time she's a woman, thanking a man for helping her, and she feels so good in my arms.

Too good.

"Thank you, Mav. Thank you," she breathes against my chest, and I feel a stab of guilt in my side that I haven't been honest enough with her to tell her my real name.

"Anytime," I reply, trying not to notice how soft she feels against me, how sweet her aroma is.

How all I want to do is kiss her.

Wait. I can't go getting ideas about kissing Amy. I'm here to hide away from the world, to take a break from my world, to consider where I want my life to go. Definitely not catch feelings for some random—but admittedly intriguing—woman.

Fighting the growing urge, I take a step back acutely aware that only seconds ago she was pressed up against me, her face nestled against my bare chest.

That was way too intimate.

"Rescue number one of the day complete," I say in a light tone that belies the way our close proximity felt.

"We're making a habit of this, aren't we?" she replies. "And I'm sorry to throw myself at you like that, what with all your shirtless-ness. I should respect your boundaries better."

"It's fine," I lie because feeling the way she did in my arms was anything but fine. "I'll be sure to remember a shirt the next time."

"There won't be a next time. You are officially off the hook when it comes to rescuing me. Promise."

"You sure about that? By my assessment, that makes it twice in two days. Are you sure there won't be a third time tomorrow?" I flash a smile at her to show her our recent closeness hasn't affected me at all.

Not. At. All.

"Of course there won't, and you didn't need to rescue me from the tree. I had it all in hand."

I can't help but laugh. "Sure you did."

"All right. Not completely in hand. I'll try a different way tomorrow."

I blink at her. "You're going to climb a tree again tomorrow?"

"Why not? I've just broken Rule number 124, and it feels marvelous."

"You've got a rule that says you can't climb trees? Is that like a family rule or something?"

"Yes. I have awfully strict parents."

"Why are they so strict?"

She shrugs. "Because they are."

"You know that's answering a question without answering it, right?"

She pauses for a moment before she says, "My family business means we need to be above reproach."

"Are they politicians or something?"

"No. We … run a foundation. It has strict moral clauses for all family members."

"What kind of foundation has so many rules?"

"An educational foundation. We need to be role models for the children. I can't be seen to be breaking any rules because it will reflect poorly on my family and therefore on our foundation."

"Huh." I've never heard of such a thing, but then they do say that the wealthy are a breed apart. They don't operate like us regular people.

I decide to leave it. After all, I don't want her digging into my identity. If she's got secrets, then so have I.

She lifts her lips into a bright and beautiful smile. "Is there any more of that coffee going? I would love a cup before we head into the town to look for jobs."

Discussion over.

"You bet."

As we make our way back to the house, I can't help but wonder what kind of life Amy leaves that the moment she's away from her strict family with all their rules she feels the urge to climb a tree.

But more than that, as she chats excitedly about finding a job and how wonderful it is to be here, I wonder just how strong the fortress around my heart will hold.

Chapter 12

Amelia

I don my goth costume and apply my makeup. Although we're in a small place off the tourist map, you never know who will recognize you, and let's face it, after the day I had yesterday, I don't want this whole adventure to come crashing down around my ears because someone sells an image of me to the media.

Checking I look appropriately dark and gloomy in the mirror, I wait for Maverick by the front door. He appears in his goth outfit, too.

"What's with the costume?" he asks.

"I could ask you the same question."

He seems to consider that for a moment. "I need to fly under the radar for a bit. PR can be … challenging."

"Do you really think someone in a small town in Malveaux will recognize you?" I ask, dubious. How high profile can Maverick's job really be?

"I guess I don't want to take that chance. How about you?"

"I simply enjoy being a goth," I say with a shrug. I pull my eye liner from my purse. "Let me ring your eyes again."

"Sure thing," he replies, and I'm relieved he doesn't question me further.

He finds a seat and I apply the eyeliner, remembering how I did this only yesterday. It's hard to believe how much has happened in such a short period of time. Twenty-four hours and I've become a goth, dodged a conman, and am now heading out to find a job.

Made up and ready to go, we leave the lake house and meander through the quaint town of Montelac on the Lac des Rêves, feeling the gentle breeze from the lake. The houses are painted in different pastels, with shutters in blues and reds, reflected in the lake. Flowerpots overflow with beautiful flowers, and I can just make out the faint toll of a church bell, echoing through the town.

I breathe in the air, enjoying the faint aroma of lavender and freshly baked bread.

I'll admit, I was embarrassed to have to get him to help me down from that tree. But he did so with such dexterity, helping me climb down without too much fuss at all. And then I threw myself at him in gratitude, forgetting that he was shirtless.

Talk about awkward.

But he seems to have moved on, and any awkwardness between us seems to have been banished from sight.

"This place is so perfect, it's like a movie set, like *The Sound of Music* or something," he says.

"Are you half expecting Julie Andrews to appear, singing about the hills being alive?"

"Pretty much. The houses are picture perfect, the lake stunning, and just look at that streetlight."

I look up at the slender black metal post with its two curved arms that support vintage lanterns. It's the sort of streetlight that's common in Ledonia, only being Malveauxian, they're a little less ornate. We do so love our decorative details in my country.

"What about it?" I ask, not sure why he's mentioning it.

"It's so pretty."

"That's good?"

"Of course it is. This place is just beautiful," he enthuses, and I'll admit that it is a very pretty town, positioned as it is on the edge of a beautiful lake.

"I'm sure the good people of Montelac will be glad you like their streetlights."

He grins at me, shaking his head. "You probably think I'm being a stupid American tourist again, right?"

"I think you're being your authentic self, and that's what matters," I reply, the fact I'm *not* being my authentic self rather putting a dent in my own enthusiasm.

Pretending to be someone I'm not is turning out to be rather exhausting. But I can't simply come out and say the truth about who I really am. Who knows what he'll do with that information? He could talk to the media, blow my cover.

Or worse yet, talk to my parents.

No. Let sleeping dogs lie, as the saying goes. It's certainly for the best.

We walk down one of the cobblestone streets lined with pastel painted buildings. I see a café whose stone walls are painted pink, with the sign reading Francine's in looping text on the pink and white striped awning. There are people sitting at tables outside in the sun, sipping their coffee and eating pastries, and not one of them even bats an eyelid at me.

Come to think of it, no one has even taken a second look at me as we've walked through the town.

Hmm.

Perhaps this town is so off the tourist map the locals either don't recognize me as a princess of the neighboring country, or they don't care.

Either way, it's an odd feeling when it finally happens. Anonymity. It's like I've stepped into a parallel universe in which I'm not a Princess from the neighboring country, whose brother is married to their new queen. I'm just me. Amy.

I spot a sign in a window of the café that reads "Help wanted" in English. Which is odd, since we're in Malveaux. But I'm not going to second guess it. Perhaps they get a lot of English-speaking workers here.

"Mav, look!" I say as I rush over to the window. "What do you think?"

He frowns, as he so often does, and says, "My friend told me I should check Francine's out to see if they were hiring."

"He must have seen the sign himself!"

"I'm not sure how. He's in the States," he replies.

We both peer through the window to see a busy café, filled with patrons, with an older woman wearing a pink, frilly apron behind the counter, busy serving customers beside a handsome young man with the sort of stubble-lined jaw my brothers love to sport.

"What do you think? Working in a café could be a lot of fun," I say, the idea solidifying in my mind. I could learn how to make coffee, get to know the locals, and work in a place that looks like a giant pink marshmallow.

"I'm not sure a café is the right place for you," Maverick says.

"Why? Because I couldn't slice the bread last night?" I wave his concerns away with my hand. "I can learn. It'll be fun."

"How about we look for something else. Maybe something that doesn't involve food."

"But I like the idea of working at the café."

"Have you ever worked at a café?"

"Well, no. But I'm a fast learner. I'm sure I'll soon master the art of making coffee and slicing bread and all those things before you know it. I mean really, how hard can it be?"

He presses his lips together, not looking the least convinced.

I turn it around on him. "Have *you* ever worked in a café?"

"Plenty."

Well, that backfired on me. "Oh."

He chews on his lip. "I guess it can't hurt to go in and ask."

I beam at him. "That's the spirit. Nothing ventured, nothing gained. That's what Father likes to say."

"You call your dad 'Father?'"

"Of course," I reply as I breeze through the front door and into the most charming café I've ever stepped inside of. The fact it's the only café I've ever stepped inside of is beside the point entirely.

This place is utterly, utterly charming, and it's all pastel pink, from the walls to the velvet seats to the flowers hanging from the ceiling.

"It looks like a big, fluffy marshmallow you just want to bite into and lap up its sugary deliciousness," I say.

In our black, Maverick and I stick out like the charred exterior of this toasted pink marshmallow.

"The place sure is pink. I didn't know *Legally Blonde* had branched out into franchising."

I regard him in surprise. "You know that movie?"

He shrugs. "I don't live under a rock, Amy. I have a sister who loves romcoms."

"Then you must agree with me that this place is gorgeous."

"Yeah, if you like the idea that a Barbie Playhouse threw up all over it."

I'm not going to let his negativity affect me, even if that was funny. "But it's lovely! And popular. Look at all the patrons. And what's more, they need help. It said so on the sign."

The place is packed to the gills with everyone from mothers with their babies to a group of elderly women, talking enthusiastically over their espressos, to men in Lycra, their bikes leaning against the outside wall.

"Maybe it's the only coffeehouse in town?"

"Or the best," I reply as the older woman from behind the counter catches my eye and offers me a bright, welcoming smile.

"Good morning," she says in heavily accented English. How sweet. She must assume I'm American, too. Perhaps it's the goth costume? "How can I help you on this beautiful day?"

"We saw your sign in the window, and we're here to offer our help," I reply. "This is my friend Maverick, and

I'm—" I stop myself before accidentally giving her my real name. "I'm Amy. Your place is absolutely gorgeous. Isn't it, Mav?"

"Gorgeous? Sure," he says, his words convincing no one.

She beams at us. "I am so glad you think so." Placing her hand against her heart, she adds, "I'm Francine, the owner of this café."

I clap my hands together in glee. "You're the owner! How wonderful. So it's you that we need to apply to for the job."

Her mouth forms an "o" shape. "You need a job?"

I imagine she's thrown by our goth appearance. "Yes, we do," I confirm.

"I am Pierre LeDuc," says the handsome man with the stubble-lined jaw, as though he's announcing himself at the palace ballroom. He takes my hand, lifting it to his lips. "I am enchanted to meet you, Amy. I am the best barista at the café,"

Seriously, this man should be on aftershave ads he's so good looking.

"Pierre," Francine warns.

"I'm simply welcoming these two strangers in the black clothing," he replies, and I wonder how many other patrons' hands have been kissed by him this morning.

"Shall we sit? We can discuss your application," Francine says, and leads us to the only vacant table in the café.

We sit, and I clasp my hands together under the table. I've never had a job interview before, and I have no idea what to say.

"Are you both looking for work?" she asks, steepling her hands that I notice are calloused, probably from decades of working here at the café she's clearly proud of.

"We are," I say firmly. "Maverick has been a barista before and makes absolutely delicious coffee."

"Oh?" Francine looks expectantly at Maverick.

"I've worked in a few coffee houses. I guess I do know my way around a coffee machine," he says.

"We can always use a barista," Francine says, looking him over.

"Wonderful!" I exclaim with a clap of my hands.

"Tell me where you've worked before, Maverick?"

"I worked at a diner in my hometown in Washington state before I moved to California, where I worked as a barista at a bunch of different cafés." He gestures at the espresso machine with his thumb. "I could make you a coffee with your machine, if you like?"

"That won't be necessary," she replies.

"One problem. I only have a tourist visa here, I think."

Francine waves his concern away. "It is no problem. We will fix that for you with the government people."

"That's so kind of you," I say. "Do I need one of those, too?"

"A work visa? You are Malveauxian?" she asks.

"Ledonian."

"Then no. We are friends."

Friends. I like that idea.

"What skills can you bring?"

I run through all the skills I've had drummed into me since birth. I imagine my understanding of how to give a royal wave, how to greet diplomats from various countries, and which tiara to wear at a state banquet aren't particularly useful skills in a café. So instead, I tell her, "I will do whatever you need me to do. I'm a quick and enthusiastic learner. I've even learned how to slice bread and wash strawberries over the last day."

Francine's brows climb her forehead. "Those are very

good skills to know," she replies, and there's a flicker of something on her face that reminds me of Max and his mischievous ways.

"I do hope you're not afraid of hard work. We are a popular café in this town, so we're always busy. My last employee left because she told me the pace here didn't fit with her Zen journey." Francine gives a delicate snort of amusement.

"Oh, she did *not*," I exclaim, my eyes wide that someone would say such a thing to her boss.

"Sadly, she did. I told her that coffee and Zen are perfectly compatible, provided that she doesn't mind moving faster than a meditating snail when serving customers."

I laugh as Maverick stifles a laugh beside me.

"I love that you have a sense of humor," I tell her. "And I assure you I'm not a meditating snail, and nor is Maverick. I'm not in the least afraid of hard work. I'm eager and willing to learn."

"She's definitely eager," Maverick echoes.

Francine pats my hand, smiling like an indulgent grandmother. "Of course you are, dear, although Shayna can be somewhat of a challenge to begin with."

"Shayna?" I ask.

She gestures toward the espresso machine, an enormous chrome contraption that indeed looks like it might be challenging. "She's been with me for nineteen years, outlasting all my marriages."

All her marriages? I wonder how many husbands she's had.

Francine looks between the two of us before her face creases into a smile. "When can you start?"

My eyes widen to the size of a couple of gold-rimmed

Ledonian state dinner plates. "Are you serious? You're going to employ both of us?"

"Yes," she replies simply.

"Thank you! Thank you! We won't let you down. Will we, Maverick?"

"No. We won't," he replies.

Francine gives us the details about when she wants us to start—at lunchtime today!—about the rules, how we have to wear aprons, right down to how much she will pay us. Most of it goes right over my head because I'm too busy buzzing over the fact I have my very first job. But I'm sure whatever I missed I will pick up on in due course.

A short while later, we say goodbye to Francine, promising to be back for the lunch rush, and step out of Francine's into the bright sunshine, both of us newly employed café workers.

The thought makes me giddy all over again.

"I can hardly believe we are both going to be working at that gorgeous place." I do a little twirl, feeling so light I want to dance through the streets. I pause in my dance long enough to see the look on Maverick's face. "Why aren't you happy?"

"I am happy," he replies, although I'm not sure whether to believe him.

"Is it always this easy to get a job in the real world?"

He gives me an odd look. "The 'real world'?"

Oops.

I backpedal quickly. "I mean, outside my family's foundation."

Quick save.

"Everything in the foundation is so structured. You need three references and a committee approval just to change the brand of paper clips."

He chuckles, then surprises me by asking, "What would you be doing right now? If you were home, I mean."

"Honestly? I'd probably be sitting through some interminable luncheon with visitors, smiling until my face hurts while listening to people discuss subsidies like they're interesting."

"Sounds thrilling," he says with a smirk.

"Oh, it's a non-stop adventure." I roll my eyes. "What about you? What would you be doing if you weren't here?"

A shadow crosses his face. It's brief, but it's there. "Meeting all the fake people I work with and pretending that they're my kind of people, all the while wishing I was here."

"That sounds positively ghastly."

"Welcome to my world. Less subsidies, more 'look at me.'"

"But you don't strike me as a 'look at me' kind of person."

"Which is why I can't stand it."

"And why you escaped."

"Exactly."

I meet his eyes and something passes between us. It's a moment of recognition that we're both refugees from lives that never feel like they quite fit.

"You know, you haven't told me what it is you do."

"Me? Oh, I'm in PR. Public relations."

I think of the palace publicists. "I imagine there are loads of 'look at me' people in PR."

"There sure are."

I hook my arm through his as we meander back toward the lake. "I just know you're going to look darling in your frilly pink apron and your goth makeup."

"I'm secure enough in my manhood to wear a frilly pink apron."

"You might need to be," I tease.

Really, this job is the perfect cover. People will never guess who I really am if I'm working in a café, of all places. What member of a royal family would do such a thing? They'll all assume I've run away to do something lavish or exotic—not choose to work in a pretty pink café in a small town on a lake in Malveaux.

"Do you think Francine will have an apron big enough for you?" I ask.

"A small pink apron. Even better. I'm gonna love that." His tone is sarcastic, but he says it with a smile, so I know he doesn't really mind.

Our wanderings take us down to the lakefront, where we find a caravan with a window, through which people are selling food—delicious crêpes, by the aroma. I've never been able to resist a crêpe, particularly one filled with chocolate and banana.

"Let's get a crêpe from that caravan and sit by the lake to eat it," I suggest. "We'll need our strength for our new jobs."

"Caravan? Oh, you mean the food truck?"

I wave his correction away with a flick of my wrist. "Potato potah-to."

We buy our crêpes, find a bench, and sit, gazing out at the lake. It's a breathtaking view of the blue water surrounded by green-blue hills in the distance, and boats bobbing.

"This place absolutely lives up to its name," I say before I take a bite. The flavors burst on my taste buds: banana and chocolate and butter. "Oh, this is amazing."

"Id iv amaving," Maverick says, and I turn to see his mouth full of crêpe, with chocolate smears around his lips.

I let out a laugh.

"What?"

"You've got a little chocolate here." I point to the edges of his mouth.

"I don't care. This is the best thing I've ever eaten in my entire life."

"It's beyond delicious. Is all food from caravans this good?"

"Are you going to tell me you've never eaten from a food truck before? Actually, don't answer that. I know what you're gonna say. This is the first time you've ever eaten anything from a food truck, right?"

"But it won't be my last. I'm going to have a crêpe every single day from now on."

We sit in companionable silence as we eat, enjoying the view and the sun on our faces. Even the temperature in this town is just right. Not too hot and not too cold. Really, despite its shaky beginnings, my adventure could not have worked out any better.

"Since you've never worked at a coffee house or practically even been in a kitchen, how about you let me help you out today."

"Really, Mav. How hard can it be? People make coffee every day. I'm certain I can handle a coffee machine called Shayna without requiring a user manual and an engineering degree."

"You'd be surprised."

"You're very kind to offer, and if it is tricky, then yes, I would appreciate your help."

"You got it."

I stretch my legs out in front of me, savoring the last bite of my crêpe. "I just know this is going to be wonderful. Learning to make coffee, serving people, wearing a pretty pink apron. All of it."

"You really have no idea what you're in for, do you?" Maverick asks, but his tone is warm, almost affectionate.

"Of course I do. You take the coffee, put it in the machine, press some buttons, and *voilà*, coffee appears in a cup." I mime pressing buttons in the air. "Simple."

He lets out a low chuckle. "Yeah, that's not quite how it works."

"Well then, my dear Maverick, it's a good thing I've got you to teach me." I bounce to my feet, too excited and full of sugar to sit still any longer. "Come on! We should head back to get ready for our first shift. I want to make sure we're not late."

"We've got two hours."

"Exactly! Barely enough time!"

He shakes his head but he's smiling and as I practically skip along the lakefront path, I can hear him beside me, his long legs easily keeping pace. I'm not sure what I'm more thrilled about: having my very first real job, or the fact that I'm actually doing something completely and utterly normal for once in my life.

All I know is this is all working out perfectly, and I cannot wait for the next part of my grand adventure to begin.

Chapter 13

Ethan

I can't believe I'm working in a café that looks like Pepto-Bismol started a Pinterest board—and then added some more pink. It's enough to give you a headache. Everything is pink. And I do mean *everything*.

Seriously, this place is so frothy pink we should be serving unicorn tears instead of coffee.

And what's worse, Francine has just handed me one of her pink frilly aprons.

"This is the largest size we have," she says in her

accented English as she holds the offending item of clothing up in front of me. She shrugs. "You will look nice in it, no?"

No is right.

If the tabloids could see me now, they'd have a field day. *Rowan Thornheart, legendary warlord of the winter realm, wearer of a pink frilly apron.*

"I'm sure it'll be fine," I say as I slip the anti-warlord apron over my head.

It's the same shade of pink as the rest of this coffee house, so at least part of me will blend in with the walls.

"There," Francine says with a satisfied smile on her face. Or is it a smirk? It's hard to tell. "You look very nice, Maverick."

"Thanks."

Francine wanders off, humming what sounds a lot like a Justin Timberlake song, but I might be wrong.

Not only does taking this job give credence to my story that I'm an American tourist, here on a working vacation, but what famous Netflix star goes to a small country in Europe to work at a coffee house that looks like a strawberry milkshake?

No one, that's who.

And, if I'm honest, there's another reason, and that reason is currently standing about five feet away from me, also wearing the offending apron—but on her the apron looks totally cute. She's wearing her usual black skirt and T-shirt, but whereas that might make someone else look plain, with her long dark hair in a ponytail, her smooth olive skin, and the only makeup her dark-ringed eyes, she looks nothing short of breathtaking.

And the way she felt in my arms when I rescued her from the tree? I blow out a breath. She felt good. Dangerously good. But I'm not going to act on my attraction to her. The last thing she needs it's me coming on to her after what happened with Greg, and besides, anything that happened between us could be nothing more than a fling —and there's something about Amy that tells me I would want a whole lot more than just that.

But no matter how much I ignore my growing attraction for her, that protective streak in me will not quit, not when it comes to my beautiful and mysterious house guest.

A beautiful and mysterious house guest who's currently being unashamedly flirted with by Pierre le Something-or-other. I didn't catch his last name. I was too busy noticing the way his eyes practically drank Amy in. The way he held her hand and lifted it to his lips in greeting, like he's freaking Pepé Le Pew.

I snort. Pierre's a culturally insensitive, lecherous skunk cartoon.

Yeah, that works.

Right now, Pierre is showing both me and Amy how to operate Shayna, the espresso machine, while taking frequent glances at Amy as though she's the best thing since sliced bread.

If only he knew she can't slice bread to save her life.

I don't know what it is but watching him flirt with her is getting right under my skin. Why does he have to stare at her so much? I mean, I get it. Anyone can see she's gorgeous. But can't he direct his eyes someplace else? Like, I don't know, literally anywhere that doesn't make me want to throttle him with his perfectly knotted necktie? Or perhaps toward the coffee machine he's supposedly such an expert with, instead of mentally undressing Amy? But no, apparently Pierre's eyeballs are magnetically drawn to her like she's the North Pole and he's a particularly desperate compass.

I study her profile as Pierre guides her in using the

machine. I know a few things about Amy, but really, what do I actually know about this woman I'm sharing a house with?

The answer to that is very little. I don't even know her last name. All I know is that she's Amy, she comes from a strict, wealthy Ledonian family who runs some kind of education foundation, and she's bent on breaking all the rules she's had to live her life by.

Well, that and the fact she's a little too naive for this world, demonstrated by her enthusiasm for virtually everything, from getting a job at this coffee house right down to the way she fell for Greg's lies.

On the plus side, there's the fact that no one in this small town seems to have recognized me. I'm sure the goth costume has helped, and Amy and I have walked freely around the town, which is easy considering it's smaller than my hometown of Maple Falls. The townsfolk have barely even looked at us. Well, other than Pierre, that is, whose eyes are Velcroed to Amy.

I don't have an ego the size of Texas. Or even Maine. I don't expect everybody watches my show. But the fact I got spotted and chased by the paparazzi in the country's capital city does suggest that at least some people know who I am. I kind of expected at least somebody to recognize me, even with my goth costume and eyeliner ringed eyes.

It's almost like I've stepped into an alternate universe in which I'm no longer famous and people don't care what I ate for breakfast, who I'm dating, or what my relationship with my famous hockey-playing brother is like.

It's refreshing, but it also feels... I don't know. Uneasy? Yeah, that's the word. *Uneasy.*

Maybe it's just that I'm not used to anonymity anymore.

But you know what? I think I'm going to like it here.

"What does this knob here do?" Amy asks, turning the knob that adjusts the steam pressure, and instantly the steam wand hisses, shooting out aerated hot water.

Amy leaps back, more shocked than anything.

"Are you okay?" I ask, but Pierre's got in there first, taking the opportunity to put his arm around her shoulders to "comfort" her.

"Did you get scalded by the hot water?" he asks.

"I think it gave me more of a shock than anything else," she replies.

"Perhaps you don't touch the machine until you're ready," Pierre says in soothing tones.

"Thank you, Pierre. I promise not to touch anything else. I'm eager, that's all," she says.

"Amy hasn't worked at a coffee house before," I explain.

But Pierre completely ignores me. "I love this eagerness in you, Amy. It is thrilling to me as a barista."

Her eagerness is thrilling to him as a barista? More like as a lecherous skunk.

Man. When did I get so jealous?

I need to chill. Sure, Pierre may be being a little bit overly attentive to Amy, he's just showing her how to do her job. And for Amy's part, the way her brow furrows in concentration, her lips parted slightly as she focuses on following Pierre's instructions is adorable. She approaches learning to make coffee with the same intensity most people reserve for defusing bombs. She wants to learn. She wants to get good at her job.

She really is an intriguing woman.

"It is good that you are learning from me today because tomorrow I must play rugby," Pierre tells her. "I play for a local club a couple of towns over."

Amy is concentrating on grinding the beans as he speaks.

"You should come and see me play," he says.

"Isn't rugby a completely insane game? Like football only without all the protective gear?" I ask.

Yeah, I hear it. I'm Ethan Roberts, an internationally recognized actor, trash-talking some barista I just met because he's flirting with a woman I've known for only a couple of days. A girl who's staying at my borrowed house and seems to have somehow hijacked my common sense in record time.

"You may see it as insane as an American, but here in Malveaux we have a long and proud tradition of rugby. It is a *man's* game," he replies, shooting me a look. Which is fair enough. I am being a bit of a jerk to him—with good reason.

"Don't women play rugby, too?" I ask, and Pierre shoots me another look, this time one I'm sure he hopes could magically make me disappear.

"You're absolutely right, Mav. I watched women's rugby at the recent Olympics. The New Zealand team won and the women performed a celebratory traditional war dance. It was very moving," Amy says.

Ethan Roberts: 1. Pepé le Pew: 0.

Francine asks Amy to help her with the food in the cabinet. "Maverick, you will make the coffee, no?" Francine asks as she passes me some customers' coffee orders.

"Sure thing," I reply.

"I will watch to see how you do," Pierre says.

I start fulfilling the coffee order. It's a little like riding a bike and I get into the flow quickly enough. I make sure there are enough beans to be ground, put the wand in place, and press the button for the dark coffee to drain into the cup. Then I prepare the milk, enjoying the feeling as I stretch and expand it to foamy perfection before I pour into the cup.

There's something about this simple job of making coffee that connects me to regular life. I'm using my hands to create something. I don't want to use a coffee pun, but making customers coffee in a small town makes me feel grounded. Authentic.

It's a nice feeling, and one I haven't had for a long, long time.

The order is for a cappuccino, which I dust lightly with powdered chocolate and present to Pierre with a proud smile. Pierre says something to me in Malveauxian that I don't understand, but the look on his face tells me he's impressed with my skill.

Either that or he just threw an insult at me and I'm none the wiser.

I then spend the next while making coffees for the customers. It's repetitious and methodical work, and I get lost in the rhythmic flow of the work.

"Oh, my gosh, Mav. I've broken so many rules today!" Amy says with obvious glee as she appears by my side. She's wearing a huge grin on her face, her cheeks flushed.

That smile. It's like getting hit with a stage spotlight at full wattage.

I hold the jug in place to heat and froth the milk. "Which rules? I thought you were doing a good job. Francine seems happy enough."

"No, I meant my family's rules. There are a whole lot of things I'm not meant to do that I've done today. Like handling money, Rule number 336. Oh, and serving people. That's Rule number 592."

I frown at her in disbelief. "You're not allowed to handle money or *serve* people? Who *is* your family?"

"I told you. They're horribly strict."

I turn the steam knob off and bang the metal jug on the counter surface a couple times to pop any unwanted larger bubbles in the milk. "There's strict and then there's having rules that would make the military say 'dial it back a bit.'"

She laughs, and the sound does something to my insides that I'd rather not examine too closely. It's bright and genuine, completely unlike the polished, practiced laughs I hear at industry events. "You're funny. Did you know that?" she says.

I'm happy to take the compliment, but don't think I didn't notice she hasn't answered my question.

I'm not going to push it. If her family is as strict and uncompromising as she suggests, I get why she won't want to talk about them, and I totally get why she wanted to escape for a while. They sound the absolute opposite of my kind, open parents who supported all three of their kids in whatever we chose to pursue in our lives.

And besides, I'm not exactly giving her my full story, either. Pot calling the kettle black and all that.

I pour the milk into the coffee cups, creating my now signature decoration.

"Mav, that's so pretty! You have to show me how to do that."

"I thought you had Pierre for that," I reply, and even I can hear the jealousy in my words.

If she notices, she doesn't mention it. "He didn't show me how to make the milk look like that. Will you show me?"

"Sure."

She beams at me. "Thanks. I'll be right back after I deliver these. Which table are they for?"

I check the note. "Table 4. I think that's over by the window."

I watch as she weaves her way through the tables filled with customers, carrying a tray holding the coffee cups and saucers. Her apron is tied in a bow that sits over her skirt, and as she sways her hips, my stomach tightens.

Amy is sexy in a completely natural, unconscious way. She's so unlike so many of the women I meet in my working life. Women who scream for you to look at them. Women who've had every nip and tuck imaginable, their lips plumped to three times their natural size.

Relationships in my world are often publicity stunts, aka "showmances." I don't know why I let Dion talk me into having a showmance with Chelsea, particularly now it seems obvious to me they're in a relationship. He even arranged all the pap shots of us allegedly on dinner dates, walking hand in hand along the beach, or walking my dog (note: I don't have a dog).

It's so disingenuous.

Amy turns and looks straight at me, totally busting me checking her out. I shoot her a smile as though I wasn't thinking about her in any way other than my housemate and co-worker, before I pull my gaze away, pretending to do something with the espresso machine.

A small voice in my head—one that sounds suspiciously like my sister—whispers: *You're an actor, Ethan. You've played dozens of roles. But this might be the first time you've been genuinely terrible at pretending not to care about someone.*

A woman who could be my ex's doppelganger, right down to the angle of her chin and long dark hair, comes and stands next to Shayna.

"Hello, I'm Giovanna Fiorelli," she virtually purrs in accented English. Italian? Ledonian? I can't tell.

"Hey there. Pierre can help you." I nod at Pierre, who's serving a customer.

"But I want to speak with *you*," she replies, and instantly my heckles rise.

Does she recognize me?

I pour some milk into cups and place them on the counter, where Amy collects them with a smile. "Thanks," she says. "Table 7?"

"You got it." I wipe my hands on my apron. "How can I help you?" I ask this woman called Giovanna Fiorelli.

She curves her lips in a smile. "A café latte, please— and your phone number."

Did she seriously just ask that?

"You want a latte and what?" I ask, wondering whether I misheard her.

"Your number," she repeats.

So, I did hear right. Huh.

I shake my head, smiling. "I don't think so."

"What? Are you saying a woman can't ask for a man's number if she thinks he's attractive?" she asks, leaning her elbows on the counter, pushing her assets together to their best advantage, and gazing up at me.

I'm no stranger to women coming on to me. I know that sounds arrogant, but when you're a well-known actor, you get more attention than you need, particularly from the opposite sex. I've been asked out, propositioned, offered underwear, been asked to sign parts of women's anatomy, you name it.

"Look, I'm flattered, but I'm just here to make the coffee. Latte, right?" I ask.

The look on her face is wounded as she straightens back up. "I thought—" she begins, but then stops.

I don't ask her to finish her sentence. It's pretty clear where it was going.

I set about making her a latte, willing Giovanna to give up and move on. Perhaps she could give Pierre her number? That would be a nice, tidy solution for all of us.

Amy appears at my side. "Time to share your knowledge, Mav," she announces.

"Who are you?" Giovanna asks.

"Hello. I'm Amy. Pleased to meet you, although you look familiar to me," she replies with a smile, offering her a hand, which Giovanna ignores.

"Do you work here?" she demands.

Amy beams at her with pride. I don't think I've ever known anyone quite so excited about working in a café. But then Amy isn't like anyone I've met. "Yes, I do." Her hand is still outstretched, and Giovanna is still ignoring it.

"Do you know Ethan?" Giovanna asks, and I snap my attention to her.

She used my name.

She knows who I am?

"No, I don't," Amy replies pleasantly. She pulls her still unshaken hand back and shoots me an uncertain look. "Should I know someone called Ethan?"

I hold my breath as Giovanna looks from Amy to me and back again.

I can't let this woman blow my cover. I need to act.

"I'm making your latte, Giovanna, and I'll bring it right over to you personally," I tell her, hoping the fact she can get some more time with me will appease her.

Her lips lift in a fresh smile. "I'll look forward to it."

I watch her walk away and let out a relieved breath.

That was close. Too close.

"What was that all about?" Amy asks when Giovanna has sat herself down at a table in direct line of sight of me.

"Your guess is as good as mine," I tell her, knowing I'll

need to manage Giovanna if she really does know who I am.

"I know her from somewhere, although I can't quite place it," Amy says.

I finish making the latte and take it over to Giovanna. Placing it down on the table, I say, "I didn't introduce myself before. I'm Maverick Mitchell. I just started working here."

She takes my hand in hers. "Maverick Mitchell? Oh, I see, darling. It is such a pleasure to meet you, *Maverick*."

"Enjoy your coffee. It's on me," I tell her.

"You're spoiling me," she simpers.

No, I'm strategically keeping the peace. I can tell from the way she said my fake name that she knows exactly who I am. The wink that followed only confirmed it.

"I'll check on you in a bit," I add with a friendly but distant smile before turning away.

This is going to be a delicate balancing act with Giovanna. I need to be polite enough not to make an enemy who could blow my cover, but not give her reason to think there's anything more than professional courtesy between us.

So far, it's worked, even if I can feel her eyes following me across the café as I make my way back behind the counter.

"Do you want me to take you through the full coffee making process first?" I ask an eager Amy.

"Pierre taught me everything I need to know," Amy replies with the confidence of someone who has considerably more food- and beverage-related knowledge than she has exhibited so far.

"Have at it." I stand back and gesture at the machine.

"Okay." She pulls her brows together as she chews on her lip. "I start by grinding the beans. Is that right?"

"Definitely."

She reaches under the counter and pulls out a large bag of beans.

I say, "There are beans in the machine already."

I watch her approach the espresso machine. "So, I just push this button?" she asks as she pushes the correct button and the machine springs to life, grinding beans.

After Pierre's unnecessarily thorough tutorial, during which he'd managed to touch her hands exactly eleven times—not that I was counting—she's practically glowing with determination.

"You got it."

"I can do this," she announces, flashing me a smile. "Pierre explained everything to me just perfectly."

I'm sure he did.

She manages to get the coffee grounds tamped down in the wand, inserts it, and soon the dark coffee is flowing.

"You need a cup," I say, slotting one underneath to capture the liquid.

"I knew I'd forget something. Right. Milk."

She maneuvers the wand to steam the milk, but unfortunately for her, it hits the liquid at precisely the wrong angle. What should be a gentle steaming process transforms into a mini cyclone as milk erupts like a dormant volcano out of the jug and shoots upwards right into poor Amy's face and hair.

I grab a nearby cloth and hand it to her as I turn the steam wand off. "Here."

She starts dabbing at her face, and when she lifts her eyes to mine she's fighting the urge to laugh, her lips twitching.

"Maybe Pierre left out a couple crucial details?" I say, trying my hardest to stifle a laugh that's threatening to burst out.

And then her shoulders begin to shake, and she lets out a snort laugh no tightly-controlled Hollywood starlet would be caught dead doing, and I lose it completely, doubling over with laughter.

If causing minor coffee shop disasters is what it takes to hear Amy laugh in such a free and natural way, I'd happily spend the rest of my life cleaning up milk geyser catastrophes.

"You know," she says between giggles. "I was promised coffee-making would be easy."

"Who promised you that?"

"Pierre. He said I was a total natural."

"That's because Pierre has a thing for you," I blurt before I can stop myself. The last thing I want to do is come across as some jealous guy when she doesn't see me as anything more than her friend.

Even if I am some jealous guy.

"No, he doesn't. He's just being nice."

I arch an eyebrow. "How nice have you seen him being to me?"

"You already know how to use the espresso machine."

It's a good point and I can't argue with her, but nevertheless Pierre hasn't exactly paid me the kind of attention he's paid Amy—and he sure hasn't spent half the afternoon gazing at me like a lovesick puppy, either.

"Maybe you could do with a different instructor?" I suggest.

Her eyes meet mine. "Are you volunteering yourself?"

"Sure am," I reply, reaching for a fresh pitcher.

As something shifts in my chest, something dangerous and warm, I do my best to ignore it.

Chapter 14

Amelia

We've been working at Francine's for four whole days now and I've loved every single moment. Both Pierre and Maverick have been so helpful in showing me the correct way to do things, from operating the espresso machine— still a work in progress—to the cash register to wrapping silverware in paper napkins and everything in between.

Francine has continued to be the best boss I could hope for, always so patient and kind. Not that I know what bosses are generally like, but I've seen enough TV shows and movies to make me think she's exceptionally kind.

Like when I dropped a tray of muffins on my way out of the kitchen yesterday. She should have been annoyed in the very least, but she didn't even tell me off. She just shrugged and said mistakes can happen and that I knew where the wall was for the next time.

Then there was the time when I was pouring beans into the grinder, pressed the button but forgot to check to see that the collection chamber was in place. Let me tell you, coffee grounds can get everywhere.

Or the time when Pierre gave me another lesson on Shayna and I didn't quite lock the portafilter into place correctly, resulting in it flying off when the pressure built and sending coffee grounds and hot water over both me and Pierre.

All Francine says is she has confidence in me and she's sure I'll get it right sometime soon.

Now that I think about it, with all my daily disasters, it's rather a small miracle I still have this job. If I made this many mistakes at the palace, I'd be sent back to finishing school before you could say *pearls on, shoulders back, pinkies out.*

"Amy? Be a darling and help me restock the food cabinet, will you? It's almost lunchtime and I want to beat the rush," Francine says to me in Malveauxian.

"It would be my pleasure." I follow her out to the kitchen, where she has a variety of food—from slices of lasagna to club sandwiches to bowls of healthy salads—waiting on the counter. I collect a plate of lasagna and then place another one balancing on my wrist, and another that nestles into the crook of my elbow.

As I'm about to head out into the café, Francine asks,

"Whatever on earth are you doing?" She has a look of alarm on her face.

"I've been watching YouTube clips on how to be a waitress. They all have plates stacked right up their arms. They're awfully clever, and I thought, how hard would it be for me to do it?'

"Why don't you take the plates out one at a time, dear?" she asks, eyeing the line of plates along my arm.

"I can do this, Francine. Promise," I reply, and as I shrug, one of the plates begins to wobble on my arm. As I go to right it, the other two plates seem to develop a mind of their own and fly off, landing with a *clank* of plates and a wet *smack* of lasagna against the kitchen floor. I look in horror from the mess back up to Francine. "I'm so, *so* sorry. I'll pay for the meals, of course. And clean them up."

"Don't worry, sweetie. The floor needed another mop anyway, and I'm certain I made too many lasagnas this morning."

Francine is a total saint! *Saint Francine.* I might just suggest it to the Pope next time he visits Father.

"Thank you. I'll be sure to take one at a time from now on." I studiously lift another plate of lasagna, and carefully walk out to the café, placing it in the cabinet.

Francine grins at me as I return to the kitchen to collect my next plate. "Well done," she says as though I've just done something extremely skilled. "We don't need fancy plate carrying here. Do we? One at a time works just as well."

I return her smile. "Absolutely. I'll stick with being a non-fancy plate carrier from now on."

She claps her hands together. "Marvellous. Just marvelous."

I continue to work, stocking the cabinet as Maverick

makes expert coffees for the patrons, and Francine looks on proudly as though what I'm doing is a lot more complicated than simply placing meals neatly behind a glass cabinet.

As I'm stacking a row of sandwiches, I look up to see an elderly woman with short curly hair and a walking stick approach the counter. Before I've even fully registered that she's struggling with some shopping bags, Maverick has darted around the counter and is at her side.

"Can I help you with your bags, ma'am?" he asks, and I wonder if the woman speaks English.

But she replies, her face flushing, "Oh, that would be lovely. Thank you, young man."

"It's Maverick, and you're welcome. Would you like a seat in the window? It's such a nice day. It would be a shame not to be able to see it."

"A seat in the window would suit me just fine, thank you, Maverick."

"Come this way." He offers her his arm as he carries her bags, and they make slow progress across the café.

Maverick places her shopping bags on one seat, and pulls the chair out for her to sit, which she does, releasing a heavy sigh.

"What can I get you, ma'am?"

"I'd love a cup of tea. Has Francine made her delicious ham and cheese croissants for lunch today?" she asks.

"She has. Would you like one?"

"That would be lovely. Thank you, young man."

"It's my pleasure," he replies, turning to leave when she calls him back.

"My Brian used to make such lovely cups of tea, you know. He was quite particular about it."

Maverick turns back to her. "Tell me about him."

The look on the woman's face tells me just how much

she appreciates the attention he's giving her, and I can't help but wonder whether she has anyone to talk to.

"He would always do one spoonful of tea leaves per person, and one for the pot. Never more, never less. He was funny like that. Then he would let it steep for two minutes exactly. He'd always put a timer on, you see. We had this funny egg timer shaped like a frog, and when the alarm went off to say that the time was up, it would *ribbit*, just like a frog. We always had a good chuckle over it."

"A frog timer you say? I've not seen one like that before. We had an egg timer shaped as a chicken when I was a kid, but it just rang a bell. Do you still have your frog?"

"Oh, that old thing croaked a long time ago," she says with a laugh.

"Croaked. You're funny," Maverick says.

"My granddaughter showed me how to use the timer on my phone, but it's not the same."

"I'm not sure anything could replace a frog going *ribbit* when your tea was ready."

She laughs. "It did make teatime all that more special."

"Earth to Amy. Come in, Amy," a voice says beside me, and reluctantly, I pull my attention from the scene to see Pierre regarding me inquisitively.

"Sorry, Pierre. Did you say something?"

"I was telling you about the Festival of Lake Lights we have here in Montelac every year, but you were too busy staring off into space," he says in Malveauxian.

"Sorry," I reply absentmindedly.

"It's so romantic."

I blink at him. "What is?"

"The Festival of Lake Lights. Were you listening to me at all?"

"Right. Of course. It sounds lovely. When is it?"

"In only a few weeks. The whole town attends."

"Well, in that case, I'm sure I'll attend, too." I return my attention to Maverick and the woman, still chatting and smiling at one another like they're old friends.

Pierre follows my line of sight. "You are looking at Mabel?"

"Is Mabel the elderly lady Maverick is chatting with?"

"Yes. She comes in here every week," he says, rolling his eyes. "She'll talk your ear off if you're not careful. Looks like your pal got stuck."

As I watch Maverick, warmth spreads across my chest. I've never met a man quite like Maverick. He's not stuck, as Pierre puts it. Far from it. He's kind and sweet, taking the time out of his day to chat with a lonely old woman.

As I'm removing my apron to take my lunch break, Maverick returns to the counter.

"You're one of the good guys. Did you know that?" I ask him.

"Why do you say that?" he asks as he collects a crois-sant stuffed with ham and cheese with a pair of tongs and places it on a plate.

"Mabel. She loved talking to you."

His smile lights up his face. "She reminds me of my grandma back in Maple Falls. She was telling me about how she can't work out how to change channels on her TV, so I offered to go help her after my shift is done."

"You're so sweet."

His gaze captures mine. "That's what every guy wants to be called: sweet," he teases.

"Well, you are. You're sweet and kind and I think you're just marvelous. Look at the way you rescued me from Greg. You offered me a place to stay and helped me find a job, not to mention helping me down from that deceptively tall tree. Admit it, Mav: you're one sweet guy."

He laughs as he holds his hands up in the surrender sign. "You got me."

I stuff my apron under the counter. "I'm on a fifteen-minute break. See you soon, Mr. Sweetie Pie."

He chuckles, shaking his head. "See you later, honeybun."

As I make my way to the kitchen, the gorgeous woman who didn't want to shake my hand when we met the other day saunters up to the counter, her eyes trained on Maverick.

And then it hits me where I've seen her before. It was at a movie premiere in Villadorata a couple of years or so ago. She was one of the minor actresses and she shimmied her way down the red carpet as though she owned the place, despite the fact her role in the movie was small to say the least.

What is an actress doing in Montelac? Other than flirting with Maverick, that is.

Without wanting to analyze my motivation, I slip through the door and stand close enough to hear what she has to say without being seen by either of them.

"Hello again," she says in English with a distinctly Ledonian accent. "Fancy seeing you here."

The way she says it suggests that finding Maverick at his place of work is about as surprising as finding a fish on a basketball court.

"Giovanna. What can I get you today?" Maverick asks, all business like. "A latte, right?"

Giovanna laughs as though he's just delivered the punchline to a delightful joke. "A café latte would be lovely, darling, but that's not why I'm here."

Darling?

"I've been thinking about you ever since our little chat the other day."

I look around the corner to see her tapping her long, manicured nails on the counter.

"I made it clear when I was here before. I would love to take you to dinner. I know this divine little restaurant over-looking the lake. Very private."

"I'm not sure that's a good idea," Maverick replies, his posture stiff, and a flash of relief envelops me.

Wait. Relief? Why should I care who Maverick does or doesn't date? He's merely my housemate, my co-worker, and my friend. We're not romantically involved in the least.

"Oh, I think it's a wonderful idea," Giovanna counters, now toying with the edge of a menu. "I notice quality when I see it, even if it is *disguised*."

She emphasizes the word "disguised" as though it would mean something to Maverick.

And then it hits me, right in the chest. I'm the one disguised. *I'm* the one pretending to be someone else, Amy, a Dutch tourist.

My heart rate kicks up. Could she be referring to me?

I watch Maverick closely, pushing a pinprick of guilt at eavesdropping away. It's for the greater good, and if Giovanna is onto me, I need to know.

"I guess dinner would be fine," he replies, and I let out an involuntary squeak that sounds a lot like an oversized mouse. Immediately, I pull away, pressing my back against the kitchen wall in case either of them looks my way, my breathing shallow.

He's going on a date with that woman?

I mean, I get it. He's a guy, and she's like some sort of sex goddess with an hourglass figure she clearly isn't afraid to show off.

But why does it bother me?

And, most importantly, will she blow my cover when they meet?

Francine breezes past me and then turns to look at me in surprise. "What are doing?"

"Stretching," I say, lifting my arms above my head and doing just that.

"I see. You'd better take your break. The lunch rush is about to begin."

"Of course."

As I make my way down to the lake, my phone rings. Max is calling.

"Why are you calling?"

"That's a nice way to greet your favorite brother."

"Oh, I thought this was Max, not Alex," I quip.

"Hilarious," he deadpans. How's India going? Do the Himalayas looking particularly Malveauxian today?" I can hear his smirk through the phone.

I snort laugh.

Wait. Did he say Malveauxian? I mean, of course he knows I'm not in India, but how would he know I'm still in Malveaux?

"How do you know where I am?"

"Palace security."

"What?" I snap, glancing up and down the street.

"Keep your hair on. I'm only joking. I saw you in an Instagram post."

My breath catches. "You what? No. No, no, no, no, no! This can't be happening. Max, I've been so careful!"

My mind races to every conclusion imaginable: there will be a knock at the door any moment and I will be dragged home by the National Guard and made to face Father, who may very well decide to re-introduce the use of the ancient palace dungeons, where he will keep me until I promise to never do anything like this ever again and instead commit my life to toeing the royal line. Either that or I will be disowned, cut off from my family forever, sent to some kind of maximum-security facility deep in the mountains to "think about what I have done."

"Relax, Ami. You were in the background of someone else's photo, and it was hard to make you out, thanks to the fact you're all in black except for a pink apron."

My shoulders drop with relief. "So, the National Guard isn't coming to get me?"

He laughs. *Laughs!* So my brother.

"The National Guard isn't coming to get you."

"Well, that's a relief." I find a bench overlooking the lake and slump down in it.

"It's the Secret Service."

"What?!" I screech, sitting bolt upright and attracting the attention of a family of ducks, who take one look at me and flap away in a panic.

"Where's your sense of humor, sis? Did you leave it behind when you escaped the palace?"

"You'd lose your sense of humor too, if you thought you were going to be dragged home against your will."

"No one's going to drag you home."

"Whose photo did you see me in?"

"Someone I've met a few times in Villadorata."

"A woman?"

"Naturally."

I roll my eyes. That certainly sounds like my brother. He's following in Alex's footsteps as the most eligible bachelor in Europe—and hardly devoid of female attention.

"Who is this woman whose photo I'm in?"

"Giovanna Fiorelli."

My heart goes *clunk*. "As in the actress we met at a film premier a couple of years ago?"

"That's the one. She's in your small town."

A quick scroll through Instagram confirms my fears. Giovanna Fiorelli is both beautiful and sexy, and completely Max's type—as well as the woman Maverick is currently talking to in the café. And not only that, the woman he has just agreed to go on a date with.

This is all feeling rather too close for comfort.

I scroll through her images until I find one of her in the town square, right here in Montelac. My face is half obscured by Giovanna's somewhat buxom assets, which she's showing off to full effect with a low-cut top that leaves little to the imagination. "I know her."

"You probably met her at the same event."

"No, I mean yes. What I mean is I've met her here at the café."

"What café?"

"The one I'm working at."

"You're working at a café?"

"That's not the point, Max. The point is she's here and she might remember who I am. She could blow my cover."

"No one will be looking at you in this photo, sis. Trust me."

"But you did. What's stopping Father or one of his people spotting me, as well?"

"I'm not sure Father would spend his time studying one of Giovanna Fiorelli's photos quite as closely as me."

He has a point.

"Have you become a goth or something?" he asks.

"It's a costume. I'm using to hide."

"You're like the opposite of a goth."

"You should ask her to take it down. The photo, I mean. That way no one else will accidentally spot me when they zoom in on her—"

"I didn't zoom," he protests, cutting me off. We both know he's lying. He zoomed for all he's worth. "But more importantly, why are you wearing a pink apron?"

I smile to myself as I think of the very first job I've had, and how much I've learned in the short time I've been here. "Because it's the uniform for the café I work at," I say proudly.

"Again, why do you work at a café? You're a princess, remember? It's not exactly in the job description."

"You wouldn't understand."

"Try me."

I chew on my lip. Of my siblings, I'm the closest to my brothers. Sofia has always been too superior and too much of a rule follower for me—at least she was until she snuck out of the palace with Marco to solve some ancient riddle. She's a much better version of herself these days. Alex and I have always been close, but he's moved to Malveaux to be with his wife, Maddie. As the two youngest and unmarried siblings, it was only natural that Max and I would become as tight knit as we are. He's my ride-or-die, as the saying goes, and I tell him everything.

Well, almost everything.

"Personally, I would have chosen a yacht on the Mediterranean, but whatever floats your boat. Do you get it, Ami? Floats your boat?"

"It wasn't exactly a sophisticated joke," I quip. "And I didn't want that kind of escape. I didn't know what kind of escape I wanted at all until I wound up here. Then I knew I wanted to see what life was like for real people, people who actually do something with their lives instead of being stuck in a palace, performing like the puppets we are."

I can hear Max shifting, probably settling into one of those leather chairs in his study. "Seriously, Ami. What's this really about? When will the novelty of making coffee as a goth in a pink apron wear off?"

The real question hangs between us. *When is Princess Amelia going to come to her senses?*

"For me it's about the woman who comes in every

morning and tells me about her arthritic hip or her grand-daughter's science project. It's about the teenage girl who sits at one of the corner tables for hours, and how I can tell whether she's had a good day by whether she orders a chocolate muffin or not.

"It's about how yesterday I completely destroyed a batch of scones and Francine just handed me more dough and said 'try again, sweetie.' Do you know how that is for me? To be allowed to fail without huge repercussions?"

"You've always been allowed to fail. In fact, you—"

"Do it all the time," I finish for him, and he laughs. "Max, you're so predictable. Remember when I mispronounced that stuffy old Archduke's name in a speech in winter and Fabiana Fontaine called me 'Princess Aimless' for a week? Father's PR machine had to issue a clarification that I wasn't, in fact, diplomatically impaired."

"You called him Duke Duckface," Max says with a chortle.

I snort as I watch the actual ducks, now recovered from my shrieks, quack their way across the lake.

"In your defense, he did look a bit like a duck. And besides, I wouldn't worry about what Fabiana Fontaine thinks of you. We all know her opinions are a waste of paper."

"The thing is, Max, here I'm just me, and when I mess up someone's coffee order, nobody writes a piece about the declining standards of the monarchy. I just make another one, usually with Mav's help."

He pounces on the name. "Mav? Who's that?"

"Maverick Mitchell. My housemate."

"You're living with a man? And his name is *Maverick*?" He whistles. "Ami, you know Father is going to have kittens."

"Not if he doesn't know. And we're not romantically

involved, or anything like that, if that's what you're hinting at. We're friends."

"Friends. Right." Max doesn't sound convinced. "Does he know who you are?"

Guilt twists in my belly. "He knows who I am at my core."

"Which means you haven't told him."

"How can I? He'll judge me as 'Princess Amelia,' like everyone else does. The pointless princess whose job it is to make a 'good' marriage and then quietly disappear."

I think of the way Maverick patiently explained the difference between pastry options to an elderly man this morning, of how he listened to Mable's stories of her husband making tea. Of the way he rescued me from Greg, offering me a place to stay.

"He's a good egg, Max. He's decent and thoughtful and smart."

"And you've got a crush on him."

"I told you, we're friends. That's all," I insist because it's true. Being friends is the full extent of our relationship. "He treats me like I'm a perfectly capable human being who happens to be on a somewhat steep learning curve when it comes to anything related to coffee or food."

"You sound happy, Ami. Actually happy, not the royal 'smiling for the cameras' happy."

I blow out a breath, surprised by the sudden thickness in my throat. "I am happy. For the first time in my life, I'm not an extension of our family legacy, Max. I'm just a person discovering that she's actually quite fond of early mornings and the smell of fresh pastry. I don't miss having to be a princess all day long. Guess what else I did."

"I get the feeling you're going to tell me."

"I climbed a tree."

He sucks in a breath. "The forbidden tree-climbing. Mummy would have heart palpitations."

"I know!" I reply with glee. "And I've broken other rules, too."

"You're not doing anything stupid, are you?"

"What do you mean? Of course I am! That's the whole point!"

"That's it. I'm coming to check on you."

Great. Because what this situation really needs is my overprotective brother turning up, bringing with him the inevitable paparazzi.

"No! You can't come, Max. Then everyone will know where I am and my cover will be blown and I'll have to go back to the palace without having experienced my grand adventure, and without even having had a torrid affair, thanks to Greg turning out to be a con artist."

"Greg? Con artist? Ami, there's no way on this sweet earth I'm not coming to check up on you now."

"Please don't." I can hear the pleading in my voice. "Don't you have some military exercise to take part in or something now that you're in the Royal Airforce?"

But Max's mind is made up. "I'll be there as soon as I can get away. I'll wear a disguise and no one will be the wiser."

"Max!"

But I know it's too late. His mind is made up.

He says goodbye and ends the call, and I'm left staring at my phone, wondering what will happen when Max turns up to ruin *everything*—and how I'll ever be able to explain any of this to Maverick.

Chapter 15

Ethan

When I arrive in the kitchen, Amy is standing at the counter, bathed in the soft morning light, munching on a piece of toast. The light is catching highlights in her hair, and as she turns to look at me, her face lifts into a smile that takes my breath away.

"Morning," I say as I make a beeline for the coffee pot, telling myself for the hundredth time that she's just my friend, and nothing more.

"Good morning, Mav," she replies brightly, and yeah, my heart skips a beat.

So much for being just friends.

"Want one?" I ask as I pull a mug from one of the kitchen cabinets.

"That would be lovely. What will we do with our free morning? I've never really had time off from a job, and I'm excited to see what it's like."

I measure out the coffee and place it in the dispenser, trying not to smile that she intends to spend her morning with me. "You've never had time off?"

"Not really. Not like this, anyway. In my line of work, we're always 'on.' Having an entire morning stretched out in front of me with nothing that I have to do and nowhere to be feels rather indulgent."

"I know what you mean," I say, because these days, I do. It's hard to get real downtime when you're known, and people want a piece of you. It's hard to get the mental space sometimes.

I make the coffee, the pot gurgling as the mixture of water and grounds coalesce into a piping hot dark brown liquid. "We can do whatever we want to do. No climbing trees, though."

"But wasn't that fun?"

"Fun" isn't exactly the word I would use to describe the feeling of her in my arms, the way my heartrate picked up, and how I haven't been able to push her from my mind ever since.

I pass her a mug and notice her nails. "You've got orange fingernails, and are those tiny spiders I see?"

She holds her hand up to inspect it as though surprised that she has such fingernails. "I know it's not Halloween, but I've always had a hankering to have orange nails with spiders and spiderwebs all over them. I bought a kit to do them yester-day. My mother would not approve." Her face is lit up, and I can tell she's enjoying breaking another one of her family's rules. "I'm not supposed to eat while standing up, either." She holds up her toast and takes another bite from it. "Cheers!"

"You're on fire today. As always."

"*Every* day, Mav. Every single day," she replies, her eyes dancing, and it's as though the force of her gaze has reached inside and tugged at my heart, my belly swooping.

Amy's enthusiasm for life is much like a puppy encoun-tering snow for the first time, and it's impossible not to get swept up in it.

I can't think about her as anything other than my friend and temporary housemate. If she feels anything for me, it's as a friend. Nothing more. I should be happy with that. With the life I lead these days, I never know whether someone is genuine about wanting to get close to me. But with Amy there's no artifice. No secondary goal. She likes being around me and I like being around her.

That's got to be enough for me, although fighting these growing feelings I have for her is not getting any easier.

I take a sip of my coffee and lean back against the counter, faking casual. "I've got an idea. Let's go explore the town some more. I saw a bookstore not far from the café. Want to go check it out?"

Her beautiful brown eyes widen. "You like to read? Maverick, I never knew this about you."

I shrug. "What can I say? I'm a multifaceted human being."

She giggles. "Looks *and* brains. You, my friend, are the total package. Let's do it."

The compliment sparks hope in my chest, and I wash it away with a sip of my coffee.

After we've both eaten breakfast and gotten dressed we

walk into the town. Amy was right, it's a beautiful morning, and I enjoy the sun on my face and the relaxed and easy vibe we have between us.

We wander past Francine's, where the owner herself is chatting with a couple of women outside. She smiles and waves at us as we pass by.

"Pierre told me about The Festival of Lake Lights they're having here soon."

"I bet he did," I grumble.

"Do you know about it?"

"Yeah, one of the regulars told me. They release these lanterns out onto the lake, hundreds of them."

"You're very sweet to give your time to the regulars the way you do."

I shrug. "It's one of the things I enjoy about working at Francine's. The people are real, you know?"

She smiles at me. "I love that about it, too."

We reach the bookstore. It's painted dark blue with a sign above the door called Forgotten Tales, written in bold gold letters. Its door is flanked by tables holding paperbacks and hardcovers, some neatly arranged, others in messy piles.

"Mav, this place is amazing!" Amy exclaims.

"I hoped you'd like it. Wanna go in?"

"Are you mad? Of course I do!"

I stand back for her to step inside, where the books are stacked high on wooden shelves, packed in like someone's been hoarding them for years. The air has that distinctive

"new book" smell, that aroma that hits you as you open a book for the first time, the promise of something wonderful inside.

It's got that cozy, somewhat chaotic vibe that makes me want to spend some time in here, much like my sister,

Emmy's bookstore back in Maple Falls. I feel instantly at home.

The elderly proprietor, a man who looks like a total grandpa cliché with his thinning gray hair, bushy eyebrows, and glasses balanced on his nose, greets us in Malveauxian. Amy responds, looping her arm through mine, and I catch the names "Amy" and "Maverick" as she speaks.

"My name is Jeremiah Bellamy. Welcome to my shop." He gestures around at the packed shelves with obvious pride.

Amy responds in Malveauxian.

He turns to me. "Ah, you are American," he says in English.

I hold my hands up. "Guilty as charged, sir. You've got a fantastic store here."

"Thank you, thank you, young man. I opened this shop when I myself was young, when my hair was dark and my goal was to read every book that came through my door."

"And did you?" I ask.

Jeremiah Bellamy flicks his wrist in dismissal. "I was young and foolish. Now, I remember only the best stories. Do you know what my favorite stories are?"

"Do tell us, Mr. Bellamy," Amy says, and I'm struck afresh by how genuinely interested she is in hearing what people have to say. She treats everyone the same, even Pierre the lecherous skunk, with his completely unnecessary flirting and long, lingering looks.

Yup, he still gets under my skin.

"My favorite stories are love stories, and I can tell by the look of you that you are very much in love," he says, his eyes crinkling at the corners.

I choke on absolutely nothing as my brain short-circuits as though I've just been asked to perform Shakespeare in ancient Greek.

Very much in love?

The words bounce around my skull.

"Oh, we're not—" I begin, my voice strangled, and at the exact same time Amy says, "We're just friends, Mr. Bellamy."

I glance at Amy. She's grinning like this is some sort of fun joke, holding onto my arm as though it's no big deal.

Me? My heartrate has jumped to an alarming speed, and I've got heat creeping up my neck, threatening my cheeks.

Seriously? I'm *blushing* now?

I've literally filmed love scenes with several of Hollywood's most beautiful women without breaking a sweat, but here I am, blushing like an uptight Victorian maiden at the thought of being in love with Amy.

That's not to say I can't imagine falling in love with Amy. Far from it. She's got so many of the qualities I want, and a few more to boot. I love the way she's so fun and energetic and full of wonder at the world. I love the way her face lights up when faced with even the most mundane of everyday tasks, as though it's all so new and exciting for her. Of course, she's also gorgeous and hot as heck, but in a totally unmanufactured, un-Hollywood way that makes her even more beautiful to me.

She's the full package, that's for sure—and totally out of bounds.

Mr. Bellamy waves away our protests with a wrinkled hand. "The eyes never lie, even when the mouth protests."

"Is that a quote from a famous book? Because that's what we're here for. Right, Amy? Books," I say, searching for a way to move on from this awkward conversation, stat.

Amy giggles beside me. Apparently, she finds my discomfort entertaining.

Pull it together, Roberts. You play a warlord. You can handle one elderly bookshop owner with romantic delusions.

"Just friends," he repeats in the same tone as someone saying "affordable housing in Los Angeles," aka he doesn't believe us for one second. His eyes sparkle with mischief, his knowing smile smug. "Of course you are."

I slip my arm from Amy's to show her just how unflustered I am, throw her a smile and tell her, "I'm gonna go see what English books are in the store."

"English books are this way," Mr. Bellamy says as he directs me to the back of the store. "We have travel books, biographies, some business books, and, most importantly, romance."

Oh, good grief.

"Thank you, sir," I say as I aim for the corner of the store.

Why am I reacting like this? He jumped to the wrong conclusion and now I'm having an existential crisis about the status of mine and Amy's relationship? She's right: we ARE just friends. Friends who met in a costume shop and now share a house on a lake in a place named after dreams. A totally normal friendship foundation.

I peruse the shelves, reading the spines of the books and pulling the occasional one out to flick through its pages. I look up and watch as Amy picks up a book and runs her fingers along the spine. Her face is lit up like Times Square on New Year's Eve when she discovers something interesting.

"Mav!" she calls out, and I wish I didn't want to run to her.

Which of course I do.

"Whatcha got there?"

She holds up a book with a title in what I bet is Malveauxian, and a picture of a lavishly decorated dining table, covered in different food, from fruit to cakes, and roasted potatoes to glasses of champagne.

"Isn't this an absolutely stunning book?"

"It's got nice pictures," I reply.

Yeah, that'll make her fall in love with me. Nice pictures.

She leafs through the book, revealing page after page of beautiful photos of different foods. "It's all famous Malveauxian foods. They do make jolly good desserts, but," she looks around the shop before she leans in toward me, and instantly my heart begins to beat like a drum.

"But what?" I ask, wondering what it would be like to kiss those soft lips of hers, to pull her against me and tell her how I feel about her, to breathe in her intoxicating scent.

"Word to the wise, Mav: don't ever drink Malveauxian tea. Or their champagne, for that matter," she says under her breath. "Dreadful stuff."

I swallow. "Got it. But I'm not sure I'll have a lot of call to drink their champagne."

"Well, if you do, add some orange cordial to it. That's what my brother always does. He's awfully clever like that."

"Why would you add orange cordial to a glass of champagne?"

"To make it taste better, silly," she replies with a laugh, as though it's the most obvious thing in the world.

"Speaking of family, my kid sister runs a bookstore a little like this in my hometown. She's a total bookworm."

"I adore her already. What's she like?"

Warmth spreads through me as I think of Emmy. "Emmy's the best. She's funny and smart and totally book-ish. Which I guess goes with the territory when you run a bookstore."

"I imagine it helps rather a lot."

"What sort of books do you like to read?"

"You're going to laugh at me."

"Why?"

"Because everyone knows chaps don't read the sort of books I like."

"Chaps?" I can't help but question, unable to stop a smile from spreading. It's adorable the way she's referring to men as "chaps."

But then I find I like everything there is to like about Amy.

"You know. You. Men."

"Right. Let me guess. You like to read romance."

"How did you know?"

"Sister, remember? She's kinda got a thing for romance books."

"See? I told you I adore Emmy already. Come with me." She leads me over to what must be the romance section, if all the illustrated covers in bright colors and men who seemed to have forgotten to put on a shirt are to go by.

I pick one up. It's got a guy dressed as a Viking, has long hair falling over his shoulders, his six-pack glistening. "Is this your vibe?"

"Oh, I'm more into romances than all that Viking stuff. I like to read about everyday people falling in love."

Why did I let her bring me to this section? It's like the universe wants me to double down on my feelings for her, right here with the matchmaking proprietor.

"It's not just romance novels. I love Hallmark Christmas movies, too. In fact, I hold an annual Christmas movie marathon every December, snuggled up in front of the fire. I used to do it with Alex—even though he pretended to hate them—but now that he's married he's not around as much, so I watch them with one of the dogs."

"Doesn't his new wife let him watch movies with you?"

"Maddie? Oh, she's lovely. She'd never tell Alex what to do. But they live here, in Malveaux. I miss him horribly."

"I tell you what, come winter, I'll do your Christmas movie marathon with you."

She lifts her gaze to mine and I swear there's something in her eyes that tells me maybe, just maybe, she feels an inkling of what I feel for her. But then it's gone, and my heart deflates like a hot air balloon come back to earth.

There's a weird tinkling sound that's getting closer, and I pull my gaze from Amy to see Mr. Bellamy holding a tray with a pot and cups and saucers. "I've made you tea," he announces proudly.

"That's so jolly sweet of you. Thank you, Mr. Bellamy," Amy says.

"I'll put it down in the reading nook for you, shall I?" He gestures at a cozy spot with a small velvet sofa.

"You're so kind," Amy says.

He places the tray down on a side table. "Sit. Drink. Stay a while. A bookshop is where wonderful things happen between the pages."

Amy beams at him. "You're absolutely right, Mr. Bellamy."

He hobbles away but not before he throws me a wink.

Now he's *winking* at me?

I blow out a breath.

"Would you care for some tea?" Amy asks.

"I thought you said Malveauxian tea was horrible."

"It is. But we don't want to be rude to Mr. Bellamy, do we?"

"Of course not. He seems like a nice man." A nice *matchmaking* man.

"I'll tell you what. You pour us some tea and I'll find some classic fairy tales, Malveaux style. We can read them together."

"Sounds ... fun?"

She giggles again, the sound tinkling and sweet. "It will be fun. Just you wait and see."

As Amy leaves to find the fairytale section—and in this store I bet you it's half the shop—I pour tea into two floral cups, feeling like a kid at a play tea party.

Yeah, you can blame Emmy for that, too.

Really, my sister has a lot to be accountable for.

I take a seat on the velvet sofa. I've always loved bookstores, particularly the small, independent stores that are so full of personality. I've taken to visiting them in LA. I guess they remind me of home and my sister's beloved bookstore, Falling for Books. But more than that they offer me an element of escape. I can get lost in a book for hours, forget about who I am and what my world has become. I can forget that I'm this hot new star that everybody wants a piece of, that everybody thinks they know me because they've read articles about me from allegedly "reliable sources."

Man, I do not miss that life one bit. In Hollywood, everything's calculated for maximum exposure, every smile some form of transaction.

Not like Amy. She's real. Authentic. There isn't one bit of artifice in her.

She returns with a stack of books and plunks herself down next to me on the sofa.

"Add lots of sugar to the tea," she says under her breath. "That way it's almost bearable."

"You're really selling it."

She adds several spoons of sugar to both our cups and stirs.

Handing me a cup, I say, "Thanks, Mom."

"Now drink up," she tells me, leaning into the role.

I take a sip, expecting the worst. It's sweet and nice enough. "I like it," I tell her.

She raises her brows at me. "You're a weirdo. Either that or secretly Malveauxian."

"You got me. I'm not American at all."

She laughs and a wonderful sense of warmth spreads across my chest.

This. This is what I'm missing in my life. This kind of closeness with someone genuine, someone I know enjoys being with me as much as I enjoy being with them.

The irony that Amy doesn't even know my real name is not lost on me.

Maybe I should tell her? Maybe it's time to come clean about who I really am?

How will she react? Even though we've grown close during our time together, how will she react to learning that I've been lying to her all along?

I watch as she takes a sip of her tea and makes a face. I shake my head, smiling. "You don't have to drink it if you don't want to."

"I don't want to upset Mr. Bellamy," she replies under her breath. "He's such a nice man and he's been so welcoming to us."

"Here." I check that Mr. Bellamy isn't watching and, seeing that he's engaged with another customer, I pour the contents of Amy's cup into mine.

"Mav! What are you doing?"

"I told you I like it. Now, read me your fairytale."

"This one is one of my childhood favorites," she says, holding up a book with a woman bundled up in red velvet, surrounded by snow. "It's called *The Winter Queen's Tiara* and it's very popular in Ledonia. Shall I translate it for you?"

"Sure."

She settles into her seat, our thighs so close they're almost touching. As she reads aloud about how a royal family's precious tiara was created when a queen saved her people during a terrible winter by venturing into frozen mountains alone, her soft voice washes over me, and I find my gaze resting on her full lips.

It would be so easy to lean in to her and place a soft kiss on those lips.

My pulse leaps at the thought.

She stops reading and I flick my gaze to her eyes. "Tell me if you're not enjoying this," she says.

"Oh, I am. You're telling it so well."

She gives me an odd look, as though she's not sure whether I'm teasing her.

"Seriously," I reassure her. "I'm enjoying you telling me the story, and the fact that you loved it when you were a kid makes it all the more special."

Her face flushes with pleasure. "When I was young I imagined one day I would be that queen, going into the frozen mountains to save my people."

"Like the movie *Frozen*."

"Other than the two stories being set in winter, I'm not sure there are any other similarities."

My show is set in winter, too, but it's a hundred times more cynical than this fairytale—a lot like the difference between my life here with Amy and back in LA.

She returns her attention to the book, and once again my gaze slides to her mouth, watching as her lips form the words, imagining … dreaming …

This is getting ridiculous. I'm like a spotty-faced

teenager with a crush on an unobtainable girl, too scared to tell her how I feel, knowing chances she feels anything for me are about as likely as Amy becoming that queen, saving her people in the frozen mountains.

"And as Queen Eleanora returned, the enchanted crystals were woven into her silver-white hair glowing with inner light that melted the snow beneath her feet. From that day forward, whenever a daughter of Ledonia wore the Winter Tiara fashioned from those never-melting crystals, the kingdom would be blessed with warmth even in the coldest seasons—not the warmth of summer sun, but the more powerful warmth that comes only from a ruler who would sacrifice everything for her people." Amy closes the book over with a wistful look in her eyes. "What do you think?"

I think I'm falling for you.

Of course I don't say it. I shouldn't even be thinking it, not when I'm only here for a month. Not when she's given me no sign she feels anything beyond friendship for me.

So, instead I reply, "It's a nice story. I can see why Kid Amy loved it so much."

Her features drop.

"What is it?" I ask, concerned I've said something wrong.

"It's raining! We're going to get soaked on our way to the café."

The moment the words leave her mouth, there's a flash of lightning, illuminating the store around us with its harsh, white light, followed a moment later by a crash of thunder.

"Woah! That was big," I say.

"We might have to stay here until the storm has blown over. I didn't bring a coat."

I grin at her. "I'm good with that. This sofa is mighty

comfy. You know, we get storms like this back home in Washington state. I shared a room with my brother—"

"Dan."

"Dan," I confirm. "He would be all stoic about the storms, pretending they didn't bother him. Not me. If I got woken up in the night I would climb into bed with my parents, where I'd usually find my sister and our two cats."

"That's a lot of creatures to have in one bed. Did Dan tough it out on his own?"

"Yup. I think he had a point to prove, being the oldest and all. You know what older brothers are like. They've got to seem like they're totally in control of everything, when I bet they're just as scared as the rest of us."

"That sounds more like Sofia. She's softened now that she's married to someone who's her complete opposite, but she still has that whole bravery thing going on. I couldn't give two hoots about whether I appear brave or not."

"That's because you're who you are unapologetically."

She tilts her head and looks intently at me. "Do you really think that?"

"Totally. It's one of the things I like most about you, in fact. The people I meet? Most of them are more concerned with how they look than who they are as human beings. They like to shout about their achievements. *Look at me! I'm freaking amazing!*" I shake my head, thinking of Chelsea and Dion and the people who surround me in LA. "You're not like that. You're real. You are who you are and you don't apologize for it."

She opens her mouth as though to reply, and then clamps her lips shut. It's as though she's on the precipice of saying something, but then thinks better of it.

"What?" I ask, but she shakes her head.

"Do you know what I like most about you, Mav?"

I scrunch my nose as I try not to get my hopes up. "My dashing good looks and charm?" I joke, making light.

She giggles. "Well, obviously. I am but a woman. What I like most about you is that you have a complete lack of pretense. You say that I'm who I am unapologetically, but that's precisely how I would choose to describe *you*."

There's a moment in which we both stare intently into one another's eyes and my heart thuds against my ribs. Should I tell her? Should I come clean? Should I let her know who I really am? Tell her I've been hiding my identity from her all this time?

I make the call. I'm doing it. I'm telling her.

I don't care about the consequences. I trust her and I want her to know the real me. No more hiding. No more pretending.

I take a breath. "Amy, I need to tell you something."

"If it's about you going on a date with Giovanna, I already know."

I blink at her. "You do?"

"I eavesdropped on your conversation the other day. I'm sorry. I know it was wrong of me, but I saw her come in and, well, I don't know why I wanted to hear. Can you forgive me?" Her features crease up.

The fact she felt the need to eavesdrop makes my stupid heart well with hope. But then it deflates again as I think of how I agreed to go to dinner with Giovanna. How can I tell her that I'm only going out with her because she knows who I am? That I'm going to use the date to ask her to keep my secret, knowing I'll probably have to trade it for something she wants from me.

"There's nothing to forgive," I say.

Her features relax. "Thank you. And I truly am sorry. Your love life is your business."

If only she knew.

"About that," I begin, needing to tell her I have no romantic interest in Giovanna whatsoever, only to be interrupted by Mr. Bellamy.

"Would you mind helping me, young man? A section of the roof always leaks when it rains. That's quite a storm out there."

"That's terrible," Amy exclaims. "What can we do for you?"

"I have some buckets in the storeroom."

"Just show us where," Amy says with her beautiful smile. "Mav?"

"Of course. We'll go get the buckets."

As we busy ourselves positioning buckets under leaks and mopping up what we've missed, I can't help feeling I've missed the chance to share my secret with Amy.

There's a certain irony in the fact that I've spent my career pretending to feel things I don't, saying lines written by someone else. But being with Amy, sharing the simple things in life, is the most authentic I've felt in years.

I'm supposed to be finding myself, not losing my heart to the mysterious woman I met in a costume store. Yet here I am, falling for someone for the first time in years. And she only sees me as a friend.

Chapter 16

Amelia

What began as a quiet royal absence has erupted into nothing short of a nationwide obsession! The hashtag #WhereIsPrincessAmelia began trending across social media platforms yesterday after Villadorata University students held an impromptu sit-in outside the palace gates.

"If our princess can find inner peace, so can we," declared organizer Selena Dupont, while posing cross-legged among two hundred similarly positioned students.

The playful protest quickly turned into something more significant when participants began sharing theories about the princess's actual whereabouts.

And now the palace gift shop reports that Princess Amelia memorabilia has sold out completely, with her infamous "Rule-Breaking Princess" coffee mugs fetching triple their value online, particularly the one featuring a cartoon of her climbing a tree with a group of foreign dignitaries.

Your faithful royal correspondent has been hot on her tail.

Several alleged "sightings" have sparked wild goose chases across Europe since the report of her dash onto a train in Tleurbonne well over a week ago. A barista in Vienna claimed the princess ordered a mocha coffee from her only last week, and a bookshop owner in Monaco insisted she purchased an armful of romance novels while wearing dark sunglasses. But quite possibly the most bizarre of claims comes from a farmer in rural Malveaux who reported seeing the princess fascinated by a chicken, as though she'd never seen one before.

All of this leads this royal correspondent to the conclusion that Princess Amelia is most certainly not currently sitting cross legged on the side of a mountain, having enjoyed a vindaloo and some poppadom for her lunch.

The royal press office's official line is that "Her Royal Highness remains on her spiritual retreat and appreciates privacy during this time of reflection."

Well, this royal reporter does not believe it for one second and I make you this promise, good people of Ledonia. I will find the truth, one way or another.

You have my word on that.

Your steadfast and loyal correspondent on all things royal,

Fabiana Fontaine xx

#WhereIsPrincessAmelia
#MeditationOrCoverUp
#AmeliaOnTheLoose

MUMMY ALWAYS SAID, *a princess's duty is to be what people need her to be*, and right now I need to be a café worker at this rather divine pink café. I will readily admit that I'm not very good at it, but you can hardly blame me. I've never made coffee before, let alone dealt with money and credit card machines, and I've certainly never served people before.

But despite my total lack of experience and expertise, I find I rather enjoy being a worker in this pretty café. There's so much to do. So much variety. I've folded napkins and wiped down tables and delivered delicious looking slices of pie and pastries and muffins to the patrons. No one has quite let me get near the coffee machine after I gave myself a milk shower with it last week, but I'm hopeful I'll get to try it once more. After all, a girl has to learn, and what better way than on the job?

There's something rather marvelous about working as a team. The patrons are all absolutely lovely, always with a ready smile and time to chat about inconsequential things. Pierre is extremely attentive and helpful, even if I do catch him watching me a little too closely at times. I suppose he's just concerned I'm going to mess things up, just like Maverick is, too. Not that I blame them. But really, how am I meant to know that a cold brew isn't just coffee stored in the fridge? It's logical, isn't it? You make the coffee and then you cool it down, hence the name cold brew. But apparently, I got that one completely wrong.

What's more, not being recognized by anyone in this town, except possibly Giovanna Fiorelli—although I've heard nothing more on that front—has been an absolute revelation. Here I'm not Princess Amelia, having to adhere to the rules that go with the title. Here I'm simply Amy, a café worker who's striving hard to get better at what she does, and enjoying every moment of it.

We have a roster for after-hours clean up, and it's my turn this evening now that the café is closed. Maverick is out on his date with Giovanna Fiorelli, and Pierre has rugby practice.

As you might imagine, I've never cleaned anything in my life—other than myself, of course, and occasionally I've mucked in with the horses in the palace stables. But I can't imagine cleaning a café bears much resemblance to wielding a pitchfork and shovel. No horse manure for a start. Or at least one would hope not.

Francine gave me some clear instructions on what she expects before she left, so I've turned all the chairs upside down and placed them on the tables, and now I'm trying to work out how to use a mop and bucket. I mean, I get that I need to dip the mop-y end of the mop in the bucket. That much seems logical. But there's this weird set of rollers at the top of the bucket that I've got no clue how to use. So, I've avoided them altogether as I've dopped the mop and sloshed it on the tiled floor, sending soapy water flying.

I suppose that's just part of the deal. You cover the floor with soapy water and then somehow soak it up. But how do you do that with a completely sodden mop? And a mop, I might add, that looks considerably grubbier than the floor I'm trying to clean with it.

I pull out my phone from my back pocket of my apron and google, "how to use a mop and bucket to clean a floor." I learn that I need to mop in sections systematically

I get to work. By the time I've dipped the raggedy old mop in the bucket a few times there's a rather large, soapy puddle forming on the floor.

I consult my phone once more. It tells me the wet floor will dry overtime. I twist my mouth as I regard the puddle. Maybe I should use a hair dryer? Surely that would work? But I can't imagine there's a hair dryer here at the café.

Perhaps I could use some tea towels? There are plenty of those in the kitchen.

Resolving that tea towels will do the trick, I then find a clean bundle in one of the kitchen cupboards. Carefully, I lay them down over the soapy puddle, forming a kind of tea towel patchwork quilt.

I stand back and look at my handiwork. It's rather pretty, if I dare say so myself, adding colors other than pink to the space. I'm sure Maverick would be relieved. He thinks this place is far too pink for his liking.

I can't help but laugh to myself as I think of him in the pink frilly apron that's part of the café uniform. He's so big and masculine, his bulk completely at odds with the apron's femininity.

But thinking of how funny Maverick looks isn't going to help me get this floor cleaned. I need to refocus on the task at hand. The puddle is now completely covered in tea towels. All I have to do now is scoop them up before I move on to the next section.

I set about the task, discovering as I do that every tea towel is now soaked through, and as I pick them up, they begin to drip down my arms and back onto the floor.

Disaster! How on earth do people do this?

I glance around wildly for a place to put the dripping towels, and in the end decide to stuff them behind a large pot plant and hope that they dry by the morning. It's a warm enough evening. They should dry out in no time, I'm sure. Not that I have any clue how long it takes a tea towel to dry.

Princess, remember?

With one patch of floor now mopped, I move to the next section. I chew on my lip. This isn't as easy as I thought it would be. How I wish I had spoken with Theresa at the palace before I left about how to do this sort of thing. She's a regular person, and very practical to boot. She'd know how to do something as simple as mopping a floor.

My fingers itch to message her. But I know I can't. I'm meant to be in India right now, silently contemplating my life choices. Not mopping a café floor only a thousand or so miles from the palace in Villadorata.

I know what I need. Music. I haven't listened to any music since I left the palace. Music will make the chore all that less cumbersome.

I pull my phone from my back pocket and search up a playlist. The top one on my list is a "mixed tape" I made for Greg and me to listen to together. Full of soppy romantic songs, I delete it quick smart.

I don't need the reminder.

But I can use Greg as the inspiration to my soundtrack for the task.

I smile as I search for *Bad Guy*, and as Billie Eilish begins to croon, I dedicate the song to Greg and his scheming ways. I think of a waltz I danced not that long ago at a palace ball. Of course it was classical music, but it had the same beat.

I sway gently to the music, holding the handle of the mop in my hands. Then my feet find the rhythm of the waltz, and I'm transported back to that ballroom, my mop a considerable improvement on those dreary, weak-chinned, self-absorbed aristocrats my parents insist on making me dance with.

I would take this mop over them any day of the week, thank you very much.

As it gets to the musical break, I spin around the mop throwing a hand out to the side, really hamming it up. It feels good to dance. Great, in fact. As I move, I push every feeling I ever had for Bad Guy Greg from my heart and from my mind, stepping one-two-three, one-two-three, picturing myself dancing in the ballroom, decked out in my Ledonian red dress.

To my surprise, I begin to feel a little misty eyed over my royal life. Odd, I know, but it's not like I hate every-thing about being a princess. I love my family, and the charity work I do. I even quite enjoy the grand events at times, but really only because I get to see Maddie, who regales me with stories of life in Texas before she became Queen.

I close my eyes and imagine my mop is a dashing man, someone who elicits so much sizzle in me I'm at risk of spontaneous combustion. My dream man. Tall with broad shoulders and kind eyes, the type you can get lost in. A man with strong arms with which to hold me, holding me against him as we step around the dance floor in our rhythmic waltz. A man who appreciates my zest for life. A man who understands what it's like to be me, both the highs and the lows. A man who understands who I am and fully accepts me, despite knowing the position I hold in the world.

A man who gets me.

And then a face pops into my mind, a face so clear it can only be one person.

Maverick.

I suck in a sharp breath, my eyes pinging open as my heart rate leaps.

Maverick? I'm fantasizing about dancing with *Maverick*?

And not just fantasizing about dancing with him—fantasizing about having a grand love affair with him, too? About him being my dream man?

I stare straight ahead, rolling through everything I've felt for him since the day we met. Initially, I was struck by how determined he looked, plodding across the shop toward me. Then, I noticed how imposing he was, with a handsome face and the kind of deep blue eyes that hint at hidden depths.

Then there's Maverick on the train. How kind he was to me in helping me with my suitcase, and how we chatted so freely as the train whisked us through the countryside.

Then I think of the impromptu picnic we had on our first evening here, how easy it was to talk to him, how I felt like I could be myself. Of course I couldn't be entirely honest with him about who I am and the life I lead, but that notwithstanding, I began to feel a closeness to him I didn't expect.

And how could I forget bare-chested Maverick when he rescued me from the tree? Don't think I didn't notice how well put together he is. Seriously, no man should look that good with his shirt off. He's all tanned abs and broad shoulders tapering to a slim waist.

And since then, we've been working together here at the café, and he's been nothing but helpful. Kind. Attentive. Always there for me through my various disasters, never judging, rather letting me mess up so I can learn.

And tonight, he's out to dinner with Giovanna Fiorelli.

My stomach twists with something unpleasant as I think of him with her, sharing a meal overlooking the lake, with romance in the air—and no doubt her dress a size too small.

It shouldn't matter to me if he goes on a date with her, or anyone else, but the heat creeping up my neck begs to differ.

Do I have feelings for Maverick? Romantic feelings? Feelings that mean I want him to be more than just my housemate, my coworker, my friend?

Could Maverick be my grand love affair?

The thought has me sucking in air.

Don't get me wrong, I like being around him, and he's more than easy on the eye. I could easily have a fling with a man like Maverick before I head back to the palace. Something fun with no strings.

But I don't want a fling. Not with him, not with anyone.

I want something so much deeper than just those sizzling feelings you get when you really fancy someone. As wonderful as those feelings are, I want more. I want to fall in love. I want to know how it feels.

I look at Alex with Maddie and Sofia with Marco and I want what they have. The way I catch them sharing little looks, smiling their secret smiles at one another. It's like they belong to an exclusive club of two, blissfully happy to be together in their little love bubbles for two.

Could Maverick be that man for me?

I swallow, my throat suddenly hot.

I've seen the way he looks at me when he doesn't know I am. I'm not blind. I know he's jealous when Pierre helps me do things in the café, and I saw the way his eyes rested on my lips that morning in the bookshop.

But does he feel something more than mere attraction to me? Because attraction can evaporate just as quickly as it forms, and I want more than just that.

Do I want more than attraction with Maverick?

And if I do, would he want that with me, too?

I shake my head, doing my best to push the image of Maverick from my mind. I let the music wash over me and I return to my waltz, refusing to picture anyone but my mop—making it rather less romantic, but certainly less frightening as well.

As I turn with a flourish, I notice a figure in the doorway.

I catch my breath. Someone's here! And not just anyone, either.

Maverick, the man I've been fantasizing about as my dance partner—and possibly more—is here, and what's worse, he's seen me dancing.

With a mop.

"I thought you'd gone on your date," I say a little too brightly, pasting on a smile that I hope says that dancing with mops is perfectly normal behavior and that him going on a date with Giovanna is totally fine with me.

Which it's not.

Obviously.

"All done," he replies, brushing his date with Giovanna away with two simple words. He holds up a brown paper bag. "I got you some Chinese. There's a place around the corner, right next to a pub that's running a quiz night I thought we could go to later in the week. But it looks like you were … kinda busy?" His lips lift into a smirk.

My heart thuds.

He saw me dancing.

I turn away and pretend to be focused on mopping the floor, my cheeks flaming.

One second I'm fantasizing about dancing with him and wondering if he feels something for me that's more substantial than just the sizzle, and the next he's here?

Talk about humiliating.

"Oh, I was just trying different techniques for mopping the floor." *And trying desperately to not feel jealous that the man I think I have feelings for was on a date with a sexy woman.*

"Different techniques? Is that what you're calling it? 'Cos tell me if I'm wrong, but it looked to me like you were dancing."

I risk glancing at him only to see that his smirk has now turned into a full grin.

"I was just being silly. It helps to pass the time when you're cleaning. That's what I always find."

I neglect to mention that this is the first time I've ever cleaned in my life.

"I would say when it came to dance technique, Mr. Mop wins, hands down," he says.

"Is that so? I'd like to see you do better."

"You'd like to see me do better dancing with a mop?"

"I would."

"Is that a challenge?"

"It's a waltz off, if you will."

He shakes his head. "That's not a thing."

"Maverick, are you telling me that you're a fraidy-pants?"

He laughs. "A fraidy-pants? How old are you?"

"You know precisely how old I am." I waggle the mop at him, soapy water flicking around the room once more.

"Hey! You're getting that on me," he complains, wiping his shirt with his hand.

He places our dinner on the counter, and as he takes

217

the mop from me, his fingers lightly brush against mine. It sends a shot of electricity right up my arm and down into the pit of my belly.

Sizzle. *Big* time.

Oh, I am in troooouuuble.

"Maverick, meet Mr. Mop," I say lightly.

"How's it going, Mr. Mop?" he says, and it makes me smile the way he so easily plays along.

"What music would you like?" I pretend to concentrate on my phone, all the while trying to get my heart rate back to normal while simultaneously ignoring the electricity currently sizzling through my veins.

It's not going well.

"Probably not this," he replies.

"Why ever not? Are you saying you're not a tough guy?"

He lets out a chortle. "Definitely not a tough guy. That's more my brother's domain. Play me something else. Something a little less intense than this."

"I know just the song." I find the Dua Lipa song, *Levitating*, and press play. Instantly, the song's catchy beat fills the café.

Maverick raises a brow. "This is a whole lot faster than the last song."

"Challenge accepted?" I grin at him, thoroughly enjoying our repartee.

"I warn you, I'm a horrible dancer," he says.

"Are you trying to get out of this challenge?"

"Nope. Just warning you."

I wait for him to start dancing, but all he does is stand there, holding the mop, looking probably as ridiculous as I did a moment ago. "Well? What are you waiting for? An audience to applaud?"

"Definitely not an audience." He takes a breath,

holding on to the mop with one hand, and then he begins to move, but it's certainly not a waltz or any other dance I recognize. It's more like he's caught in an earthquake, jiggling around with the occasional pronounced movement thrown in for good measure.

I press my lips together to stop from laughing, but it's no use. A giggle escapes, my hand instantly flying to my mouth.

He stops in his tracks. "I told you I was a horrible dancer."

"You're just sort of ... jiggling."

He puts his hands up in the surrender sign, the mop handle balanced against one of his shoulders. "I've not got any clue how to do the kind of dancing you were doing."

"Don't you attend balls back home in America?"

"You mean like Prom? That was a few years ago for me, and we sure didn't do any waltzing."

"Why not?"

"'Cos this isn't the 19th century?"

"Everyone should know how to waltz, at the very least."

"Is that so?" His eyes are dancing.

At least one part of his anatomy can do it.

"Let me show you." I reach for the mop only for Maverick to take my hand in his. The touch of his flesh against mine has exactly the same effect it had on me earlier when our fingers brushed, and my breath catches in my throat.

Maverick shoots me a puzzled look. "Did you ...? Were you ...? Did you wanna dance with the mop?" he asks, clearly embarrassed, and struggling to find the right words —but I notice he hasn't let go of my hand.

I make a snap decision. After all, I've escaped the palace to have a grand adventure. I'm going to be brave.

Although I never expected to feel anything for Maverick, despite his obvious masculine appeal, I now have a case of fireworks going off in my chest.

As our eyes lock, I know the last thing I want to do is dance with a mop.

"I'm certain you would be offended if I chose a mop over you. So, would you care to dance with me, Maverick?" I ask.

He slots the mop into the bucket and pushes it away with his foot. "You'll have to show me what to do."

"It would be my pleasure," I respond, more than happy that I can finally show him something I know how to do that he doesn't. "Place your left hand on my upper back, just below my shoulder," I instruct, trying to sound authoritative despite the fact I know exactly how it feels to be touched by this man.

His hand settles lightly on the T-shirt covering my back and heat spreads from his fingers.

I clear my throat. "Now take my outstretched hand in yours." I place my own hand on his shoulder and hold out my other.

"Like this?" he asks, taking my hand in his.

We're now a mere handful of inches apart, and I can't help but breathe in his woodsy, citrusy scent, the skin of his hand soft and warm against mine.

"Now what?" he asks, and I crane my neck to look up at this large hulk of a man for whom I have sudden feelings I don't know quite what to do with.

Well, other than the obvious. But I can't kiss him. I simply can't! The mere thought has heat rising in my cheeks once more.

"Are you okay?" he asks.

"Of course I am." It comes out a little snappier than I intended, so I soften my voice and add, "Now, we move.

It's just three counts. One-two-three, one-two-three. You move forward with your left foot first, and I move back."

We begin to move, awkwardly at first, his height making him decidedly gangly. But after a few steps and clear instruction from me, we fall into a rhythm.

"See? You're getting it," I say a moment too soon as he steps on my foot, making me wince.

"I'm so sorry, Amy! Are you okay?"

"I'm fine. My brother stood on my feet more than once when we were learning to dance. Ready to try again?"

"As long as you're comfortable with potentially losing a limb."

"I'll take my chances."

Maverick's brow furrows in concentration, those impossibly blue eyes of his focused entirely on me as if I'm explaining nuclear physics, rather than a simple waltz.

But after a couple more missteps he begins to get into the rhythm, and we move around the floor between the tables as Dua Lipa and DaBaby's music fills the air.

"Not bad for someone who moments ago thought dancing was just jiggling on the spot," I tease.

"I did not jiggle," he protests.

"If you say so," I reply, and we share a smile.

The frenetic song ends, morphing into the artist's slower, more romantic *Anything for Love*, and suddenly standing so close to Maverick, alone in the middle of an empty café, feels intense. Far too intense.

I pull away, working to regain my composure. "And that's how to waltz," I say as lightly as I can manage.

"I think I got it. Like, one-two-three, one-two-three, one-two-three." He takes the steps, holding his hands in place, dancing with an invisible partner.

"Well done."

As I watch him move, I wonder if he felt it, too, this

thing that seems to have come from out of the blue, hitting me like a jolt of electricity.

Surely something so strong must be reciprocated.

But then I think of how, up until this evening, he was just Maverick to me, my new friend, my housemate and fellow café worker. Nothing more than that.

Now? Now he's morphed into an object of desire, someone it would seem I fantasize about as I'm dancing around with a mop.

I blow out a breath.

"How did your date go with Giovanna Fiorelli?" I ask as jealousy squirms in my belly.

He stops dancing and turns to me. "We've agreed to be friends."

The rush of relief brings unexpected tears to my eyes. "Friends?" I reply, aiming for casual indifference, and knowing my face is probably giving me away.

"Friends," he echoes, his eyes soft, and I'm hit with my feelings for him with full force, right in my chest. He takes a few more dance steps and smiles at me. "So? What do you think?"

I think I've got a big, fat crush on you that will mean I'll spend my entire time thinking about what it would be like to kiss you while you're blissfully unaware.

I lift my lips into a brave smile, doing my best to push these new-found feelings I have for him down until they're flattened into nothing more than a paper-thin reminder on the café floor. "You're a total natural, Mav. A total natural."

Chapter 17

Amelia

Through eating Chinese and taking the walk back to the lake house, lying awake and staring at my ceiling before a fitful sleep, and all the rest of the next day, working alongside one another at the café, I can't stop thinking about Maverick.

As I watch him making coffees for endless customers, always with a ready smile, taking the time to listen to their stories, I scroll through everything I know about him.

I know he's an American from a small town in Washington state with the most whimsical name of Maple Falls.

I know that he lives in Los Angeles and has a job he doesn't particularly like, surrounded by fake people.

I know that he's kind to lonely customers in the café.

That he listened to me read him my favorite fairytale, even though I'm sure he thought it childish.

That he's patient in teaching me basic life skills, like how to wash strawberries and how to make a coffee without spraying myself with milk foam.

That he's saved me more than once, like some fairytale knight in shining armor.

I know that he looks irresistibly cute as a goth, and totally out of place, that he's tall and handsome, with the most kissable lips I've ever had the good fortune to see.

I know all these things, and added together it makes him the most perfect man of my acquaintance.

No one has even come close to having all the qualities Maverick has.

No wonder I've got feelings for the guy.

And they're growing by the day.

"All set?" he asks, holding the mop he'd caught me dancing with only last night, the mop I'd imagined was *him*.

"Nearly." I busy myself with rearranging the condiments shelf—the shelf I'd already arranged before he appeared at my side—to buy me some time before I need to look him in the eye.

Because looking Maverick in those deep blue eyes and seeing the warmth that lies there?

Hmm, *so* not a good idea.

"You finish up. I'll go put your dance partner in the supplies closet."

I chance a look at him. He's smiling at his joke, looking

impossibly handsome in his close-fitting plain white T-shirt that shows off his muscular arms, his pecs, his wide shoulders, his abs... oh, all of it. It shows every inch of his enviable torso off to perfection. All I can say is thank goodness he's still wearing his pink Francine's apron, because otherwise I might very well throw myself into his arms and confess how I feel.

"Sure. Okay," I manage before I return my attention to the condiments that certainly don't require a further rearrangement—but they're getting another one anyway.

I don't quite know how I've got through the last day in his presence, my new feelings for him swirling around inside of me like water going down a drain. And now it's closing time and we're heading back to the lake house, where it will be just him and me and those swirling feelings.

I blow out a breath.

Why did I have to go getting a crush on someone who's not only my work colleague, but my housemate, too?

And I haven't even told him who I really am.

Maverick strides past my position behind the counter, locking the door. "Front door and windows secured. Shall we head out the back?" he asks.

"Of course," I say with a smile.

This is just Maverick. He's my friend. Nothing more.

"After you, mademoiselle," he says with a bow that wouldn't look out of place in the State Room at the palace.

"Thanks," I say as I traipse through the kitchen and out the back door.

"Aren't you forgetting something?"

"What?"

Instead of answering, I feel his arms reach around my waist. My heart stops. *What's happening? Is he—?* But then I look down to see him untying the long strap of my apron before he loops it over my head and hands it to me.

"Thanks," I murmur, trying to get my breathing in check.

He hangs my apron on a peg and locks the door behind us, and then we begin the walk home along the cobblestone streets. Him taking his long-legged strides and me toddling to keep up.

We reach the town square, which is busier than usual at this time of day. There are people lounging on the church steps, others paddling in the fountain, and still others snapping selfies with the pretty town backdrop.

"Must be tourists," Maverick murmurs, but no sooner have the words left his lips when music begins and I notice for the first time that many of the people in the square are dressed similarly, in ripped jeans, head bands, and fluoro colored shirts.

Justin Timberlake begins to tell us about a feeling he seems to have in his bones, the catchy beat thrumming, and instantly, the people dispersed around the square clamber together and begin to move in unison, facing us.

"What the—?" Maverick says, reflecting my exact thoughts.

"It's a flash mob!" I say, excitement rushing through me. "I've heard of these but never actually seen one."

The singer is now telling us to dance, dance, dance, and I can't help but move to the music, the atmosphere around us electric.

"Isn't it marvelous?" I ask Maverick.

"It sure is something," he replies, his brows pulled together in his characteristic way.

What can he be worried about? It's a flash mob, not *the* Mob.

By now, the dancers are in lines, the music pulsating around us, waving their hands then clapping them in unison before moving into a turn. They slide to the right, then shimmy to the left, slowly making their way toward us both.

It's mesmerizing. Everyone is in perfect harmony, their outfits working together to make them look like a professional dance troupe.

"Have you seen one of these before?" I ask as I move from side to side to the music.

I notice someone in the crowd, dancing along with the others. "Oh, my. Is that Francine?"

"Where?" Maverick questions, and I point at the short, round figure of our boss, dressed in a flouro skirt and white shirt, her hair teased to twice its usual volume. "Francine is involved in this?"

"Look! That's Mr. Bellamy from the bookshop!" I exclaim as I spot him moving stiffly to the music, his movements small and rigid. "Perhaps it's a whole town event they put on annually?"

"Maybe? They're getting closer." Maverick places his arm protectively around me, and I can't help but wish he was doing so for another reason.

I smile up at him and see his jaw is clenched tight. "What are you worried about?"

"Nothing. I'm fine," he mutters, sounding anything but.

"Don't you like flash mobs?"

"It's just … why are they all looking at *us*?"

I watch the dancers. "It could be that we're the only spectators here. It makes sense that they should all focus on something."

Maverick pulls me closer to him, pressing me up against his firm, muscular body, which I am determined to ignore and instead focus on the rather wonderful spectacle playing in front of my eyes.

By now the dancers have spread out in a semi-circle around us and it's hard not to feel backed up against the wall. Quite literally, as it happens, the stone wall outside the pharmacy is mere inches from our backs.

And then, just as suddenly as it had started, the music stops and everyone begins to disperse casually, as though they weren't just dancing in perfect synchronicity for an audience of two rather bewildered café workers.

"Oh, my goodness," I say as I recognize two more dancers, one man, and one woman.

The man approaches me and offers me a red rose at the very same time as the woman approaches Maverick and does the same.

Giovanna, looking more like Sophia Lauren than ever in her full skirt nipped in at her enviably slim waist, places a kiss on Maverick's cheek, and a knot in my belly twists painfully.

"A beautiful rose for a beautiful rose," Pierre says to me, his eyes trained on mine as he holds the rose out for me.

"Thank you." Automatically, I take it from him as I have taken countless flowers from people on royal promenades, my eyes sliding back to Maverick. Giovanna is now smiling her confident smile at him, completely oblivious to the jealousy raging inside of me.

"You are a rose without thorns, and I am your perfect match," she purrs as she pushes her long dark hair back, exposing the soft skin of her shoulder.

Maverick smiles at her as he takes the flower somewhat awkwardly, and I'm pleased to say it's one of his smiles that doesn't reach his eyes—not like the ones he gives me.

"You will think of me when you hold it, yes?" she asks, looking up at him bashfully.

Huh! Giovanna Fiorelli is about as bashful as a hungry cat at a seafood buffet.

"Do you like it?" Pierre asks, dragging my attention back from Maverick and Giovanna.

"Of course I do. It's lovely. Thank you, Pierre. You're very sweet." I lift the rose to my nose, but its scent is too faint.

"All this was for you, to show you how special you are, Amy," Pierre says as he takes my hand in his and presses a kiss to my palm. It's alarmingly intimate, and I force myself not to snatch my hand away. Years of royal training has taught me to deny my instincts in such situations and instead paste on a banal smile.

"The flash mob was absolutely amazing. Thank you both so very much," I say.

"Amy's right. You guys nailed it," Maverick says. He slips his arm around my shoulders, giving me a thrill, even though I'm sure it's only because he wants to double down on his message to Giovanna that they can be nothing more than friends.

Whatever his motivation, I'll take it—as desperate as that sounds.

Thankfully, Pierre lets go of my hand, and I wipe my damp palm on the back of my jeans.

"It was all for you, Maverick," Giovanna says in her heavy Ledonian-accented English.

"Pierre said it was all for *me*," I say.

I couldn't resist it. Take it up with my lawyers.

"It's for both of you, our special Montelac visitors," Pierre says with an outstretch of his arms.

"Really? Do you put on flash mobs for all your visitors? Because if you do, you must be exhausted," I say, genuinely interested in this dance. "But on the other hand, it could be quite the tourist attraction. I'm certain people would come from all over Europe to witness your dancing."

"We … err, we did it for you," Pierre repeats.

Strange.

"Well, you did a great job, guys," Maverick begins. "But we've got to go, right, Amy?"

"Right," I say, still luxuriating in having his arm held around my shoulders.

"I've got that salmon back at the lake house I promised to cook you tonight. Remember?" he says.

"The salmon. Of course." I know absolutely nothing about some salmon, but I'm not going to let a minor detail like that get in the way of getting Maverick away from Giovanna channeling Sophia Lauren, even if he's told me he's not interested in her.

He's but a man, and she's a woman most would be powerless to resist.

"Thanks again, you two. Splendid work. Just splendid," I say.

"See you guys later," Maverick adds.

I look over my shoulder when we're at a safe distance to see them both watching us, Giovanna with a distinct scowl on her face, and Pierre looking … well, if I didn't know any better, I would say he looks confused.

"What was *that*?" Maverick asks, a laugh rumbling out of him as we reach the edge of the town.

"A terribly complicated way to tell someone you like them?" I offer, giggling.

"But that would have taken so much time to pull off. Even though it's clear as day Pierre's got a thing for you."

"I've disagreed with you about that before, but now

evidence would point to you being right." I hold up the rose.

"You think?"

"And Giovanna certainly hasn't got your 'let's just be friends' message, if you did indeed communicate that to her."

"Of course I did," he replies, his tone indignant.

"What I mean is, she doesn't speak terribly good English, and you don't speak any Ledonian, so perhaps it got lost in translation?"

His arm is still around my shoulders, and as he comes to a stop, he pulls it away, looking into my eyes.

I look up at him, my heartrate kicking up a notch. "Did I say something?" I ask.

"No. It's … I—" he begins, only to be cut off by Francine's voice.

"Hello, you two," she says, and Maverick instantly takes a step back from me as though singed.

Nooo! I'm dying to know what he was going to say! Of course the chances that he was about to tell me he feels the same way about me is probably one in a million, but even if there's a tiny, miniscule, barely perceptible outside chance that he might have feelings for me, I need to know.

"You were amazing, Francine," he replies smoothly. "You sure are a dark horse. A woman of many talents. Café owner and dancer."

She smiles, pleased with the compliment. "It's just a bit of fun, don't you think?"

"It was so fun. I loved it," I reply.

Francine beams at us, clasping her hands together. "I'm so glad! We wanted to make sure you both felt welcome here. It's not every day we get such special visitors."

There's something about the way she says "special"

that makes me wonder if she knows more than she's letting on.

But that's impossible. No one here knows who I am.

Do they?

I glance at Maverick. He's turned pale, as though he's seen a ghost.

"What a thoughtful town you have. I've never felt so welcome anywhere," I say, not pulling my gaze from Maverick.

What's got into him?

"Anything for our favorite visitors," Francine says, giving us a little wave before hurrying away from us, up the street.

As Maverick and I resume our walk toward the lake house, I can't help but steal glances at him. He's twirling Giovanna's rose between his fingers, a thoughtful expression on his face.

"Are you going to keep it?" I ask, aiming for casual and hoping I'm successful.

"What? Oh, this?" He looks at the rose as though surprised to find it in his hand. "Probably not. Seems a bit much, don't you think? The whole way they gave those roses to us, I mean."

"It was rather elaborate," I agree.

We walk in comfortable silence for a while, the evening surprisingly light as dusk settles. I'm acutely aware of every inch between us, the way our hands occasionally brush as we walk side by side.

"So," he says finally, and my heart soars. Is he about to tell me what he was going to say before Francine interrupted us?

"About that salmon."

The salmon. Right.

"I may have stretched the truth a bit."

"You don't have salmon waiting at home?" I ask, already knowing the answer.

"I don't even know how to cook salmon."

We share a smile.

"Let's stop by the market and pick something else up," I suggest.

As we turn toward the market, roses in hand, I realize with startling clarity that I'm in real trouble here. Because this isn't just a crush anymore.

I'm falling for Maverick Mitchell.

A man who lives an ocean away.

A man who could never fit into my real life.

A man who doesn't even know my real name or how I live my life.

But as he smiles at me, his eyes crinkling at the corners the way they do, I can't bring myself to care about any of that. Not yet. Not when everything about this moment feels so perfectly, impossibly right.

For now, I'll allow myself this—this adventure, this connection, this feeling. The rest of it can wait for tomorrow.

Or maybe the day after that.

Chapter 18

Ethan

I spot her across the street and my brain just kind of stops working. Amy in shorts and a black tank top, her hair falling across her shoulders instead of the practical ponytail she wears at work. Her hair catches the final rays of sunlight for the day as she walks toward me, falling in waves that somehow look both perfectly messy and completely intentional. Her olive skin practically glows, and those eyes? *Man.* Those eyes could probably make a guy confess his darkest secrets without even trying.

My secrets might not be dark, but I sure do have them.

Not that I'm staring.

Except I totally am.

I blow out a breath.

It's officially over. I'm done for. I'm falling for this woman who moves with such easy confidence, like she owns the sidewalk but doesn't need to make a big deal about it. There's something about the way she carries herself that's incredibly sexy, and I wonder how I didn't see it before that day she climbed the tree and my feelings hit me in the gut.

My heart does that ridiculous flutter that I've officially given up fighting.

Talk about inconvenient feelings. But try as I might, I just can't seem to get this beautiful girl out of my head—or my heart.

Yeah, I said "heart." I may find her incredibly sexy, but she's so much more than just hot. She's the full package. Smart. Classy. Fun. Easy to talk to. Full to her very brim with a joy for life you just don't see in people. Well, not the people I meet.

My mind flits to Giovanna, a woman in such stark contrast to Amy they may as well be from different planets. We cut a deal at dinner a few nights ago, although it felt a little like selling my soul.

As I'd suspected, she knew exactly who I was, and shared with me that she was an actress too.

I knew where that conversation was going.

She assured me that what we could have together wouldn't be just a "showmance" because she genuinely found me attractive. And oh, would I mind dressing up as Rowan Thornheart for her someday?

The thing is I've met a hundred Giovannas in my time. I knew I could appease her by agreeing to pose for a bunch of photos, making it look like we were an item, and she didn't take any time snapping the first few with her phone, like the expert selfie taker I bet she is.

She agreed reluctantly not to post them until my time here is done, after which I promised to be available for more photo shoots in Villadorata, the capital city of Ledonia where she lives.

The things we're forced to do.

She did say something weird though. She told me she had come to Montelac to see me, and when I asked her how she knew I was here, she acted all evasive and wouldn't reply. Of course my mind leaped to the worst, and I've been a little on edge ever since, always on the lookout for paps.

The last thing I need is for the world to know I'm here, particularly when I want to get as much time as I can with Amy before this whole thing has to come to an end.

"You're staring," Amy says as she approaches, totally busting me, her luscious lips—painted siren red, *have mercy* —lifted in a soft smile.

I clear my throat. "I was thinking about work, actually," I lie.

"Work?"

"Yeah. I think I left the cleaning supplies out on the counter when I cleaned up earlier."

Smooth, Roberts. Real smooth.

Immediately I want to kick myself for coming up with such a lame excuse.

"Do you want to go to the café to check? It's just around the corner."

"Nah. It can wait until tomorrow. Shall we go? The quiz starts in about five minutes."

"Are you ready for it?" she asks, bumping her shoulder against my arm as we walk down the street.

"I'll admit, I'm not great at quizzes, but I'll try my best. You?"

"I love quizzes! Especially if they're about European history, which I majored in at university. Either that or Taylor Swift."

I arch an eyebrow at her. "You're a Swiftie? And here I was thinking I liked you."

"How could you not like Taylor?" she replies, as though the two of them are on a first-name basis. "She's a talented musician, terribly clever, and such a positive role model for girls and women alike. The question should be why you would *not* like her."

"She's so mainstream."

"By which you mean she's successful."

She's got a point.

"Yeah, maybe."

"You can't dislike someone because of their success."

I think of the way some publications find the worst possible angle on me time and time again. "You're right," I reply.

We arrive at the pub, the place warm and buzzing with activity. It looks like what I expect a typical British pub would look like, right here in Malveaux, from its red carpet to forest green walls, and gold trimmings. There are rows of beers on tap at the bar, and photos of the town in the olden days on the walls.

"Amy! Over here!" Pierre calls out, waving at us from a table where he's sitting with Francine and Giovanna.

Huh. I wonder how they know each other.

"Shall we join Francine's team?" Amy asks.

"We could make our own. Just you and me?" I suggest.

"But wouldn't it be more fun with a larger group? Besides, look around. All the other teams have at least six people. We want the best chance possible to win this thing."

"I never knew you were so competitive."

"With a family like mine it's impossible not to be. Come on." She takes me by the hand and leads me weaving through the crowds to Francine's table. It feels nice to have her touch me, even though I know it doesn't mean anything to her. She's just my friend.

Although I want her to be so much more.

I catch myself. She can't be anything more. Soon I'll need to head back to my life, and Amy and our time here and everything between us will be relegated to memory.

But I know I want more.

A whole lot more.

"We're so glad you made it," Francine declares as we arrive at the table.

"Amy, come sit next to me," Pierre says, pushing his hair back from his face and throwing a dazzling smile at her like it's some kind of sexy weapon. Seriously, this guy belongs in an aftershave commercial—preferably one that's filming far, far away from here.

Yup, my new friend, Jealousy, has come back to visit for a while.

It's weird because up until now, I never got jealous. Not over a woman, anyway. And I'll tell you right now, I don't like this feeling.

Be that as it may, I'm not gonna let Pierre win. Not tonight and not with Amy.

"We'll take these seats here," I tell him as I pull a chair out for Amy. She will be safely encased between me and Francine, and right across the table from Cologne Commercial.

I take my seat next to Amy, and immediately feel a hand on my arm.

"I love that you're sitting next to me," Giovanna purrs, moving closer.

In my need to keep Amy from Pierre, I landed myself right back in Giovanna's hot water.

"We can whisper sweet nothings into each other's ears all night long," she says.

I smile at her.

Not gonna happen, lady.

"What's your area of expertise, Giovanna?" I ask.

I half expect her to reply something like "love making" as though she's a Bond girl from the '60s, but instead she says, "Ledonian agricultural and horticultural practices of the 20th century."

I blink at her in disbelief. "That's rather specific."

"It's a fascinating topic. Much like *you* are, Maverick Mitchell."

And we're back to overt flirtation.

I shoot her a meaningful look, but she just simpers at me. I lean a little closer and say under my breath, "We've got a deal, remember?"

"Oh, I remember," she coos.

"Then lay off it a bit, okay?"

She shrugs. "I'm just being me."

I don't quite know how to reply, so instead I turn my attention elsewhere. "What's your specialty, Francine? Any areas you know a lot about?"

"Me? I'm hoping they'll be easy questions. I never went to university or anything like that," she says.

"You don't have to bother with university to know about life," Pierre states with conviction. "I didn't go, and I like to think I have a pretty full understanding of things." He gives Amy a look that's much like the looks Giovanna has been throwing me.

It's like we've stumbled onto the flirtation table, where

the only rule is that you must flirt with your words, with your eyes, or—as I am now experiencing with Giovanna—by pressing yourself inappropriately against my arm.

I pull it away and instead clasp my hands on the table, my elbows tucked in at my sides. I feel like I'm a kid again, closing up my body space to protect myself from being wrestled by Dan. He was always bigger, older, and stronger than me, so I never got to win.

"What about you, Amy? Anything that you are particularly knowledgeable about?" Francine asks.

She opens her mouth to reply when someone in a top hat and a very bright jacket taps on the microphone. "Is this thing working?"

"Yes!" several people call out.

"Oh, it's about to begin," Giovanna says, clapping her hands together in glee.

"Good evening, ladies and gentlemen, and welcome to the Winchester Arms' Quiz Night!" the quizmaster says.

There's a round of applause with people cheering.

"Popular event," I comment.

"We don't have that many events in this town, so everyone comes out for Quiz Night. It's almost a religion," Francine says.

"Tonight, you will be competing in a quiz about the Royal Families of Europe: Tiaras, Scandals, and Secret Lives!"

The room erupts into murmurs, someone calling out, "But I don't know anything about them!" as another says, "My favorite topic!"

I lean back in my seat. "I'm going to be totally useless at this quiz."

Amy has gone suddenly stiff in her chair.

"You okay?" I ask, leaning toward her. Her face is drained of color.

"She probably doesn't know anything about European royal families. Don't worry, sweetie," Francine says as she pets Amy's arm. "We'll help you out. Won't we?"

I shrug. "I don't know anything about them either, let alone any scandals or tiaras."

Amy gives me an odd look. I don't know quite what to make of it.

"What about the royal family of Ledonia?" Pierre asks, and receives a glare from Francine. Why, I couldn't tell you.

"Nope. I'm American," I say by way of explanation, which I think is a totally plausible reason why I wouldn't know much about the Ledonian royal family. Why would I? We've got enough going on in our own country not to worry about what a bunch of wealthy people born into extreme privilege get up to on the daily.

I glance at Amy once more. She still looks like she's freaking out. She did say she was competitive. Maybe she knows as much about European Royals as I do and takes quizzes super seriously?

"I think I might leave," she says.

I try to reassure her. "Don't go. It'll be fun. You'll see."

"You're not thinking of leaving, are you?" Pierre asks, stricken at the thought his object of desire might not stick around. "You've got to stay. I'll buy you a drink. Wine?"

"I don't know," Amy replies in a very uncharacteristi-cally Amy way.

What's got into her?

"Wine it is then," Pierre says as he leaves the table.

I notice he doesn't offer me a drink. But then why would he? He's not exactly my biggest fan.

"You don't have to stay if you don't want to," I tell her. "But can you tell me why?"

"First question of the first round is on general royal

knowledge," the quiz master begins before Amy has the chance to respond. "Which European monarchy is considered the oldest, continuous hereditary monarchy in the world, dating back to 900 AD?"

"I've got no clue," I say.

"Is it England?" Francine asks.

"I think it might be Monaco," Giovanna offers. "Monaco is my spirit animal," she says.

Can a country be a spirit animal?

"I just love it there. Don't you, Maverick? The casinos are fabulous," she says.

"I've never been," I reply.

"I'll take you there," she offers.

Yeah, I'm good.

"Let's say England," Francine suggests as she begins to write the answer down on the table's quiz sheet.

Amy leans closer to me and I catch the aroma of her scent, an enchanting combination of vanilla and flowers and … *her.* "It's Denmark."

"Denmark? Are you sure? I didn't even know they had a royal family there," I say quietly.

"I'm sure," she says simply.

"Why don't you say it then?"

"Can you?"

I shoot her a confused look. This is so unlike Amy. She's more of a *charge in with all sirens blaring* kind of person, not this little mouse she seems to have suddenly morphed into. But she's clearly rattled by something, and the last thing I want to do is upset her.

"It's Denmark," I tell Francine. "Not England."

"Demark. Of course. You're right, Maverick," Francine replies, and she crosses out "England" on the sheet and replaces it with "Denmark."

I lean back toward Amy. "Is it weird the way everybody here is speaking English?"

"I suppose," she replies.

"You sure you're okay? You're being weird."

"I'm fine," she replies, sounding anything but.

"Question two: Monaco's Prince Rainier III's marriage to which American actress in 1956 was dubbed 'the wedding of the century' and watched by 30 million people?" the quiz master asks.

"Definitely Grace Kelly," Giovanna pronounces with confidence as Pierre places a glass of red wine in front of Amy.

She immediately takes a gulp, and then another.

She sure is rattled.

"How do you know it's Grace Kelly?" Pierre asks as he takes his seat.

"Because I've have spent some time in Monaco and I know a lot about the country, including about how Grace Kelly married the prince," Giovanna replies.

I lean closer to Amy, enjoying the proximity. "Is that right?" I ask her under my breath, and she nods.

"It's Grace Kelly," she replies, her voice small.

I slide my arm around the back of her chair and give her shoulder a squeeze. She looks at me, her face blanched white, and I ask, "Are you sick?"

"No. I'm not sick. I'm just … Is it hot in here? Or is it me?" she says, her speech rapid.

"I think it's warm. Not surprising with so many people, I guess."

The quiz master announces another general knowledge question—this time about how many rooms the palace in Villadorata in Ledonia has—and Amy tells me the answer once more, under her breath.

This carries on for the rest of the first round, by the

end of which she has completely drained her glass of wine, and I offer to buy her another one.

"It's probably not a good idea," she says.

"Why don't you come to the bar with me and I'll get you a soda?" I offer.

"All right."

We make our way over to the bar, where we wait in line to place our order. I take the opportunity to check in with her again.

"Look, if you're not enjoying this we can head back to the house."

"It's just—" She bites down on her lip and my heart goes out to her. She's clearly bothered by something. I just don't know what it is.

She looks around the room.

"Tell me."

She takes a deep breath, her forehead creased with worry. "I don't want you to think ill of me."

"I could never think ill of you." I repeat her phrase, meaning every word of it. "Never."

If only she knew how I really felt about her.

"Round Two is about to begin, so please take your seats," the quizmaster announces.

"Amy?"

She looks up at me, her brown eyes wide. She opens her mouth to speak when Pierre hooks his arm around her shoulders and hands her a glass of wine.

"For you, my lady," he says, and my lip curls.

"Thank you," Amy replies, and I can tell her smile is forced.

"Let's head back. Round Two is about to begin and I have a feeling we're going to win this thing," Pierre says as he guides Amy back to the table.

I order a beer, and the quizmaster begins the second round.

"Round 2 is royal historical trivia. Question one: Which royal family adopted the surname 'Windsor' in 1917, replacing their German family name?"

Arriving back at the table, everyone has agreed that it's the British royal family.

"I've watched *The Crown*," Francine announces as she writes on the quiz sheet.

"Question two: Both the Ledonian and Malveauxian royal families are known for their annual tradition where members participate in what unusual athletic competitions?"

"Is it the waffle race, where people have to run down a hill holding waffles?" Pierre asks.

"No, silly. It's an egg and spoon race," Giovanna corrects.

"I think they chase wheels of cheese, don't they?" Francine offers.

"There are two: the Wife Race and the Cheese Race," Amy announces to the table. She stands abruptly. "And now, I really do need to go."

"Why? Aren't you having fun? You know all the answers!" Giovanna says.

"Stay. I'll get you another glass of wine," Pierre offers.

"Thank you, but no. I have a sudden headache. See you all at the café tomorrow. Sorry, Francine." She shoots me a look before she dashes from the table.

Without even thinking, I leap out of my chair and chase after her, yelling goodbye to everyone over my shoulder. I burst out of the pub and look up and down the street. I can see her receding figure rushing away. "Amy! Wait!" I call out as I pound the pavement, chasing after her.

I catch up quickly. Reaching for her arm I say, "What's going on?"

"I need to tell you something, and I don't know how you're going to take it, and if you are upset with me I would understand completely because you would be absolutely right and I'm so, so sorry." She looks up at me with worry written right across her face, and I want to smooth it away with my fingertips and tell her everything is going to be okay.

That I'm here for her, no matter what.

Chapter 19

Amelia

Of all the pubs in all the towns in all of Malveaux, we had to walk into one hosting a quiz about my family. What are the odds?

Low, I'm sure. Infinitesimal, even.

But you know what? I'm glad it happened, because it means I get to finally open up to Maverick about who I am. I need to be fully honest. Vulnerable.

I blow out a breath.

Will he hate me?

Will he think I've been playing some elaborate prank?

Will he think less of me for lying?

Not that it matters what he thinks. Except, of course it matters. It matters tremendously. What Maverick thinks of me is… well, right now, it's everything.

Mummy always says honesty is the best policy. Though I doubt she meant "confess your fake identity to a man you have feelings for while on an unauthorized holiday from your real life."

The fact of the matter is, as exciting as it's been to pretend to be someone else, the closer I've got to Maverick, the more I've felt like a fraud.

I've not been my authentic self.

I've not fully been *me*.

I suppose I've wanted the best of both worlds: working at the café, sharing a house with Maverick, enjoying the anonymity of being a regular person, but at the same time being Amelia.

Not the princess. The woman.

Right now, as I look at the expectant and concerned look on his face, I'm like a shaken bottle of champagne, ready to pop.

"Do you want to go back to the house and talk?" he asks, and I shake my head.

"No. I need to tell you now, before my resolve melts faster than ice cream at a summer garden party."

He gives me an inquisitive look.

"That happened at a garden party I was at one summer. It made a terrible mess," I explain, wondering why I'm babbling on when I should just get to the point.

He reaches out and I slip my hand in his, marveling at how small it feels, wrapped protectively in his big, strong hand. "You can tell me anything, Amy. Anything at all."

I nod, pressing my lips together as my nerves jangle.

Maverick waits quietly for me to speak. He's giving me space. I would appreciate the gesture more if it didn't make what I'm about to do even harder.

There's no use dragging this out like a particularly dreary state dinner.

Do it, Amelia!

I take a breath and say, "I'm not quite sure how to tell you this, so I think I'm just going to come straight out with it."

"Sure. Whatever you want." His eyes are kind, which is both lovely and utterly devastating.

Am I about to hurt him, this man I've got feelings for, feelings that are growing day by day?

I look him squarely in the eye. "The reason I can't do all the things regular people do every day isn't because I have some strange affliction caused by my mother. Well, not exactly. It's because I'm ... I'm a princess. An actual, literal, tiara-wearing princess. And I've never had to cook or clean or serve people or any of the things I do every day now because there are people who do that for us. Which sounds absolutely ridiculous and elitist now that I'm saying it because I work in a café, but there it is. The truth."

I hold my breath. He looks at me with that adorable half-smile, waiting for the punchline. When I say nothing more, he asks, "A princess of what?"

Ugh. He thinks I'm joking. Well, to be fair, it does sound like the opening line to a particularly unimaginative fairy tale.

"What I'm trying to tell you is that I'm a princess. As in a member of a royal family." I speak in slow, measured tones to ensure he gets every word.

"How does that work exactly?" he asks, his brows drawing together.

"How does it work?" Odd question, but I'll run with it.

"Well, I suppose it works because I was born into the royal family, and that automatically made me a princess."

I'm not being deliberately obtuse, but really, how else does one become a princess?

"Back up the bus here. Is this a joke or what?"

"I'm trying to tell you the truth, Maverick." I meet his gaze directly. "My name isn't Amy. It's Amelia. Amelia Astrid Kristiana Eugenie Canossa, Princess of Ledonia."

He gawks at me, and I can practically see the cogs turning behind those beautiful blue eyes. I can't blame him. Why would a grown woman make up a story about being a princess?

"Are you serious?" he finally asks. "I mean, to be fair, it would explain a lot."

"What would it explain exactly?" I ask, feeling oddly affronted. Does he think princesses are all bumbling idiots who can't operate coffee machines? Because if so, he might actually be right, at least in my case.

"It's just that you have this whole wide-eyed thing going on, like everything is new and exciting to you, even the most boring things."

I feel my cheeks flush with embarrassment. Is that how he sees me? As some sort of royal fish out of water, gawking at peasant life like it's a zoo exhibit?

"I thought you were just a super enthusiastic person," he continues. "But now? Now maybe it makes sense."

I take another deep breath. In for a penny, in for a crown.

"I am the third-born daughter of King Frederic and Queen Astrid of Ledonia. My older brother, Alexander, is married to Madeline, the Queen of Malveaux. My older sister, Sofia, is also married, and she is my father's heir, so she will be Queen of Ledonia when Father retires at sixty-five."

"Me? I'm just plain old Princess Amelia. I won't be queen of anything, and I'm unlikely to marry any heir to a throne because there simply aren't any more left." I attempt a laugh that comes out more like a nervous hiccup.

Maverick leans back on his heels, crossing his arms. "Prove it."

I bite my lip until my mind lands on an idea. "You noticed the sticker on my luggage. Remember? That's covering up my family crest, the Royal Ledonian Crest. It features a pheasant, the national bird. I can show it to you when we get home."

He doesn't look convinced. I can't blame him. Expensive luggage with crests doesn't make one royal—though in my family's case, it certainly helps.

"Even better, I'll show you on my phone." I pull my phone from my purse and tap through to the royal family's Instagram account. I turn the screen toward him, displaying a photo from last month's charity gala. It's of me with my hair in an elaborate updo, wearing a simple but unmistakably expensive dress, with appropriate princess-approved makeup.

My facial features, however, are unmistakably the same.

Maverick takes my phone and stares at it for a long moment. Then he looks up at me, his jaw dropped. "You're … you're telling the truth."

"I told you," I reply, but there's no satisfaction in being right.

I've spent my entire life following the rules, pleasing others, being what everyone needs me to be. The one time I tried to break free—to just be plain Amy, and most certainly not Princess Amelia—I've ended up hurting someone I've come to care about deeply.

The irony isn't lost on me. I ran away to find something

genuine, and now, when I've finally found it, it's been built entirely on a lie.

He knows my biggest and worst secret. The thing I've been holding close to my heart, protecting my privacy like a lioness protects her cub.

Maverick is still staring at me with those impossibly blue eyes of his, waiting for me to say something more. But all I can think is that I've finally found someone who sees me—the *real* me. The person beneath the title and the privilege and the royal protocol. Me, plain Amelia.

And I might have just ruined it forever.

Chapter 20

Ethan

Amy being a princess is the last thing I ever expected. It's true she'd glossed over parts of her life and kept others entirely to herself. But a bone fide princess, with a long name and parents who are the King and Queen of a small European country?

Nope. I did not see that coming.

But as I look into her beautiful big brown eyes, I see nothing but truth.

It's the same truth that's been there all along, just wearing a tiara I didn't expect.

My mind may be scrambling to make sense of her words, but my heart is steady. Amy's true identity makes no difference to the way I feel about her.

She's chewing on her lip, her brows knitted together. "Say something, Mav. Please. I know you probably hate me, and I wouldn't blame you at all if you did. But I hope you don't because I never meant to hurt you. You must believe me. I was pretending to be someone else so I could live a different life for a while, and then I met you and you helped me with that awful Greg and offered me a place to stay and, really, you're the kindest, sweetest, most generous man I've met in my whole life, and I—"

Before I even properly know what I'm doing, I collect her in my arms and hold her close against me. With my heart banging like a shutter in the wind, I gaze down at her, fighting the urge to just kiss her, and kiss her good.

But I can't do that. Not until I tell her my truth. Not until she knows everything she needs to know.

"Does this mean you forgive me?" she whispers, gazing up at me, and I can see tears pooling in her eyes in the glow of the streetlights.

"Forgive you? There's nothing to forgive."

She swallows. "But I lied to you about who I am."

I press a kiss to her forehead, my own guilt twisting in my belly. "I need to tell you something myself."

"You're a secret American prince?" She chokes out a laugh.

"Walk with me?"

She nods, and I take her hand in mine, leading her toward the lake, down the stone steps, and onto the beach. The moon is streaked with clouds, trying its best to shine, casting a strip of light across the still water. Somehow, the scene is lit like a movie set, and once again I'm struck by how this place is the perfect romantic backdrop.

Now, it's my turn to tell her who I am. My turn to come clean.

She's opened up to me about who she is, and that had to have been super hard for her. And it's a doozy. This woman I met purely by chance, has run away from her life to be here in this town, with me.

Yeah, I know. She's not *with me*. But I know I want her to be, even if it's only for the next couple weeks. Even if that's all we have.

"Look!" says Amy—I mean Princess Amelia. And no, I'm nowhere near used to that yet.

I follow her line of sight to see our footsteps in the sand glowing, like someone sprinkled glitter in the indentations of our footsteps.

"I think I read about this," I say, leaping on the reprieve from having to deliver my own confession. "It's this totally cool natural phenomenon about the Lac des Rêves."

"That's right. The lake has bioluminescent organisms in the water and sand that glow when disturbed. That's why you can see our footsteps. Isn't it magical?"

"It is, if you think stepping on bug larvae is magical," I joke.

She makes a face. "We just stepped in bug larvae? The poor bugs!"

That is so Amy. I mean Amelia. Princess Amelia. *Gah.*

"I prefer to think of it as fairy dust."

I smile at her. "Yeah. Me too."

There's a sudden high-pitched screeching noise that pierces the serenity, that has us pressing our hands over our ears.

"What's that noise?" she yells.

"I have no idea!" I reply, and just as suddenly as it began, the noise stops.

I look around, searching for the source. But all I can see is the darkness of the lake, punctuated only by the full moon's reflection, streetlights running along the shore, and the glow of the town.

"Maybe it's the bugs?"

"Do you really think bugs can make a noise that loud?" I ask.

"You've obviously not been to the Amazon."

"Of course I haven't been to the Amazon," I reply on a laugh. "We really do lead different lives, don't we?"

"I imagine there are more similarities than differences."

We share a smile.

"Yeah. I bet so, too."

We walk hand in hand along the beach, and I try to work out how to tell her that she's not the only one who's been less than fully honest here.

"Now that I know you're a princess, it explains so much. Why you're so accomplished with some things and seem to know nothing about others at the same time, like how you tried slicing bread with a weird mallet karate chop!"

"That was embarrassing."

"It's because you've never sliced bread in your life, right?" I ask and she nods.

She counts them off on her fingers. "Never sliced bread. Never made coffee. Never worked in an actual job. Never done anything regular people do every day."

"Your rules make sense now, too. Princesses probably aren't allowed to climb trees or serve people or stand to eat at a kitchen counter."

"I've been breaking rules all over the place and marking them off in my journal as I do," she says, and I can see the pride written across her face.

The signs may all have been there, but how could I have guessed? It's not exactly every day you meet a woman by chance while escaping paparazzi, and she turns out to be royalty.

"What do I call you now? Your Majesty?"

She laughs. "No. Definitely not. Officially, I'm 'Your Royal Highness' or 'ma'am,' but Ami will do nicely."

"Ami," I say. "Not too different from Amy."

"Exactly."

I know it's my turn to come clean.

I take a deep breath and begin my confession. "You're not the only one hiding something. I've wanted to tell you for a while now, but ... well, the truth is I chickened out."

"What is it?" she asks, her voice shaky. "Please don't tell me you're a con man like Greg and you want me to invest in something. I couldn't bear it."

"I'm not a con man like Greg. You have my word on that."

"What have you been hiding?" The worry in her eyes is clear to see, and I know I just need to come out and say it.

"I'm not Maverick Mitchell. I made the name up. I'm Ethan Roberts. I'm an actor on a Netflix show back in the States. I came here to get away from all the publicity and craziness that my life has become over the last few years, and I pretended to be someone else to get that."

She blinks at me, those kissable lips of hers forming an "o" shape. "Ethan Roberts? That's your real name?"

"It is."

"And you're an actor?"

"Yup."

She takes a step back from me. "Does that mean you've been acting this whole time?"

"No! No. I promise you. It isn't like that."

"But why did you need to pretend you were someone else with me? I have no idea who Ethan Roberts is. Well, I do now, but I wouldn't have known you when we met."

"I know it looks horrible, but I didn't know who to trust. That day we met in Tleurbonne, I was being chased by paparazzi. They had already published a picture of me having breakfast at a café in the city, so I knew they were hot on my heels. That's why I dived into the costume store that day."

She blinks at me. "That's why *I* dived into that costume shop."

"Wait, what?"

"I thought they were onto me, the princess who had escaped the palace. I thought my cover was blown and that my image would be splashed all over the media, and then my parents would realize I hadn't gone on a silent meditation retreat in India with my cousin, and I'd be wheeled back to the palace and be thrown in the metaphorical dungeon. Quite possibly the literal one, too."

"That's a lot to take in."

"Welcome to my life."

"But they were chasing me. I'm sure they were."

She pulls her lips into a hint of a smile, shrugging her shoulders. "Maybe they were after both of us."

She could be right. "Maybe. Look, I'm sorry I didn't tell you who I really was. The closer we've got the more it's played on my mind, and I've wanted to tell you."

"Me too," she admits.

I shake my head. "I can't believe we were both pretending to be other people. What are the odds?"

"Not high, I'm sure."

The atmosphere around us has shifted, and here we stand, two people exposed. Vulnerable. Sharing our truth.

"Wait. Are you telling me that you genuinely thought your family would buy that you were on a silent meditation retreat?" I ask.

"Why not? I can be silent if I want to be." Her eyes flash, and we both laugh, any lingering tension between us evaporating into the night air.

"That's why you wore your goth costume out of the store that day," I say as everything begins to fall into place. "There was no children's party."

"Why would I go dressed as a goth to a children's party?"

"You had to be scarier than a clown."

"Clowns aren't scary. At least they're not where I come from."

"You obviously haven't seen the Stephen King movie, *It*."

"Is it a romcom?"

"Horror."

"Well then clearly I haven't seen it, Mav." She catches herself. "I mean Ethan."

"I guess it's gonna take some time to get used to." I add, "Ami." I feel the shape of her name on my lips. "That's a nice name, and it's a whole lot easier for me to get my head around than Princess Amelia Astro Christine something."

"Astrid Kristiana Eugenie," she corrects.

"Hey, give a guy a break. That's a lot of names to get used to in one hit."

"You know you can just call me Ami. In private, that is. To the rest of the world, I still need to be Amy."

I like the idea of having a name for her that only I get to use.

"Ami," I repeat, looking into her eyes. I feel as though I'm really seeing her for the first time. The world around us blurs as I gaze at this stunning woman with me here on this magical beach, under the moonlight.

There's something both terrifying and freeing about this moment. Our masks are gone. With her, I'm not hiding anymore. The tension in my shoulders I've been carrying around for weeks, even months, eases. I feel a sense of peace. Of warmth.

Of acceptance.

She's gazing back at me, not as Princess Amelia, not as Amy, but just as herself—Ami, the woman who climbs trees when she thinks no one can see her breaking the rules.

"All this time, we were both hiding. And somehow—" My eyes drop briefly to her full lips before I find her gaze again, so certain about what I want. "Somehow I found you anyway."

"We found each other," she says. She swallows, her breath ragged.

I move a little closer, giving her every chance to step away if this isn't what she wants. I hesitate before I gently brush a strand of hair from her face, my fingertips grazing her skin.

She sucks in a breath and the air between us suddenly thickens.

I cup her face in my hands and lean in, my eyes not leaving hers until our lips graze, the slightest touch sending a bolt of electricity through me so strong, it leaves me breathless.

I pull back and search her face. I need a clear sign that she wants this as much as I do. That she feels this thing between us that keeps growing and growing. This thing I didn't ask for. This thing I never expected to feel.

This thing I want more than anything.

"Ami, I want you to know that you're everything I could possibly want, and so much more. We might have been pretending to be other people, but I know the essence of you, of who you are, and I'm yours if you want me. Body and soul."

The corners of her full mouth lift into a smile that lights up her whole face. "Kiss me again, Ethan Roberts," she instructs.

And it turns out, when it comes to a royal command, I am not a man who needs to be told twice.

And this time there's nothing tentative in our kiss. This time, I pull her against me, wrapping my arms around her, feeling her soft curves meld against me, breathing in her intoxicating scent. She's taking short, shallow breaths, and as I tangle my fingers up in her hair, I crash my lips against hers greedily, full of the intensity of the desire I feel for her, claiming her as mine.

She responds by tightly clasping the collar of my polo shirt, kissing me long and hard and deep, so I'm in no doubt whatsoever how much she wants me.

How much she needs me.

And the kiss? Let's just say it's better than perfect. I never want it to stop. I want to get lost in her, right here on the shore of this lake, with our fairy dust footprints and our confessions.

"As Maverick and Amy we were friends, and now that we are Ethan and Ami—"

"We're so much more than that," I finish for her.

We share a smile, and my heart feels as though it could double in size for this incredible woman in my arms, this woman who likes me and accepts me for who I am.

So what if she's really a princess, I'm an actor, and we're both escaping our regular lives? What we have is real. We're two souls who have found each other, connected in the most beautiful and pure way, with no hidden agendas, no feelings based on our positions in the world.

We're just two people, falling for one another by this perfectly magical lake of dreams.

Chapter 21

Amelia

Blissful. That's how I feel. Utterly and completely blissful.

Can you blame me? Not only am I having a wonderful adventure away from the rules of my life, but I've found myself falling for the most wonderful of men, a man who knows the real me and doesn't give two hoots about my royal birth or my social standing or any of that nonsense.

Who would have thought a random meeting in a costume shop could lead to so much happiness?

I'd always dreamt of having an exciting love affair with

a man who could elicit such passion in me it could barely be contained. And now I have such a man in the rather dashing, incredibly handsome, and awfully manly Ethan Roberts.

Talk about Sizzle with a capital "S." I'm like a steak on a grill, sizzling with feelings and desire for him.

It's more than I could ever have hoped for when I left the palace for my month of freedom. I'd hoped that Greg would live up to my expectations, but of course he ended up being a total disaster.

In a way, I'm thankful to him. If it wasn't for Greg turning out to be a conman, I would never have found my way to Ethan. And now that I have, my life has become a wonderful, romantic dream I never want to wake up from.

I still trip up every now and then and call him Mav, of course. It's only been a week since he told me who he really is. But he's definitely an Ethan. Not that I had any clue what an Ethan would look like before we met. Now that I know him, I would have to say that Ethan is quite clearly the name for a ridiculously handsome, tall, funny, smart, kind man who is a rather splendid kisser.

The *most* splendid, in fact.

Believe me, I know. We've been doing rather a lot of kissing this past week. And it's been nothing short of incredible.

In between all that kissing, we've been talking a lot, as well.

After all, we can now be completely and wholeheartedly honest with one another. No more hiding our true identities. No more Maverick and Amy. We can be who we are, fully and completely, but away from all the rules and conventions that surround our usual lives, free to learn everything there is to learn about each other.

I've shared how I was born into a position I never

asked for, and although I understand how privileged I am, I want the chance to be just me, Amelia. The woman, not just a princess.

He's shared his life as a TV star and how he hates how intrusive and facile fame is, despite loving the work. For him, fame has been an unwanted side effect of pursuing his acting dream.

There's an odd parallel to our lives. We both find ourselves in roles we never wanted, and neither of us know how to handle them so that we retain our souls.

Of course I've Googled him. More than once, as it turns out. Anyone would do the same if they found out they'd been unwittingly sharing a house with a famous Hollywood actor. The oddest thing is that I've watched his show in the past. Not a whole episode, you understand. Blood, gore, and the worst side of humanity isn't exactly my viewing preference.

Give me a good romcom any day, thank you very much.

But I've seen bits and pieces of episodes nonetheless, and I didn't recognize him. He looks so different on the show. He wears an awfully severe white-blond wig, his face covered in prosthetic scars—although he does spend quite a remarkable amount of time shirtless, considering the show is set in continual sub-zero temperatures. Still, why let a bit of snow get in the way of a jolly good view? That's what I say.

You know what beats Rowan Thornheart in all his bare-chested, long-haired glory? The real Ethan Roberts, the man whose smile sets my heart aflutter, whose kisses make my belly swoop with desire. The man who understands me, who lets me be me.

My Ethan.

Oh, I feel giddy just at the thought that he's mine.

We've barely spent a single moment apart since that evening on the lake shore, our footsteps glowing in the sand. It helps that we not only live in a house together, but we work together, too—where we share secret smiles and even steal kisses in the kitchen when no one's looking.

Not that it's stopped Pierre flirting with me the way he does, nor Giovanna turning up and flashing her pearly whites, among other assets. But neither of us pay them one iota of attention. We're too wrapped up in each other and this new, wonderful, utterly blissful thing between us.

We're sitting side by side at the lake house on the swing seat on the patio that overlooks the lake, our fingers entwined as we talk about nothing and everything. It's been a week to the day since that magical night where we admitted to one another who we really are. One week of falling deeper and deeper for this man who once dressed as a goth and stole my heart while I wasn't looking.

"Do you wanna hear a weird thing?" Ethan asks as I'm snuggled up against him, hearing the rhythmic pulse of his heart in his chest.

"Of course I do," I murmur.

"Even though I pretended to be someone else, I've been more myself around you than I have with anyone for a long, long time."

I tilt my head to look up at him. "That's not weird to me. You know why?"

"Tell me."

"Because I feel exactly the same. The first thing you knew about me was I was some random stranger in a costume shop, not that I was Princess Amelia of Ledonia. You treated me like an everyday person."

"I'll try to remember to curtsy more often around you in the future," he teases.

I giggle. "Please don't, and not only because I don't

want you to see me as a princess, but because a man your size curtsying would look really quite ludicrous."

"Hey, I met 'ludicrous' head on the day I put on that pink, frilly apron that's too small for me at Francine's."

I giggle. "I think you look adorable in that apron."

"And we all know 'adorable' is what every self-respecting guy aims for."

"In that case you nailed it, my darling Ethan."

"I think I like my real name on your lips."

"You do? What else do you like on your lips?" I tease.

He leans in and kisses me softly. "Does that answer your question?"

"It doesn't, I'm afraid. You'll need to show me again."

He lets out a laugh, and I decide his laugh is the most wonderful sound in the world and I never want him to stop laughing the way he does here at the lake. "In that case, let me show you again and again."

"And again."

He presses another kiss to my lips, and I pull him against me.

This. This is what I was searching for. A genuine connection with a man who sees me not as a member of the royal family, but as a woman. And the sizzle? It's burst through the atmosphere with a sonic boom and is currently on its way to Mars.

Ethan shifts, and I nestle back into his warm chest. "You know what's ridiculous? Last year, my agent made me attend a party where they served water from different elevations of Mount Everest. People were discussing the 'mouthfeel' of water from 20,000 feet versus 25,000 feet, whatever a 'mouthfeel' is."

"Oh, I can do better than that on the ridiculous scale. We held a state dinner for the Irish Prime Minister where we served authentic Celtic cuisine from the 10th century."

"What was it?"

"Bland porridge and tough meat. The ambassador from Ireland kept eyeing the exit."

Ethan chuckles. "Did anyone actually eat it?"

"Of course. We all did. You have to so as not to offend anyone."

"Well, at least your events serve a purpose. Last month I had to attend the premiere of a movie I wasn't even in because my agent thought the movie's 'brand presence' would help my social media metrics."

"Brand presence? Whatever is that?"

"It's some completely nonsense term for having famous people standing around pretending to care about things. I spent three hours taking selfies with people who kept calling me by my character's name."

"Oh, Rowan Thornheart," I say, throwing my hand against my chest and pretending to swoon.

But instead of laughing along, Ethan's face creases into the frown I've not seen since before we confessed our true identities to one another.

"What is it?" I ask, concerned.

"I guess it's the thought of going back to my old life. I'm contracted as Rowan Thornheart for another couple seasons. I know it won't be worth trying to break it, but—" He breaks off.

"But what?" I ask, giving his hand a squeeze.

"I don't know. That character could be so much more than some tough warlord who gets around without his shirt, you know?"

"So why don't you ask the producers for character development for him? You could give him some more depth and vulnerability rather than just him being the brooding, shirtless warrior he currently is."

"They'd never go for it."

"Do you know that for certain?"

He pauses for a beat before he replies, "No."

"Nothing ventured, nothing gained. That's what my father always says, and he's absolutely right. Imagine if you hadn't decided to get away from Hollywood and come here? We would never have met."

"You're my something ventured and something gained?" he asks, his frown lifting, his eyes soft.

I smile at him, my chest filling with warmth. "Just as you are mine."

"Maybe I will talk to them," he says. "Hey, I want to tell you something. You know how you said not many royals have carved out careers outside of royalty?"

"Other than charity work, which of course is very important. Oh, and sports. Some royals have been awfully good at sports."

"I compiled a list for you."

"A list of what?"

"It's of members of royal families across Europe in which younger brothers and sisters who don't inherit the throne have achieved something outside of being royal. Want me to read it to you?"

"I know who you're going to talk about. Prince Harry from Britain and his Invictus Games for war veterans. I've been to those games. They're jolly good. Hazza did a fine job."

"Actually, 'Hazza,' as you call him, didn't make the top ten on my list."

I pull back to look at him. "Oh?"

He holds his phone up and reads a note. "First up there's Princess Anne of Britain who was an equestrian rider. She won medals, she was that good."

"Oh, I knew about her, too."

"Did you know about the Spanish princess, Cristina,

who was an Olympic sailor? She competed and won at the 1988 Olympics."

I blink at him in surprise. "No."

He reads his screen. "What about Princess Mabel of Orange-Nassau who's a human rights activist?"

"Really? I didn't know that."

"Princess Madeleine from Sweden is a children's book author and works for the World Childhood Foundation. Prince Félix from Luxembourg runs a successful vineyard in France. Here's a good one: Prince Constantine from the Netherlands works in technology and innovation and heads up TeachLeap, which helps Dutch start-ups. Then there's Princess—"

I place my hand on his arm, my head spinning, and not just with the list of impressive achievements by members of royal families across Europe. Ethan's taken the time to research this for me, to show me that I can carve out a life for myself outside of my family. That I can be my own person.

Suddenly, my throat grows tight. "The fact you did this for me is … well, I so appreciate it," I say, my voice strangled. Tears have welled in my eyes, and I try to blink them away rapidly. "I so appreciate *you*."

"Ami, are you okay?" he asks, concern etched on his face.

"You're just so lovely doing this for me. Thank you." My voice cracks and to my embarrassment an errant tear slides down my cheek.

He pulls me closer against him, planting a kiss on my forehead. "Hey, don't cry. This is good, Ami. This shows there are so many options for you outside of charity work and all the things royals traditionally do. You have options. Lots and lots of options. You can follow your heart."

I nod, not trusting my voice to speak again.

"You don't have to be penned in. Use your position for whatever you want to do with your life."

"But my parents—"

"I'm sure your parents want what all parents want for their offspring: for you to be happy."

"You don't know my father. He can be awfully strict, not to mention the fact that we have generations upon generations of history and tradition to live up to."

"But you told me the story about how your dad was behind the whole ancient scroll adventure Sofia and Marco went on, right? A man capable of that level of intrigue and fun isn't all about the rules and duty and tradition and playing it safe."

I roll the idea around in my head. "That was a complete surprise for all of us."

"Maybe he'll support you in doing what you want?"

"Maybe," I reply, chewing on my lip. The thought of returning to the palace and my old life, to confronting my parents, asking them to support me in whatever my choices may be has my belly tying in elaborate knots.

"Do you know what you want to do?" he asks softly.

I've been thinking about this very thing, trying to work out what I can take from my time away from the palace. As magical as it's been to get to know Ethan and develop such strong feelings for him, this experience has changed me as a person, as well. I can't imagine going back to my old life and simply accepting it. I'm different now. All I wanted when I left the palace was to have an adventure, do exciting things with interesting people.

It turns out what I got instead was a deeper understanding of who I am.

"I don't quite know how it looks yet, but I think I want to do something with people. I know that's vague, but I've loved working at the café, connecting with people. I would like to do something along those lines."

"Run your own café?"

"I can't imagine my parents would go for that idea. Can you imagine? A princess running a café? They'd make sure I was surrounded in security detail as I made cappuccinos, with their grim expressions and dark glasses and weapons at the ready."

"That might destroy the laid back café vibe."

"Exactly. I can't imagine anyone would want to come to that café."

"The way I see it, you can do whatever your heart desires, Ami."

"But what if my heart desires to be with you?" I ask, my voice small, my heart hammering in my chest.

The edges of his mouth lift into a hint of a smile, his deep blue gaze intense. "Then I think we should give your heart just that," he says, brushing the hair from my forehead before he leans closer to me, our breath mingling, and brushes his lips against mine in a deeply emotional kiss. It wraps me up in its warmth and sincerity.

"I'm falling for you, Ami," he whispers against my lips. "I'm yours, body and soul. I've never felt like this before."

My breath hitches in my throat. "I'm falling for you, too," I tell him, never more certain of anything in my life.

"Just as well," he says, his eyes teasing.

"How do we manage being together when we go back to our real lives, when this Montelac bubble bursts?"

"Who says it needs to burst? We've got today, tomorrow, the next day, and the day after that, and the day after that."

Does that mean he doesn't see a future with me? Does that mean the time we're spending now is enough for him? That there's no future beyond the next few days for us?

"And besides, I'm sure I could fit in a trip to Ledonia."

My sagging heart leaps at his words. "You could?"

"Or we could meet halfway. Paris sounds good to me."

I beam at him. "I would love to visit Paris with you. And London. Oh, and Barcelona."

"And Milan and Dubrovnik and Dublin." He gives me a kiss before naming each city.

"And Brussels and Amsterdam and Prague," I add, doing the same.

"I'm going to run out of cities to name," he says with a laugh, and it's like his laugh has tentacles that can reach inside my heart and squeeze. "I want nothing more than for us to make this work, however we do that. We can face it together. We will find a way."

I wrap my arms around him. "I do, too. However we do it."

And that's the big question. How will we do it? We lead such different and demanding lives, his as a famous actor in America, and mine as a princess of Ledonia.

But as I look into his eyes, I see nothing but sincerity and truth, and I know somehow, with both of us wanting this so desperately, we will make it work.

Chapter 22

Ethan

Prepare yourselves for an intriguing development in the continuing saga of our mysteriously meditative Princess Amelia.

As you know, there has been much speculation in the press that our Amelia has not been meditating on a mountain halfway across the world and instead has escaped the palace, spotted in various locations around the continent.

And now Prince Maximilien, aka our new Prince

McGorgeousness, was spotted just yesterday departing from his Royal Air Force base in a private aircraft, destination undisclosed. The timing couldn't be more curious. Just as whispers about his sister's whereabouts grow louder and louder, our dashing prince makes a hasty exit from his military duties.

Coincidence?

This journalist thinks not.

"It's simply a personal matter," insists a palace spokesperson with that tight smile that always suggests there's more beneath the surface. *Much* more. And don't we all know by now that "personal matter" is palace speak for "situation we'd rather not discuss?"

This royal correspondent is certain Princess Amelia is the "situation." What are they hiding? I have a few theories of my own:

She's got a secret boyfriend in some exotic locale with whom she's having a torrid affair.

She's had plastic surgery that's gone horribly wrong, disfiguring herself in the process and needs to hide until it can be corrected.

She's joined a cult and will next be seen dancing in a field with heavily bearded men and women in pinafores.

Who knows! What we do know is that my inside-the-palace source tells me the King has requested twice-daily updates from the meditation retreat—a meditation retreat that forbids all communication.

Interesting.

Apparently, His Majesty has been taking, and I quote, "a shot of whiskey rather than a cup of tea before bedtime."

Well! Those familiar with our dear King Frederic know that whiskey is reserved only for matters of significant royal distress.

Princess Amelia's presence will be required at next week's annual Summer Ball along with the rest of the royal family.

I will leave you with this question. Has Max been dispatched on a royal retrieval mission, destination yet unknown?

This is one royal mystery I am determined to solve for you all. And mark my words when I say I most assuredly will.

Yours with binoculars and a notepad at the ready,

Fabiana Fontaine xx

#RoyallyDispatched
#SiblingBailout
#MaximumRoyalIntervention

My phone vibrates against the counter as I'm wiping down the espresso machine. I've developed a peculiar fondness for this routine. The methodical cleaning of coffee grounds and milk residue is somehow more satisfying than memorizing lines for a character who spends half his screen time brooding in sub-zero temperatures and the other half in compromising positions with his shirt off.

Francine's is enjoying one of those magical lulls between the morning rush and the lunch crowd, with only a few locals lounging at tables. Francine is humming the song the flash mob performed not so long ago while arranging pastries in the display case. Across the room, Pierre is pretending to inventory sugar packets while eyeing Ami with the subtlety of a flashing neon sign.

I check my phone and see a notification from Ami.

Check your messages.

I shoot her a puzzled look across the café. Why didn't she just come talk to me?

I swipe to open our text thread, and my stomach plummets faster than a badly steamed latte.

She's forwarded a message with the heading "from my brother." It reads *Arriving in Montelac in one hour. Meet me at your café. I'll be in disguise. Max xx*

Ami's brother is coming here? A prince, here in Montelac, coming here to check in on his sister—but we all know he's going to end up judging me.

Just what I need.

What's more, won't his presence compromise Ami? Sure, he said he would be in a disguise, but how do we know he won't be recognized and her cover completely blown?

But then Ami hasn't been recognized here in Montelac, not even once. Which has always struck me as weird—weird but convenient for us, that is.

Sure, she looks different from the photos I've seen of her in her princess persona, in a pair of black jeans and a T-shirt, her hair tied up in a ponytail. But she doesn't look *so* different that you wouldn't see some similarities.

Not that I'm complaining. She's been able to enjoy her anonymity here for the past three weeks, and we are both grateful for it.

Ami arrives by my side as I finish making a mocha and a latte for a couple of regulars. Her dark hair is pulled back in her characteristic ponytail that makes her look both younger and weirdly more regal. Maybe it's because I know that she is regal now—which sure is something I've had to wrap my head around since that night on the lake shore when we shared our secrets.

But you know what? It hasn't changed how I feel about her. Not at all. Sure, she was born into privilege and tradition, her life dictated by rules and expectation. She'd told me all that when she was Amy. She just left out the royal part.

None of it changes who she is as a person.

She's still the gorgeous woman I met who artfully ringed my eyes with eyeliner, the woman who made me laugh despite myself. The woman who's been right here at my side for this crazy adventure.

Don't get me wrong. I know her royal status complicates things. What kind of a future can we have with both of us leading lives in the spotlight? Both of our actions relentlessly scrutinized?

But I'm determined to find a way. The way I see it, you don't get that many chances to find your person. And when it comes to Ami, I know deep in my heart that she's my person.

"You saw the message?" she asks.

"Meet me out the back after you deliver these, 'kay?" I say, and she nods as she collects the cups and turns to walk away.

I tell Francine I'm taking a quick break and head out the kitchen door to the alleyway. A moment later, Ami arrives.

"Your brother's coming here in an hour?" I question.

She pales, her eyes widening to cartoon proportions. "Less than that now. It's a terrible, terrible idea. I tried to tell him to stay away, but he's insisted."

Anxiety pings against my skull as I pace. "The King of Malveaux is coming here?"

"No, not Alex. Max," she replies. "He's not the king of anything, and nor will he ever be."

"But he's still your brother, and having a sister myself, I

know how protective we brothers can be, and I also know what jerks guys can be."

She brushes my concern away with a flick of her wrist. "Oh, Max isn't like that."

"Ami, *every* brother is like that. Did you know he was coming to visit?"

She chews on her lip. "He threatened it a while back, but I told him not to."

I push out a breath, placing my hands on her arms. "His arrival here will… well, it has the potential to seriously mess things up for us."

The exposure of Ami's real-world identity could pop her carefully constructed Montelac bubble—and destroy mine, too.

"I know," she replies, looking up at me with those big brown eyes. "But he did say he would be in a disguise, and besides, no one has recognized me here. Perhaps the same will happen for Max?"

"Is it just me, or is that weird? You're a princess from a neighboring country that has close ties to Malveaux, right? I get that Montelac is a small, sleepy place, tucked away from the world, but not one person seems to have reacted to you, a princess, working in a café."

"Perhaps they have, and they simply don't care? Perhaps they've decided to turn a blind eye because they knew I'd run away and that I need the anonymity?"

It sounds more wishful thinking than anything, but it could be that the past few years have made me cynical.

I give her arms a squeeze. "I hope so. And I hope I pass the test with Max."

She smiles up at me. "Of course you will. With flying colors."

The door swings open and Pierre steps outside, coming to an abrupt stop when he spots us. He narrows his eyes, flicking them between Ami and me. "You two are now … lovers?" he asks in his Malveauxian accent, stretching the "r" to three times its usual length.

Busted.

I glance at Ami. She straightens her shoulders and slips her arm around my waist.

"We're together," she replies, and the pride in her voice makes my heart double in size.

We both watch for his reaction, but all he does is shrug as though it's no big deal and says, "Okay."

Considering he's made flirting with Ami a professional sport since we got here, that wasn't the reaction I was expecting.

"There's someone here to see you," he says as he checks his already perfectly styled hair.

Ami and I share a look before we dart back through the kitchen and into the café. I scan the room, my eyes landing on a solitary figure by the counter. And his disguise? Let's just say it wouldn't take a rocket scientist to work out who Max is.

Waiting with casual confidence, one arm leaning on the counter, is a man a couple inches shorter than me in a colorful Hawaiian shirt, cargo shorts with multiple bulging pockets, an "I 🖤 Lac des Rêves" hat he probably bought moments before arriving, and a bushy, obviously stuck-on, fake mustache.

That's his disguise? A mustached tourist?

That's it.

Game over.

We're done.

At least we had the originality to disguise ourselves as goths. Max's outfit makes him look like he's an extra from an Adam Sandler movie, and what's worse, he sticks out amongst the locals like a sore thumb.

"Good morning, café staff of this very pink café," he says in English in a sonorous voice, his accent matching Ami's. "My name is Chip and I'm from Arkansas in the United States of America," he says, sounding nothing like someone from Arkansas. Or the United States, for that matter. "I'm here for the Festival of Lake Lights and I wondered if I could order a pot of Malveauxian tea, since I'm a tourist here in your fine country."

Wow, this guy may as well have the words "prince in disguise" spelt out in three languages in a flashing neon sign above his head.

Ami can barely contain her grin as she replies, "Might I suggest a cup of coffee instead, Chip?" She touches my arm. "Maverick here makes a fine cup."

Max's eyes—the same brown as Ami's—slide to mine. His fake mustache twitches as he raises his (real) brows at me. "I think I would enjoy a cup of Maverick's coffee. Are you both goths?"

"We are," Amy says with pride as I make my way to Shayna. "What can I getcha … Chip?"

The name in itself must be sending everyone's warning bells into a symphony.

"I'll take a half-caf, venti, three-pump vanilla, one-pump caramel, no-foam, extra-hot, light-whip, oat latte with a caramel drizzle in a to-go cup, but double-cupped with a sleeve."

I blink at him in wonder. He what now?

"I can fix you a latte?" I offer.

His mustache puckers as his lips lift into a smile, and I bet his initial order was some kind of joke I didn't get. "A latte would be great."

As I get to work on Shayna, a sleek yellow Ferrari glistens in the light outside. It's parked with total disregard for parking rules, taking up what appears to be a space and a half directly in front of the café.

Subtlety, it seems, is not a royal trait, at least where Max is concerned.

"Can I offer you something to eat?" Francine asks with her welcoming smile. "Tourists get hungry, you know."

"Oh, I know. I've been a tourist from America in your fine country for a good few days now, and I find I'm hungry often," he replies, his eyes not leaving mine.

Yup, there it is. The anticipated brother scrutiny, only it's from a real-life prince whose car is a yellow Ferrari, who's disguised as a tourist with a false mustache that could drop off his face any moment now.

Seriously, you couldn't make this stuff up.

As Francine takes him through the various food offerings, Ami and I share a look. Her face is aglow, and I can tell she's happy to see her favorite brother—and just as bewildered and amused by his disguise as I am.

Finally, after Francine has chewed his ear off about where "Chip" has visited in Malveaux—which he answers with confidence, adding in specific details that suggest he's actually been to the places he mentions—he takes his latte and a panini to go, and announces he will be by the lake for the next hour or so, admiring the scenery.

"Your brother should have visited our costume store," I say to Ami under my breath as Max marches out of the door.

She beams at me. "I like that you call it 'our' costume shop. And he's going to adore you."

Ten minutes later, Francine suggests we both take our breaks before the lunch crowd turns up, so we head for the lake, where we find Max in all his "Chip the American tourist" garb, sitting on a bench. He stands when he sees us, and Ami rushes over to him, throwing her arms around his neck with sibling affection. "I can't believe you actually came!"

"I said I would, didn't I?" he replies, returning her hug while maintaining eye contact with me over her shoulder. It's an impressive multitasking feat to show brotherly love while simultaneously communicating *I know seventeen ways to make your disappearance look like an accident.*

Once Ami has released him from her grasp, he extends his hand to me. "You must be Maverick Mitchell, although you look a lot like Rowan Thornheart, the Winter's Curse Wielder to me."

Ami and I share a look.

"He *is* Rowan Thornheart, Max. Or rather he's Ethan Roberts, the very fine actor who plays the role. But he's pretending to be a goth called Maverick Mitchell right now," Ami explains.

Hearing my identity summarised like that tells me Max is going to be even more suspicious of me now.

Max sizes me up. "What do I call you, then?"

I wipe my suddenly clammy hand on my jeans before shaking his. "Ethan is fine, Your... um, Royal Prince."

Ami snort laughs. "I should have taken you through royal protocol, but I'm sure Max will be happy if you call him by his first name. Right, Max?"

"Yes. Max," he says, his tone confirming every one of my fears.

"Max it is," I reply.

"You're wearing eye makeup," he says.

I'm being totally scrutinized by a man in a Hawaiian shirt and a fake mustache. And that's not something I can say has happened to me before.

"It's part of the goth costume, silly," Ami says.

"I think you have some explaining to do," he says to his

sister, sounding more like a parent than a brother. "Why did you tell me his name is Maverick Mitchell?"

"It's a long story," she replies.

"I've got time. Perhaps you could start with how you didn't realize he was Ethan Roberts from the get go," he says.

"You know me. I don't go in for that sort of show," she explains. "Too much fighting and not enough loving for my appetite. Although the shirtless scenes aren't terrible," she adds with a mischievous glint.

"You've watched my show now?" I ask.

"Just a few clips on YouTube. I wanted to see what all the fuss was about. You're very good," she tells me, and I can't help but flush with pride.

"Ami prefers Hallmark Christmas movies, don't you? She once made me watch three in one night. I now know more about small-town bakeries and Christmas tree farms than any human should."

"Traitor," she says as she prods his arm.

"Hey! No violence against the American tourist, please," he says. He turns his attention to me. "So, what's this long story that's had you changing your name to something that sounds like it's from a *Top Gun* movie?"

I should be pleased that he gets the reference, but instead I feel like a bug under a microscope.

"Neither of us knew who one another was at first. We were both hiding, I guess, playing roles for anonymity's sake," I explain.

"Hiding,' Max repeats, raising an eyebrow in a way that reminds me so much of Ami it's startling. The royal DNA is strong with this one. "And now?"

I glance at Ami, who gives me an encouraging smile that somehow makes the whole bizarre situation feel manageable. "Now we're not hiding from each other anymore, and we're no longer Amy and Maverick."

Ami and I share a smile.

"We're just us, Ami and Ethan," she says.

"Wait. You were 'Amy?'" Max asks. "This gets weirder and weirder by the minute."

"I was pretending to be Amy and Ethan needed a break from the Hollywood spotlight. That's why he was pretending to be Maverick," Ami adds.

He crosses his arms and levels me with his gaze. "So, you've been lying to my sister."

"Settle down. It's not like that, Max. Can't you see? Neither of us could be fully honest in the beginning. But now things are different. We've come clean about who we really are." She turns her gaze to mine. "It's been wonderful to finally be our full selves."

"It has," I reply, my chest warm under her gaze.

"Tell me, Ethan, do you always make a habit of rooming with strange women you meet in costume shops?" Max asks, but the sting is sucked from his words as one side of his fake mustache becomes unstuck.

"Max!" Ami warns.

"It was more like—" I search for an explanation that won't sound like the plot of a romantic comedy. "I guess it was more like a series of unlikely coincidences."

"Ethan saved me from that awful con man, Greg. He's been nothing but a gentleman. Well, most of the time," she adds with a teasing smile that sends my mind to some decidedly ungentlemanly moments we've shared since we came clean about who we are and how we feel about one another, if you can count totally hot making out as "ungentlemanly."

Max raises his brows, his eyes boring into me.

"Your mustache has come unstuck," Ami says and Max

rips the rest of it from his face and I get a good look at him
—mainly because his unflinching stare is trained steadily
and uncompromisingly on me.

He has the same thick dark hair as his sister, although
his is cropped. His cheekbones are just as high as Ami's,
the shape of his mouth an almost direct replica. He has the
kind of square jaw you see on leading men in Hollywood,
combined with his obviously athletic physique and I can
see why he's regarded as Europe's most eligible bachelor.

"So, I take it you two are romantically involved now?"
he asks.

Ami slips her hand into mine, beaming at her brother.
"We are," she says simply, and I know I'm about to get the
brotherly third degree on top of already having been taken
through my paces by the guy.

"How about you and I go for a little chat, man to
man," he suggests, sticking to my anticipated script.

The phrase "man to man" has never sounded more
ominous.

But I was prepared for this. Well, as prepared as you
can be with fifteen minutes notice that the brother of the
woman you have recently become romantically involved
with is about to turn up in your life.

Here comes the royal inquisition.

Are dungeons still a thing in modern monarchies?
What about the rack?

"I figured you'd say that. Wanna take a walk?" I offer.

"Max," Ami warns, her voice taking on a tone I've
never heard before.

"Just a friendly chat,' Max assures her, though the glint
in his eye suggests his definition of "friendly" might
include interrogation techniques banned by international
treaties.

We make our way down the shoreline, ironically

heading to where his sister and I shared our first kiss only seven short days ago.

"So," he begins. "You and my sister."

I clear my throat. "Ami and I have become close."

"Close," he repeats, his expression neutral. "Is that what the kids are calling it these days? I've been training at the Royal Air Force academy, so I might be behind on the current euphemisms."

Is that his less than subtle way of telling me he has military skills he can and will use against me?

"Look, Max. I care about your sister. A lot."

"I'm sure you do. Everyone cares about Ami. She's the best."

"I know. She's an amazing woman and I'm lucky to have her in my life." I can't help the smile spreading across my face. "Look, I get it. I've got a sister, as well. You're feeling protective over her. But this thing between us may have started off on—"

"Lies?" he offers, cutting me off.

"Just one each."

"Quite a big one, wouldn't you agree?"

"We're past that now. We both gave each other the full picture about who we really are and what we're doing here in Montelac. It's brought us closer together. A lot closer. Max, I know you've just met me and all of this is a lot to take in, but what we have is real. It's not about her being a princess or me being an actor. It's about who we are when all that falls away. When we're just two people making coffee and dancing with mops in the café after closing." I smile at the memory.

He knits his brows together. "You dance with mops?"

"Just that one time," I reply, remembering the way she looked at me that night. It gave me a glimmer of hope that maybe she felt the way I did about her.

Turns out that hope became reality in the most beautiful way.

Max studies me for a moment, then does something unexpected.

He smiles. "You seem genuine, despite the twisted path that got you here."

"I am genuine. You can trust in that."

"The thing is, Ethan, I've watched my sister get her hopes up before. People tend to see the title, not the person. The tiara, not the woman wearing it."

"But that's the thing. I fell for her when I thought she was just Amy," I tell him honestly. "Finding out she's a princess was... well, it was a shock, but it didn't change how I feel about her. If anything, it made me admire her more. Here she is in this small town, living a normal life, learning to do things she's never had to do before, all with this incredible grace and humor."

He nods. "That sounds like Ami. But tell me this. What happens when this little vacation from reality ends? When you go back to Hollywood and Rowan Thornheart's catchphrases, and she returns to her royal duties?"

It's the question I've been avoiding answering myself, the one that sometimes wakes me in the middle of the night.

"The truth is, Max, I don't know. What I do know is I want to figure that out with Ami."

He nods, considering my words.

"I know you're her brother and you're worried about her. I get it. If I met some guy pretending to be someone he's not, sharing a house with my sister in a foreign country? Yeah. I'd turn up on his doorstep, demanding answers, too."

"We're protective, us brothers."

"Right? That's exactly what I told her. The thing is I

get that I haven't known your sister for that long, and for some of that time, we were pretending to be other people. The irony is that I've been more my true self with Ami than I have with anyone in a long, long time."

He sizes me up, but I can tell he's softening toward me. "You care for her."

"So much."

He nods. "I'm glad to hear it. Ami deserves someone to love her."

Love.

The moment the word leaves his mouth, I know that's what I feel for Ami.

Love.

I love her.

I'm *in* love with her.

My entire body buzzes with the realization, my face morphing into a smile.

"There's something else you should know. The palace is starting to ask questions. Father isn't buying the meditation retreat story anymore."

"I was amazed anyone would believe that in the first place, to be honest."

"You're right. It's shocking that anyone believed Ami would voluntarily stop talking for more than twenty minutes," he replies with a laugh. "There are rumors circulating in the press, too."

My stomach tightens. "What kind of rumors?"

"The usual. Secret boyfriend, hidden pregnancy, plastic surgery gone wrong," he says with a dismissive wave of his hand, just like Ami does. "Although the secret boyfriend one seems to have been right on the money."

"I guess it is."

"Some are even speculating she's joined a cult."

I can't help but laugh at that one. The absurdity breaks

through whatever tension is left between us. "A cult? Ami wants to break every rule in the rule book. She'd be a horrible cult member."

"You'd be surprised what people will believe about royals," he says with a wry smile.

"I'm not sure I would." A gesture at myself with my thumb. "Hollywood actor right here."

"Yes, I suppose that does make you uniquely qualified for understanding what it's like for us."

I glance across at Ami, waiting patiently for us on the bench. Something inside me solidifies, a certainty I didn't know I was capable of feeling.

A certainty about us.

"I know it won't be easy for her and me. Nothing worth having ever is," I say.

"That sounds a lot like a line from your show," he replies, but there's less edge to his voice now. That is until he leans forward, suddenly serious again. "Just so we're clear, if you hurt her—"

"You'll have me thrown in a dungeon?" I suggest, only half-joking.

He grins, but it doesn't reach his eyes. "Don't hurt her."

The hairs on the back of my neck tingle. "I won't. You have my word."

Clearly tired of being patient—not a characteristic that's overly developed in her—Ami trudges over the sand toward us. "Are you playing nice with my boyfriend, Max?"

Boyfriend.

It's the first time she's called me that out loud, and despite the circumstances, I can't help but smile like I've just won an award for something far more meaningful than any golden statue could.

The thing is, as I look at this beautiful woman I love, I know I want to be more than just her boyfriend. I want to be the man she shares her day with, the man who is there for the little moments as well as the big. The man she relies on, who she can trust completely.

The man who is with her through the full length of her life, loving her, cherishing her, always being there for her.

I swallow down a lump forming in my throat.

I want to be her everything. And despite the obstacles in our way, I want nothing more than to make that happen.

Chapter 23

Amelia

This just in. This royal correspondent has received reports of a yellow Ferrari being driven by a handsome young man meeting Prince Max's description in Malveaux. It was spotted in the small town of Montelac.

Coincidence? Perhaps. But we all know everyone's favorite royal bachelor has a fondness for ostentatious vehicles.

But this does beg the question, what is our prince doing in a town so far off the tourist map?

Certainly Montelac is located on a very picturesque lake where they're about to hold their annual Festival of Lake Lights. Could Max be there for the festivities?

Or, far more tantalizingly, could this be where the princess has been hiding out all along in plain sight? And now that Max has appeared, could it be that he's in town to rescue his sister from the clutches of an evil meditating kidnapper?

I don't know about you, but I have a sudden urge to take a dip in a mountain-fed lake in Malveaux.

Watch this space, fellow royal spotters.

Yours quickly packing her suitcase,

Fabiana Fontaine xx

#MaxOnAMission
#PrincessRescue
#DontChooseAYellowFerrariIfYouWantToHide

"Tell me, Max. Do you like him? As in really like him?" I ask, my heart in my throat as I wait to hear my brother's verdict.

I've had to wait a full day to hear this verdict, thanks to the fact Max took off in his ever so subtle yellow Ferrari soon after he'd had his "little chat" with Ethan on the lake shore. He said it was to put the media off, but I imagine any journalist would have easily been able to work out who the loudly dressed American tourist called Chip was.

Really, my brother could have dressed as a clown, complete with oversized shoes and a bright red nose that honks when squeezed and been less obviously disguised.

Thankfully no one seems to have cottoned on, but with Max looking as subtle as a drunk uncle at a royal wedding, I can only hope that doesn't change.

Ethan gave me the full run down on their conversation, so I know that things started out somewhat tentatively but ended on a positive note, at least as far as my brother's approval of Ethan goes.

The media speculation and our father's suspicions certainly raised alarm bells. But I'm determined not to allow anything to distract me from Ethan and what's left of our time here in Montelac, because I know that it will be over far too soon.

Our time together is precious.

Max finally turned up at the café again after the lunch rush, this time in a pair of chinos and a polo shirt—his more usual off duty outfit—appearing at the back door to the café. Luckily, I was the one to open the door, and I bundled him out into the alleyway as quickly as I could to interrogate him.

"Ethan's a good guy," he replies.

I throw myself into his arms, saying, "You like him! Oh, Max, I'm so glad."

"Steady on. You could wind a chap." He uncurls my arms from around him.

I let him go, but I'm never letting the way I feel go. It's nothing short of miraculous. I escaped the palace to have a grand adventure, hoping to find excitement with a con man, only to find something so much better, so much deeper, so much more profound with the man I met by accident in a costume shop in the capital city of Malveaux.

My Maverick. My Ethan.

And now he's won my brother's approval, which makes me feel like dancing I'm so giddy. Not that I needed Max's approval, of course, but it's nice to get it all the same.

"He seems genuine in his feelings for you."

"I know he is. Oh, Max, I've never felt like this before. It's like everything I hoped for has come true. This is exactly what I wanted when I escaped the palace."

He offers me a wry smile as he scrunches up his nose. "To work in a café that backs onto an alleyway full of rubbish bins?"

I bat him on the arm. "He really is wonderful, isn't he?"

"Us chaps don't tend to say other chaps are wonderful, but yes, I like him. Just as long as he treats you the way he says he's going to."

I roll my eyes. "You're more like Alex day by day."

He shrugs his broad shoulders. "I guess I'm growing up?"

"Don't rush it. You're two years younger than me."

He grins. "It's only twenty-two months, actually, and I am light years more mature."

I let out a giddy laugh. Quite frankly, Max could say anything today and I wouldn't care.

His features drop. "Did he tell you about the media interest and Father's suspicions?"

"Yes. Father I can handle," I say with at least a hundred percent more confidence than I feel.

"What's your plan? You're going to return when Stefania gets back from India and pretend you were there with her all along?"

I chew on my lip. The truth is I've been ruminating on how to handle my return to the palace, which is approaching at an alarmingly fast rate. Our last night here in Montelac is the Festival of Lake Lights tomorrow night. As much as I want to stay here in Ethan's and my lake of dreams bubble, I know I'll have to return to reality soon.

"I'm going to come clean with him. With both of them."

His brows ping up. "Ami, is that wise? They'll not only be infuriated that you lied to them and put yourself at risk, but now, I'll be an accessory to your crime."

"The thing is, Max, I'm not the same Amelia I was when I left the palace, and I don't just mean because I'm working in a café and wearing goth clothes and an apron every day. Being here in Montelac with Ethan has changed me in ways I think I'm only just beginning to understand. For starters, I've learned so much about all the things that normal people do in their everyday lives, things that you and I have never had to do. We've got people to wash our clothes and make our food and do everything we ask."

"Are you saying you're going to help out around the palace once you get home?" he asks, his eyes dancing. "You could scrub the marble floors, maybe hand wash the velvet curtains in the State Room."

I roll my eyes. "You make me sound like Cinderella. What I'm saying is that I appreciate what everybody does for us. Theresa does anything I ask her at any time, day or night. What an intrusion that must be on her life! Before coming here, I thought the kitchen was some magical place where food was created with some sort of chef wand and delivered to us in the dining room."

"No, you didn't."

"Well, not a wand exactly, but I had no idea what went into preparing food. When I first arrived, Ethan asked me to slice some bread, and I had absolutely no clue how to do it. I thought it involved a mallet and brute strength."

He snorts.

"I'm ashamed to say I never thought about what it would be like to be anyone other than myself, and I spent my time rebelling against the rules and the way we live our lives, never really appreciating what I've got. And I mean *really* appreciating it, not just saying 'oh, I know I'm privileged.'"

He narrows his eyes. "What are you saying exactly?"

I take a breath, trying to order my thoughts, the thoughts that have been building like a stack of bricks in my mind since arriving in this little town on the lake. "I'm saying that in pretending to be someone else, I've learned who I really am."

He blinks at me. "That's rather profound for you, Ami."

I nod. "I know it is. During this time away I've realized that I'm more than just a princess, someone in the public eye who cuts ribbons and smiles, never giving away my true feelings about anything. Someone who dreams of breaking free and becoming someone else, even just for a month. Someone for whom their greatest achievement will be making an appropriate marriage to some weak-chinned aristocrat and producing several children. I want to be just Amelia."

"What are you going to do?"

"I don't know yet. What I do know is that whatever it is I do, it will be on my terms."

The edges of his mouth lift in a smile. "I'm proud of you," he says, taking me by surprise.

"I'm proud of me, too," I say back.

"And on that note, I need to get back to the base."

"I thought you were staying for the Festival of Lake Lights?"

"That was just my cover. The media is already talking about me and my yellow Ferrari."

"Yes, thank you for that," I reply, my tone dipped in a pool of sarcasm. "Couldn't you have hired a silver hatch-back instead?"

"So not my style, Ami," he says with a wink.

"Let's hope you didn't lead them here with your bright yellow beacon."

"I think you'll be safe. You're more goth than princess these days." He pulls me into a hug. "Take care of yourself. Promise me?"

"I will. I hope you can see how happy I am. I've really landed on my feet here."

"You've landed on your sneaker-clad feet," he says looking down at my shoes.

"So much more comfortable than sensible heels paired with a twin set and pearls, even though I know that life is waiting for me."

"But on your terms."

"On my terms," I echo, warmth spreading through me.

"I'm happy for you, sis."

"Hey, Max," Ethan says, appearing in the doorway. "You leaving?"

"Yes. Great to meet you, Ethan," Max says, extending his hand.

"You, too, Your Royal ... Max."

"That's a new one," my brother says, grinning.

We say our final goodbyes and I can hear the rumble of his attention- seeking, brightly hued vehicle as he drives away.

Ethan collects me in his arms. "Are you okay?"

I smile up at him, my heart full to the brim and bursting for both the person I've become and the man who holds me so closely in his arms. "I'm more than okay," I whisper. "I've got you."

He brushes a soft kiss against my lips. "Right back atcha."

The kitchen door swings open once more. "Look at

you two lovebirds," Francine says, and we pull apart like we're guilty.

"We were just … you know," Ethan says weakly.

And this guy's a famous actor?

Francine simply smiles at us. "Amy, you will run a quick errand for me, no?"

"Of course."

"Good girl. I need lemons. You can get them at the market." She hands me some cash.

"I'd be delighted to," I reply. "See you soon, Maverick."

He shakes his head, smiling. "See ya, Amy."

I literally skip down the alleyway and out into the sun.

Life is good. No, scratch that. Life is *great*. The threat of the media discovering my whereabouts and my parents' reaction when they know I didn't go to India fades as I think about the time I've spent here with Ethan in this pretty town on the edge of a beautiful lake, and how, when I must return to the palace, I intend to never give either my newfound self or Ethan up.

As I turn onto the main street, I almost bowl someone over, clasping their arms to stop us both from toppling over. "I'm so sorry!" I gush.

"You!" a familiar voice says in Ledonian, startling me with its undertone of disgust as apples and oranges go flying.

Giovanna is scowling at me as though I'm the bad guy in her soap opera.

"Yes, me," I say lightly. "I'm so sorry, Giovanna. I wasn't concentrating. I didn't hurt you, did I?"

"You made me spill all my shopping!"

"Let me help you." I drop to the ground, collecting her fallen produce. As I offer them to her, she snaps them away, stuffing them back into her brown paper bag. "I really am sorry. Some of those pieces of fruit will be bruised. Please let me buy you some more."

She levels me with her gaze. "You would like that, wouldn't you?"

That's an odd thing to say.

I won't be deterred. Just because she's clearly in a terrible mood doesn't mean I shouldn't be kind. "I'd simply like to help. It was my fault you dropped them, so it's only fair I should pay for more."

She lifts her chin and squares her shoulders. "Do you really think you know anything about fairness?"

I open my mouth to reply but she doesn't give me a chance.

"*I'm* meant to be with him!" she spits.

So this is about Ethan. I should have guessed.

"What do you mean?" I ask, genuinely confused.

Giovanna thinks she's *meant* to be with Ethan? Is it some sort of weird actor thing? Are they all meant to date one another or something? I know that used to be the rule for royalty a hundred or so years ago, but for actors?

She throws her hands on her hips. "*I* should be kissing him, not you. I should be the one having romantic strolls along the water's edge, seeing our glowing footsteps in the sand, hearing him whisper sweet nothings in my ear. I'm perfect for him. Perfect! You were never in the plan, and yet here you are, messing everything up for me."

The plan?

And how does she know about our glowing footsteps in the sand?

Confused, I ask, "Giovanna, what are you talking about?"

She crosses her arms and glares at me, her nostrils flaring. "You were never meant to be here," she says in a menacing tone I'm certain she's used on the soap she stars in.

"I'm … sorry," I say, although I've got no clue what I'm apologizing for. But it seems to go some way to placate her, when her features suddenly drop, and her bottom lip begins to quiver.

"Giovanna, it's okay," I say, reaching for her hand. "There'll be other chances with other men for kisses and strolls and sweet nothings whispered in your ear. Look at you. You're utterly gorgeous. Men must fall over themselves to be with you."

She sniffs. "They do. Sometimes quite literally."

"See? You'll be all right. Maverick isn't the man for you, but I guarantee you'll find your person someday."

She eyes me as though she has something else to say. But all she does is nod, pulling her lips into as thin a line as she can—which isn't thin at all, and I strongly suspect significant artificial enhancement now that I'm up this close.

"Now, about the fruit," I say.

She waves her hand in the air. "I don't care about fruit."

"I would be happy to get you some more and I'm on my way to the market for Francine right now. She needs some lemons, you see."

"No. I must go. My time here is done," she declares with dramatic flair.

"Your time here?" I question, wondering whether this means she's leaving Montelac.

But all she says is, "Good luck to you, Ami."

I blink at her in disbelief.

Ami? She called me *Ami*?

She turns to walk away, and I call out, "Giovanna, wait!"

Looking back at me, she replies in Ledonian, "Look out for yourself. You never know about people."

You never know about people? What the heck does that mean?

She turns to walk away once more, and I rush after her.

"Why did you call me Ami?"

"Did I? My mistake. I meant Amy. It's my accent, you see. Ledonian." She shrugs as though that explains it.

But of course it doesn't explain it because not only am I Ledonian too, but we're literally speaking the language.

As I search her face it seems utterly implausible that she wouldn't know who I am. She's from Ledonia. She's met both me and my brother before. It might have been a couple of years ago, but surely she'd remember?

No. I'm not convinced. She knows exactly who I am.

I swallow. "Do you know who I am?" I ask tentatively.

She seems to contemplate my question for a beat before she looks up and down the street and then leans closer to me and says, "Things are not always as they seem."

Well, that doesn't answer my question in the least.

"What do you mean? Giovanna, please tell me."

"Just … watch your back, princess," she replies under her breath before she turns and walks quickly away.

I suck in air.

I was right! She knows exactly who I am!

Her words echo in my mind like a warning bell. Something isn't right. First the flash mob and roses, now Giovanna's cryptic threats. Could they be connected? Or am I just seeing a link that isn't there?

I hurry to the market, eager to get back to Ethan and the café. But no matter how much I try to dismiss Giovanna's words, I can't shake the feeling that soon our glorious little bubble of happiness at the Lac des Rêves might be about to burst.

Chapter 24

Ethan

The entire town feels alive tonight, with the townspeople milling around, listening to live music, with food trucks selling food with delicious aromas, and street performers pulling in the crowds. There's a living statue whose clothes are painted entirely in gold, a magician doing card tricks, and jugglers, juggling multiple items from oranges to balls and even knives.

That last one we steered well clear of for obvious reasons.

Tonight is the Festival of Lake Lights and Ami and I walk hand in hand through the crowds, sampling drinks and snacks, stopping to chat to locals, simply happy to be here with one another. An accordionist plays what Ami tells me are traditional Malveauxian folk tunes, that echo across the cobblestone streets, creating a unique atmosphere I've not experienced before.

We stop and have our caricatures drawn, laughing at the way he draws Ami's eyes so huge she just looks like the Disney princess I once thought she resembled, and my jaw so exaggerated I look like Joe Swanson from that cartoon, *Family Guy*.

I'm aware that this perfect time we've had together here in this town is going to be over tomorrow, and I'll have to face some hard truths. Like the fact that Ami's a princess, with royal duties and a life full of rules, who lives in a country thousands of miles from my home. That I'm an actor, committed to the next two seasons of the show, and whatever other projects Dion has scoped out for me in all his agent wisdom.

We've come so far, Ami and me. From strangers to housemates and work colleagues, to both developing feelings for one another in secret, to then admitting who we really are and deepening our connection beyond anything I've experienced before.

It sure has been a journey, but you know what? As I look at Ami, smiling and nodding her head as Francine tells her about the lanterns on the lake, the destination we've reached has made it all worthwhile.

I've not told Ami that I've fallen in love with her yet, this beautiful woman with the sparkling smile and zest for life, the princess who treats everyone with kindness and respect. Ami is one in a billion. I am so thankful we found one another, and I never want to let her go.

And tonight, for our last night in Montelac, I have a plan.

Everyone tells me the lanterns on the lake are beautiful, the perfect backdrop for showing her my heart, for whispering the truth that I've fallen in love with her, deeply and completely.

"Francine has promised to make those delicious cinnamon buns again tomorrow. We can come by and have some before we have to leave," Ami says, her eyes bright. "Isn't that right, Francine?"

"For you? Anything," she replies, smiling at Ami like an indulgent grandmother.

"I adore you, Francine. You're the best boss I've ever had, and I'm going to miss you." Ami gives her a hug.

The fact she's the *only* boss she's ever had doesn't need mentioning.

"I have so enjoyed having you at my café," she says.

"It's been a blast. Thanks for everything," I reply, giving her a hug, too.

As I place my arm around Ami's shoulders, Francine says, "Did you know tradition holds that wishes made during the festival, when the water glows bright, will come true?"

"How wonderful," Ami says before she adds quietly for my ears only, her breath tickling my neck, "I know what I'm going to wish for."

"World peace? Wait, you're not a beauty pageant contestant."

"See you later, Francine," Ami says, and we make our way over to the growing crowd.

"Tell me what you're going to wish for," I say.

"You'll have to guess."

I come to a stop and turn to face her. "How about I tell you what my wish would be instead?"

"I have a feeling we might be wishing for the same thing."

"To always be like this, just you and me at the Festival of Lake Lights, here in Montelac on the beautiful Lac des Rêves, our little sanctuary."

Her eyes are intense in the soft evening light. "Our little sanctuary," she echoes, her beautiful lips pulled into a smile that lights up her entire face.

Someone barks out a laugh nearby, pulling us back from our shared wish.

"Come on. Let's see what's caught everyone's attention," I say, leading her to the performers.

It turns out they're traditional Malveauxian folk dancers, dressed in regional costumes that make them look Germanic to me, dancing in couples. They twist and they turn, the women leaping into their partners' arms who twirl them around in death defying moves.

"They're amazing," Ami says. "So talented."

I kiss the top of her head as I stand close behind her, watching the dancers, my arms held around her waist.

This. This is what I've been missing from my life. A deep connection to another human being, honest, vulnerable, and true. No agenda. Nothing but a desire to be together, sharing the small moments in life.

I can't remember the last time I felt this happy, this complete.

They finish their dance and curtsy and bow to the applauding crowd.

"Do you want to go eat? I saw a crêpe truck back that-a-ways that smelled pretty good," I say, gesturing with my thumb over my shoulder.

"Eating street food is absolutely forbidden, you know."

"Let's break that rule in two."

She grins at me. "You are a man who speaks my language."

I take her hand and lead her through the crowd until my hand snaps free. I look back at her to see her staring at something, tensed up, her face thunder.

"What is it?" I ask.

"It's *her*," Ami replies, her face blanched white.

"Who?"

"That woman with the blonde hair and glasses over there. That's Fabiana Fontaine, the columnist who always writes about my family. She's a notorious royal gossip columnist. What is she doing here?"

I look over to see a petite woman, her blonde hair held in a ponytail, wearing a pair of glasses, speaking rapidly with a man.

"Do you think she knows I'm here?" Ami asks, her face creased with anxiety.

"If she doesn't already, I think we'd better get out of here before she does."

Ami nods rapidly. "Yes. Good thinking."

Quickly, and without looking back, we make our way to the food truck and order our crêpes: mine a traditional ham and cheese, and Ami's goat cheese and honey with walnuts.

Ami's on edge, her eyes constantly flitting around the crowd.

"Let's head down to the lake. I bet it's busy down there with people watching the lanterns. We can merge into the crowd."

"Ethan, she can't expose me. We'll be headline news, and my parents?" She sucks in a breath. "My parents will be apoplectic."

Her words hit me in the chest. Hard. I don't want what we've shared here to become public. This is our time, our space. We only have tonight, and then tomorrow this will all be over. I don't want to lose what precious time we have left.

"Let's not panic, okay? She might just be here for the festival," I say, but Ami shoots me a look that shows she doesn't believe me.

She hides behind a tree as I pay for our dinner, and then we high tail it down to the lake, not looking back.

When we reach the lake's edge, the shore is lined with people, just as I'd expected. Hundreds of lanterns are floating on the lake, like little stars, bobbing in the water. The lighting, like always in this town, is soft enough to fit the evening vibe, but bright enough so we can see one another clearly.

"I think we'll be safe here," I say, looking around.

"I hope so. I don't want that woman destroying our night."

I take her hand in mine. "I won't let her," I reply, not knowing how I'll manage it, but knowing it's important that I find a way. "I've got your back. Always."

She smiles at me, her features softening. "I know you do. And I have yours."

Some people vacate a bench seat overlooking the lake, and we claim it. Sitting side by side, our dinner in our hands, I look out at the lanterns on the lake.

"Could this spot get any more romantic?" I ask, hoping to lighten her mood.

She shifts closer to me and leans her head on my shoulder. "It's absolutely perfect. You know my sister went to a town festival in the Ledonian mountains and fell in love under the lanterns. I can see why. They're so … luminous."

"Lights that are luminous? Wow," I tease and I'm thankful to hear her laugh. "Let's eat and then head back to the house. We'll be safer there."

"Good plan." She lifts her crêpe to her nose and breathes in the aroma. "I think this is the best smell in the world. Well, other than you, that is."

"I beat out crêpes in the smell stakes? *Winning*," I reply, and win a smile from Ami.

"I missed your smile for a moment there."

We both unwrap our crêpes, biting into the soft, buttery treat.

"This is easily the best thing I've eaten in my life," Ami says around her mouthful.

I let out a soft laugh, filled with the most incredible sense that this woman at my side, her mouth full of crêpe, is my person.

"What? Have I got something on my face?" She lifts her hand to her cheek, and I gently wrap my fingers around her wrist and place it against my chest.

"I can feel your heartbeat."

My heart is thudding with the certainty of the way I feel. I look into her eyes and say, "I know we've only known each other for a handful of weeks," I begin.

"Four. It's been four," she says.

"Four weeks. It's not long, but it's long enough for me to know that the time I've spent with you has been the best of my life, and I don't want this to end."

Her gaze is intense as she looks back at me. "I don't want it to end, either," she says, her voice breathless.

"I love you, Ami," I tell her, my heart beating like a drum, swept up in the moment. Swept up in *her*. "Body and soul, I'm yours."

Her lips curve into a smile, her eyes glistening. "I love you, too, Ethan," she breathes, and before you can say "forgotten crêpe," we've closed what distance there was between us, and become wrapped up in the most emotional and heartfelt kiss.

"I love you with all my heart, and I want us to stay together when all of this goes away, when we're back in our regular lives. I want it so, so much. More than I've ever wanted anything."

"I want that more than anything, too," I say. I pull back from her and look her square in the eyes. "Let's make it happen. No matter what. You and me."

She lets out a gurgling laugh as her tears make tracks down her face. "You and me."

I pull her against me and kiss her once more, my heart so full of love for this incredible woman in my arms, it could explode, right here on the shores of the Lake of Dreams.

"I'm so glad I walked into that costume store," I tell her, and I can feel her soft laugh reverberating in my chest.

"You're not the most convincing of goths, you know."

"Hey, I'm an actor. I take professional offence at that."

There's a sudden high-pitched squeal that takes us by surprise, just like the night we walked along the shore, our footsteps glowing behind us.

"There's that noise again!" Ami yells over the screeching.

Then, as suddenly as it began, it stops.

Ami snuggles against me. "It must be the bugs again."

I hold her, my mind racing. The sound is familiar not because we've heard it by the lake before, but because it's a noise I've heard on set.

Audio feedback.

But that's crazy. Why would there be audio feedback here in Montelac? We're not on set. We're outside on the edge of a picturesque lake with the entire town gathered for the festival.

But there are other things I've noticed, things that add up to… I don't quite know what.

"Ami?" I ask softly. "Have you noticed anything … weird about this town?"

"Like what?"

"I don't know. Like how the lighting is always perfect wherever we go. How people part so we can walk through. That flash mob that performed just for us, like they knew we would walk through the square at that exact moment."

"People are just nice here, and maybe a little eccentric. That's all." She pushes herself up to look at me. "What's with the sudden paranoia? Is it because I saw Fabiana Fontaine here? Has she put you on edge, too?"

"I don't know where it comes from. I guess it's just this feeling in my gut that things aren't quite right here. It's like they're almost too perfect, you know?"

"We're not in some spy movie," she says as she reaches up to kiss me. "It's perfect because this is a beautiful place, the place we fell in love."

I let out a breath, my shoulders relaxing. "You're probably right. I'm adding two plus two and getting paranoia."

"I know exactly how to fix that." She pulls me into another kiss, the kind where I could forget my own name.

Pulling back, I grin at her. "That did the trick."

"I thought it might," she replies with a smile.

Something captures my attention over her shoulder. "Is that bush moving?"

She swings around to look. "I think you're seeing things, Ethan."

But my curiosity gets the better of me. "I'm gonna go check it out," I say, rising to my feet and striding over to the bush. Something catches the light, and I reach in, my hand landing on something warm that doesn't feel as though it belongs in nature.

"What is it?" Ami asks, arriving at my side as I clasp the smooth surface and give it a yank.

I pull on the object and it pops out of the bush, a red light flashing. There are dark cables connecting it to something, I don't know what, and immediately my heart begins to thud.

"It looks like a camera," I say. I turn to look at the bench we only just vacated. "Someone was filming us," I say, hardly believing my words.

"Why would they do that?" Ami asks, her voice breathless with anxiety. "Could it just be a security camera?"

I don't reply. I'm too busy rolling through the possibilities in my mind.

A camera hidden in a bush.

That shrieking audio feedback sound we've heard more than once.

The lighting that creates the perfect ambience but is always bright enough that we can see one another's faces.

The fact that this place is always picture-perfect, like a TV set.

A TV set.

My actor's instincts recognize the setup.

My belly ties in knots.

I swing my attention around, noticing for the first time that people have stopped watching the lanterns bobbing on the lake, and are instead watching us.

"What's going on here?" I demand. "This is a camera!" I hold the offending item up as evidence.

"Ethan, who are you yelling at?" Ami asks.

It's then that I notice a figure dressed all in black, half obscured by one of the tree trunks that line the promenade. The person sees me looking and immediately darts behind the tree.

I dash over and manage to grab the person's arm.

"Hey, let go of me!" the guy yells, his eyes wild.

"You're American?" I ask.

"Canadian, but whatever," he replies.

"What are you doing here?" I demand and the guy's panicked gaze immediately flicks toward the crowd.

I follow his line of sight to see the woman Ami was so thrown by back in the town square. Fabiana Fontaine, the columnist Fabiana Fontaine. She's standing beside a middle-aged man, also dressed in black, whose eyes are trained directly on me.

And then it all clicks into place

"Why are you doing this?" I ask in shock.

His face blanches. "Don't ask me. I just work here."

"Who should I ask then?"

"Him." He gestures toward the middle-aged man next to Fabiana Fontaine.

"Ethan? What's going on?" Ami asks, appearing at my side, her voice strangled with fear.

I stalk toward Fabiana and the man, my jaw set, my belly clenched. "Why are you filming us?" I demand.

I don't know whether it's the man or the columnist looking for dirt on Amelia, but whoever it is and whatever their motivation, I'm determined to find out—and make them pay.

The man in black crosses his arms, glaring. "You're fired," he calls out, and I swing around to see the guy I was just talking with scuttle away.

It's then I notice things I hadn't given a second thought to. Things that don't fit. Bushes that look out of place, doubtlessly concealing camera equipment. Streetlights that illuminate their paths to studio level perfection. I look up to see a boom, held in place by wires overhead.

How could I not have noticed? Now that I see it, it's everywhere, screaming at me that this isn't just a town where the people are unusually hospitable, where flash mobs occur for no reason, and people offer roses like they're on a reality TV show.

Wait.

A reality TV show?

The world tilts on its axis.

"You *are* filming us," I accuse, aghast, my words barely audible over the frenetic drumming of my heart, like thunder in my chest.

I'm Truman Burbank, living in the *Truman Show*, an unwitting participant in the record of the past month of my life.

I dart my accusatory gaze between the man in black and the columnist for my answer.

"You've been even better than we'd hoped," the middle-aged man says in English, his accent American.

It's like the air has been sucked from my lungs as my brain crackles with electricity, trying to make sense of what's been going on.

I look back to see a frightened Ami, watching on.

"Why can't you just leave her alone? All she wants is some time to herself away from people like you." I glare at them both.

The man's face lights up. "Oh, you think this is all about your little princess girlfriend?"

"How dare you demean her like that!" I spit, outrage tensing every muscle in my body.

"It's all been about you, Ethan. The princess was just an unexpected added extra."

His words shatter like glass around me.

It's all been about … *me?*

My mind scrambles.

Me "accidentally" choosing Malveaux on Chelsea's map.

Chelsea's suggestion to stay at her "friend's" lake

house, a friend who turned out to be my slippery agent, Dion.

Ami and I getting the first job we applied for, without having to produce a CV or prove our skills, both of us thinking we were disguised in our goth costumes.

The old bookshop where the proprietor tried to match-make us over tea.

The flash mob, the townspeople's dance moves so perfectly synchronized as they danced for our entertainment.

The roses we were given at the end of it by Giovanna the actress and Pierre, the smooth guy who looks like he should be in an aftershave ad.

The town, like a European Hallmark movie set.

And then my heart seems to stop altogether.

Ami.

Ami.

Is she part of this? Was she pretending all along? The so-called Dutch tourist who just happened to be in that costume store that day and then turned up on my train.

The bored princess who wanted to escape her life and break all the rules.

Could she have been pretending all along?

My mind whirring, I'm pulled back to the present as the man passes me a phone. Out of instinct, I take it, lifting it to my ear.

"Ethan! Dion," the disembodied voice says at the other end. "This thing has been better than we even *dreamed*. You, falling in love with a princess? It's gold! Gold!"

"W-what?" I ask, dumbfounded, barely able to speak.

"I told you to leave everything to me, but you? Man, you hit it out of the park! This thing is gonna go viral. You're made, my friend. Made!"

His words come into sharp focus. "You? You're behind this?"

"Of course I am. Don't forget you gave me free reign. Ha! That was a royal pun. Do you get it?"

He's making jokes now?

I fight to get my pulse under control. "Let me get this straight. You set up a reality TV show to follow my every move while I was on a break from work, a break you agreed I needed to take, and now you're happy that you think this is going to go viral?"

"You're welcome," he replies with his smarmy, superior voice. "Just think of the money, the exposure! The fact you didn't know about it? Heck, you'll forget that soon enough."

My anger boils over as I clutch the phone to my ear, my entire body tense. "Dion? You're fired." Without listening to his response, I throw the phone at the man, who catches it, a self-satisfied smirk on his face.

"You'll thank us one day," he has the gall to tell me.

"Thank you? I think you mean *sue you*," I spit, my anger clutching at my chest, forcing my breath to shallow.

"Why are you here, Fabiana? Is Ethan right? You've been filming us?" Ami asks, her voice trembling.

Fabiana Fontaine lifts her hands in surrender. "I had nothing to do with this, Your Royal Highness. I promise you that."

"How could I ever believe you? You're always looking for a story about my family, but I didn't know you would stoop so low as to do this!" Ami says, her eyes wide with shock.

But I'm not thinking about Fabiana Fontaine and her alleged underhand tactics.

No. I'm too horrified that this crew has been capturing

our movements, cataloguing our intimate moments, captured for nothing more than entertainment.

My life, laid bare for all to see.

With my breath ragged I force myself to ask the question that's burning through my brain. The question I don't even want to know the answer to.

"Are you a part of this?" I ask Ami, my heart beating so hard it could shatter my ribs.

She turns her gaze to mine, her eyes wide, a look of utter bewilderment on her face. "I could ask you the same question."

"What?"

"You're the actor. How do I know you didn't get me to come here under false pretenses to be part of this—" she gestures around at the crowd, everyone gawking at us, any pretense that this is a town festival now gone. "This fiasco?!"

It's like all the hubbub around us, all the people watching us, Fabiana Fontaine and the producer and the cameraman and people in black managing lighting and booms. All of it merges into the background, blurred so there's only me and Ami.

"Think about it. Why would I do something like that? I came here to get away from all of this," I ask.

"I don't know. I just don't know," she replies, her voice strangled and small as tears pool in her eyes.

And then Max arrives, pulling Amelia away, and the ensuing shouting and flashes and noise meld into a disorienting blur.

And I'm left standing alone, my mind spinning in a thousand different directions, trying to make sense of it all.

Everything I thought was real—this town, our connection, our love—suddenly feels manufactured.

Was any of it authentic?

Or were we both just pawns in someone else's game?

I search the dispersing crowd for Ami's face, but she's gone, swept away back to her real life, just as I'm being pulled back to mine.

The realization hits me like ice water.

I don't know who to trust anymore.

Not my agent.

Not this town.

Not the woman I just told I loved.

And maybe, worst of all, I can't even trust my own feelings, my own judgment. Because if I could fall for something this orchestrated, this fake, what does that say about everything I thought was true?

Chapter 25

Amelia

Well, what a to do! Your royal correspondent is positively *pulsating* with exclusive news that will make your royal-watching hearts soar.

Princess Amelia has finally returned to the palace after her mysterious absence, just in time for tonight's Summer Ball.

After my bombshell revelation about Prince Max's suspicious yellow Ferrari sighting (you're welcome, readers), Princess Amelia was spotted in tears being escorted from a town festival by none other than her Brother in Shining Armor, looking decidedly *un*-festive.

Even more scandalous? She was dressed all in black, making her look more like a goth at a funeral than a happy festival goer.

And yet more scandalous? The tall, handsome man dressed as a goth she was seen canoodling with has been identified as none other than Ethan Roberts, star of the American fantasy series, *It Came One Winter*.

Be still my beating heart.

Talk about a royal-Hollywood liaison that would utterly tantalize even the most cynical among us.

What will happen now that the two alleged lovers have been forcibly separated?

Will King Frederic ban all Netflix subscriptions at the palace in retaliation?

And will our Amelia ever get all that dreadful goth eyeliner off?

Stay tuned, my devoted readers. Answers will follow as soon as this royal correspondent uncovers them.

Fanning herself with Summer Ball invitations,

Fabiana Fontaine xx

#MadMaxOnAMission
#PrincessReturned
#GrabTheMakeupRemover

I haven't slept. I've barely eaten. My mind is a battlefield, two sides fighting it out, both determined they're in the right.

The last eighteen hours have been a blur.

Max arriving at the lake, whisking me away.

His insistence that I do not return to the lake house, leaving my belongings behind.

The short flight on the royal jet back to Villadorata.

The way the palace feels both familiar and suddenly alien.

The realization that I may be back where it all began but I can never go back to the person I was before.

And now, being in the family drawing room with Max, Sofia, and my parents, all watching me with concern in their eyes.

Memories of last night fill my mind. Ethan and I together, enjoying the festival, sharing crêpes by the lake. Ethan telling me he loves me. Me telling him I love him back.

Ethan.

I look down at my hands in my lap. Gone are my Montelac clothes: my goth outfit and comfortable shoes. Instead, I'm in my "off duty royal" outfit, the clothes acting like a straitjacket.

"We are so grateful that you were there, Max, but the fact you had gone to visit your sister without telling us?" Father replies.

"I know. I should have told you. But I thought I was doing the right thing by Ami. She asked me not to say anything to you, and I was respecting that because I understand why she wanted to escape for a while. The moment I learned Fabiana Fontaine was at the festival, I headed back as soon as I could. That woman has a lot to answer for."

"But don't either of you see? This entire thing was utterly foolhardy. You could have been hurt. Or worse." Mummy's voice cracks as she speaks, her hand flying to her mouth.

Max bows his head. "I know. It was irresponsible and I apologize."

Mummy purses her lips and nods, and I can tell she's only just holding back a flood of emotion.

"It's a good job we knew where you were all along, Amelia, even if we didn't know about the filming," Father says.

My jaw drops. "How did you know where I was?"

"You might have invested in a 'burner phone,' as they call it, but we had palace security following you when you spent a day in Tleurbonne, and then on the train to the coast. We had to scramble when we saw that you took a helicopter of all things to Montelac, but we followed you there, too."

My heart sinks to my toes. "So I never really escaped."

"As I said to Sofia when she left the palace herself, you are a member of our family and you are important. You need protection, whether you like it or not."

I lift my eyes to Sofia's and see concern etched on her face. "I've been so worried about you, Ami."

I want to yell that I didn't need their protection, that I could look after myself, but I know that Ethan stepped in to save me more than once. If he hadn't been there? I don't even want to think of what might have happened.

"You're both grown-ups. We understand you're not children anymore. But you need to accept that you're not normal people, either. You are royalty, and with that comes a different set of rules," Father says, his tone harsh.

"I know. I won't do such a thing again. You have my word, Father," Max replies.

Father turns his attention to me. "Amelia? What do you have to say for yourself?"

I take a breath and lift my eyes to his. Swallowing, I prepare to recite the words I've practiced in my mind. "I know what I did was both inexcusable and foolish. I deceived you in pretending I was going to India with Stefania. She had no idea of my plans. The only person I told was Max, and I only told him because I thought I needed a safeguard in case anything went wrong."

"Which it did," Father says, his features pinched.

"It did," I confirm, my heart aching. "I know I did wrong, and I accept full responsibility for my deception. I'm prepared to face whatever consequences you deem appropriate."

The room falls into silence, and I return my attention to the clasped hands in my lap, my heart sinking like a heavy brick, settling in my belly.

"You do remember that I left the palace myself and no harm was done," Sofia says, coming to my defense.

"You needed to be pointed in the right direction, darling," Mummy says. "You were planning on marrying a man you didn't love. We needed to help you see what true love was."

"But can't you see this might be the same thing for Ami?" She turns to me. "Because you love him, don't you?"

I nod, my throat tight. Because I do love Ethan. I know we had a moment of doubt during the chaos at the festival, but that's all it was. A moment. I love him and I trust him. Wholeheartedly.

"Why did you do it? Why did you leave?" Mummy asks, her voice small.

"Because I wanted to experience life beyond the confines of the palace walls, beyond all the rules that go with being me. I wanted to live, *really* live." I take a breath. "I know you won't understand, but I knew I couldn't do what I wanted to do as Princess Amelia. I needed to escape my everyday life, so I could have that experience. I got to do things I never would have done, experienced life as a regular person, extracted the joy out of little things."

My heart aches as I picture Ethan in his pink Francine's apron, his smile lighting up his face, the deep pools of his eyes sparkling—with love.

Love for *me*.

I escaped my life and fell deeply in love with the worthiest of men.

A man who, the last time I saw him, questioned whether I had betrayed him.

Pain twists in my belly.

I look down, my shoulders slumped, defeated. "I know you won't understand."

"And what of this Ethan Roberts?" Father questions. "An actor who had cameras recording your every move. When we learned about that—"

"Don't blame Ethan!" I say with gusto. "I know he had nothing to do with the filming. He was just as shocked as I was with what we discovered. And besides, he helped me more than once, starting on that first day when he saved me from the con man."

Mummy sucks in air as Father harrumphs.

"It's not exactly reassuring that you willingly went to a house with a strange man who rescued you from a *con man*, Amelia," he scolds.

"You weren't there. You don't know. Ethan is the kindest, most genuine—"

"Most duplicitous man you have ever had the misfortune to meet! A man who double crossed you to take advantage of your status as a princess to make a quick buck," Father spits.

"No! He would never do that. It was Fabiana Fontaine and ... and ... some other people," I insist, not having any clue who the other people might be but knowing, as I know myself, that Ethan would never do anything to hurt me, let alone exploit me for notoriety or financial gain. "Ethan made me feel like he saw me, *really* saw me. Not as Princess Amelia. Not as a member of the royal family. But just as *me*." I press my hand to my heart, looking imploringly at my parents.

There was truth in all of it. I know there was.

Father paces the room and comes to a stop in front of me. "We didn't realize how unhappy you were, Amelia," he says in a tone so much softer than I was expecting that it brings tears to my eyes, my throat tight.

"I was unhappy, but this time away has shown me that I'm capable of so much more than just cutting ribbons and being a figurehead of charities. I can do more. I can *be* more, and with your help, I'd like the chance to show you and the country who I really am."

My parents share a look.

"I think we understand, darling. It's not easy being a member of this family," Mummy says.

I press my lips together, holding back my tears at the unexpected understanding.

Father says, "Let us bring more meaning and purpose to your role. We can make adjustments to your royal duties. We can find you more substantive charitable work, something you can be passionate about."

Astonished, I reply. "I ... I have some ideas of my own."

I'd expected punishment, to be well and truly told off, and deservedly so. Not this. Not *understanding*.

Mummy moves to sit next to me, wrapping her arm around my shoulder. "We love you, darling. We want the best for you."

Her touch opens the floodgates, the tears I've been

holding back for so long now falling freely down my cheeks.

"Oh, Ami," Sofia says, coming to sit on my other side and taking my hand in hers. "It will all be okay. You'll see," she soothes.

"As members of the royal family, we all share responsibilities," Father says. "We will do what we can to accommodate your wishes, Amelia, on one condition."

I know what his condition will be before the words even leave his mouth.

My already sunken heart sinks further, hitting the floor with a thud.

"As long as you have nothing further to do with that actor," he says.

"But Father," I begin only for him to cut me off.

"That man participated in filming you without your consent. He exploited your position, Amelia. If we had known about it, we would have pulled you out of that town immediately. I cannot countenance you having any contact with him whatsoever from this day forward."

I rise to my feet and take a breath, resolved, empowered by my new sense of self-worth, my new sense of who I am as a human being. "Ethan loves me, and I love him. That I know is true."

"You cannot see him," Father says, his nostrils flared.

I clench my hands at my sides.

I am Princess Amelia. I am a strong woman in charge of my own destiny. I may be part of this family, I may have a royal duty, but that will not stop me from being the person I've become.

I don't care if Father forbids me to see Ethan again. I've never been one to do as I was told. Not without a fight, anyway.

And I'm not going to start now.

How many times in your life do you get to feel the kind of love Ethan and I share?

I'm not going to allow it to slip through my fingers.

"I can't accept that, Father. Ethan has taught me what love is. He's taught me that if you love someone, *truly* love someone, you let them be who they are. You support them in whoever it is they choose to be. I've been put in a box, labelled as a princess since the day I was born. And I thought that was my destiny and there was nothing in my power to change it. Ethan helped me see that I can be more than just that label. I can be *me*."

"You can be you without that actor," he replies.

According to my father, Ethan is the villain of my story, and there's no changing his mind.

"Ethan seemed to me like he had Ami's best interests at heart, Father. I saw him arguing with that Fontaine woman and the producer. He was as blindsided as Ami was," Max says.

I throw him a grateful smile.

"Ami might be impetuous at times and loves to break the rules, but it seems to me she's fallen in love with this man, and he reciprocates that love," Sofia says.

Both my siblings' support falls on deaf ears.

"We will support you in a new role, Amelia, but that's where it ends," Father says. "Now, we must all prepare for tonight's ball."

I look into his eyes and see his commitment to his words. "In that case, Father, you leave me no choice. I know Ethan is true and that he had nothing to do with the filming. I love him and he loves me. If you can't accept that, then I will be forced to pack my bags and leave to find him."

"Amelia!" Mummy exclaims.

"I will attend the ball tonight, but after that, I will go," I say, the reality of my words hitting me with brute force.

I'll be leaving my family, my home, my life.

But I'll be leaving it to find the man I love, the man my parents misguidedly see as the villain in my story. The man I know is true.

Ethan is not the villain. He's the hero.

"But darling, what if you're wrong? What if he was involved in filming you? What then?" Mummy asks.

I shake my head, confidence in who Ethan is hardening my resolve. "He won't be. You'll see."

Father studies me for a beat. "Don't leave. We'll invite him here to the palace. We can meet with him and he can explain himself."

The tension I've been carrying around with me since last night at the lake lifts, my heart filling with hope. "Then you'll see that he's not the man you think he is. You'll see that he's a good man, the *best* man, and I cannot believe my luck that he's fallen in love with me."

Father frowns, his lips pulled into a thin line. "We'll see about that."

I lift my chin and smile at him. "Yes, Father, we will."

A COUPLE OF HOURS LATER, I make my way to the ballroom in my red satin gown that sweeps the floor, silver embroidery like feathers climbing up toward the fitted bodice that hugs my waist, emphasizing the fullness of the skirt. My hair is swept up, and on top of my head sits a sparkling tiara, my face fully made-up, my lips glossy red.

Anyone would feel regal in this dress. Powerful. Beautiful.

I'm announced and join the ball, smiling and greeting our guests like I've been trained to do all my life.

"Good evening, your Royal Highness," a man says as he bows before me. Looking up, I recognize him as Victor, the Duke of Carmania, a man I have suffered through several balls with, and a man who loves to drone on and on about his horses.

"Hello, Victor," I say with a fake smile.

"I must say it's jolly good to have you back in the fold where you belong. A fine filly like you shouldn't be let loose to roam the countryside."

"Thank you," I reply, ignoring the fact he just referred to me as a horse.

"I heard you were working at a café of all places, serving people drinks and food. Surely that's not true? A princess serving others? It's unconscionable."

I think of Francine's and how happy I was there, waiting tables and folding napkins and dancing with mops with Ethan at my side.

I lift my chin and reply, "That's right. I did work at a café, Victor."

He gives a derisive snort, his top lip curling in judgement. "Wasn't that a little beneath you? You're a princess, not a common worker."

I picture Francine's with its extreme amount of pink, like a big fluffy marshmallow. I picture the people I worked with, Francine and Pierre, the regulars that came in, always with a smile and a happy hello.

But mostly I picture Ethan, in his goth costume with a pink, frilly apron tied around his waist. How he knew how to use that espresso machine. How he took to being a barista so easily even though he had found fame as an actor. He didn't think working in a café was beneath him. Not for one minute.

"Actually, Victor, working in that café was the most rewarding thing I've done in my entire life."

He blinks at me as though I've just told him that I am in fact an alien and I'm now going to suck his brains through a straw.

"And before you ask about Ethan Roberts—which I know you will, because everybody is talking about him and me and this town we lived in—I want you to know that he had nothing to do with the filming, and that he's the best man I have ever, ever known."

He opens his mouth to reply when there's a sudden commotion and whispers ripple through the crowd.

"What's going on?" Victor asks, clearly unimpressed.

And then the guests part and my heart stops as I look across the room. Standing in the doorway, inexplicably here at the palace, at this ball, is Ethan.

My Ethan.

Our eyes lock across the crowded room and everything else fades away.

He came for me. Ethan came for *me.*

My eyes slide over him as he takes his long-legged stride across the room, aiming for me. He's wearing a black dinner suit with a white shirt, the standard uniform of men at these events, but on him it looks beyond debonair, a handsome vision in formal attire.

When he comes to a stop, his eyes are focused solely on me with such intensity it feels like my heart has stopped.

"You're here," I breathe.

"I couldn't stay away."

He came for me.

"How- how did you get in?" I ask, knowing these are invitation-only, exclusive events, and there's no way Father would have allowed Ethan on the list.

"Max," he replies simply. "Ami," he says and there is

such a depth of emotion in the way he utters my name that all I want to do is throw myself into his arms and tell him I love him again and again and again, never letting go.

Instead, with my heart beating like a drum, I simply stare at him.

"I had to come back for you. I love you," he says.

"I love you, too, and I'm sorry I let even the tiniest amount of doubt creep in. I trust you and I love you and everything between us has been true. Everything. I promise you that."

"I'm sorry, too. I accused you of something you're totally innocent of and I've been kicking myself ever since because I let you go."

"Amelia!" Father's voice cuts through our moment, his face is like thunder, his anger barely contained.

Max appears at his side, his eyes darting between Ethan and me.

"Your Majesty, Your Royal Highness," Ethan says as he bows. "Please forgive the intrusion."

Someone has learnt his royal protocol since I last saw him.

"I'll do more than forgive it. I'll have you thrown out!" Father exclaims, and if they weren't watching us before, every person stops and stares to see what will happen when the actor meets the King.

Chapter 26

Ethan

"Sir, please hear me out. Then I will leave, if that's what you want," I say, nerves jangling in my stomach.

I can feel Ami's father's cold fury, filling the palace, but he surprises me by agreeing with a short nod of his head.

A quiet hush falls across the room.

"The first thing I want you to know, sir, is that I love your daughter with all my heart." I shift my gaze briefly to Ami, to see her watching me closely, her eyes bright, her face lit up in her beautiful smile.

The moment I saw her across the room she took my breath away. She's always beautiful, no matter whether she's in one of her goth outfits, hugging the branch of a tree she can't get down from, or wearing her Francine's apron, surrounded with all things pink.

But tonight? Tonight she looks like the princess she is, almost intimidatingly beautiful, the red of her dress telling the world that she's of royal Ledonian birth.

Yeah, I did my homework. I figured it would be handy armor tonight.

"The time we spent together in Montelac has been the best time of my life because of your daughter. I went there to escape, to take a break from my life. I thought I would spend my time contemplating my choices. Instead, I spent it working in a café with your daughter, teaching her how to operate an espresso machine and slice bread."

There's a rumble of surprise in the room and I'm sure some of the assembled guests are shocked to learn that the rumor is true: Princess Amelia did work in a café. Shock! Horror!

"It's also true that when we first met, I pretended I was someone else."

This time the rumble is louder, people in shock that I lied to their princess.

A woman bearing a striking resemblance to Ami appears at the King's side, and I can only assume she's the Queen.

I swallow, my mouth dry. "I did so because I was running from my own fame, not for any other reason. I'd had enough of being Ethan Roberts, famous TV star. I wanted to be anonymous once more, like I was before fame found me. But what I didn't bank on was falling for Ami, and then I knew I had to tell her who I really was.

"It was at that point, once we shared our true identities,

that we really let one another in, and I fell hard, and I fell fast." I turn to look at Amelia. "I fell harder than I've ever fallen for anyone in my life."

She smiles at me, that beautiful smile that lights up her whole face, the smile I've missed since like a part of me is gone. The smile I know I want to see every single day of my life.

"Sir, I was able to be my authentic self with your daughter in a way I haven't been in a very long time. She may be a princess, but she's as real as anyone can get. Real and funny and kind and clever and full of the joys of life. In the short time I've known her, I have grown to not only love her, but admire her, too. Sir, your daughter is nothing short of incredible."

The people around us burst into chatter, silenced only when the King lifts a hand.

"And what of the filming? My sources tell me it's a reality television production," he asks, spitting out the words as though their taste is bitter.

I reach into the top pocket of my rented tux jacket and pull out a folded document. Passing it to the King, I say, "This is a document drafted by my lawyer this morning. I am suing the production company and my agent for filming me and your daughter without our consent."

The King's eyes scan the paper briefly before he lifts them once more to mine. "You didn't know about this?"

"I swear on my life that I did not, sir."

The room erupts into chatter once more, and instinctively Ami and I move closer to one another. She slips her hand into mine, and I relish the softness of her skin. As our gazes meet, we communicate our love for one another without the need for words. We simply stand, looking into one another's eyes as the room swirls around us.

Ami takes a deep breath, and I nod at her, knowing she wants to say her piece.

"Father," she begins. "I know you have forbidden me to see Ethan again. But I'm a grown woman with choices of my own. I choose Ethan."

My heart swells to twice its size, as the room bursts into loud chatter. Thanks to my lawyers, it's unlikely they'll get our reality show, but they sure are getting a show tonight.

The King calls for quiet by lifting a single hand once more.

"Mr. Roberts. I cannot accept the way with which you met my daughter, nor the way in which your relationship developed in secrecy regardless of this lawsuit."

Amelia's hand tightens in mine.

A figure catches my eye, and I see Max shift to our side. He's followed in silence by what I can only assume are other members of Ami's family: her sister, Sofia, who I recognize by the way she holds herself; her husband, Marco, a guy who looks as out of place in the opulence of the ballroom as I feel; her older brother, Alex, who shares Max's good looks but with a maturity in his features Max has yet to grow into; and his wife, Maddie, the Queen of the country where I just spent the last month of my life, who throws me a wink and a smile as she stands beside Ami, giving her arm a squeeze.

The King's eyes widen as he takes in the scene. All his offspring and their spouses, standing shoulder-to-shoulder with Ami.

"Father, you sent Marco and I on a wild goose chase to give us every chance to fall in love. Can't you accept that Amelia is doing this on her own terms as well?" Sofia says.

The King glares at her as the Queen whispers something in his ear.

He clears his throat. "Tell me something, Mr. Roberts. What are your intentions towards my daughter?"

That old line?

I've got this.

"To love her and respect her as the woman she is. To let her be whoever she wants to be, and to support her in that." I smile at Ami.

"That's all very well, but do you intend to make her your wife?" he asks.

His words hit me in the solar plexus.

I swallow as I square my shoulders. "With your permission, yes," I reply.

People gasp while others cheer and shout their approval. A man who looks a lot like a weasel scoffs and walks away.

But I'm not paying attention to any of them. Instead, I'm looking at the woman I love, seeing the emotion written across her face.

"Really?" she breathes.

"Really," I reply, never having been more certain of anything in my life.

We share a smile.

"Do you understand what it means to be a part of this family? Amelia is a princess. She has certain royal duties and expectations," the King says.

"Which of course I will support her in meeting, as long as it's what *she* wants to do," I reply.

He levels me with his stare, but I stand tall, confident in the strength of my love. "You've already won Amelia over, and the rest of my family, by the looks of things," he says, giving his grudging but genuine acceptance.

My belly clenches, my heart beating out of my chest.

"Does that mean what I think it means, Father?" Ami asks, and to my surprise, the King's face lifts in a smile.

He reaches for her hand. "Your happiness is more important to me than anything, as it is with all my children. If you have chosen this man, he must be worthy."

"He is, Father," Ami says, and she turns to me. "I promise you that."

"In that case, what are we all doing standing around? The show is over. Let the music begin and let us dance!" He gestures with his arms dramatically, and in an instant the music begins, and people begin to dance around us.

"May I have this dance?" Ami asks me.

"It would be weird if I said no, right?"

"Weird and a touch humiliating."

"In that case, it's a good thing I had all that experience dancing with the mop."

She laughs and it ends in a snort. "Just don't dip my hair in a bucket and I think you'll have this."

"I'll try to remember that part," I say as I pull her softly against me.

We begin to move around the room, following the steps Ami taught me that night in the café.

"Who would have thought back then when I caught you dancing, we would be here tonight, dancing together with your father's blessing?"

"You know, that was the night it hit me that I had feelings for you."

"In that case, I win."

"What do you win?"

"I had feelings for you long before then."

"Since when?"

"Since that time I rescued you from the tree."

She grins, and I take the opportunity to spin her around, capturing her once again and holding her close in my arms. "I'm so glad I broke the no climbing a tree rule."

"Less so for me."

"Why?"

"I was worried I might drop you, that's why," I say on a laugh.

"But you didn't. You held me in those big, strong arms of yours."

I smile at the memory. "I remember."

"Do you know what?" she asks.

"What?"

"You saw me for who I was even before I was brave enough to find the words to tell you."

"I could say the exact same thing about you."

"There's a certain synchronicity to that, don't you think, Maverick?"

"Oh, I do, Amy. The most wonderful synchronicity of all."

And then I kiss her, right there in the palace ballroom.

Epilogue

Amelia

Good People of Ledonia! What a positively scandalous few months this has been! Not only did Princess Amelia dupe us all with her "Indian expedition"—which turned out to be a goth hop-skip-and-a-jump to neighboring Malveaux—but she's gifted us with a love story so deliciously improbable that even my romance-novel-addicted great aunt would have dismissed it as far too far-fetched for her book club.

Let's recap this royal madness, shall we, darlings? Our

princess masqueraded as a Dutch tourist with an affinity for black clothing and dramatic eyeliner, while her soon-to-be Hollywood heartthrob was simultaneously pretending to be someone else entirely as he sported the same goth attire.

Our Amelia and Ethan Roberts took jobs at a quaint lakeside café and fell madly in love, all the while being filmed for a reality show that, alas, we mere mortals will never be blessed enough to witness.

Yes, good people, it's been confirmed: Ethan Roberts' legal team, with the support of our very own royal family, has triumphed in their battle, and we will be forever denied the exquisite pleasure of watching our princess and her movie star burn up the screen with their romance. The footage shall remain forever locked away like the crown jewels—but infinitely more tantalizing.

This royal correspondent finds herself torn between journalistic disappointment and reluctant respect. While I would willingly crawl across burning coals just to glimpse that reportedly magical first kiss by the Lake of Dreams, even I must concede that royals deserve some modicum of privacy (though I do say this while simultaneously stockpiling heat-resistant clothing, just in case).

And what about Prince Max, our dashing royal knight? Not only did he gallantly rush to his sister's rescue when he suspected Ethan Roberts of orchestrating the filming debacle, but then, in a romance novel twist, he helped that very same Ethan crash the Summer Ball! I was there, darlings, clutching my complimentary champagne, when Ethan professed his love with such passionate eloquence that Rowan Thornheart looked positively amateur by comparison.

Now one wonders how to engage Prince Max's rescue services? I'm asking purely for journalistic reasons, you understand, though I have compiled a list of scenarios requiring princely intervention that I keep in my bedside drawer, just in case opportunity knocks.

And now we have a princess entangled with a Hollywood star and we've become accustomed to spotting our Amelia with the devastatingly handsome Ethan Roberts *sans* eyeliner jet-setting across continents—Paris, London, Barcelona, New York—looking so besotted it makes my heart double in size.

Which brings us to today, good people, because today marks our princess's triumphant return to Montelac as her true self, Princess Amelia of Ledonia, where she will be meeting the real townsfolk, minus the hired actors.

Sadly, the media has been banned from the event, but your favorite royal correspondent has an insider who has promised to reveal all.

I remain, as always, your devoted and somewhat envious royal correspondent,

Fabiana Fontaine xx

#SummerBallScandal
#EthanEverAfter
#PrincessGotGame

As the car pulls into the small town on the side of the lake, I'm struck afresh by how utterly picturesque the place is. The deep blue of the lake contrasts with the pretty painted buildings, clustered together on its shores, with snow-capped mountains in the distance.

This town might have been used as a set to capture Ethan's life, but it is certainly beautiful in its own right.

"You ready?" Max asks, sitting beside me in the back seat.

"I can't believe I'm back here. It all looks—" I glance down the street towards Francine's, thinking of all the time I spent here and how much it changed me. "It looks familiar and yet so very different at the same time. You know?"

Max smiles at me. Looking handsome in his Royal Airforce uniform, I can only imagine how much Fabiana Fontaine will be salivating over him in her next report. "I understand. There's been a lot of water that's passed under the bridge since you were last here."

"We have arrived, Your Royal Highnesses," our driver, Sergio, says.

He met us in Côte-des-Papillons, but this time, I didn't catch a train with an officious guard and a handsome goth to help me with my suitcase. Max and I flew on the royal jet from Villadorata to the coast, where Sergio met us, whisking us through the beautiful countryside to Montelac.

"You are very welcome," Sergio replies. "I will wait here for you to return in no more than thirty minutes."

As my feet make contact with the cobblestone street, my breath visible in the cool winter air, nostalgia for this little town and everything that happened in it fills my chest. It's not unlike the first time I wandered these streets, with Ethan masquerading as Maverick and me as Amy. Back then I had only just escaped the palace and was on my grand adventure. Everything felt so new and exciting. Seeing the pastel coloured buildings for the first time, spotting that "help wanted" sign in the window of Francine's, learning how to make coffee, getting to know the locals, and everything that passed between Ethan and me.

This visit is so very different from that first time and not only because I'm now so familiar with the town. This visit is official, and although Sergio is waiting for Max and me in the car, we're by no means alone. Palace Security is already here, watching my every move—much like the cameras did.

The irony is not lost on me. Even in disguise, masquerading as Amy, a Dutch tourist with a ridiculous, made-up name, I was watched.

But at least this time I'm fully aware of it.

We walk down the familiar street, arriving outside Francine's. Of course the café is closed, no patrons filling the seats outside, chatting in the sun. We peer inside, the pink interior making me smile. Ethan was right, this place is so pink it looks like Pepto-Bismol started a Pinterest board.

I visualize Ethan in his pink apron, a size too small for his large frame, standing at "Shayna," as he makes coffee, and my heart squeezes.

Who would have thought I would fall in love with a man who looked so out of place here in this pink café, and yet somehow has become intrinsically sewn into its very fabric for me?

But fall in love I did, and it has turned out to be just as magical as I'd hoped when I had sat in my room at the palace, gazing out the window, feeling hemmed in, dreaming of more.

The last few months have been a whirlwind. After Max helped Ethan gain entry to the Summer Ball that magical, wonderful night, we've being together as much as has been humanly possible—which has proven to be rather challenging, what with my duties and Ethan's filming schedule back in Los Angeles.

We knew it would be tricky from the start, but we are

so deeply in love that a long distance relationship, in which we only see each other a couple of times each month, isn't a hurdle for us.

Ethan stayed at the palace for a few days directly after the Summer Ball, during which time he not only won all my siblings and their respective partners over, but he managed to eke his way into Mummy's affections. Even Father softened toward him.

Yes, Father still loves to carry on about how I'm a princess and how I'm different from normal people and how difficult it will be for Ethan and I to continue our love affair in the spotlight. But what he doesn't take into account is one very important point in all this: Ethan and I are so deeply in love, nothing can come between us.

I escaped the confines of my royal life to have a grand adventure, and I found more than I could ever have hoped for. I found Ethan, I found love, and I found myself.

Perhaps Maddie was right, I did pull a bit of an *Eat, Pray, Love* after all?

"It's a little odd knowing that neither Giovanna or Pierre will be here," I say as memories of both of them enter my mind. "Both of them were hired actors."

"I still can't believe Ethan chose you over the gorgeous Giovanna. True love clearly is blind," Max says and receives a sharp shove from me. "Hey! Just joking!"

"She was hired to act as Ethan's love interest. There was nothing genuine about her being here. And nor Pierre, for that matter."

Both Pierre and Giovanna were the only hired actors here in Montelac, planted to be Ethan's and my romance storylines. That's why Giovanna told me that day in the market that she was meant for Ethan. It was quite literal. Apparently, the producers scrambled to find Pierre for me once they knew I'd accompanied Ethan to the lake house his duplicitous agent had rented, pulling him from an after-shave commercial he'd been hired for in Milan.

"He's been in a bunch of commercials. I'm surprised you didn't recognize him," Max says.

"Ethan did always say he looked like an aftershave model—which, incidentally, turned out to be true—but I just thought he was being jealous."

Seeing Ethan—Maverick at that time—acting jealous whenever Pierre showed me attention was the first sign that he felt something for me other than friendship.

"The thought of anyone getting jealous over my sister is not something I want to think about. Brother, remember?"

"The best brother I could ever, ever have," I say, giving him a squeeze.

"Ami, it's been over three months since I helped Ethan get to the ball. You don't need to keep thanking me. It's time you got over it," he says, straightening his uniform.

"Well, I would have gone and found him myself the very next day if he hadn't been there."

"I'm sure you would have."

"Your Royal Highnesses," a voice says behind us and I turn to see Steve, one of those dark sunglass-wearing palace security guys in a black suit. "You are expected at the town square in less than a minute."

"Thanks, Steve," I say with a smile, and although I'm sure he'd never admit to it, Steve's lips quirk.

"Ready?" Max asks me.

"Ready," I confirm.

We make our way to the town square, where a waiting crowd erupts into applause and cheers, waving both flags of our respective countries, Ledonia and Malveaux. We smile and wave as we step up onto the small stage, and I spot Francine in the crowd, grinning at me, along with Mr.

Bellamy from the bookshop, and a bunch of the café regulars.

It seems as though every person who lives in Montelac is here in the town square to see me, and emotion swells inside as I look out at them all.

I adjust the microphone. It makes that horrible screeching sound that reminds me of the evening on the lake shore when Ethan and I shared our true identities and feelings with one another—not to mention our very first kiss.

"Good evening, Montelac!" I say as though I'm a rock-star about to perform, and people cheer and wave their flags in response. "I cannot tell you how wonderful it is to be back here in your beautiful town. And I also can't tell you how nice it is not to have to wear all that black eye makeup, too."

"But you looked so cute as a goth," Francine calls out, and people murmur their agreement.

"Thank you, Francine," I say with a smile, and she winks at me. "Everyone in this town was nothing but wonderful to both me and Ethan while we were here, and I want you all to know that although we were pretending to be other people, the connection we both felt to you all and to this town was very real. I only wish Ethan could be here with us now, but he's promised to return when his schedule allows."

I place my hand over my heart, emotion tightening my throat. "You were horribly taken advantage of by the production team behind the reality television show, insisting you all sign non-disclosure agreements and forbid-ding you to talk to the media. It makes me so upset to even think about it, although I'll admit, the fact the media had no idea we were here did mean that Ethan and I could be anonymous people, escaping our everyday lives. We fell in love here, among you, the people of Montelac, and I will always have a very special place in my heart for you all.

"Today, I bring with me my little brother," I say, knowing he will hate the word "little."

Predictably, Max shoots me a quick look before he turns and waves and smiles at everybody.

"Although you might remember him as Chip, the Hawaiian shirt wearing tourist who visited us in his yellow Ferrari."

The crowd laughs at the memory, and Mr. Bellamy from the bookshop says, "His disguise was much worse than yours!"

"You're absolutely right about that, Mr. Bellamy," I reply with a smile.

"These days, I've been lucky enough to have had the opportunity to create a program that provides hospitality training to people who need a second chance in life. Through this program, I have met and worked with some wonderful people, and I am proud to announce that on my return to Villadorata tomorrow, I will be opening the Ledonian branch of Francine's." I grin at Francine, who beams back at me.

When I'd had the idea, I asked Francine if it would be possible to replicate the café that meant so much to me. She was deeply touched, agreeing to give the manager and staff some pointers, including what shade of pink was the most conducive in a café environment.

"I am also thrilled to announce that my darling sister-in-law, aka Queen Madeline, has officially recognized Montelac as a cultural landmark with historical protection."

There's a cheer from the crowd.

"I'm aware that you have already had greater tourist numbers than ever before, bringing tourist Euros, thanks to the fact Ethan and I inadvertently shone a light on your beautiful town. This cultural landmark protection means that Montelac will always retain its unique character, and that no developers can enter here without your express consent."

I step off the podium and tug on a gold rope that pulls velvet curtains open to reveal a gleaming brass plaque, naming Montelac as an official Cultural Landmark of Malveaux.

Another cheer erupts from the crowd, and I smile at them, my heart full to the brim.

Returning to the podium, I say, "On a personal note, I want to thank each and every one of you for the welcome you gave both me and Ethan. You were all so kind to us, despite the invasion to your town by the production company and everything that went with it. For me, it was the most incredible time of my life, not just because I fell in love with a wonderful man, but because this place and the people in it gave me the chance to grow."

Tears well in my eyes. "Thank you. From the bottom of my heart, thank you," I say, and the townsfolk rise to their feet, applauding and cheering, and my tears pour down my cheeks.

Max and I spend the next few minutes mingling with the crowd, me giving tearful hugs to Francine and Mr. Bellamy and several of the café regulars, and Max answering questions about his role in the Royal Air Force.

"Thank goodness that horrible Fontaine woman isn't here," Max says.

"No press, remember? But between you and I, I did spot a blonde head and a pair of glasses in the crowd."

Max's jaw clenches.

"Why does she bother you so much?"

349

"Because she writes about us all the time as though we're public fodder, there only to entertain people."

"It's the women in the two royal families she doesn't care for. She likes *you*."

"No, she likes Alex. She was the one who labelled him Prince McHottie, remember? Dreadful woman."

"Freedom of the press and all that," I say lightly, because not even the gossipy Fabiana Fontaine can diminish this wonderful day.

And then the most incredible thing happens. The crowd moves to either side of the square, forming a tunnel at the end of which stands a man. And not just any man.

Ethan.

My heart leaps at the sight of him. Gone is his goth eyeliner and dark clothes, replaced with a pair of chinos, a polo shirt, and the handsome, grinning face I love.

We move toward one another, meeting in the middle, where he sweeps me up in a kiss, the crowd cheering around us.

"What are you doing here? I didn't think I was going to get to see you until next month."

"Is that anyway to greet your boyfriend?" he asks with a grin. "We've had a break in filming and I figured why not hop on a plane and go visit my favourite person in all the world. That's you, in case you were wondering."

"I can't believe you're here, back where it all began."

His eyes sweep over me. "You're looking good, princess."

I glance down at my outfit. Gone are the prim and proper princess dresses with the high neck, paired with a string of pearls, replaced with my version of smart casual: a pair of dress jeans, a cute top, and a flattering blazer.

Another thing my parents agreed to along with my new career.

Suddenly aware how quiet the square has become, I look around to see that we're the only two left. "Where did everyone go?" I ask.

Ethan takes my hand in his. "Come with me. I've got something to show you."

He leads me from the square down to the lakefront, and we chat.

"How's Rowan's character transformation coming along?" I ask.

"Less bare chest and more bare emotions," he says with a laugh. "I'm so glad the producers were open to my ideas."

"I'm so glad you're enjoying your job so much more."

"Getting some creative freedom has really helped with that, as has getting an agent who isn't a slime ball."

"How is Nicole? I loved meeting her last month. You've really landed on your feet with that one."

"She's great. She's getting me the kinds of scripts I'm interested in and she's totally in my corner in a way Dion never was."

I give his hand a squeeze. "I'm so glad, my darling Ethan. Oh, by the way, I read in the news that a man has been arrested for conning women out of money for a winery that doesn't even exist."

"Greg Smith?" he asks.

"That was an alias. His real name is Malcolm Muggeridge. Apparently, he's likely to be a guest of the Malveauxian Crown for some years to come."

"A guest of the Malveauxian Crown?"

"That's a euphemism for 'in prison.'"

"Nice."

We arrive at the lakefront where, only just over three months ago on what should have been a magical night at the festival, we had learned the truth about the reality TV programme about our lives.

With the sun setting, the lake is awash in pink, orange, and yellow, and I look in wonder at the lights strung between the lamp posts, the trees wrapped in fairy lights, and a single table set for two, covered in a white tablecloth.

I turn to Ethan, wide eyed. "What's going on?"

"I figured you might be hungry after your speech, which was very good, by the way," he says in response, gesturing at the table.

"You were there?"

"I wouldn't have missed it."

He pulls a chair out for me and as I sit, music begins to play.

"Is that—" I question.

"*Anything for Love*," he replies. "I figured a touch of nostalgia was appropriate for this, our first night back in Montelac. Without the mop."

"You're a romantic, Ethan Roberts."

"Only with you, Ami."

We share a smile, and then he pours us a drink.

He takes my hand as he looks out over the lake. "We shared so much here on this lake of dreams."

"Our glowing footsteps on the beach."

"Your tree climbing."

"Washing strawberries with soap."

"That time in Mr. Bellamy's bookshop." He squeezes my hand as I take a sip of my drink. "Can I ask you something?"

"Anything."

"Anything?"

"Of course. With you, I'm an open book."

"In that case," he says as he pulls his chair out and lowers himself to one knee. Taking a small box from his pocket, he snaps it open, and immediately, my hands fly to my mouth, my eyes the size of the full moon over the lake.

"Ami, we met by chance in a costume store. We became friends, and from that friendship sprang the deepest of loves. I love you with all my heart and I cannot imagine wanting to spend the rest of my life with anyone else but you."

Tears prick my eyes, my heart beating out of my chest.

"Amelia Astrid Kristiana Eugenie Canossa, Princess of Ledonia, and queen of my heart, will you marry me?" His voice trembles with emotion as he gazes up at me, his Adam's apple bobbing, his deep blue eyes intense and full of love.

"Yes, I'll marry you, Ethan. Of course I will!"

With my heart thudding in my ears, he slides a sparkling diamond ring onto my left hand, and collects me in his arms, pressing the most incredible, emotional kiss against my lips.

"I love you so much," he whispers into my hair, sending a shiver down my spine.

"I love you, too," I reply, pressing my lips once again against his.

It's only after we've kissed and kissed some more that I notice the applause echoing around us and turn to see the townspeople, stretching down the street, clapping and whooping and grinning at us.

My shoulders shake with a combination of pure, unadulterated joy and embarrassment—but mainly pure, unadulterated joy—as I capture Ethan's gaze, and he grins back at me, his eyes dancing.

"They insisted when I told them what I had planned."

"They knew?" I ask, agog.

"Someone had to help me get the lights strung up and the music playing."

I laugh, giddy and happy and utterly content, and in my mind I write my final princess rule. Rule number 1,251: *A princess should escape her palace life, find herself and what truly matters to her, and fall deeply in love with her perfect match to get her happily ever after.*

THE END

Do you want to know what happens next? For a BONUS EPILOGUE set in Amelia and Ethan's future, follow this link: https://BookHip.com/ZWLPZSA

The final Ledonian royal sibling, Max, will be getting his story later in 2025, so sign up to Kate's newsletter to learn when here: https://kateokeeffe.com/newsletter/

More in the Royally Kissed series

Don't miss out on reading what happens next with the four royal
Ledonian siblings, Alex, Sofia, Amelia, and Max:

The Backup Princess

Royally Matched

The Royal Runaway

Max's book is coming in late-2025!

Acknowledgments

I can barely believe this is my 30th book, and I feel SO lucky to get to do this with my life. Thank you to you, my reader, for reading and loving and reviewing and talking about my books. It goes without saying that without you, I wouldn't be doing this (but there, I said it anyway), and the fact that even one reader has enjoyed my stories is still simply incredible to me.

I dedicated this book to my sweet sister-in-law, Donna, who has supported my writing from the very beginning, reading each and every book. She's always full of enthusiasm and positivity. Thank you for everything, Donna. You're just wonderful.

Amelia is easily one of my all-time favourite characters, and I always knew this would be one fun book to write. Her zest for life spurred me on to give her the story she deserved, away from the palace and all its rules she grew to despise. Having her escape the confines of her life was so satisfying for me as a writer, as was allowing her to blossom over the course of the book.

Of course Amelia deserves a worthy man, and I loved pulling a minor character from another one of my books in to serve as that man. Ethan Roberts, as you may have picked up in the story, is Dan Roberts's brother, hero of one of my ice hockey romances, *The Rebound Play*. Ethan appears in the book, but only briefly, and expanding him from a bit-part player into a fully fledged, flawed, but nevertheless swoony hero was a lot of fun.

As always, my incredible critique partner, Jackie Rutherford, gave me invaluable feedback on how to make this story what it became, and for that I'm truly grateful. Jackie is as smart as a whip and understands story and character in such a way that never fails to astound me. Thank you, Jackie. You're a total rock star!

I ran a couple of competitions to find names for two minor characters in this book, Giovanna Fiorelli and Pierre le Duc. Thank you, Linda Wright from my readers' group, Kate's Cupids, for Giovanna's name; and thank you to Ann Diener from my newsletter for Pierre's name. I adore them both, and I hope you enjoyed seeing the names in this story.

Dylan from Simply Dylan Designs made the figures on the cover once more, and Sue Traynor added the facial features. Thank you both for your creativity and willingness to work with this picky author with a preformed vision of what her characters look like.

Until book number 31, thank you so much for reading, and I hope you stay royal with me for Max's story.

Kate xoxo

Also by Kate O'Keeffe

Royal Romcoms:

The Backup Princess
Royally Matched
The Royal Runaway

Hockey Romcoms:

Mistletoe Face Off
The Rebound Play

Small Town Romcoms:

Faking It With the Grump
Faking It With My Best Friend
Faking It With the Guy Next Door

Romcoms Set in Britain:

Dating Mr. Darcy
Marrying Mr. Darcy
Falling for Another Darcy
Falling for Mr. Bingley (spin-off novella)
Never Fall for Your Back-Up Guy
Never Fall for Your Enemy
Never Fall for Your Fake Fiancé

Never Fall for Your One that Got Away

Romcoms Set in New Zealand:

One Last First Date

Two Last First Dates

Three Last First Dates

Four Last First Dates

No More Bad Dates

No More Terrible Dates

No More Horrible Dates

Styling Wellywood

Miss Perfect Meets Her Match

Falling for Grace

Co-Authored with Melissa Baldwin:

One Way Ticket

Writing as Lacey Sinclair:

Manhattan Cinderella

The Right Guy

About the Author

Kate O'Keeffe is a *USA Today* bestselling author known for her fun, feel-good romantic comedies brimming with humor, heart, and happily ever afters. A native of New Zealand, Kate has crafted numerous popular series, garnering a devoted international readership.

With a flair for witty banter and irresistible heroines navigating the ups and downs of modern dating, Kate's novels showcase strong friendships, comedic entanglements, and the of course sometimes bumpy but always hopeful road to love.

When she's not writing, Kate can often be found reading romcoms, binging her favourite shows, or spending time with her friends and family in the beautiful Hawke's Bay region of New Zealand.